THE PAIUTES WERE ACTIVE

Ben Hollister emerged from the tall pines onto the trail. Ahead of him lay a narrow canyon strewn with boulders and scrub, a perfect place for an ambush. The Pony Express mounts were the best in the land, specially bred for speed and stamina. He urged his horse forward, hunching low in the saddle to make himself as small a target as possible.

The first arrow missed him by a foot. His horse reared and pulled to one side, keeping three more arrows from finding their intended mark. Ben fought to control his horse with one hand, while sliding his .45 out of the holster with the other.

Five braves rose from behind a cluster of rocks. All were heavily daubed with war paint and stringing fresh arrows. They had counted on felling their victim with the first volley.

Ben fired three times in quick succession, killing two and sending the other braves fleeing. He did not go in pursuit. Getting the mail to the next relay station on time was more important.

WILLIAM W. JOHNSTONE
THE ASHES SERIES

OUT OF THE ASHES (#1)	(0-7860-0289-1, $4.99/$5.99)
BLOOD IN THE ASHES (#4)	(0-8217-3009-6, $3.95/$4.95)
ALONE IN THE ASHES (#5)	(0-8217-4019-9, $3.99/$4.99)
WIND IN THE ASHES (#6)	(0-8217-3257-9, $3.95/$4.95)
VALOR IN THE ASHES (#9)	(0-8217-2484-3, $3.95/$4.95)
TRAPPED IN THE ASHES (#10)	(0-8217-2626-9, $3.95/$4.95)
DEATH IN THE ASHES (#11)	(0-8217-2922-5, $3.95/$4.95)
SURVIVAL IN THE ASHES (#12)	(0-8217-3098-3, $3.95/$4.95)
FURY IN THE ASHES (#13)	(0-8217-3316-8, $3.95/$4.95)
COURAGE IN THE ASHES (#14)	(0-8217-3574-8, $3.99/$4.99)
VENGEANCE IN THE ASHES (#16)	(0-8217-4066-0, $3.99/$4.99)
TREASON IN THE ASHES (#19)	(0-8217-4521-2, $4.50/$5.50)
D-DAY IN THE ASHES	(0-8217-4650-2, $4.50/$5.50)
BETRAYAL IN THE ASHES	(0-8217-5265-0, $4.99/$5.99)

THE
PONY RIDERS

Guy N. Smith

Pinnacle Books
Kensington Publishing Corp.
http://www.pinnaclebooks.com

PINNACLE BOOKS are published by

Kensington Publishing Corp.
850 Third Avenue
New York, NY 10022

Copyright © 1997 by Guy N. Smith

Pinnacle and the P logo Reg. U.S. Pat. & TM Off.

First Printing: March, 1997
10 9 8 7 6 5 4 3 2 1

Printed in the United States of America

For Pat LoBrutto
who helped me to saddle up
and ride the Overland Trail

"He (Joseph A. Slade) was so friendly and gentle-spoken that I warmed to him in spite of his awful history. It was hardly possible to realize that this person was the pitiless scourge of the outlaws, the raw-head-and-bloody bones the mothers of the mountains terrified their children with. And to this day I can remember nothing remarkable about Slade except that his face was rather broad across and the cheek bones were low and the lips peculiarly thin and straight. But that was enough to leave something of an effect upon me, for since then I seldom see a face like that without fancying that the owner of it is a dangerous man."

—*Mark Twain*

Love your friend and never desert him. If you see him surrounded by the enemy do not run away; go to him, and if you cannot save him, be killed together and let your bones lie side by side.

—*Native American Saying*

Prologue

The woman came through from the back of the wagon, somehow kept her balance in spite of the bumping and lurching, and lowered herself down on to the seat alongside her husband. Her figure was full and her bosom was rounded. She gazed around her, shading her eyes with her hand from the glare of the setting sun.

The line of wagons had straggled, due to the Callaghans having lost a wheel. Some had waited and helped them with the repairs; others had lumbered on ahead in their impatience.

"Where's that boy got to, Bart? He should've been back by now." There was concern in the woman's voice.

"Boy's a man now, Prudence." Bart Hollister made a conscious effort not to appear to be worried about their son. It would only add to his wife's uneasiness. Bart's features had a pallor about them which bespoke a lifetime spent indoors; the elements were only just beginning to make their mark on his complexion. His accent was clearly British, with just a trace of a Massachusetts drawl if you listened hard enough. The Hollisters had only been three years out of England, and Bart's lined features reflected his regrets. It had been a mistake leaving his job as a gunsmith in Birmingham, the gun capital of Britain; even Colts were now being manufactured under license there. He had started as an apprentice at the Proof House, moved to small premises in Steelhouse Lane and set up business on his own. It had seemed that every

aspiring gunsmith had followed in his wake and his share of
the available work had slipped. He'd seen America as a kind
of Utopia—the army and the pioneers were fighting the redmen, and every man needed a gun. The potential for a skilled
gunsmith was unbelievable.

Setting up in Boston was Bart's second mistake. A gunsmith needed to go west where the Indian wars were being
fought. Everybody, it seemed, was going west. Now he just
hoped that he wasn't making his third big mistake.

"You hear me, Bart?" Prudence might become hysterical
if their son did not show up soon. "This is no place for a
boy fresh out of Boston. They say the country is crawling
with savages."

"Ben rides and shoots as good as any man on this train,
mebbe better'n some. And he can mend a gun almost as good
as I can, and he's only just turned eighteen. He's ridden on
ahead, mebbe joined up with Harker. Call it hero worship."

"That colonel in St. Louis warned us about travelling with
Harker." Prudence's misgivings were far from vanquished, as
she squinted anxiously in the early evening sunlight. "What
was it he said . . . a trapper looking for a quick buck. Last
train he guided only a dozen wagons made it. Indians killed
some of the movers, others drowned because he tried to cross
a river in full flood. No experience, that was what the man
said."

"If we'd left it any later, we'd never've made it afore the
snows come." Bart was unmoved. They'd argued all this out
a dozen times before. "Sure, Pinner's the best wagon master,
but he's probably up past Fort Hall by now. If we hadn't gone
with Harker, we'd've had to wait for spring." And maybe by
then, after a winter of arguing, they'd've changed their minds
and gone back to Boston. Women can be mighty persuasive
if you listen to them for too long, and in the end you give
in to them for the sake of peace and quiet.

"*I* didn't want to leave Boston, anyway," another female

voice complained from inside the wagon. Something toppled and fell. She cursed whatever it was she had knocked over.

Bart groaned. Now Sarah was coming to sit up front to support her mother. Prudence edged up the rough seat to make room for her.

"There won't be any dancing schools in Portland." Sarah seated herself and stared straight ahead. "After I'd finished in Boston, I could maybe have gone on to New York. They said at school that I was good enough to go."

"There'll be opportunities aplenty in Oregon." Bart had been through all this one, too. It was getting tiresome. He glanced sideways at Sarah. She would mature into a beautiful woman, even at sixteen she was striking to look at. Her features were finely molded, her hair was the color of ripened corn, and her eyes were a deeper blue than a midsummer sky. Her every movement was supple and graceful, her posture a perfection that had been attained at the dancing school in Boston.

"Dance halls and saloons," she replied scathingly. "As soon as I'm old enough, I'll travel all the way back to New York. That's *my* ambition!" She flicked a strand of hair off her face angrily.

"When you're old enough, you can please yourself with what you do." The road was rutted, the wagon lurched so that both women clung tightly to the seat. "But, as I've told you a hundred times, there'll be opportunities out west for all of us. Back east, places like Boston, St. Louis and New York are crowded, outgrowing themselves. Stores and factories are springing up right next to each other, so folks are hard put to make a living. There's that many gun stores that everybody who needs a gun has one and soon there'll be nobody left to sell to. And there's that many repair places that if every gun breaks down, and even if you happen to be the best gun doctor in the business, you'll only get a small share of the trade, just how it was back in England. Out west, it'll be different. Everybody needs a gun, either for protection or for huntin'. They need somebody around who can do repairs fast and efficient. There'll be army contracts to be had, too. And as for dancin'—there'll be a demand for that, too, as new towns spring up."

Sarah turned her head away. She was tired of arguing with her father. If Mom couldn't make him change his mind, then what chance did she stand? Anyway, it was too late now; they were all sold up in Boston, just like they had been in Birmingham, and ten miles out of Fort Laramie. There wouldn't be any going back, no matter how much she and her mother protested.

"There's a rider coming." Prudence tried to stand up, was thrown back on to her seat. "It looks like Ben."

It was Ben.

He reined in alongside his parents's wagon, sat his horse like he was an extension of the animal itself. In spite of his small size—he could not have weighed more than 135 pounds and was surely no taller than five feet four or five—he gave the impression of a boy who had become a man before his time. He was lithe and strong; a muscular body rippled beneath the shrunk and faded plaid shirt and buckskin trousers. A Colt Navy .36 nestled in his holster, and he gave the impression that he could use it as well as any man on this wagon train. There was a steely glint in his blue eyes that matched that of his sister, a determination to succeed at whatever he did. Long yellow hair fell around his collar and his handsome face was dust grimed, but there was a smile on his lips.

"Been lookin' out for me?" He had noticed the concerned looks of his mother; his father's expression was inscrutable. Bart Hollister had a rough tongue when the occasion demanded, and you never pushed your luck with him.

"There's Indians from here on." Prudence Hollister was unable to conceal her nervousness. "Mister Harker warned us this morning before he rode on ahead. It's dangerous country, Ben. You'd best stay right alongside your family—just in case we need you."

"I've been ridin' with Sep Harker most of the day." Ben sat proudly upright in his saddle. "We been lookin' for injuns." Ben had easily dropped his British accent, mimicking the Americans he'd gotten to know.

"Oh!" Prudence paled, and became tight-lipped. "You see any, Ben?"

"Plenty o' signs but Sep reckons the war party has probably moved on up towards South Pass. Cheyennes. Don't reckon they'll risk tanglin' with us."

Bart wasn't convinced. This train was a small one: twenty wagons and no more than a hundred movers. Much larger trains had been massacred by both the Arapahoes and the Cheyennes. What Prudence had said was right, but he'd never admit it to her. That colonel in St. Louis had correctly advised them that Sep Harker lacked experience. Right now, though, they were only just a few miles out of Fort Laramie and there was a helluva way left to go. But there was no turning back; it was too late for that.

"We'll doubtless be striking camp soon." Bart eyed his son carefully.

"Sure thing, Sep's waitin' up ahead, 'bout a mile, circlin' the wagons as they arrive on an open stretch of land close to the river. River'll protect us tonight on one side—we just have to watch the other, but he reckons the injuns are gone. He says we'll cross at first light."

"Oh!" Prudence's hand went to her mouth. "Is it . . . narrow and shallow?"

"Wide'n deep, an' fast flowing," Ben answered. He'd been taught as a boy not to tell lies. And, anyway, there was no point in allaying his mother's worst fears now only to confirm them later. Prudence Hollister had a phobia about water. "We'll be okay, though, we'll float the wagons across, make rafts to carry the supplies, if necessary. Movers always cross rivers that way." So Sep Harker had told him.

Like Ben had told them, Harker had drawn the wagons up into a half circle spanning the river bank. The current swirled muddy brown, dead branches sped downstream. Somewhere far upstream there had been heavy rain, maybe a cloudburst the day before. Ben licked his dry lips. Crossing this lot was going to be tricky. Still, he'd leave the worrying until tomorrow.

Sep Harker delegated the night guard—two men to lie beneath the wagons and watch the scrubland that stretched back to the hills and bluffs. There was no point in watching the river; they'd see enough of that in the morning. The guide was a man of few words who kept to himself—as if he was afraid of being asked too many questions that he couldn't answer, Bart decided. He couldn't get that colonel's advice out of his mind. Somehow the guide's image as a trapper turned guide didn't fit.

"There's plenty injun signs." Harker was of small build, wore buckskins and boots of deerhide, with a skin cap pulled tightly down on his head. His features were mostly hidden beneath a bushy grey beard. His eyes were never still, flicking this way and that. If he noticed you looking at him, he jerked his gaze away—like he was afraid you might be shrewd enough to read his thoughts. "But they're two, mebbe three, days old. They's probably followin' Pinner's train, joinin' up with a big party. They mebbe don't even know we're here, or if they do, then we ain't worth botherin' with."

Harker had spent his life trapping, but the beavers were mostly gone now. And with the settlers coming west in numbers, there was a good living to be made by guiding them. The Oregon trail had been opened up. You only had to follow it—if you knew the route—and one guide was as good as another. He didn't tell the movers that, though. The less you told 'em, the better.

"All the same, we hev to keep our eyes skint. It'll take us most o' tomorrer to cross the river."

Sep Harker never lingered around the campfire; he was a loner. He turned and walked away into the gathering darkness

Nobody really knew where Sep spent his nights. Or if he slept at all.

Bart Hollister oiled a heavy Adams .45 revolver, one that he had brought with him from England, checked that the cylinder spun freely and the hammer cocked smoothly and effortlessly. "Time'll come when cap'n ball guns will be outdated." It was a theory he frequently expounded and elaborated upon if his audience was attentive. A lot of folks just nodded and thought him crazy. "Look at the time it takes to reload, especially if you've got a war party hollerin' round your wagon. Now, if the powder and balls was already loaded in shells that fitted the cylinders, all you'd have to do would be to slide 'em in and keep pullin' the trigger. If you had enough shells you could keep shootin' all day. After all, they've done it with shotguns, paper cases even if you do have to keep 'em dry. Paper's no good for rifles, though. It needs to be metal. Brass, mebbe. When it eventually comes, the guns we're usin' now will be museum pieces. You see if I'm not right one of these days. I'm workin' on the idea, maybe I'm not all that far away from it." The original idea was spawned in his Steelhouse Lane workshop, and he was still trying to figure it out.

Ben nodded in the darkness; he saw the sense in what his father said. All Bart Hollister had to do was to convince others that it would work. But he would also need financial backing. That was the hardest part.

Sep was standing on the opposite river bank by the time the camp stirred. Even the sentries had not seen or heard him cross. There was a length of strong rope spanning the foaming waterway, securely knotted to a stout tree on either side. Doubtlessly, he had pulled himself across along it, having lassoed a rock on the other side first. The wagon master, however, was not one to divulge his knowhow to others. The line would be used to assist the movers in their crossing. In the grey light of dawn, the assembly saw how his clothing clung wetly to his body.

They lost the first wagon. The current took it and whirled it downstream. It was a loss but not a crisis; the contents had already been off-loaded. Fortunately, they did not lose any more, and by the middle of the afternoon, the last of the wagons was hauled up the bank.

That was when the Indians attacked.

The braves had been lying among the rocks and scrub no more than a hundred yards from where the movers were reloading their wagons in preparation for the tortuous journey that lay ahead. A war party of about thirty Cheyennes had crept there under the cover of darkness and had lain motionless throughout the long, hot day. A scout of Pinner's experience would have checked the cover out at dawn, and he would probably have known they were there. He would have smelled them.

Harker paid the price for his negligence—he was the first victim. An arrow took him in the butt, spun him round. A second embedded itself in his groin, and he went down kicking and screaming.

The movers were caught out in the open; they didn't even have a circle of wagons to defend. Most of their rifles were on board. They only had their handguns.

The Indians streamed out of the rocks, loosening arrows as they came. Three whites went down with the first volley, while horses reared and threatened to bolt with the driverless wagons.

"Get down!" Bart pushed Prudence and Sarah under the wagon and fired his .45 at an onrushing Cheyenne. The warrior fell headlong in a cloud of dust and didn't move again. Three more shots came in rapid succession and two braves sprawled. One began to crawl forward; Bart needed a second bullet to finish him.

Bart changed the cylinder and handed the empty one to Prudence to recharge. Sarah slay on the ground beneath the wagon, her eyes were closed, her face deathly white. Prudence shook her and was relieved when her daughter's eyelids flickered open. For an awful moment, she feared that Sarah had fallen victim to the ambush.

Ben Hollister fired from behind the tailboard and saw a painted brave drop. He ducked to reload. The Indians had had the advantage of surprise, but they had not capitalized fully on it. Maybe the Hollisters's deadly shooting had halted the human stampede. Now the attackers had ducked for every scalp of available cover. They would trade arrows for bullets. They outnumbered the whites, and it was only a matter of time before . . .

A second war party arrived on the scene within the hour, riding half-broken ponies and heavily daubed with paint, yelling and brandishing lances and tomahawks. Those Indians crouched in the cover of bushes and rocks fired a hail of arrows. Meanwhile, the dust screen kicked up by the galloping hooves rendered the braves uncertain targets for the desperate defenders of the wagon train.

Bart Hollister squeezed off three shots at half-naked wraiths in the dusty gloom. One fell, but the others disappeared. Then Sarah was screaming hysterically and he turned to see Prudence writhing on the floor with an arrow protruding from her bosom. Her dress was quickly saturating with scarlet, her lips moved as she tried to speak. She never made it, her head fell back.

Bart held her, shocked and dazed. He was dimly aware that up above Ben was shooting fast. Yet the sound of the shots might have been distant echoes from across the plains, as everything was so unreal. Sarah was speaking, shouting, screaming at her father, wide-eyed with grief and terror. Something struck Bart between the shoulder blades and threw him forward. He felt his revolver drop from his fingers, started to black out before the searing pain hit him.

Ben wondered why the gunfire from under the wagon had ceased. His father wouldn't have run out of powder and shot.

An arrow must have got him, in which case his mother and sister needed protection. The shooting all around was spasmodic, the white casualties had been heavy. Ben risked another look over the tailboard; the dusty air smelled acrid with smoke, his eyes smarted and he could barely see.

The Indians had begun torching the wagons.

Somebody screamed; the shriek was female. Ben knew instinctively that it was Sarah. A gun in either hand, he swung down from the seat of the wagon. Shapes, silhouettes, came and went—some on foot, others mounted. He fired a shot and a darting Indian dropped.

Suddenly, a mounted brave materialized out of the smoky half-light, leaned down and grabbed up something from beneath the wagon even as Ben swung his gun. Ben's finger hesitated on the trigger as the Cheyenne lifted up a limp form from the ground, pulled it aloft so that it shielded him. For one God-awful second Ben had almost shot Sarah as she was being hoisted up on to the plunging mustang, held by her captor as a shield. The Indian saw him, grinned evilly, and then he was gone into the thickening smoke with a drumming of unshod hooves.

Just the memory of those leering daubed features remained to mock and torture Ben Hollister. The smoke was so dense it was almost impossible to breathe. A glance showed Ben his parents lying under the wagon in an embrace of death. They had died together; they would have wanted it that way. At least they had been spared the knowledge of their daughter's fate. The thought had Ben feeling mentally and physically sick. He picked up his father's .45, stuck it in his belt.

A thundering of hooves had Ben whirling, crouching, but the mount was a riderless one. It saw him, panicked and reared. He leaped, grabbed its mane and pulled himself up on to its back. It plunged, wheeled and bucked in an effort to throw him, but Ben could ride almost as well as he could shoot. He clung on, using his knees to bring the animal under control.

Ben fired from the hip as a warrior rushed towards him and saw the Indian go down even as his mount bolted. The pony was gun shy; its previous master had only fired arrows. Ben let it have its head, direction was immaterial, anywhere was preferable to this hell of blazing carnage. Another rider passed him, heading in the opposite direction. Ben only had a momentary glimpse but it was enough to show him that the beast carried two riders. One sat bolt upright, pulling on the rope reins, while the other was slumped and hung like a rag doll. Then an eddy of smoke hid the riders from him; when it cleared there was neither beast nor burdens to be seen.

Ben rode low and fast, letting the animal have its head until he was clear of the massacre. At the bank of the wide river, he urged the mustang into the water and let it swim with the current.

Far behind him he heard the Cheyenne still yelling and shrieking as they began the mutilation of their victims. He tried not to think about Sarah but it was impossible. He had heard and read about what Indians did to captured white women.

Book One

Now he gazed at the landscape far and near,
Then, impetuous, stamped the earth,
And turned and tightened his saddle-girth;
But mostly he watched with eager search,
Lonely and spectral, and sombre and still.
He springs to the saddle, the bridle he turns;
A shape in the moonlight, a bulk in the dark,
And beneath, from the pebbles, in passing, a spark
Struck out by a steed flying fearless and fleet
That was all! And yet, through the gloom and the light,
The fate of a nation was riding that night;
And the spark struck out by that steed in his flight,
Kindled the land into flame with its heat.

—*Henry Wadsworth Longfellow*

One

The Hollisters had sailed from England in 1854 and left Boston in 1857. That was over two years ago, but to Ben it seemed an eternity. He had considered returning to England, but he discarded the idea. He had no living relatives and few friends, for he had spent his boyhood helping his father in their small gun business.

He had to make a living somehow. He thought about repairing guns—he had learned enough about the trade during his apprenticeship to have started up a business on his own—except that he did not have any tools nor the money with which to buy them. Nor could he afford to rent a workshop.

His only other skill was with horses, so he took a livery job in Fort Kearney for a while and then moved on down to Marysville when he became bored. There were also rodeos. He proved his horsemanship on several occasions but the prize money was only a pittance.

He still grieved over the loss of his family. His parents's bodies would have been mutilated and scalped by the Cheyennes. He had heard of a wagon train being looted and burned a few miles out of Fort Laramie. It had to be the one Sep Harker had unwittingly led into an ambush. Ben hadn't ridden out to look; he did not want to see.

It was Sarah's fate that plagued him most. He could not get out of his mind that momentary glimpse of a mounted warrior with a female slung across his mustang. Was Sarah alive or dead? He had recurring nightmares about it, wandering in the thick smoke looking for his sister but never finding her. If she had been dead the brave would not have taken her corpse—he would have scalped her and left her body to be consumed in the fire.

Night and day, Ben was plagued by that smoky vision. He got to blaming himself. He should have shot her, spared her the atrocities which must have followed. But he had held his fire. Shooting one's own kin is not something that is done on a snap decision. While there was life, there was hope. Was there any hope now for Sarah?

He should have gone back to the wagon train afterward—except that there would have been nothing to see except burned out wagons and charred bodies. At least he would have known for sure whether or not Sarah had died along with their parents. He blamed himself for a lot of things but chiefly for escaping when he should have stayed and died with the others. He should have searched for a trail and followed the war party. But he wouldn't have known what to look for; he had never been further west than Boston before that day.

Excuses to satisfy his conscience? Whatever, they left him with a feeling of guilt. He managed to convince himself that Sarah was dead by now, that it was pointless to go looking for her after two years.

It was something which he would have to live with for the rest of his life.

Horses came a close second to guns in Ben's life. Livery work was tedious and didn't pay well. He wasn't experienced enough to go on a cattle drive, and rodeos earned only a few bucks, if you managed to stay on a crazy, unbroken mount longer than any of the other contestants. He had almost given up the prospect of a riding job when he saw a notice in Atchison advertising for stagecoach drivers for the Butterfield Overland Mail Company. It was worth a try.

It wasn't as difficult Ben had imagined. The horses were quality stock; if you handled them right, they responded.

"Start tomorrow." The florid-faced agent scribbled something in a book. "You'll be riding with Floyd, he's the best in the business. Learn from him and you won't go far wrong. If he says you're okay, that's good enough for us."

Floyd was small and wiry and he knew how to handle a team. Ben sat between him and the guard for the first two stages and then Floyd handed over the reins.

"Hosses have sense." The driver seldom smiled. There was little to smile about when you were on the road day in and day out. "Mostly they're used to the route, they jest want to get to the other end 'cause they knows there'll be food and water fer 'em. Yep, they got a lot more sense than most of the folks who ride the stage routes."

Butterfield had been carrying transcontinental mail since 1858 using the Oxbow Route, which travelled south from St. Louis via El Paso and San Diego. The more direct Overland Route was still unsuitable for coaches. The return coast-to-coast trip took a minimum of three weeks, sometimes longer because the route was plagued by Indians and gangs of outlaws. The government paid Butterfield a subsidy of $600,000 to maintain the service.

In January, 1860, Ben made his first run from Fort Smith to Fort Belknap. It was trouble free, and even though Floyd did not praise him, the fact that he didn't criticize him meant that Ben had passed the test.

"Won't always be this easy." Floyd had a quiet voice, he wasn't used to talking much. "There'll be road agents; sometimes injuns attack the coaches. That's the guard's job, you jest keep drivin' and hopes you don't git hit by a bullet or an arrer. The army ain't makin' much of a job keepin' the injuns quiet. They chase one lot an' while they're gone, another lot goes on the warpath. Mebbe, though," he spoke even softer so than Ben had to lean forward to catch the words, "the coaches won't be carryin' the mail much longer—not accordin' to what folks are sayin'."

"Oh?" Ben was curious.

"Jest talk, rumors at the moment, but where there's smoke, there's fire." Floyd glanced about him like he was afraid of being overheard. A man came out of the stables. Floyd waited until he had gone back inside before continuing. "I'm only tellin' yuh what I heard, jest in case you got to thinkin' you'd got a regular job an' it didn't turn out like that. They reckon that there's a plan afoot to carry the mail on horseback, in stages, usin' the Overland Route. 'Cause it's shorter and quicker. Can't see it workin' myself." Floyd spat on the ground. "But I was talkin' to a guy from back east who'd read in the newspapers that the government is puttin' up a million dollars if the idea works. If it does, you'n me won't be ridin' no more stages. Still, newspapers spread rumors jest like folks, you can't believe anythin' until you sees it with yer own eyes."

In those early months of 1860 Ben worked his way up and down the stage line from St. Louis to Fort Yuma. It was during this spell that he established his reputation with a gun. The legend began on a run between Fort Chadbourne and Tucson.

Eb Wyer rode guard that day. He was another of that dying breed of mountain men who had forsaken their former domain and probably wouldn't even be going back to the legendary reunion at Bent's Fort this year. There weren't many of his kind left. Times were changing and you tried to make the most of what was left. Like Ben, Eb had to make a living.

He was a grizzled, grey-bearded figure of indeterminable age. The coaches were his only means of making a living. He found it impossible to stay in one place more than a few days. Most nights he slept in the stable with the horses, relay cabins were "jest too civilized" for him. Pack horses and mules were the extent of his horsemanship, but he knew how to fight injuns. He'd tried to get a scouting job, but the army had told him he was too old. How the hell did *they* know how old he was? He wasn't even sure himself 'cept he was around forty, give or take a year or two, when the Alamo fell. He'd've liked to have been there, he told Ben, but he only heard about it a year or so afterward. News travelled slow in the mountains in those days.

Butterfield wasn't particular about a man's age, just so long as he could shoot from a swaying, jolting box. Eb regarded the shotgun loaded with buckshot with contempt. He could still knock an injun off'n a gallopin' mustang at 200 yards with his Hawken .54. He only used the scattergun if they got too close. Ben glanced at the other's rifle and recognized it only too well. He'd seen several during the time he'd helped his father in their Boston workshop: a stock of plain hard maple, stained dark and fitted with oval cheek-pieces, the octagonal barrel with a slow twist bored to .54; flat barrel wedges, forestock tips, Kentucky-style butt plates, scrolled trigger guards and double-set triggers; breech tangs were long and strong to reinforce the wrist of the stock. The best Indian and buffalo rifle that a plainsman could buy.

Everything was real peaceful when Ben set out from El Paso. Eb appeared to be dozing beside him, but it was the old timer who saw the Apaches riding out of the scrub first, jerking upright. "See 'em, boy!" Eb grabbed up the Hawken, cradled it across his knees. "They're goin' to try to beat us to the road—cut us off. Keep goin'. I'm jest gonna give 'em a taste o' what we kin do before they get closer. Mebbe they'll change their minds!"

Ben shied from the cloud of smoke. Out of the corner of his eye he saw an Apache go backward off a mustang. The others never faltered; they kept on coming.

Eb reloaded fast but Ben couldn't help remembering his father's theory about ready-loaded shells. Maybe it *would* become reality one of these days. If Eb had been loading up with cartridges probably two or three more Indians would

have parted company with their mounts before they reached
the road.

The coach hit a pothole, lurched, and threatened to overturn, but miraculously it kept its balance. Ben concentrated
on his driving. If they spilled, they were done for. Their only
hope was to outpace the war party. It looked like an impossibility—lithe, buckskin-clad riders on fresh ponies could
easily catch an unwieldy coach and team.

The Apaches were almost at the road when Eb fired again.
A pony rolled, its rider somersaulted, came upright instantly,
and began running in the wake of his yelling, galloping companions.

The guard pulled his shotgun out from under the seat,
rested his feet on it to stop it sliding. Buckshot was deadly
at close range.

"They've beat us to the road, boy!"

Ben didn't reply. Eb had spoken the stark truth. The war
party was already fanning out into a half circle across the
rutted track up ahead. As the stage approached they would
close in and swarm aboard.

One of the braves was aiming a gun awkwardly. It belched
a puff of smoke but the ball did not even strike the stagecoach. Ben urged his team to an even greater effort. Their
only hope was to burst their way through the Apaches blocking the road.

The Indians sat their horses, waited, lances, tomahawks
and arrows at the ready. They thought the driver would brake
to a sliding halt in a cloud of desert dust or slew off the road
and overturn. Only when the rattling wheels showed no signs
of slowing or changing direction did the warriors realize that
the driver was going to ram them—charge right through their
midst. Even a fearless Apache can be forgiven for pulling
his mount over in the face of an onrushing, hurtling stagecoach.

Eb's Hawken bucked and spat its ball with devastating

accuracy from the jolting seat. A brave's mustang reared and threw its now lifeless burden and bolted.

Eb grabbed up the double 10-gauge and pulled both triggers simultaneously. The nearest Apache's torso opened up and those closest to him shrieked as they were peppered by the fringe of the twin blast.

A gap appeared in the bunched horsemen and Ben headed his coach and team straight for it. An arrow embedded itself in the woodwork at his feet, others thudded into the side of the coach as it thundered through.

The Indians were in disarray. Temporarily.

Suddenly, old Eb wasn't there any more. Ben hadn't seen nor heard him go, he was gone, just as if he had never been there at all. An arrow had gotten him probably, or a very unlucky ball from that ancient piece. Whichever, it was of no consequence. All that mattered was that the stage no longer had a guard and the Apaches had re-grouped and were hollering in full pursuit. They were fast catching up to the stagecoach as it lumbered in full flight. Ben knew only too well that he stood no chance of outdistancing his pursuers.

He stood precariously to look behind over the top. Just at that moment the leading Apache drew level, leaped and secured a grip on the roof, then began to haul himself up.

Ben held the reins with one hand, tugged his .45 from his belt with the other. It was an instinctive snap shot as the painted face hove into view over the rear of the coach. But it was enough; those features exploded and disappeared.

The shotgun slid and clattered over the side. There was no time to reload it, anyway. Another Apache was drawing level, arm upraised to hurl a tomahawk; at close range it was deadlier than an arrow.

Ben shot the rider from the saddle.

The team was flecked with sweat, but they would keep going until they dropped—they were scared to hell. Ben just had to keep them on the road and ensure that they did not career off into the desert where the stagecoach would topple on the uneven terrain.

Ben kept standing up to look behind, just in case another unwelcome boarder might have grabbed a hold. It was a hazardous exercise as the pursuing Indians were trying to pick him off. A number of arrows quivered in the roof already.

The hammer of the .45 clicked on a spent chamber. Ben slid it back into its holster and grabbed the .36 out of his belt. He heard another arrow thud into the roof.

The horses were tiring. The long run at full speed had sapped the team's stamina. The Indians were close behind, crouched low over their mounts. They made no move to jump aboard. They had no need to now for their quarry was tiring. But they respected their foe—at their cost they had learned how he drove at an unbelievable speed and killed with terrible accuracy at the same time. They were wary of him. They had already named him.

Slayer Who Rides With the Wind.

Ben knew that as soon as his gun was empty they would swarm aboard and pull him down by sheer weight of numbers. He did not have another spare chamber; there would be no chance to reload. Only his deadly gunfire, combined with that incredible drive, had saved him so far. Now the slowing horses were no match for the pursuing mustangs.

Within minutes it would all be over. Ben reckoned that he had one shot left and he would use it on himself. He had heard coach crews at the relay stations relating terrible accounts of Apache tortures—they were the cruelest of all the tribes.

He looked behind one last time and stared in disbelief. Only seconds earlier the braves had been gaining rapidly on him. Now they had dropped back, wheeled and bunched their mounts, sitting staring after the trundling coach. For some unknown reason they had abandoned the chase just when their quarry was within their reach.

Ben squinted through smarting eyes up the trail ahead of him. A cloud of dust was approaching and in it he could make

out horses and riders. He groaned his despair aloud. The
Apaches weren't hurrying because more of them were headed
this way, the stagecoach was caught between two fires. He
had ridden into a clever trap. They had played a cruel game
with him like a cat plays with a mouse. Now another war party
was closing in on him for the *coup-de-grace*.

Ben hauled on the reins, brought the horses to a walking
pace. Speed was of no importance any longer. His fingers
closed over the butt of his revolver. Just one shot was left to
him . . .

Once again he stared in disbelief. Was the desert playing
cruel tricks on him now, creating a mirage to torture him
still further? Those riders approaching were not mounted on
half-wild ponies—they sat astride thoroughbred stock. They
wore jackets and leggings and wide brimmed hats to shield
their faces from the sun and the dust. They carried rifles and
pistols, too.

Ben was laughing uncontrollably by the time they reached
him. They all watched the Indians retreat.

"Heard the shootin'." Ben recognized the big man with
the moustache as the boss of the relay station a mile or so
down the trail. "Thought mebbe you was havin' trouble with
them Apache bastards."

"Thanks." Ben returned the .36 to his belt. "Things were
gettin' a mite desperate. They got poor old Eb some way
back. I got maybe four or five of 'em, though."

They shook their heads in amazement. Way back down
the road they could see a couple of Indians lying dead. They
didn't doubt Ben's word that there were more.

That day the legend of Ben Hollister was born among both
red and white men. His name would be mentioned in awe
from St. Louis to Sacramento.

Slayer Who Rides With the Wind.

TWO

April 3, 1860

Ben Hollister, like most other folks, it seemed, had arrived in St. Joseph, Missouri. Floyd had been right about there being no smoke without fire. Posters had gone up in every town from St. Louis to Sacramento announcing that Russell, Majors & Waddell were experimenting with a new method for the transportation of transcontinental mail. Instead of the despatches going by stagecoach along the lengthy southern route, the mail would be carried in pouches on *horseback* over the central Overland Route. William Russell's target was to complete the run in a maximum of ten days.

John Butterfield was reported in most newspapers as saying that the feat was impossible. Today the journey would be attempted. Inside two weeks the result would be known.

Crowds thronged the sidewalks of St. Joseph. Today could well be an historic one. If it wasn't, it would be ignominiously forgotten, and the stagecoaches would continue to carry the mail.

Ben had another reason, apart from curiosity, for being in St. Joseph today. His job hung in the balance. Ten days from now he might not have one.

William H. Russell, wearing a top hat and tailed coat, stood on a podium outside the company's office. He stroked his short trimmed beard, glanced across at the clock over the courthouse. A late start was not a good omen, nevertheless the special messenger bringing the despatch had been unavoidably delayed. Russell made light of it and smiled. What was an hour or two in ten days? It worked, everybody laughed.

The maiden run of the Pony Express had received maximum publicity. Standing beside Russell, the first westbound rider showed signs of nervousness. Johnny Fry, a Kansas ranch hand, had won several major horse races. This was to be the biggest of his life. He was dressed in tight-fitting jockey clothing for lightness and wore a skull cap on his head, its long peak designed to protect him from the elements. The only addition to his usual racing attire was a holstered .45, for the trail was not without its dangers.

Russell began to speak. Ben had to strain to catch the words for some of the assembly were already cheering him. He detailed the contents of the pouches which were strapped in readiness on the mount: 49 letters, copies of eastern newspapers specially printed on tissue for lightness, 5 private telegrams and numerous telegraphic despatches destined for Californian newspapers. In total, the contents weighed 15 pounds. The delivery charge was $5 for every half ounce. This drew gasps of disbelief from the listeners. How could the Pony Express expect to attract business with such exorbitant prices? The government had guaranteed a million dollar subsidy. If the experiment was a success, Russell said as he smiled confidently, that would enable Russell, Majors & Waddell to reduce their charges.

William Russell was red-faced and shouting in an attempt to make himself heard. "Furthermore, if Congress grants that subsidy, we might get the stagecoach contract, too, and that would reduce charges still further."

This time the cheers drowned his words.

Johnny Fry swung himself up into the saddle. Nineteen hundred miles away in San Francisco, another Pony Express rider, Billy Richardson, also mounted his horse, ready for the eastbound ride. In all, thirty riders would be used.

William Russell glanced around and received a nod from the man who stood alongside a brass cannon across the street. This epic ride would be started in true style.

Russell added that the Pony Express would, in any case, only be short-lived. The telegraph lines already reached from St. Joseph to Fort Kearney, Nebraska. From San Francisco they had progressed as far as Carson City. There was still a gap of 1600 miles between Nebraska and Nevada. Once this was joined up, and the telegraph was fully operative from coast to coast, there would no longer be any need for riders to deliver dispatches.

The cannon boomed and Johnny Fry lightly touched the flanks of his mount. His epic ride had begun.

April 13, 1860

Crowds gathered in the streets of Sacramento. There was a murmur of excited chatter—word had been received that the westbound rider was on his way from Placerville and that he was ahead of schedule.

A banner stretched across the street read: HURRAH FOR THE CENTRAL ROUTE.

A brass cannon, similar to the one that had fired when Johnny Fry left on the first stage of the journey in St. Joseph, was primed in readiness.

Voices were hushed, ears were strained. At last, a pounding of hooves was heard, growing louder by the second. A cheer went up before the oncoming rider rounded the last bend and came into full view. There was no mistaking the skull cap of the boyish figure crouched low in the saddle.

The cannon saluted Will Hamilton, the final rider. It was 5:25 P.M.

Hamilton ignored the applause; he was not finished yet.

He paused just long enough to transfer the pouches to a fresh horse and then he boarded the waiting steamer *Antelope*.

Hamilton arrived in San Francisco just over seven hours later.

William H. Russell had proved that the central Overland Route was far quicker on horseback than the southern one was by stagecoach.

Even so, John Butterfield was not giving up without a fight. The Pony Express trail would be impassable in winter, he claimed, but his own stagecoach route would not.

William Russell presented two men to contest this point. Charles R. Morehead, Jr. (Russell's nephew) and James Rupe, a former army captain, had returned from Russell's Leavenworth headquarters last winter in atrocious conditions without undue problems.

Congress accepted the facts and findings. Russell, Majors & Waddell were granted a subsidy of a million dollars to run the Pony Express up until such time as the telegraph stretched from coast to coast.

Within a week, Butterfield was laying off drivers. Ben's legendary encounter with the Apaches counted for nothing—the firm was only retaining a few of their longest serving men. A few coaches would still run the southern route; a reduced private service had replaced the transcontinental mail run. The was no longer a back-up support of over half a million dollars.

Ben had his horse, guns and about a hundred dollars left over from his wages. He had no ties; he could go where he pleased. With time on his hands, his thoughts returned to Sarah—not that they had ever truly left her.

There were numerous reports of white women living as captives with the Indians. Virtually every tribe, it seemed, had one. In some cases, the unfortunates had been stolen as babies and brought up by the tribes. They seemed more Indian than white.

Nobody bothered to investigate these reports. In most cases, the women had no wish to escape. Their treatment on their return to a white settlement would be far worse than they had experienced in an Indian village. No self-respecting man wanted a woman who had shared a redskin's blanket.

"Take it from me," Tucker at the trading post at Marysville told him, "if'n your sister's living with the Cheyenne, you best leave her there. Don't go lookin' for her, she won't thank you for it. And, in any case, if by some miracle you found her, you wouldn't like what you saw. Lord, you probably wouldn't even recognize her!"

His words lingered with Ben like a mountain echo that went on and on.

You wouldn't like what you saw. You probably wouldn't even recognize her.

Ben came to the conclusion that there wasn't any point in hanging around. He didn't have a job. A lot of folks headed west in search of a new future. That was where he'd been going with his family when the wagon train was wiped out. Maybe there was a better future for him in Oregon.

He had driven the Butterfield stagecoach as far as Fort Yuma on one occasion. It looked like good country, maybe beyond there it was even better. He saddled up and followed the old southern trail.

That was where he came upon the posters advertising for Pony Express couriers. To Ben Hollister, it sounded better than driving stagecoaches.

He decided to ride on to Sacramento.

The loneliest place is in the midst of a crowd. That was how it was with Ben Hollister that bright sunny day—surrounded by excited chatter, being jostled yet ignored. He had never been a mixer and it was too late to start now.

A poster had been affixed to the notice board outside the St. George Hotel. Necks were stretched, obstructing the view of those at the rear. Some stood on the balls of their feet in an attempt to see. There were many who were unable to read relying on those who falteringly muttered the printed words aloud.

Mostly the gathering was of young men. An excitement about them might spill into something uglier when the bars opened. Those who had read began pushing their way back through the packed bodies.

Ben let the human tide take him until he stood before the announcement. It read:

PONY EXPRESS
Applicants are invited to apply for the position
of couriers and will be interviewed at the
St. George Hotel, Sacramento, today. The
requirements are:
1. Weight around 125 lbs.
2. Age 16-25.
3. Strength and stamina.
4. A sense of responsibility.
5. Good horsemanship.
6. Pay - $50 a month.
Horsemanship will be tested in the corral
adjoining the St. George Hotel.
Mormon youths will be interviewed and
tested in Salt Lake City.
Successful applicants will be required to
sign the Alexander Majors pledge of honesty,
loyalty to the company, sobriety, decent speech and
gentlemanly conduct.
Signed: Alexander Majors

Ben fitted the bill, but he didn't dare raise his hopes too high. There would be a lot of applicants and the Pony Express could afford to be discerning. They would only take the very best.

The corral had been erected on a stretch of waste ground adjacent to the hotel. Spectators lined its perimeter. It was like the whole of Sacramento had turned out to watch. A rider had just been thrown, and two men were attempting to rope the careening horse while another was helping the unfortunate man to his feet.

The animal was caught and restrained. Another prospective rider clambered into the arena—there was a nervousness about his walk.

The horse threw him almost immediately and a flailing hoof missed him by inches as he rolled.

Two more were unseated in the next few minutes.

Ben pushed his way to the front. The still atmosphere stank of sweat. One of the fallen riders was being helped back over the rails. It looked like his arm was broken.

Ben eyed the latest animal. Unbroken stock. Wild horses caught up for the purpose of putting riders to the stiffest test. At a rodeo, you won ten bucks for staying on for two minutes. Success here was rewarded with a chance to ride for the Pony Express. Failure was probably a broken limb. Or worse.

"Only one made it so far." A slim but powerful young man standing next to Ben turned and spoke. His features had a maturity about them but his voice sounded as though it had scarcely finished breaking. A boy who had grown into manhood too quick for his years, Ben thought. Like he had himself.

The unexpected friendliness took Ben aback. The other wore fringed buckskins that were a mite too large for his frame. His boots were polished leather like he took pride in them. Maybe he was just another spectator.

"Riders worth their salt won't be in any hurry." The stranger spoke with a soft, articulate voice. "Let the hosses tire themselves throwing the riff-raff. They'll handle reasonable then. Providing, of course, you can ride." He laughed.

"Come the end of the day the queue of applicants will be considerably reduced. You gonna give it a try?"

"I guess I've nothing to lose." Ben's initial disappointment returned. "I need a job but I don't reckon I'll find one here. They're asking an awful lot."

"Which'll sort out the bums." The other's expression was serious. "There's a number of stipulations that won't matter if you can do the most important thing they're looking for. You ride hard'n fast, and gettin' the mail through's more important than your life even. What's your name?"

"Ben Hollister."

"Think I might've heard of you. You were a Butterfield stage driver, weren't you?"

"That's right." Ben waited for an explanation but none was forthcoming. "Mebbe I've heard of you, too?"

"Doubt it." The other smiled disarmingly. "Name's Will Cody but that won't mean anything to you. Now, suppose we go and get ourselves a drink, and when this lot've finished gettin' throwed, we'll see if we can stick on one o' those wild horses for a mite longer'n anybody's managed so far."

Three

Cody was much younger than he had thought, Ben decided, as he watched the other vault the fence and drop down into the corral. Those slightly oversized buckskin clothes were deceptive. The frame inside them was lithe and powerful, but Cody had not yet matured enough to fill them. A kid still growing, fifteen or maybe even fourteen. It didn't matter except that Pony Express posters stated that you had to be a minimum of sixteen to be taken on. Good luck to the boy if he managed to fool 'em.

In the arena, the boy became a man. There was no getting away from that. Cody climbed straight into the saddle and took the reins from the liveryman like it was something he did every day. Will looked totally relaxed, almost to the point of arrogance.

The horse was half wild and didn't take to having a rider on its back. The moment the gate was lifted it shied and reared. Cody went with it like he was part of it, a centaur. The front hooves hit the ground, the head went down and Cody leaned back to counter it. He wasn't in any hurry. The horse could set the pace; he would just go along with its every movement.

Dust hung in the air. There was no wind to disperse it. Horse and rider were a silhouette. If those hooves stirred up any more the contestant would be hidden from the watchers.

Ben watched closely. He had already seen several riders

thrown, and he was no mean horseman himself, but perhaps Cody would show him a few things on how to stay in the saddle. This was tougher than any of the rodeos in which Ben had competed. These animals had been specially picked for their meanness and wildness. No fakers would make the grade.

Cody's mount was going crazy. Its eyes rolled and it was flecked with foam. It bucked and wheeled, trying to crush its rider against the fence. Cody anticipated it, swung a leg free and lay almost flat. It saved him, otherwise he would surely have been crushed. The animal backed off and he came upright again.

The horse ran out of tricks and tried the old ones again. They did not work any more now than they had previously. It realized that it was not going to unseat its burden and reluctantly decided that it was easier to play along. It snorted its protest as it cantered round the perimeter, not even bothering to try to crush its rider again. It wasn't tamed, but it was beaten for now.

"You'll do." One of the men grabbed the reins. This guy could ride, all right, and letting him continue any longer was just a waste of time with so many others waiting for a chance. "Go report to the office. Next one!"

Ben was atop the fence in readiness. He caught Cody's eye briefly. The other winked and nodded. Then Will was lost from view as he pushed his way through the crowd.

The horse which two men were bringing out looked much fresher than the last, Ben noted with some misgivings, like they had saved it up specially for himself. They struggled to hold it. Its eyes had a wild look in them and it bared its teeth in what could only have been a snarl. It hated captivity and it hated humans even more. It pulled and kicked, tried to bite as the halter was removed. A nasty, vicious animal, it was looking for trouble.

It plunged and reared as Ben hit the saddle. Somehow he stayed on. He had seen more than one rider unseated right at the start. You needed a slice of luck as well as good horse-manship to pass the discerning Pony Express test. Still, he stayed on, and having learned from what he had already seen, he lifted a leg just in time as the horse crashed against a fence post.

The horse bucked and twisted every way, it might even have tried rolling him if Ben hadn't kept a tight rein. The dust clouds had his eyes smarting. He could hear the crowd but he could not see them. He ignored them—he could not risk any distractions.

Ben had to fight his mount every second, every inch of the way. He kicked its flanks, then he was wrestling with it to stop it from bolting. It seemed to guess what he had to do and was determined to disqualify him. He leaned back as it went down on its front legs, hauled it back up.

Cody had been lucky. He'd gotten the last ride on a horse that had probably been used three or four times today. Ben had drawn a first timer. It would go through half a dozen riders before it showed any signs of tiring.

Ben lost all track of time, every second that he stayed in the saddle was a bonus well won. He heard somebody shouting. It was a few moments before he realized that it wasn't from the watchers.

"That'll do! Yuh cain't stop there all day. There's others waitin'." One of the judges was impatient. He was not interested in watching any fancy riding once the two minutes were up. Rough hands seized the reins. It took the two men all their time to hold the crazed horse, as it almost dragged them off their feet as Ben leaped dawn.

Ben was glad the dust was thick and swirling so that nobody could see how much he was shaking.

"Get to the office!" A slip of paper was thrust into his hand. "C'mon, next one, we ain't got all day!"

Ben had to fight his way through the crowd which was still swelling. If they had witnessed his feat, they had already forgotten it. They cared only for themselves and how each one of them would make out. They liked to see a rider thrown; it lessened the competition.

A side room of the hotel served as a temporary office. It was gloomy inside, or maybe it was the coating of dust on Ben's eyes. There were three men in the room, the one dressed in city clothes sitting behind a trestle table. Ben looked around for Will Cody but there was no sign of him. Will had signed up and had left. Ben might never see him again. Their trails had crossed and now parted again.

"Name?" The man at the desk took the crumpled piece of paper, his eyes fixed on an open ledger in front of him.

"Hollister. Ben Hollister."

The other wrote with a slow and neat hand.

"Age?"

"Nineteen." As far as Ben could remember, he had not kept much track of time recently. He had told Butterfield he was eighteen and that had been about a year ago.

"Read the pledge and sign it."

Sweat and dust blurred the printed words. Ben wiped his eyes with the back of his hand. The pen shook between his fingers. It had been a long time since he had last scrawled his name. Gradually his eyes focused.

ALEXANDER MAJORS PLEDGE
While I am in the employ of Alexander Majors, I agree not to use profane language, not to gamble, not to treat animals cruelly, and not to do anything incompatible with the conduct of a gentleman. I agree that if I violate any of the above conditions to accept my discharge without my pay for my services.

So help me God.

Ben scratched the quill on the paper and rested his hand on the adjacent Bible. He was a Pony Express rider.

It was the shorter of the two men standing behind the clerk who attracted and held Ben's attention. Ben felt compelled

to meet the stare and for some inexplicable reason wanted
to drop his gaze and shy away—except that he could not. It
was a kind of hypnotism, like one coming upon a rattler in
the brush. He tensed and his breathing quickened. He experienced a pang of fear that went as quickly as it had come.
Ben was still trembling. He told himself it was because of
his ride on that half wild mustang. It had stretched every
muscle and nerve in his body. Deep down he knew that that
wasn't the reason.

The man was watching Ben closely with grey eyes that
were deep and menacing in a fixed, unblinking stare. He was
stocky, with a broad face and low cheekbones, his sallow
complexion all the more noticeable because of the short
brimmed hat that shaded his features. His lips were thin and
straight. Ben could not imagine them ever smiling.

He wore a dark frock coat that was filmed with dust, and
matching trousers tucked into scuffed riding boots. His garments were neatly patched, meticulously cared for, as though
he was unable to afford to buy new ones. His age was difficult to guess, but Ben thought he was probably in his early
thirties. There was no sign of a gun but you knew instinctively that he could use one just as a rattler carried and spat
instant death. There was a definite similarity. Ben shuddered.
He had never backed off from anybody in his life before.
He wasn't going to now.

There was an atmosphere of tension in the room. Ben
sensed that the other two men were watching apprehensively.

"This is Mister Slade," the clerk spoke nervously, cleared
his throat.

"*Captain* Slade!" The dark clothed man had a surprisingly
soft cultured voice, but there was no mistaking the icy tone
in the reprimand. "Captain Joseph A. Slade." Soft as the
words were spoken, they were like lightning crackling amidst
thunder clouds.

"Yes . . . of course. Captain Slade." The clerk shifted uneasily in his chair. "Division Superintendent of the Rocky

Ridge Division. That's east of South Pass." His gaze shifted to Ben. "Horseshoe station is the division headquarters. Captain Slade's headquarters."

An uneasy silence followed, a clock was ticking loudly in the foyer beyond the partly open door. Ben had not noticed it before.

"Hollister will be based at Horseshoe station." Slade spoke in a matter-of-fact tone, but it was undoubtedly an order—just in case they had other plans for their latest employee. The other two men glanced at each other; neither would dispute Slade's statement.

"Oh . . . sure." The clerk made a note in his ledger, his hand appeared to tremble slightly, though it might have been a trick of the light. "No problem, Captain. He was going to be based at Horseshoe, anyway." An approval-seeking tone with hindsight. Clearly these employees of the newly-formed mail service were subservient where the road boss of the Rocky Ridge division was concerned.

Slade's expression was inscrutable. Slowly, arrogantly, he completed his own assessment of the company's newest recruit. It was impossible to read his findings in those cold eyes. He flicked some dust off his sleeve, a deliberate action rather than an habitual one. "That completes the Horseshoe postings." It was obvious that he had no intention of remaining here any longer. His gaze flicked over the recruiting agents. Neither man offered any dissent. Ben sensed a relief in both of them that this strange, commanding man was about to leave.

"Start riding for Horseshoe in the morning." Slade turned back in the doorway, adjusted his high crowned, short brimmed hat. Elsewhere his appearance might have seemed comical. Not here, though. He exuded something that transcended respect—fear.

"I'll start out at first light." Ben spoke steadily even though his pulses were racing.

"Bromley and Clute," J.A. Slade said, nodding in the direction of the two agents, "will fill you in on the regulations. You've already signed the Pledge. Don't ever think of breaking it. At least, not on the Rocky Ridge division!"

Then he was gone, closing the door quietly, gentlemanly, behind him.

Ben was aware that he was sweating. So were Bromley and Clute. The latter was fidgeting with his pen.

"The pay's fifty dollars a month, plus board and food." Clute spoke a mite too fast for one who was wholly at ease. "The company is hiring an initial eighty riders. You're one of 'em and you've seen how many out there have failed today. Don't ever lose sight of that. And Slade's taken the best of 'em."

Ben looked questioningly from Clute to Bromley. His expression asked the question.

"Never heard of Slade!" Bromley shook his head in amazement. "Thought everybody'd heard o' J.A. Slade."

"I'm new to these parts." Ben felt at a disadvantage. "Spent most o' my time in Boston. Came from England originally."

"Then I guess you'll find it a mite different out here." There was a hint of a sneer in Bromley's tone. "You've passed the horsemanship test, but you've still to prove you can cope, and that doesn't jest mean deliverin' mail along trails infested with Indians and outlaws. You gotta survive Slade for a start."

"And just who the hell is this guy Slade?" Ben felt himself becoming angry. He had never cowed to any man in his life—Slade had just taken him by surprise. He'd handle it okay from now on.

"Cap'n Slade, and don't you ever forget to call him 'cap'n,' 'specially if he's bin drinkin'." He glanced back towards the door as though he was afraid lest the man he was talking about might suddenly reappear. The Pony Express official lowered his voice, just in case Slade was still within earshot. "Though nobody's ever *proved* that he was a captain but you call him that just the same. They say he killed his first man when he was jest twelve years old. An old German. Killed 'im with a stone." He glanced doorwards again, "Rumor has it that there's a warrant out for his arrest in Illinois. Suspected of *twenty-six killings!* Mind you, rumors spread and grow west of Boston but there's no smoke without fire. Me, I wouldn't care to be stationed at Horseshoe with Slade. No, sir!"

Ben met Bromley's gaze. The other dropped his eyes.

" 'Course, Slade *might've* bin a captain when he served with Captain Killman in the Mexican War." That was just in case Slade happened to be listening outside. "I'm not sayin' he wasn't, jest that I don't know fer sure. There's tales about his courage in the fightin'. I don't doubt 'em—when it comes to gunplay there's nobody to match J.A. Slade, and he's still here today to prove it. That's why Russell Majors've appointed him road boss o' the Rocky Ridge division. It's the worst stretch of all the Overland fer injuns and outlaws and they gotta keep it open if'n they're gonna get mails through regular. And I'll tell you, Slade's the man to do jest that."

Ben's thoughts flitted to his folks and Sarah. He knew only too well what the Indians did to white settlers.

"Slade got married after the war. If he still has a wife, then she ain't followed him out here. Sober, he's a gentleman and an educated one, too. Drunk, he's a devil. You seen him sober today, tomorrow it might be different. Take a tip from me, Hollister, don't never argue with him, no matter how sure you might be that you're right. Slade was freightin' for a while in Missouri. Killed one o' the few friends he ever had in a drunken argument. He drifted after that. Don't take no chances with him. It's too late when you're dead.

"Keepin' trails open ain't nothin' new to Slade. Hockadays hired him to protect their coaches in fifty-eight. He was a Division Superintendent then, just as he is now. He hates injuns worse'n he does outlaws. Story goes that one day a bunch o' renegades attacked one o' the coaches that Slade was ridin' in. The guard was wounded but he lived. Slade opened up with that old Army .44 o' his, shot four o' the redskins outta the saddle. The rest high-tailed it. Slade made the driver stop the coach so's he could get down and scalp the dead injuns. The run was completed half an hour ahead o' schedule with Slade drivin' and a row o' injun scalps hangin' from the roof!"

"I expect I'll get along fine with him." Ben heard somebody come in from the corral. It was a small man with half his face skinned and bleeding, but grinning in spite of it. Another applicant who had made the grade—at a price. "Like I said," Ben said, moving toward the door, "I'll start out for Horseshoe at first light."

"Good luck." Clute's outstretched hand took Ben by surprise. "You'll need it, Hollister. West of Fort Laramie, good shootin' and hard ridin' is only half the battle. Only the lucky ones survive. J.A. Slade will be either the best or the worst thing that ever happened to you."

Four

Ben was riding east on the big black, heading for Pyramid Lake soon after sunup. He wore the .45 in a holster high on his hip, tilted slightly forward. That way, he could draw and shoot with either hand if the occasion demanded. A Colt Naval .36 was stuck in his belt. He carried spare cylinders for both in his pocket. A Hawken .54 was booted and loaded, too. He was not taking any chances. Ben had heard reports of Shoshone and Paiute raiding parties between Carson City and the Great Salt Lake. He rode easily, watchful all the time.

Twice, he saw Indians and made detours. They were not wearing war paint and appeared to be just hunting parties, but he wasn't taking any chances.

Already there was evidence of the formation of the latest means of communication across the breadth of the continent. Ben had been briefed in Sacramento and now he saw it with his own eyes. Several times, both eastbound and westbound riders passed him, small men crouched low in their saddles, coaxing their mounts to maintain maximum speed. Once a horse got into full stride, you kept it there, you didn't tax it beyond its limits because it would tire quicker that way.

Some of the messengers wore tight-fitting clothing and jockey caps, others were clad in buckskin shirts and leggings, whichever they felt most comfortable in. The choice of garments was optional, except for those whose runs began or ended at St. Joseph. The latter couriers wore silver mounted trappings and a silver plated horn, fancy leggings and jangling spurs. Usually, they changed in or out of this attire on the steamboat. William Russell had ordered a ceremonial outfit to be worn, If the riders were seen to be wearing it in and around St. Joseph, he was satisfied. This requirement, a whim of Russell's, was not enforced along the Overland Trail.

The riders were armed, Ben noted, as they thundered past him—a belted revolver and a booted rifle. Even with his own expertise and fascination for firearms, it was impossible to tell at a glance what calibers were being issued by the Pony Express. He would find that out once he arrived at Horseshoe station.

Stations were being erected at approximately fifteen-mile intervals along the trail. Some were just "swing" stations, a shack and a stable. Others were "home" stations designed to accommodate riders who had completed their relays for the day. The latter had sleeping accommodations, a cabin with pole bunks and a stove on which to cook food. Palisades were also erected for protection against Indian attacks. Ben used a couple of these home stations for his overnight stops, resting up at both Cold Springs and Sutler's Store in Fort Halleck. A small regiment of soldiers was stationed here in anticipation of Indian troubles. Many of the tribes along the Overland were becoming restless, seeing the influx of white settlers as a threat to their lands and their way of life. The Pony Express might be the flashpoint to a bloody uprising, but as yet the fort was under-manned and ill-prepared for an all-out war.

Benjamin Ficklin was responsible for getting the express routes operating. Ben glimpsed him briefly at Fort Halleck—a neatly dressed humorless man who rarely smiled. Perhaps this was due to the heavy responsibility which had been placed upon him; in all, 190 stations needed to be built, 165 "swing" stations under the control of a stableman where the mail pouches were simply transferred to a fresh mount, and 25 "home" depots. Crews were hired to build new stations or to renovate those which had existed in the days when the Overland Trail had been a stagecoach route. Ficklin had appointed five division superintendents to supervise the work. Within a few months, it was hoped that every station would be fully operative with relays on a 24-hour basis. Critics claimed that once the snows came the route would be impassable. Russell's nephew, Charlie Morehead, however, had been freighting supplies to Utah in 1858 to quell the Mormon rebellion, and he had made it back to headquarters at Fort Leavenworth through drifts and blizzards. Russell claimed this feat proved that the route would be passable for riders during the winter.

Only the winter could settle that claim.

Stations were being erected as fast as the gangs could fell and pull timber from the forests. In Nebraska, where there were few forests, they used sod. Adobe dwellings were built along the desert stretches, and in some places, steep hillsides were dug out to make swing stations.

From Carson City to Fort Kearney, every station had a stout stockade. The roofs were also covered with soil, for already the pioneers trekking west had experienced the dangers of fire arrows.

The building of relay stations for the Pony Express along the Overland Trail was not the only work that Ben witnessed as he rode eastward. Construction gangs were erecting the telegraph, sometimes managing as much as twenty miles of poles and wire in a single day. One day the eastbound and westbound telegraph gangs would meet up and that would herald the end of the Pony Express. The dispatch riders had already reduced the time of communications from east to west from three weeks to ten days. The telegraph would reduce it to mere seconds.

Ben was aware that his new job was only a temporary one. Some said it would be three years before the telegraph was working fully; others claimed that it would be completed in half that time. Regardless of whoever was right, the riders lived from day to day and many would die before the job was finished.

Ben knew the morning he rode out from Sutler's Store that he would complete the last lap of his long journey that day. He would reach Horseshoe station before nightfall.

He had already noticed some smoke signals in the hills. He rode at an easy canter, watchful of every bend in the trail, every bush and tree that might hide a brave with a strung bow. From time to time, Ben's hand strayed instinctively to the butt of his holstered .45. Every movement, every rustling of foliage by the breeze, presented a threat to his existence. He would not be taken unaware.

By late morning, there was more smoke in the high hills, and he knew that he was deep into hostile country. The stableman at Sutler's had warned him that the Paiutes were active. A telegraph gang had beaten off an attack by a small war party and only the westbound express rider's speed had enabled him to outdistance pursuing braves. The Pony Express mounts were the best in the land, specially bred for speed and stamina. Still, Ben knew that the black horse he rode could in no way equal them. He had to rely on caution.

Several times he left the trail and followed animal tracks through the wood. The Indians knew that the whites followed the Overland Trail and that was where they would lie in ambush.

Ben emerged from the tall pines on to the trail. Ahead of him lay a narrow canyon strewn with boulders and scrub, a perfect place for an ambush. There was no way around it unless he embarked upon steep and treacherous unknown tracks through the mountains. That way might take him days to reach Horseshoe and he would probably become lost.

He had no alternative other than to travel the canyon, doubtless he would have to run the gauntlet here many times in the ensuing months. He drew a deep breath. He might as well make a start right now. He urged his horse forward, hunched low in the saddle in order to make himself as small a target as possible.

The day was warm, with hardly a breath of wind. Bees hummed in the undergrowth as they searched for pollen. Everywhere was still. Too still. Ben's eyes darted from rock to rock, bush to bush. There was cover enough here for a small army to lie unseen.

The first arrow missed him by a foot. The black shied, reared and pulled to one side, which was why another three arrows went wide of their intended mark. Ben fought to control his horse with one hand, while sliding his .45 out of the holster with the other.

Five braves rose from behind a cluster of rocks, heavily daubed with war paint and stringing fresh arrows. Their mustangs were probably tethered in a clump of trees close by. They had counted on felling their victim with their arrows without the need to ride in pursuit.

Ben fired three times in quick succession. The advantage of the Adams .45 over the Colt .36, still belted, was only too apparent. The former was self-cocking. All Ben had to do was to keep on squeezing the trigger.

A Paiute sprawled, clutching a gaping wound in his stomach. The second shot missed. The third caught an attacker in the head, crumpling him to the ground.

The braves hesitated, never before had they experienced such rapid and accurate fire. Even the man who dressed in black, the one they had named Man Who Likes Killing, could not shoot like this.

A cry of dismay from the young warrior in the lead was silenced by Ben's fourth shot. The two surviving Indians fled, leaping over boulders, dodging and weaving, as they headed back to where their ponies were tethered.

Ben lowered his smoking revolver. The air was heavy with the stench of powdersmoke. His horse stood quietly, used to the sound of gunfire. He could, with luck, have picked off the last two fleeing warriors but he saw no reason to slaughter indiscriminately. The ambush was broken, and that was all that mattered.

Ben dismounted and approached the wounded Paiute, gun at the ready. He was not taking any chances. The other was lying on his back, splayed fingers vainly attempting to staunch the flow of blood from the ragged wound below his navel. There was no trace of fear in the Paiute's expression. Nor pain. Just defiance and amazement.

"You shoot faster than Man Who Likes Killing!" The dying Indian mouthed. Blood trickled from his lips as he spoke. His bow lay a few feet away, a knife close by. Ben kicked it away.

"I haven't heard of him." Ben answered. He hoped fervently that the brave would die quickly and spare him having to administer a close range head shot.

"Man who hunts and kills warriors, scalps them. Shoots fast. But not as fast as you. Dresses in black clothes. Likes killing."

An image sprang immediately into Ben's mind—one of a sallow faced man in a dust-filmed frock coat. "That'll be Slade," he muttered to himself. "Couldn't be anybody else."

The Indian's eyes closed. Ben's relief was short lived when they opened again. The Paiute stared fearlessly up at the man who stood over him. He would not ask for mercy, just to die how a warrior should, defiant to the last.

"I am called Slayer Who Rides With the Wind." Ben squatted beside the dying man. "The Apaches gave me that name. But I do not like killing. I only shoot to protect myself. I would not have harmed you if you had not attacked me."

If the brave understood, he gave no sign. He continued to stare up at the white man who had cut him down. He bore him no malice, for death was part of life to a warrior. He accepted his fate. Today he had been destined to die, and nothing could have changed that.

"My sister was taken by the Cheyenne." Ben's pulses

raced as he spoke. He was probably wasting his time, but he had to ask. "Do you know of any white woman living with the tribes? Anywhere."

The brave regarded him stoically, his eyes closed, struggled to open this time, and when he spoke it was in a barely audible whisper. "There are white squaws in some of the villages."

"Where?" Ben tensed, he could not stop his hopes from rising.

The Paiute's lips moved but this time no sound came from them, not even a whisper. His dark eyes had glazed over.

"Where?" It was as much as Ben could do to stop himself shaking the other, yelling at him.

The Indian's head fell back, lolled to one side. His body twitched once, then became limp.

Slowly, Ben straightened up. Almost certainly Sarah was not among the white women to whom the brave had referred. Many white women had been captured by the Indians since the great trek west had begun. It was a long shot, but it had been worth a try. Ben would keep on asking, searching, for the rest of his life or until he had the answer he was seeking. Sarah was probably dead, but he would not rest until he knew for certain what had become of her.

Ben carefully reloaded his .45 and slid it back into its holster. He stood there looking down at the three dead Indians. If he had had a shovel with him, he would have buried them. But he did not have one and the ground was too stony even to scrape out a shallow grave and cover them. He had no alternative but to leave them for the coyotes and the buzzards.

He climbed back into the saddle and set off at a steady pace toward Horseshoe station.

Horseshoe was the largest relay station on the Rocky Ridge division. After the wilderness through which Ben had travelled, it seemed like a small town with its array of wooden buildings. There was a sizable bunkhouse and stabling, and it even had a store which, according to the board over the doorway, served as a saloon, too. The palisade was stout and encompassed an area larger than Pony Express requirements. A smaller building, set apart from the others, bore the sign "Division Superintendent." J.A. Slade had his own quarters separate from the other employees.

Dusk was still an hour away and the stockade gates were open. Men sat on the steps outside the buildings, smoking and talking. One pointed toward the approaching rider and they all stood up, shading their eyes against the glare of the setting sun. They knew from Ben's mount that he was no incoming relay rider. They watched, hands resting on gun butts. West of Fort Laramie, nobody took any chances where strangers were concerned.

"Ben Hollister," Ben called from a distance and reined in the black. "I'm posted here."

The watchers relaxed and a burly unshaven man, whose stomach bulged over his gunbelt, stepped forward. "Bin expectin' you, Hollister. We wuz told you'd be arrivin' yesterday. Slade said so."

"I came as fast as I could." Ben sat his horse, sizing up each one of them in turn and then swung down from the saddle. "It's a long ride from Sacramento."

"Pony riders hev to cover four twelve-mile stretches in a day. Or thereabouts." The big-bellied man grunted. "Yuh'll need to ride faster'n that, Hollister."

"I will." Ben smiled, he was not going to enter into any arguments. Not yet, anyway. "Next time I'll have a faster horse." He nodded over to where a number of small, lithe horses were corraled alongside the stables.

"See any injuns?" A small man who was obviously a rider resting between relays asked.

"Five jumped me in a canyon about fifteen miles back."

Ben began to loosen his saddle girths. "I got three. The other two escaped."

"You got . . . *three!*" The overweight man's jaw dropped open. Then his eyes narrowed in disbelief. "Where's the trophies, then?"

The circle of men closed in on Ben, eyeing up his saddlebags.

"Trophies?" Ben met their contemptuous expressions. "What kind o' trophies am I supposed to have?"

"Skelps. What else?"

"I don't have any." Ben was unable to keep the scorn out of his voice. "I don't scalp and I don't steal from the dead. Isn't killing them enough?"

"Take your hoss over to the stable." The big man turned away. It was clear that he did not believe this newcomer's boast that he had killed three Indians. "Amos'll look after it. Then get yourself some grub. You'll sleep in the bunkhouse like everybody else here. You're on the eastbound ride tomorrow at eleven. You'll hand over at Willow Springs. And mebbe yuh'll kill a few more injuns on the way!"

Ben ignored their laughter and led his horse across the dusty compound in the direction of the stables. He let his horse drink from the trough, listening to the sound of horses munching hay out of the racks. And it was only when his eyes adjusted to the gloom that Ben realized he was not alone.

A man stood in a corner watching intently, his negroid features rendering him almost invisible in the near darkness.

"You must be Ben Hollister." The stableman had a southern drawl. "The boss man was all riled up when yuh didn't show up yesterday."

"Slade?"

"That's right." The negro's eyes rolled. "When the cap'n gits mad, yuh duck for cover. Me, I sits in the corner there and hopes he doesn't see me, then p'raps he'll take it outta somebody else."

"Slade around, is he?"

"No, thank the Lord! He took one o' the hosses, rode out just after sunup this mornin'. No tellin' where he's gone. He don't tell nobody and if yuh got any sense, yuh don't ask where he's a-headed. And yuh only knows he's back when he comes ridin' in an' hollerin' at everybody, usually at poor old Amos, to come and see to his hoss. Mebbe Slade's out checkin' the trail. Or lookin' to see where you's a-got to. Or jest huntin' injuns like he does most days. The Paiutes call him Man Who Likes Killing." The stableman licked his lips and there was a tremor in his voice when he spoke, "Just as the Apaches call you Slayer Who Rides With the Wind."

Ben started. "News travels."

"Me, I've travelled, too." Amos began to fork some fresh hay into the racks. "No choice, had to keep on the move. If'n they ketch me, they'll take me back to where I don't wanna go back, or sell me to some place worse, like they do with runaway slaves. My master was a good man. I'd've stayed if he was still alive. He died. His son took over the plantation and he was the meanest, most cruel man yuh'd meet from Alabama to Missouri. He beat yuh every day, just so's mebbe yuh'd work harder the next day, even though yuh'd worked as hard as yuh could the day before. One day I made a run fer it, jest like that. Didn't stop to think about it, and when I did get to think 'bout it, it was too late. I left mah Annabel an' mah two kids behind." Amos's voice cracked, he was close to breaking down. "If I'd gone back . . . then I guess the master would've punished me wuss than ever. Mebbe sold me to one o' the farms, that way I'd never see mah Annabel agin, anyway. Or hanged me as a lesson to any o' the other slaves who might think about escapin'. I figured the Pony Express was the best place to hide. Russell, he won't stand for no ill-treatment of runaway slaves. There's talk that one day all slaves'll be set free. There's a fellah name o' John Brown. We heard stories 'bout him on the plantation some time back. He wants all slaves freed an' he'll fight fer 'em if he has to. Last we heard, this Brown fellah, he done raided a military arsenal on the Shenandoah. That'd be 'bout fifty-nine. Mebbe he's still around, mebbe they've shot or hanged him, I dunno. But if he is still around, I tell yuh, Mister Ben, from what I heered, if he can arm the slaves, there'll be an uprising, make no mistake 'bout that!"

Ben nodded. It was probably the one and only time Amos had recounted his story since he'd left wherever he had been kept in slavery. He had been storing it up and it had to spill out some time. He had to get it all out of his system and he'd just needed the right man to tell it to. Ben felt honored.

"Your secret's safe with me." Ben was at a loss how to console him. Amos stood out plain enough as a runaway slave and nobody could change that. Not yet, anyway. "Seems mine ain't much of a secret, though."

"Did you really kill three injuns, Mister Ben?"

"Yeah." Ben nodded. Somehow this latest fight with the Paiutes seemed worse because it had been a close encounter. Shooting redskins from a wagon train under attack or a stagecoach being pursued was less personal. "That's the way it is. They come at you and you don't have any choice."

"The cap'n goes huntin' injuns most days." Amos forked some more hay. Ben could not see his expression in the darkness. "Day in, day out. Comes back with their scalps. Then he goes to the saloon and gets drunk like he's celebratin'. After that it's watch out, Amos. Me, I don't know nothin' 'bout injuns but I reckon that if Slade didn't keep huntin' 'em they wouldn't be half so mad. He fires 'em up. Mebbe if he laid off 'em it might be possible to live peaceably with 'em. But, like I says, I never seed an injun till I got clear o' Alabama."

"I've heard a lot of stories about Slade." Ben leaned up against the rail. He had not realized how tired he was until now. "Only met him the once, a few days ago in Sacramento. He was picking the best of the riders out of those who passed the test. Tell me, Amos, you ever hear of a guy name of Will Cody?"

"Sure, he was here till the day afore yesterday. Rode out, goin' east, reckoned he wasn't goin' to take no shit from Slade. I saddled Cody's hoss fer him. He said he had a chance of another posting. Somewhere close to St. Joseph. He told me while I was fixin' the saddle. Kennekuk, somethin' like that. Anyhow, he said he'll be back this way in mebbe a week or so when he's on the westbound ride. Never can tell, though. They make out schedules, then a rider falls sick or gets kilt and afore you know it you're takin' over and miles away."

"Right now I need some food and sleep." Ben straightened up. "They tell me I'm ridin' out to Willow Springs tomorrow morning."

"Watch out fer yourself." Amos lowered his voice. "An' I don't mean jest to look out fer injuns and bandits. The cap'n can be wuss than either o' them when he's riled. An' he was madder'n a nest o' hornets when he rode out this mornin'. Usually, he only comes back like that. I tell yuh, Mister Ben, he wuz in a bad mood. Very bad."

Five

Ben woke up soon after daylight the following morning. Breakfast was warmed up pemmican stew left over from the previous night's supper. He ate leisurely; it would be several hours before he would be setting out on his first relay run. After eating, he headed across the compound towards the stable. He needed to persuade Amos to care for the black during his absence. Ben did not envisage any problems, Amos had obviously taken a liking to him.

"Hollister!"

His name hit him like a bolt of lightning crackling across the compound, a command loaded with venom. The voice was low and yet it carried. It demanded obedience, the way one might have spoken to a mischievous dog. Had Ben been wearing his gun he might have instinctively reached for it and that would have been a dangerous thing to do when it was J.A. Slade who was bawling you out.

Ben turned slowly and saw Slade standing in the open doorway of his office. He looked just as he had been when Ben had last seen him, the same dust-filmed frock coat and hat, those pallid features and thin lips. Twin red spots of anger were starting to blotch the cheeks. This time, the division superintendent carried a gun. It was strapped high on his waist, only just visible beneath his coat. Something dangled from his left hand but from that distance Ben could not make out what it was.

"Where've you been, Hollister?" A low hiss but Ben heard it, all right. "You were supposed to report for duty yesterday."

Ben took a deep breath, let it out slowly. His pulses had begun to race but he fought to get himself under control. You didn't get angry with Slade; neither did you cower before him. Somewhere in between there was a balance that allowed you to keep your self-respect. Ben found it before he spoke. "I wasn't given a day or a time. I came as fast as I could. I'd've been here sooner except that I ran into some Indians on the way." Not that the Paiutes had delayed Ben for long, but the excuse spilled out before he could check it. He hated himself for making excuses, but Slade had that kind of effect on a man. All the same, Ben hadn't conceded anything to the bullying road boss.

"So it was *you* who shot them Paiutes!" Slade's tone altered—it was the nearest he was ever likely to get to paying anybody a compliment. "Three of 'em." His thin lips curled and the hint of congratulations was gone as quickly as it had come. "But you just left 'em where they fell." Those grey eyes narrowed, bored into Ben. Clearly the corpses on the trail had, for some reason, incurred Slade's displeasure.

"That's right. I didn't have anything to bury 'em with and, in any case, the ground was too hard. I wouldn't've had the time, else I'd've been even later getting here."

"Well, I finished the job for you!" Slade sneered as his left hand came into full view. Ben started, almost recoiling as he saw three blood-soaked scalps. "When you kill an injun, Hollister, you scalp 'im and leave the body for the others to find. A warning. That way one o' these days it'll get through to 'em what happens if they get to raidin' on the Rocky Ridge division. Get it?"

Ben nodded. He understood, all right, but he wasn't going to be goaded into an argument with J.A. Slade.

"You're takin' over from the eastbound rider at eleven." Slade's tone was softer yet still commanding. The red marks on his cheeks were fading. These were routine orders he was giving now. "There's a set of clothes in the store for you. Take a revolver if you need one, or carry your own if you prefer. You seem kinda handy with it—a heavy caliber judging by the wounds on those injun corpses. A .45, I'd guess, without diggin' out the bullets. One revolver only is allowed. Rifles have been withdrawn as of today. We go for lightness. Get yourself kitted out and report to the office. I'd better brief you before you leave."

Slade turned on his heel, went back indoors and closed the door behind him. He had reprimanded the latest recruit at Horseshoe station, enforcing his own brand of discipline. He had let Ben Hollister know who was boss around here right at the start. Just in case the new rider was in any doubt about that.

Ben collected his riding clothes and changed in the bunkhouse. The jockey cap was light and skull tight so it would not blow off. The shirt and breeches were close fitting yet supple enough to allow easy movement. They would not catch on branches or undergrowth. All the same, he experienced an almost naked feeling after his customary thick shirt and hide trousers. He strapped on his .45 and slipped a spare cylinder into his pocket. After that was used up, he had only the speed and stamina of his mount to rely upon.

Slade was sitting behind his desk, a pile of paperwork in front of him, when Ben walked into the office. The road boss's broad cheeks were deathly pale, there was no sign of those twin red spots that heralded uncontrolled anger. His lips were bloodless, unsmiling, but his posture was almost relaxed. Those few moments of anger had passed, but Ben knew that they could return in an instant, if the occasion demanded. He was determined to play down their earlier confrontation.

Ben's eyes roved the small room and saw the bunk in the corner. Clearly Slade used the place as his living quarters as well as an office. There was no sign of the Paiute scalps. He wondered what Slade had done with them. There was no spare chair—when Captain Slade summoned you, you stood before him. It was all part of his ruthless code of discipline.

"I'd better brief you on how we work here." Slade spoke softly, it was as if it was a recitation which he had learned by heart for the benefit of new recruits. "The mails are our priority. We've only been running a couple of weeks and the Rocky Ridge record is the best on the entire Overland. I intend to keep it that way. Other divisions have already lost riders. The mail is more important than riders. Riders are dispensable, and there is a long waiting list. There's outlaws and there's injuns. The injuns are our worst problem. The Paiutes have gone on the warpath. Blood Arrow, their chief, is determined to stop the whites moving west. Apart from attacking Pony riders and stagecoaches, the injuns are cutting down the telegraph poles and stealing the wire to make necklaces and bind tomahawks. The mails have to go through, the telegraph has to be joined up all the way from St. Joseph to Sacramento. So, our job, as well as deliverin' the mails, is to make life tough for the redskins, teach 'em a lesson so that they'll leave the mails and the telegraph alone. An' there's only one way to do that!"

"Couldn't we try to make peace with them?" Ben asked.

"Peace!" It was almost a shriek from Slade. He stiffened, it might have been a trick of the light but Ben thought he detected a pinkish tinge on those pallid cheeks. "You can't make peace with savages! You have to hit 'em, and hit 'em hard, all the time. The army ain't exactly havin' much success. Right now they're fightin' the Cheyennes and the Arapahoes around Fort Laramie. They chase one bunch and another moves in. Out here it's the Paiutes that are causin' the problem. If they join up with the Shoshones and the Bannocks, then we've got a full scale war on our hands." Slade's thick neck was thrust forward, his sunken eyes seemed to burn. "It's me they're scared of most, Hollister. Man Who Likes Killing is what they call me and I'm livin' up to that

name. I heard the Apaches got a name for you, too, so mebbe you'd better spread the word on the Rocky Ridge, and let your guns do your talkin'. By what I've already seen, you can shoot some. What's that gun you're carryin'?" Slade's hand reached out across the desk.

"An Adams forty-five." Ben slid the revolver out of its holster and handed it over butt first. "Best handgun you'll come across, take it from me, and I was in the gun trade once. It was my father's. He brought it with him from England. My family was killed in a Cheyenne raid outside of Fort Laramie . . ." Ben's voice trailed off.

Slade examined the weapon with a curious expression on his usually deadpan face. "English," he muttered scornfully, noting the markings. "What do the English know about Indian fightin'?"

"It has several advantages over that Dragoon forty-four you're carrying," Ben said.

"The Army forty-four is the best gun ever made, specially this one!" Slade snapped. He half rose from his chair, snatching out his own gun with amazing speed and laid it on the desk alongside the Adams.

"Yours was made in England, too," Ben leaned forward, the English markings were clearly visible on the worn but well maintained Dragoon model. "Made under license in London around 1850. Could never understand why Colt never switched to the forty-five like Adams."

"So, how's yours got an advantage over mine?" Slade's voice was low, his anger threatened to return. Nobody had ever criticized his gun before. The dead were proof of its speed and accuracy.

"For a start," Ben explained, "yours has a separate barrel, whereas with mine, the barrel and frame are a single unit. Mine's less likely to get damaged if it's dropped. The cylinders are virtually identical. See the shield there—that stops a chain fire reaction, one cap setting off all the others. But the main difference is in the method of firing. Mine is self-cocking. I just have to keep on pulling the trigger, whereas you have to cock your hammer for each shot. I can get off two shots for every one of yours."

"Nobody can shoot faster'n me, no matter what gun they're usin'!" Slade thrust the Adams back at Ben with contempt. "I've had this gun o' mine ten years, mebbe longer, and there's a good many lyin' in their graves, red and white, who'd testify to it if they could get up an' speak!"

"One day they'll make cartridges for revolvers and rifles," Ben continued. "They're already making them for shotguns."

"Shotguns!" Slade might have spat his contempt but for his gentlemanly upbringing. "Scatterguns! You just blast everythin' in front of you."

"Imagine just loading cartridges, no cap and ball to recharge when you've used your spare cylinders." Ben was unruffled. "Cartridges, combined with a self-cocking revolver or rifle, just think about it. The Indians and outlaws wouldn't know what'd hit 'em. Mark my words, that's how the frontier will be won in the end. I should know, I used to repair and sometimes help to make guns in England. I've witnessed the early experiments. They haven't got it quite right yet, but they will. Somebody will find a way."

"I'll believe it when I see it with my own eyes." Slade was skeptical. "But even then I'll stick with my Dragoon."

"Every man to his own choice." Ben knew it was time to back off, Slade would never be convinced. It wasn't worth an argument that might escalate to a terrible conclusion. "I'll stick with mine, you stick with yours."

Slade returned his own gun to its holster. The flush that had threatened faded and his grey eyes became thoughtful. "There are times when I could use some help, Hollister. Not that I can't cope, but this division is a big one. I can't be everywhere at the same time. Like I said, there's bandits and injuns . . . But your job is to see that the mails get through, your first run is Willow Springs. If everythin' goes okay, you'll be back here tomorrow. And there's another problem cropped up where I could mebbe use you . . ."

Ben was uneasy. He watched the other closely. Slade was a strange man: he spoke with a cultured voice—he was no two-bit gunman—yet he was a far more fearsome prospect than any of the armed ruffians that littered the western territories. Educated, yet as ruthless a killer as you were ever likely to meet. He made no attempt to disguise his hatred for the Indian tribes. He killed them with callous indiscrimination, just as he would kill anybody who angered him. Some time, something in his early life had changed him. Maybe it was killing an old man when he was twelve, revelling in the power of life and death. Or being hounded by lawmen and posses, outwitting them, and killing them. Or the Mexican War, another bloodbath. War changed a lot of people. Slade had tasted blood and he couldn't live without it.

"The horses," Slade snapped, jerking Ben out of his reverie, "that's another problem we have here. The company buys the best stock available. In this division we buy 'em from Jules Reni, a French-Canadian trapper. He's got a ranch a day's ride from here between Halfway House and Fremont Spring. A shanty town they call Julesburg after Reni, a hideout for any outlaw on the run. Reni trades with the injuns, too. The company pays two hundred dollars a beast," Slade sneered, " 'bout four times what they're worth. A few come from army stock at Fort Leavenworth and Fort Kearney, but mostly they end up with Jules Reni. Hosses are frequently stolen from the Pony stations." Slade's eyes narrowed, his mouth was a bloodless slit. "If you catch a hoss thief in these parts you either hang 'im or shoot 'im. Often it's half-breeds workin' as stable hands with the company, sneakin' the hosses out. Some were stolen from Mud Springs last week. They turned up here two days ago—bought from Jules Reni!"

Ben nodded seeing what Slade was driving at. "Steal 'em and sell 'em back to the Pony, eh?"

"You got it, Hollister. I think mebbe when you get back

here tomorrow, you and me'll take a ride out to Julesburg, ask a few questions, see what kind of answers we get. It'll be good experience for you. Right now, though, you'd better get ready to ride. Don't even think about anything except the mails until you get back."

Ben smelled that only too familiar odor as he lay in his bunk that night. The smell had never left him since he and his family had emigrated from England. A reminder of his homeland, his boyhood—it came back to him from time to time. In the darkness of the bunkhouse, he was almost convinced that he was back in his father's workshop in Steelhouse Lane—a whiff of gun oil combined with linseed oil that had been used to treat the stocks, its sweetness soured by the acrid stench of stale black gunpowder from barrels in the rack on the wall that had not been ram-rodded recently.

He breathed it in deeply, savored it, and then it went as quickly as it had come. It was only nostalgia that had wafted three thousand miles, and at such times, when he closed his eyes, he could see his father's workshop as clearly as if he had still been there.

The workbench beneath the tiny barred window was littered with an untidy assortment of spare parts and discarded broken ones, a heap of springs and locks. "Never throw anything away." Bart Hollister's voice came to him clearly as his father bent over a tricky re-stocking job. "You never know when it might come in handy. Just when you need it, you find you've slung it."

Ben could never remember his father looking any different, faded oily overalls, hair thinning when you saw him without his cap.

A rack of guns lined the rear wall, all chained together through the trigger guards, their owners's names tagged on them. Those propped up in the corner were for testing after the repairs had been completed. There was a bed of sand in the walled yard behind the workshop for firing into. Most of the Steelhouse Lane gunsmiths had one. Those that did not used the Hollisters's. Saturdays were reserved for testing after the week's repairs had been completed, and the gun trade area of Birmingham sounded like a battue at one of the big pheasant shoots.

Ben carried out most of the testing for his father. Shotguns, rifles, revolvers all had to be tried and approved before being handed back to their owners. Ben did not just blast away into the sand, though. He drew targets with a stick, and the gun wasn't right until he had hit what he was aiming at. It gave the job an added interest. It also taught him how to shoot. It was an unprecedented opportunity to learn to use every weapon with a degree of accuracy that was to stand him in good stead later on.

Ben experimented, too. One day he dripped tallow from a lighted candle into some birdshot. The merit of every shotgun was in the way it "patterned", the density of the pattern of shot at thirty yards. Ben wondered how it would be if the shot charge held together and did not start to scatter until it got to thirty yards. In theory, that would increase the range and striking velocity, enabling it to kill a deer where otherwise it would only wound. He blew most of the sand out of the pit at his first attempt and had to sweep it up and shovel it back. The idea sure worked.

"Damn young fool!" His father had shaken an angry fist at him. "Lucky for you that gun was bored out to improved cylinder. Full choke, even half choke, and that shot charge, all stuck together as it was, would've burst the barrel and blown your damnfool head off!"

Ben had always learned from his mistakes. He had learned that day that waxing shot was fine, provided the gun barrels weren't choked.

Memories like these were both sweet and painful. They made him homesick for England and angry because of what had happened to his family. On occasion, he cried and was grateful for the darkness of the bunkhouse because nobody could see him.

Above all, it brought back his fears for Sarah. He would never be at peace until he found out what had happened to her. And that was as good a reason as any for riding with J.A. Slade.

Six

The incoming rider was a few minutes ahead of schedule. Amos had the fresh mount ready, and it was restless, eager to go after having been rested for a couple of days.

"Looks like Pony Bob Haslam." Amos shielded his eyes against the glare of the midmorning sun. "An' he's all of a lather, bin ridin' like the devil himself was on his tail."

"Injuns!" The rider came to a halt in a cloud of dust and slid from the saddle. Ben noticed how stiff the man's posture was; it certainly belied his agility on horseback. "Shoshones. I managed to shake 'em off but there's a lot o' smoke in the hills, like they're talkin' to the Paiutes. Keep your eyes skinned, fellah. There's no knowin' what's east o' here."

"You go eat and rest, Mister Bob." Amos lifted the pouches off the steaming mount.

"Slade around?" Haslam grunted, his eyes scanning the compound, coming to rest on the closed door of the division superintendent's office.

"He was in his office earlier," Ben answered. "I haven't seen him leave, so he's probably still there, catching up on paperwork."

"An' he can stay there!" Haslam grunted and stalked away in the direction of the bunkhouse.

"Mister Bob, he don't like the cap'n." Amos spoke in a rasping whisper. "One day they wuz arguin' over the schedule. Almost got to shootin'. Might've done 'cept Bolivar

Roberts was staying over and happened to be around. He stepped between 'em. Master Roberts, he set up a lot o' the stations, his division is east of Carson City. The cap'n wouldn't go against Roberts, else the bosses would fire him. Roberts, he don't like Cap'n Slade, either."

"Does anybody like Slade?" Ben smiled. He guessed it depended whether or not you were afraid of the road boss.

"Watch." Amos lifted the mochila off the tired horse, slapped it on the fresh one. "Let me show you, Mister Ben. Next time you'll have to do it yourself. You gotta change in less'n two minutes an' sometimes the cap'n stands and watches with his timepiece in his hand." Amos looked quickly in the direction of the office. The door was still closed. He gave an audible sigh of relief.

Ben was surprised how light the mochila was. It could not have weighed more than ten or twelve pounds. But it could account for an awful lot of mail and a substantial sum in freightage revenue for the company. The standard charge was five dollars a half ounce. Maybe on the long ride, he would try and work out the cost of his cargo.

"See them pockets." Amos had the mochila, which was also part of the light saddle, on the new mount. "You jest have to lift the whole lot off'n one hoss onto the other, cinch it tight, an' you're ready to go."

"Thanks." Ben swung himself into the saddle.

"Good luck, Mister Ben. An' keep your eyes skinned for injuns."

"See you tomorrow, Amos." Ben touched his horse's flanks and the animal surged away without any further bidding.

The horse's strength and stamina were only too apparent to Ben before he was out of sight of Horseshoe station. His mount knew what was expected and it sensed that its rider could handle it. Teamwork between man and beast was half the battle.

Ben made the twelve-mile ride to Box Elder without any

problems. He saw smoke signals in the hills, but there was no sign of any Indians. He had an uneasy feeling that, like Pony Bob Haslam had said, the tribes were planning something, and in the meantime, kept a low profile. Maybe a full-scale uprising. Pony Express riders were not worth ambushing—yet.

"You must be the new man, Hollister." The stableman at Deer Creek was waiting with Ben's change-over mount. Ben lifted the mochila off his sweating horse on to the fresh one. It was as easy as Amos had shown him.

"That's me." There was no time to stand talking. Ben was five minutes ahead of schedule. He intended to improve upon that by the time he reached Red Butte. He swung up into the saddle.

"Heard o' you, Hollister. Them three injuns . . ."

Ben wheeled his mount and sped away. Like Slade, his own reputation appeared to be growing along the Overland Trail, and he wasn't sure that he liked it.

There were no more Indian signs after Deer Creek, not so much as a puff of smoke from the hills. Ben relaxed, and his thoughts turned to his destination. If the other riders were all on schedule then all he had to do was to eat and sleep, then take the westbound mail back as far as Horseshoe tomorrow. He wondered why Slade wanted him to accompany him out to Julesburg. The road boss was not the type to enlist help. A shoot out with a bunch of horse thieves was all in a day's work to J.A. Slade, and it would only serve to add to the reputation with which he seemed obsessed. It was as though Ben was being put to the test again. He had proved his horsemanship, now he had to prove his marksmanship. He had already shot three Indians—maybe Slade thought that his latest recruit had ambushed them, gunned them down from cover, and with no witnesses was capitalizing on his feat. Outlaws with guns were another matter. Ben pushed it from his mind, he would meet it when the time came.

As Ben rounded a bend, there were Indians blocking the

trail ahead of him. Just three, on foot, arrows strung. His horse reacted instantly, wheeled and shied just like the black had done in the last ambush. As before, it saved Ben from the first volley and then he was plunging for the cover of nearby scrub trees.

The Paiutes yelled, but they were too cunning to rush in pursuit. They had counted on taking the pony rider by surprise, but their plan had failed. Now they must stalk him.

Ben tethered his mount to a tree. He dared not risk it bolting with the mails. The braves were doubtlessly after his horse. Pony Express horses were worthy prizes for the Indians, as they were far superior to half-wild mustangs.

He drew his .45, stepped back into the undergrowth and listened. Any movement he made would give away his position. The Paiutes knew roughly where he was. They would, in all probability, split up and crawl upon him from different directions. They only needed a glimpse of him. He would make a much easier target than a wheeling horseman.

Somewhere a jay screeched. The noisy bird was warning its feathered friends that Man was abroad. Red or white, it mattered not to this colorful guardian of the woods. Ben noted that it had called from some distance away to his left. Perhaps the Indians had left the trail, headed uphill and were making a detour to approach him from behind.

Another jay called to his right. That confirmed Ben's thinking that the braves had separated. Nobody was in a hurry; it was going to be a long wait.

Ben saw a pine tree about ten yards away, towering high above the scrub birch trees. It grew tall and straight, its stout branches thick with foliage. It would be as easy as a ladder to climb.

Ben considered the advantages and disadvantages. Altitude was a definite advantage but it also made him a sitting target with nowhere to hide if he was spotted. The Indians were in thick cover, on the ground they could crawl unseen within striking distance before he became aware of their presence. He opted for the tree.

He had to cross a stretch of open ground, but the surrounding scrub would shield him. He crawled from one tuft of coarse grass to another, reaching the huge trunk in a matter of a few minutes. The flattened blades of grass would tell any woodsman, red or white, what he had done but by the time his stalkers got close enough to read his tracks it wouldn't matter.

He eased himself up, a bough at a time, tested each one with his weight before pulling on it. One crack of dead wood would be sufficient to seal his death warrant.

Ben made it to about fifteen feet above ground, straddled a bough with his back leaning against the mighty trunk. That afforded him protection from the rear, the thick foliage concealing the rest of him but still giving him a wide arc of fire.

The only sound was that of wild bees in the bushes below. The jay no longer shrieked. Having delivered its warning, it had flitted silently away to a place of greater safety.

Ben's horse swished at troublesome flies with its tail. Then, suddenly, it snickered and Ben's finger curled around the trigger of his .45.

There was no sign of any of his stalkers. They would not risk stealing his horse until his body lay upon the ground with arrows sticking out of it. But Ben knew that the Paiutes were somewhere very close.

A swarm of bees rose up into the air, buzzed angrily and settled again on the bushes where they had been gathering pollen. They had been disturbed momentarily. That was behind Ben where the tree trunk both protected him and denied him vision. He resisted the temptation to turn around and peer. He had to let the Paiutes come to him.

Another long silence followed. They were watching, listening, as still as statues, trying to figure out just where he was. They reckoned they should have spotted him by now.

The one who showed himself would be the first loser in this deadly game of hide and seek.

Ben was becoming edgy, not just because there were three Indians out there after his scalp, but because he should have been well on his way to Willow Springs with the mail. Yet patience was the only thing that would save both himself and the mails.

The tethered horse snickered. Only Ben's eyes moved, they were stinging where sweat had trickled into them.

For just one fleeting second, he glimpsed a coppery arm. It was withdrawn as quickly as it appeared, as if the Paiute sensed that he was being watched. The brave was behind a bush but Ben did not dare risk a shot. Even if he killed the Indian, his shot might bring an arrow true to its mark.

They sensed that he was very close but did not know exactly where. They would sit him out for as long as it took. They were in no hurry.

A faint faraway sound reached his strained ears. There was no mistaking the drumming of hooves, those of a shod horse rather than an Indian pony. Somebody was travelling the Overland Trail. The westbound Pony Express rider? No, whoever it was rode in the opposite direction, and he was not riding at full gallop. The noise became louder. Closer.

The Indians heard it. Ben saw the foliage move on the bush which he had been watching intently even though no breeze had got up. Possibly the Paiutes thought he had somehow managed to crawl away, found another horse and was escaping. It puzzled them, distracted them, and they were less cautious.

A brave emerged from cover. A second one joined him, and they headed to where Ben's horse was tethered. There was no longer any danger. The white man had escaped but they did not want to lose a prize so valuable as a Pony Express mount.

Ben fired twice, as fast as he could work the self-cocking Adams. Both Indians dropped. Then Ben was lying full length along the thick bough, anticipating an arrow from the third Paiute at any moment.

Instead, his ears picked up the sound of leaves and branches being pushed aside. The remaining Indian was leaving—he was not prepared to take on one who could shoot so fast and with such deadly accuracy.

The horse on the trail had come to a standstill. Ben did not move. He was trying to work out what was happening out there.

Crack.

Ben recognized the heavy report of a .44. It could have been a .45, but apart from his own gun, he did not know of any in use in these parts. Then came the crash of a body falling amidst dry undergrowth. Whoever the stranger was, he was dismounting from his horse, walking into the brush.

Ben climbed down from his lofty perch as swiftly and as silently as possible. He saw at a glance that both Paiutes were dead. Undoubtedly the third had been killed by the mysterious horseman. But there was still a need for caution, the unknown man could well be a road agent who had chanced to meet up with the fleeing Indian.

Ben moved stealthily, using every scrap of available cover to his advantage, his .45 at the ready. This time, he would not dare risk shooting at any movement in the bushes until he had identified whoever it was.

Realization dawned upon Ben that the other shooter was stalking him. Faint rustlings of overhanging foliage came from behind him, as though the other knew that he was there and had made a detour to approach from the rear. Ben licked his dry lips, crouched down with his back against a tree trunk in order to make as small a target of himself as possible. Again, he waited, this game of cat and mouse had become decidedly sinister. Time seemed to stand still. The only sound was the hum of the bees as they carried on their work undeterred.

Ben stretched out a hand, felt along the ground until his fingers closed over a sizeable pebble. He tossed it as far as he could, heard it crash through the undergrowth, bounce and roll.

Crack-crack.

The two shots were so close together that they might have been one. Whoever it was out there, he had cocked and fired his revolver with amazing speed. Bullets whined, ricocheting off a rock. Ben fired in the direction from which the double shot had come, but there was neither a cry of pain nor the sound of a falling body. The other must have leaped to one side as he fired.

Ben did likewise, but no answering fire came his way. In his own mind, he was convinced that it was an outlaw out there, a lone bandit who had arrived at just the wrong time. Possibly the gunman had figured out that there were mail pouches on the tethered horse, but he needed to kill the Pony Express rider before he could steal them.

There was no way any two-bit thief was going to get the mochila except over Ben's dead body and Ben determined that *he* wasn't going to die.

A stone clattered in the bushes a few yards to Ben's left. He smiled to himself, he certainly was not going to fall for his own trick.

However, it had provided the distraction which the other sought. Too late Ben realized that his adversary had circled round behind him yet again. The first he knew about it was when a gun barrel appeared round a nearby tree. Ben half turned, stared death in the face.

"In just two seconds I'm gonna blow your head to mulch. Or mebbe I'll hang yuh instead. Yuh killed a rider, you'll pay for that, but at least yuh haven't got away with the mails."

There was something very familiar about the hate-filled soft voice. It was no idle threat, the other was gloating, savoring the killing, prolonging it those few seconds which ultimately saved Ben Hollister's life.

"Slade!"

The uttering of the road boss's name saved Ben's life. The

other's finger was already tightening on the trigger of his Army Colt.

"Hollister!" J.A. Slade's gun was lowered.

Ben turned around slowly, knew he was shaking and didn't give a damn this time. The two men stared into each other's eyes. Slade's blazed with killing lust that was slowly turning to anger. He had been thwarted, even made a fool of.

"What the hell are yuh doin' here, Hollister, when you should be at Willow Springs handin' over the mails?"

"Indians. They ambushed me. Maybe you haven't noticed." Ben inclined his head in the direction of the two Paiutes who lay sprawled on the ground.

"Yuh got delayed by injuns!" Slade's lips were barely visible in his contempt. "Jest *three* of 'em?"

"They were blocking the trail."

"Then yuh should've ridden through 'em, shot 'em as you went, like all the other riders do. Yuh don't stop for injuns. How long've yuh bin holded up here?"

"Too long." Ben holstered his gun.

"Then get ridin'!" Slade shouted. "What're yuh standin' about for when you're already over an hour late?"

Ben shrugged, untethered his horse and swung up into the saddle.

"Get goin'!" Slade yelled after him as he rode away. "An' when yuh git back to Horseshoe I might just dock some o' your pay. An' there's another job waitin' for yuh when yuh get there."

Ben looked back just once. J.A. Slade was bending over one of the Paiutes, nicking around the dead brave's scalp with his Bowie knife. It did not disturb Ben this time. He might have ended up that way if it had not been for the sound of Slade's horse. It had come mighty close. He knew only too well what the Cheyenne had done to his parents. It was the frontier that had made J.A. Slade what he was.

Ben knew he was fast heading that way himself.

Seven

Ben's return relay with the eastbound mails passed without incident. He made up time between Box Elder and La Bonte, and was five minutes ahead of schedule when he galloped into Horseshoe station.

"Cap'n Slade is fair ragin'." Amos's worried features were streaked with sweat as he glanced furtively in the direction of the Division Superintendent's office. "He came in with three fresh injun scalps yesterday."

"And told you he'd shot three Paiutes?"

"Cap'n Slade, he didn't say nothin' 'bout that. Like I said, Mister Ben, he's ragin'. There's bin some more hosses stolen two nights ago. From Rock Creek. They wuz only bought last week, too."

"Indians?"

"Mebbe. Indians like Pony Express horses. That's why I sleeps in the stables with the hosses. Cap'n Slade says not to let the hosses outta ma sight, sleepin' or wakin'."

Ben was uneasy. Right now he needed food and rest, and he had not forgotten what Slade had in mind. Indians or not, the theft would be blamed on Jules Reni, and the road boss's vengeance would be swift. If J.A. Slade needed one more scapegoat, it would make very little difference to the eventual outcome.

"There'll be a full scale injun uprisin' if Cap'n Slade don't stop shootin' and scalpin'." Amos began to lead the exhausted mount in the direction of the stables. "Bin drinkin', I smelled whiskey on his breath. That's when the cap'n's at his worst. You get bedded down, Mister Ben, and pray he don't come into the bunkhouse. If'n he does, pretend that you're asleep."

"Hollister!" It was clear to Ben that he was not going to make it as far as the bunkhouse. Slade's voice was not loud but its force hit Ben like a physical blow.

Ben stopped and turned to face J.A. Slade standing in the open doorway of his office. The road boss did not look any different from how he always looked but his coat tails were pulled back, the Army .44 in full view, strapped high. Slade's hand rested on the butt.

Ben Hollister and J.A. Slade eyed each other in an unspoken duel of personalities. Slade was the boss, he had just bawled out an employee of the company. That employee was uncowed. Even defiant in his very bearing.

"May the Good Lord preserve us." Amos muttered and urged the tired horse to hurry. This was no place to be standing around.

"You goin' somewhere, Hollister?"

"Eatin' and sleepin' mostly," Ben drawled. "After that it'll be tomorrow, and I'm on the westbound run. Leastways, accordin' to *your* schedule, I am."

"We'll be back here in time for you to ride with the mails." Slade's thin slips stretched in the nearest he ever got to a smile. He was done with fuming, now his anger was cold and calculated and he was savoring every second of it. He was a thousand times more dangerous that way. "Four hosses stolen from Rock Creek, only bought a few days ago, and I'd bet every cent of my pay packet as to where we'll find 'em. Have Amos saddle up a fresh hoss for you. And pack that other gun o' yours and some spare cylinders. And take a carbine, too. Before we're through with this, there'll be plenty o' shootin' and not much time for reloadin'."

"He's goin' after Jules Reni," Amos whispered, when they

reached the stable. "Reni's bad, Mister Ben, so I've heard, and so are his sons. And there's bad men that hang around with them, too. I've seen some of 'em when they'se brought hosses here, an' they're mean and evil. I didn't like the way they wuz eyein' me up, like they wuz figurin' out how much bounty they'd get for handin' in a runaway slave. You jest be careful out there, Mister Ben. Mebbe it's a good thing Cap'n Slade's-a-goin' with you. You keep a-prayin' to the Lord 'cause you'll need Him around, too."

"I will." Ben helped Amos to saddle a fresh lithe grey. Ben was both tired and hungry, and neither condition helped one's reflexes. He was still wearing his tight-fitting company issue clothing and there was no time to change. He stuck the Navy .36 behind his belt and went across to the bunkhouse where there was a rack of long guns: a few Hawkens and a couple of carbines. A double 10-gauge shotgun stood at the far end, its damascus steel barrels brown and shiny like it had never had much use. Ben lifted it down. It was a breech loader. He slipped two fingers into the end of the barrels. They were open-bored, true cylinders to aid the shot spread. That was fine in this instance.

A half-full carton of rimfire shells with paper cases stood on the shelf above. Ben tipped the contents into his pockets. He booted the scattergun and took the reins from Amos.

"You jest keep a-prayin', Mister Ben," Amos whispered hoarsely.

"I just started." Ben swung himself wearily up into the saddle. "I'm prayin' that I'll be ridin' the westbound mails tomorrow."

Slade was sitting his horse impatiently across the compound. He did not wait for Ben to join him, instead he set off at a steady canter through the open gate, a strange black clad figure riding ramrod straight. If he had not snatched any sleep since his return to headquarters, it did not show.

Ben caught up with Slade and rode alongside him. A glance showed Ben that the Division Superintendent's features were an inscrutable mask fixed on the trail ahead, scanning trees and bushes on either side. His nostrils flared as if he was scenting for Indians and unwashed outlaws who might be lying in ambush.

They saw nobody except a Pony Express rider coming from the opposite direction. Slade scarcely glanced at the courier as he thundered by. Instead the road boss's eyes elevated—there were smoke signals in the far hills.

"Paiutes talkin' to Shoshones and Bannocks, for a guess." It was the first time that Slade had spoken. It was almost as though he was muttering to himself. "Guess they're tryin' to get together, but tribes don't join forces easily."

It was some time before the road boss spoke again. "I said boot a rifle, not a shotgun!" He had not turned around since they had ridden out of Horseshoe station and for the first time he noticed that Ben was packing a ten-gauge.

"Best weapon there is for close work," Ben replied. "And it fires *cartridges*. I can get half a dozen shots off with this in the time it takes to stoke up a Hawken."

"Not necessarily goin' to be close shootin'. Might be we'll pin 'em down in the shacks, have to smoke 'em out. Depends how many are hangin' around out there, which of 'em stays to fight alongside Reni and who runs for their skins. Shotgun'll only pepper 'em if we don't get in close."

"Then we'll use our handguns."

They were needling each other. Maybe Slade saw it as a way of firing up his companion, for an angry man made the best gunfighter. Eventually they lapsed into silence and Ben dropped slightly behind his companion. They had said all that there was to say.

It was the best part of a full day's ride out to Julesburg. They rode through the Upper California Crossing on the South Platte, a dangerous crossing during the winter months but now the water was shallow and they forded it easily.

Julesburg was in complete contrast to the image which Ben had conjured up. The name sounded important, smacked of a growing settlement. In truth, it was no more than a cluster of untidy, hastily erected shacks. A large corral was situated on one side in which a number of horses grazed the short scrub grass. Behind was a dark and gloomy pine forest that stretched as far as the nearest hills.

A number of men were lounging in front of the buildings. They watched the approaching horsemen with interest. They recognized Slade. The road boss had doubtless come to haggle over another consignment of horseflesh. It was not a matter for concern.

Slade reined in, his eyes flicked over the horses in the corral. "That's them." Only Ben was near enough to hear. "Them two grey would stand out anywhere. I'll warrant they're carrying army brands like they were at Rock Creek. Stolen from the army, sold to the Pony, then stolen back again. And ready to be sold back to the Pony."

Ben stiffened. He knew his companion was about to ask some unanswerable questions of the men who sat watching them. Accusations and denials, heated arguments would follow. But for the road boss, it was all cut and dried already.

"Let's go." Slade nudged his mount forward.

Some more men came of the shacks. Ben counted eight of them, a motley bunch of ruffians all with belted guns and knives, the dregs of the trek westward who had opted for an easier life this side of Fort Laramie. They bunched together.

"It's Slade," somebody called out, a warning to anybody still indoors who was not yet aware of the road boss's visit.

Slade brought his mount to a halt. "Where's Reni?" His voice was barely audible, yet every one of them heard it. A couple of them glanced furtively back at the doorway behind them.

A squat figure with a hunched back shambled out on to the rickety verandah. His features were mostly hidden behind a thick, unkempt beard and what was visible was grimed with dirt. He wore stained hide clothes, and a homemade skin cap was pulled down tightly on his head.

"Somebody looks for me?" Stumps of blackened and yellowed teeth showed when he spoke. Jules Reni was one of the many French-Canadian trappers who had come down out of the mountains with the decline of the beaver trade. He had traded with the Indians for a while, but horse dealing was much more profitable, particularly since the formation of the Pony Express.

Ben had already noticed that two younger men standing close to Reni bore a striking physical resemblance to the older man. They were equally as filthy. Doubtless they were Jules Reni's sons.

"Them horses in the corral," Slade began, his eyes never shifted from the other, "they were sold to Rock Creek station 'bout a week ago. Then stolen back."

For a few seconds there was a tense silence. The watchers' hands had edged nearer to their holstered guns. Then Reni gave a rumbling laugh that sounded nervous and forced. "You're mistaken, Slade, I bought them from the army coupla days ago."

"*Captain* Slade." Slade's hand rested on his high strapped .44 like everybody else's had suddenly done.

"Yuh can go'n' check the brands if you think I'm lyin', *Captain* Slade."

"They'll have army markings, all right." Slade's voice was little more than a whisper now, the hiss of a snake about to strike. "Those hosses were marked in the first place before they were sold to the Pony. Still got 'em, even after they've been to Rock Creek'n back."

Reni's features suffused with blood. Ben saw that the other was not carrying a gun. He had probably come straight from his bunk where he had been sleeping off a drinking session. "You callin' me a liar, Slade? An' a hoss thief?"

"Damn right, I am, Reni. Me'n Hollister here are takin' those hosses' back. An' a few more with 'em to make up for what you've stolen before."

There was a deathly silence followed by rasping intakes

of breath. One of Reni's sons spat in the dust. "Nobody calls my ol' man that!"

"I do." Slade swung down from his horse and Ben followed. " 'Cause it's true. You—" He nodded to one of the sons. "Git them four hosses roped an' two more besides. Then we'll be leavin'. Now!"

J.A. Slade's sense of anticipation and reactions were a second ahead of everybody else's. With the experience of scores of gunfights behind him, he knew just which one of these disreputables was going to reach for a gun first. The taller of Reni's two sons reached first, but never even cleared his holster.

Slade dropped to a crouch, fanned the hammer of his Army .44. It is doubtful whether the Adams self-cocking .45 could have gotten off the shots any faster. The outcome would have been little different, though. The first bullet tore into the forehead of the son who had gone for his gun. The second took the shorter of the two and smashed his chest. Both crumpled to the ground with their revolvers still holstered.

Ben had drawn and was firing by the time his companion was moving on to the others. The self-cocking Adams was as fast as Slade's Colt. Five shots raked the men on the verandah. Three went down, and Slade dropped another two. They had their guns out but did not manage to get off a shot between them. There was a heap of writhing, bleeding, screaming and cursing bodies either on the raised structure or on the ground in front of it. One of the wounded managed a couple of wild shots. The bullets ploughed into the porch roof above.

Dust cut up around Ben and Slade. It was panic shooting from the others, only an unlucky ball would have felled one of the Pony Express men. Slade dropped on to one knee and changed a cylinder. Ben gave him covering fire and another of the horse thieves crumpled, a heart shot that threw him back into the open doorway where he lay motionless.

The rest ran, zig-zagged for the buildings at the rear and

the woods beyond. Ben dropped another of them and then his hammer was clicking on a spent cylinder. He shoved the Adams back in its holster and snatched the .36 out of his belt. Its filed trigger meant that he could work it faster than a standard model, but by this time the surviving outlaws had made it either to the tumbledown shacks or to the shelter of the trees.

Slade fired once more to dispatch one of the wounded who had risen to his knees. None of the others moved.

"So much for that scum." Slade stood up, he was smiling the only way he knew how. "Like I told you, Hollister . . ."

"Slade!" Ben's Colt was trained on the open doorway.

"What?"

"We didn't get Reni. He must've made it indoors." There was no sign of the French-Canadian.

Ben marvelled at his companion's agility as he launched into a crouching run, leaped up on to the verandah and flattened himself alongside the doorway. Ben was close behind him.

"Reni," Slade called. "Yuh better come out, your hands where I can see 'em. Else we're comin' in shootin'."

There was no reply. Ben listened intently, hearing a laborious breathing from somewhere inside, the wheezing of lungs and a sound like somebody was straining not to cough. Slade cocked his .44 loudly and ominously.

"You hear me, Reni, you humped bastard?"

A few moments later the listeners heard dragging footsteps and a spasm of coughing that could not be contained any longer.

"You got it all wrong, Slade." Reni was still protesting his innocence from indoors.

"A heap o' dead bodies out here says I didn't." Slade's revolver was trained on the open doorway. "You comin' out or are we comin' in?"

"Don't shoot!" Next second Jules Reni appeared in the opening, a shambling hunchbacked figure with his hands held high. His cap was missing, long matted greasy dark hair spilled and straggled around his thick neck. There was no mistaking the terror in his eyes.

Ben was certain that Slade was going to shoot—the barrel of his .44 was no more than two feet from the horse thief's head. A dead-white finger curled around the trigger, took a first pressure, then it relaxed and the gun was slowly lowered. Reni was clearly unarmed.

"Step outside," Slade hissed, "and keep your hands where I can see 'em." He addressed Ben without turning his head, "Hollister, go bring a length o' rope from that tangle that's lyin' around out there. An' cut a piece to tie his hands."

"You takin' me back to Fort Kearney?" There was panic in Jules Reni's voice. He was hoping that he would be handed over to the army and that his worst fears would not be realized. "Colonel Rork will explain everythin' . . ."

"I might mention it next time I see him." Slade was gloating openly now. *"If* I remember. Chances are I'll've forgotten all about it by then."

"What . . . what yer gonna do?" Reni had gone deathly pale, he was shaking in every limb and his eyes were rolling.

"You should know." Slade laughed mirthlessly. "Your sons were lucky, we made it too quick and easy for them. Else they'd've sure got what your gonna get. *I'm gonna hang yuh, Reni, like we hang all hoss thieves on the Rocky Ridge division."*

"No!" Jules Reni might have attempted a stumbling bid for freedom in his sheer panic if Ben had not pulled the French-Canadian's arms behind his back and begun to bind his wrists tightly. "Look, I can explain . . ."

"Shaddup!" Slade struck his prisoner hard across the forehead with the barrel of his cocked .44. It was a miracle that the cap did not detonate. Reni whimpered, sagged. "Get a move on, Hollister, we ain't got all day."

Jules Reni sat hunched on the back of one of the stolen horses as Slade led it across to a lone tree that grew in front of the cluster of buildings. The road boss slipped a noose around his captive's neck and pulled it tight. Then Slade deftly tossed the loose end up over a stout branch and pulled on it to secure it.

"The crows and buzzards'll come after we've gone," Slade jibed, "an', if they ain't too particular, they'll peck your eyes out before they eat your dirty stinkin' flesh. An' your skeleton'll rattle here on windy nights until the rope rots and lets you down."

Reni's eyes were closed. He had given up all hope. He just wanted to get it over now. Slade gave the horse's rump a slap to send it charging forward.

Jules Reni was jerked into the air, left swinging and twisting, his feet kicking wildly at first, then slowing.

"Round up as many o' them hosses as you can, Hollister." Slade turned away. "An' tie 'em together so's we can take 'em back with us. An' while your doin' that, I've just got one small job left to do . . ."

As Ben went about his task of catching up the stolen horses, a backward glance revealed J.A. Slade stepping amid the slain, skinning knife in hand, collecting his trophies. Just in case anybody should doubt his word.

The only reason that Jules Reni's scalp remained on his head was because he swung gently out of Slade's reach. It was too much trouble to climb up and collect it.

Eight

J.A. Slade pulled his horse into the cover of a clump of trees on the side of the trail somewhere between Ward's and Badeau's stations, some fifteen or twenty miles from Horseshoe. His keen ears had picked up the distant drumming of hooves. There was no mistaking the hoofbeats of a Pony Express mount, faster and more decisive than any other. A sense of purpose and urgency, the rider determined to reach the next station on schedule at all costs. Nothing would stop him.

It was the eastbound rider, low in the saddle and going hell-for-leather, his dust-grimed features a mask of determination, partly hidden beneath the long peak of his jockey cap. Slade recognized Warren Upson, the son of Lauren Upson, the editor of the *Sacramento Union*. A wild youth but the kind that the company needed, Warren had joined the miner's rush to the Washoe mines in Carson Valley, spurning the safer job of a newspaper reporter. He always looked for a new challenge, and Bolivar Roberts had hired him at Friday's station. Warren Upson was one of the best riders in the Pony Express. Grudgingly, Slade admired him, but he told himself that the individual didn't count—all that mattered was that the mails were delivered on time. All the same, you looked to your best men. The road boss admired Ben Hollister for the same reasons, but he would never have admitted it to anybody. A Division Superintendent had to remain impartial; he could not afford to enter into personal relationships.

Slade watched Upson disappear around the next bend and grunted his satisfaction aloud. Then he pulled a gold timepiece from his vest pocket and noted that it was approaching mid-day. Hollister was due along this same stretch in about half an hour, riding westward.

Slade eased his horse out of the thicket. He would have plenty of warning of Ben Hollister's approach, which would give him time enough to take cover again. And to watch unobserved. Apart from clearing the Rocky Ridge division of outlaws and Indians, it was the Division Superintendent's job to keep a check on his riders.

There was a stagecoach due within the hour as well, also eastbound. The safety of both bullion and passengers was his responsibility, too. He would watch without being seen.

There were more Indian signals in the hills than Slade had seen for some time. Blood Arrow, the Paiute chief, had called a council, as his braves were in favor of all-out war on the whites. The chief had talked to both the Shoshones and the Bannocks, but these tribes were still undecided whether or not to join forces with the Paiutes. If they did, they would become a formidable army hell-bent on slaughtering every settler west of Fort Kearney.

The Indians resented the westward trek by the whites, the way their land was being taken from them by the pioneers. The Paiutes had an additional reason for war—the telegraph. The construction gangs needed timber for the poles upon which to string the Wires that Speak, and trees were being felled all along the route. The Paiutes relied upon nuts for their staple diet, and vast tracts of nut trees were being cut down along with the pines. After one of the severest winters in living memory, the Indians had almost reached starvation point. In other places, the Paiutes had learned, the whites were slaughtering the buffalo. Only interested in selling the hides, they left the carcasses to rot. The coming of the white man heralded the end of the life which the tribes had known for generations. They would fight for it until the last brave lay riddled with bullets. It was far better to die nobly in battle than to starve to death.

Numaga, the Paiute chief up until a few months ago, had pleaded with his warriors for peace. Arrows were no match for guns, he said, and the pony soldiers would defeat the tribes the length and breadth of this great land. Far better to plead for somewhere to live peaceably than to be annihilated. But Blood Arrow had rallied the braves for war and Numaga had been forced to concede the leadership of the Paiutes to his warmongering rival. The former chief had loaded up his travois, and with his wife and young son dejectedly following him, he had set off for the Great Salt Lake to a self-imposed exile. This was the beginning of the end of the redmen, he told those who sadly bade him farewell, not just the Paiute tribe.

Now Blood Arrow was screaming for white scalps, particularly that of the Man Who Likes Killing. The warrior who succeeded in taking J.A. Slade's scalp would become a legend from the Rocky Ridge to the Great Salt Lake. They also coveted the hair of Slayer Who Rides With the Wind, yet they respected him as a worthy foe who did not fight for sport. Had not this golden haired white man twice killed Paiutes single-handedly when they had ambushed him? Slade killed at every opportunity, ambushing hunting parties and slaying lone braves who offered no threat to the whites. All that would change, Blood Arrow promised his followers as they donned their war paint and called upon their neighboring tribes to change their minds and join them on a trail of bloody death.

Slade could not get Ben Hollister out of his mind. It angered him—Hollister was just another employee, except that he could ride and shoot better than most. The only other person Slade had ever befriended was Andrew Farrar, whom he had killed in a drunken bout in St. Joseph when they were in the freighting business together. Slade had never gotten over that. He had had to live with it ever since; it tortured him, sleeping or waking. In a strange sort of way, Ben was a replacement for Andrew. Slade tried not to think of Ben that way, but that was how it was working out. Maybe that was one reason why the road boss was out here now, checking on Ben. Protecting him. Slade refused to admit it even to himself— even if it was true.

J.A. Slade's guts knotted when he recalled that fight with the three Indians a couple of weeks ago. He had sneaked up on Ben believing that the other was a road agent and had come within a trigger pressure of shooting the younger man. It must never happen again. But Slade had no control over his actions when a drinking session roused his killing lust.

Ben would be his protégé. Of course, Ben would never be his equal, the road boss told himself repeatedly, but Hollister could mend guns as well as use them, and that could be mighty useful out here. Slade touched the butt of his Army Dragoon .44 reassuringly. He had had the gun for ten years, maybe more. It had served him well in both the Mexican War and the Mormon Uprising. You got attached to a gun, he thought. It became an extension of yourself. If it should go wrong in any way, then Ben Hollister would be around to repair it. He was the kind of man you liked to have by your side in a fight when you were outnumbered; the gunfight at Julesburg had been an example of that. There were good reasons for looking after Ben, and Andrew Farrar's death had nothing whatever to do with it. Slade almost succeeded in convincing himself of that.

In about ten minutes, Slade decided, he would pull off the trail, sit his horse in a thicket, and watch as Ben Hollister sped by. At least he would know that the other was safe this far.

Slade's deep thoughts had dulled his customary alertness. There was no sound of approaching hoofbeats. The Paiute smoke signals were too distant to be an immediate threat to his safety.

He saw nothing, heard nothing—until a hammer blow to his chest had him reeling in the saddle. The pain was instant, unbearable, just as though a thousand tiny arrows had embedded themselves in his torso, burning him with the heat of a blacksmith's furnace. He was unable to breathe, his fingers slipped from the reins. He made a grab for them and missed.

He felt himself sliding sideways from the saddle. The sky above was darkening fast like night had come early. He was surely blinded.

He was aware of a double explosion that sounded as one, a booming that had his ears ringing as he thudded to the ground. He sprawled in the road, unconscious and bleeding.

The westbound rider was overdue at Badeau's. Ben waited impatiently, walked to and fro, shaded his eyes and stared down the trail. Listened. For every minute that the other was late, Ben would have to try to make up time between here and Ward's. And if he failed to do that, then he would be late arriving at Horseshoe. Slade would apportion the blame no further than Ben. No excuse, however valid, was acceptable. The road boss might even dock him some pay like the last time.

"There's a lotta Indian signs." Ben fidgeted outside the stable. "Just look at those smoke signals up in the hills."

"And can yuh blame 'em?" Sam Booker was small and wizened. He had driven coaches for Butterfield until the company said he was too old for the job. "The whites are takin' their land an' their food. The army aren't makin' much headway right now but they will. Soon there won't be no food left, no nuts for the Paiutes, no game. The deer'll be gone from these parts jest as the buffalo are fast disappearin' elsewhere. The injuns are desperate. They're proud, too.

They'd sooner die fightin' than surrender and spend the rest o' their lives in near starvation on some barren reservation. Best thing the army can do is to make some kind o' treaty with the tribes and stick to it. Give 'em the best land and let 'em live in peace. That way it'll save a lot o' lives on both sides. Mostly the injuns, but the army won't be satisfied till they've wiped the injuns out to the last man, woman and child. Government can't see it, or don't want to. The injuns have lived here for thousands of years. Kin yuh blame 'em for fightin' for what's theirs?"

"Guess you've got a point." Ben remembered Booker from the Butterfield days, the old timer had always been known as an "injun lover." The stage crews used to josh him about it. Still, there were two sides to every issue, and your sympathies lay with whichever one you happened to be on. Ben would not make his own mind up until he had found out what had happened to Sarah.

"Slade's stirred up the trouble on the Rocky Ridge." Booker drew hard on a blackened pipe, blew out a cloud of strong smelling smoke. "The Paiutes call him Man Who Likes Killing and that's jest what he is, a killer. He goes huntin'n injuns, ambushes small huntin' parties that ain't doin' no harm to nobody and guns 'em down. Skelps 'em, too. He's as bad or worse'n they are. They're savages, never know'd nothin' else, but Slade's educated. There's a good many others like him. It's the whites that are the savages, not the injuns. The injuns are jest pertectin' what's theirs, doin' what they've allus done." Booker stabbed the air angrily with his pipe. "An' I reckon yore not far behind Slade, Hollister. Slayer Who Rides With the Wind, uh!"

"You could be right, Sam." Ben avoided the other's gaze. "I'm as bad as the rest o' them 'cause I don't have any choice right now. At least, not until the telegraph's finished and the Pony's disbanded. Like the soldiers, they have a job to do, and they got their orders. I pledged to carry the mails and I'll do just that. Anybody tries to stop me, they get shot. My folks were killed in an attack on a wagon train. The Cheyenne took my sister. I'm just praying that one day I'll find her."

"Mebbe you'd better pray yuh don't, and I'm not speakin' ill o' the injuns." Booker spat in the dust. "Could be that your sister now *prefers* livin' with the injuns. Don't necessarily mean they've treated her bad, jest made her one o' their own, and there's no way back from that. Few years back I'd've said she was better off livin' with a tribe, now I'm not so sure with the whites out to exterminate 'em." He paused, sucked on his pipe and bubbled nicotine in the bowl. " 'Nother thing, whites don't take kindly to one o' their own who's bin with injuns, even if they took her against her will. If'n they get their hands on her, they'll do wuss to her than ever the injuns did. You take my advice, Hollister, and leave her where she is. Remember her as you used to know her. That way yuh'll both be better off."

Ben's mouth tasted sour. Suddenly, he didn't care whether the westbound rider showed up or not. Everything else seemed insignificant in the light of the stableman's philosophy. All the same, Ben would never abandon his search for Sarah. He could not, if he was ever going to be able to live with himself.

"He's comin' now." Sam Booker's eyesight was still as keen as it had been when he was riding the stages. "It's Charley Cliff by the look o' him, allus lies across his hoss like he's makin' ready to slide off."

"Injuns!" Charley Cliff dismounted in one lithe movement, leaving Booker to transfer the mochila on to the fresh horse. "The rider from Scott's Bluff got an arrow in his leg. He made it through, though."

Ben was mounted and ready, the horse did not even need its flanks touched to get going. It surged forward, knowing what it needed to do.

Ben reckoned he could still make up the lost time before he reached Horseshoe. If there were Paiutes on the trail he would give them a run for their money.

Ben did not slow on the bends, just dropped a hand to his gun. He would shoot any Indians that tried to block his way, otherwise he would rely on speed. Sam Booker had put everything into perspective. For now.

As Ben rounded a bend his mount was suddenly shying and rearing, pulling to one side. His .45 was drawn instinctively, his eyes searching the scrub for any signs of an ambush. Sometimes a sensitive horse smelled Indians before it saw them.

There were no Indians, just a black clad figure sprawled face downwards on the road. Ben grunted. Recognition was instantaneous, there was no mistaking that inert form in the frock coat and the short brimmed hat.

Ben was off his horse and kneeling by the unconscious J.A. Slade. His first thought was that the road boss was dead. Gently, he rolled him over, Slade's shirt was saturated with blood, his head fell to one side and his eyes were closed. Ben tore at the buttons, bared the torso and grimaced at what he saw.

There were a dozen, maybe twenty, small wounds that seeped blood. Flies buzzed and swarmed at the blood. Ben swatted at them. He knew at once just what had happened to the man the Indians called Man Who Likes Killing. Somebody had ambushed him from the cover of the trees that lined the trail . . . Ben tensed, his revolver across the place from where the ambusher had hidden but there was nobody there. The cowardly act done, the gunman had fled. It was the only way anybody would ever out-gun J.A. Slade, Ben reflected bitterly.

They were shotgun wounds—probably a double blast had knocked the road boss out of the saddle. Now he lay where he had fallen.

"Slade!" Ben gave way to panic, shouted and shook the limp body. He could not believe that J.A. Slade was dead. But there was no response, not so much as the flicker of an eyelid.

J.A. Slade was dead, gunned down by a cowardly road agent. Some two-bit outlaw had cheated the Paiutes out of their most coveted scalp.

Ben leaned his head on the bloodied chest, all he could hear was the roaring in his own ears. He was aware of how his temples pounded, his pulses raced. Then he detected a slight vibration from within the still body. He had to listen hard and long to be sure. Yes, there was a faint heartbeat, barely perceptible but it was there, all right.

Slade lived, but for how long?

Never before had Ben felt so utterly helpless. His first responsibility was to the mails, had the road boss been able to speak then he would have ordered the rider to continue on his way and leave him here to die. But right now J.A. Slade had no say in the matter; he wouldn't be giving orders to anybody for a long time to come, if ever. Ben anguished over his dilemma—he had no medical supplies, no means of administering to the badly wounded man.

Ben looked for Slade's horse but there was no sign of it. It had either bolted or wandered away. The ambusher might have stolen it. Ben had no time to go looking for it. He considered trying to lift the injured man on to the Pony Express mount, maybe riding double all the way to Horseshoe station. Almost certainly Slade would not survive the journey. He would be dead, for sure, by the time they arrived at division headquarters. All the same, Ben could not leave the road boss here to die, to be scalped by the Paiutes who were sure to find him.

As Ben agonized over a decision, he became aware of a distant rumbling. At first he dismissed it as a roll of thunder, there were frequent storms up in the mountains. Except that the noise went on and on, grew louder with each passing second.

Realization dawned upon him and he almost shouted his relief aloud. The eastbound stagecoach was approaching! He slid his hands beneath the unconscious man's armpits and

with some difficulty dragged him to the side of the trail. At
the speed the coach would be going they might both be run
over if they remained in the middle of the trail on a bend.

The grating and grinding of iron rimmed wheels became
louder and louder. Ben stood astride the crumpled heap that
was J.A. Slade, arms uplifted. He felt the ground beneath
his feet begin to vibrate.

The scarlet painted stagecoach hurtled round the bend.
The driver was not sparing his team for he, too, had seen
the smoke signals. There were aplenty in these goddamned
hills and the sooner they reached Fort Laramie the easier he
would feel.

Ben waved frantically. The driver saw him, started to
brake. The wheels locked and the coach slid to a halt in a
cloud of dust some twenty yards down the trail.

"Slade's been shot!" Ben yelled as driver and guard scram-
bled down from the box. "He's in a bad way . . . get him
aboard . . . try to get him some help at one of the stations."

They lifted Slade into the coach. There were no passengers
so there was ample room to stretch him out on the floor. He
would only have rolled off the seats with all the bumping
and jerking.

"I'll ride inside with him." The guard shook his head as
he gazed on the still form. "Don't look good to me, seems
like he's not for this world much longer." Nobody liked the
road boss. Many hated him and everybody feared him. They
would only miss him because he was handy to have around
with the Indians on the warpath. "We'll do what we can fer
him, though, once we get to Badeau's. If he makes it."

As Ben remounted, he heard the coach pulling away in the
opposite direction. The driver was taking it as steadily as he
could along the rutted trail.

Ben galloped away at full speed, as he had even more time
to try to make up now. The arrival of the eastbound stage
could not have been more timely. He had done everything
possible. All the same, he resigned himself to the fact that

he would probably never see Slade again. Sam Booker's words echoed in his brain. "Man Who Likes Killing, an' that's jest what Slade is. He's worse'n the injuns."

Nevertheless, Ben Hollister experienced a feeling of sadness. He and Slade had grown as close as anyone was ever likely to get to the Division Superintendent of the Rocky Ridge division. Ben would miss him, but at least Slade's boast had been fulfilled—nobody had gunned him down in a straight fight. It had taken a cowardly ambush to kill him.

And that gave Ben Hollister a strange kind of satisfaction.

Nine

There was no news of Slade except that the stagecoach crew had taken him as far as Cottonwood, a home station beyond Julesburg. There were better medical supplies for use in emergencies there than at swing stations. Nobody seemed to know what had happened to the road boss after that. If he had died, then surely news of his death would have travelled with the westbound riders.

About a week later there was a new arrival at Horseshoe station. Ben had a "rest day" and watched as a dapper little man wearing city clothes stepped down from the westbound stagecoach. There was something military about the stranger in his straight back and measured strides, an air of authority about his every movement. The way that Amos carried his bags across to the Division Superintendent's office seemed more like an obedience to an order than the carrying out of a request.

Ben was puzzled. Often passengers alighted at Horseshoe for a meal in the saloon, but their baggage remained in the rack on the coach. The very fact that this man had instructed his baggage to be unloaded indicated that he was not continuing with his journey.

Ben watched the man enter the office and close the door behind him. Half an hour later, he still had not emerged.

Ben decided that the stranger was probably one of the telegraph construction officials who frequently travelled the line, possibly one of the bosses from back east who had come out here to check on the progress the gangs were making. Nevertheless, the guy wouldn't just have taken up residence in Slade's old office; he would have booked into the saloon. It was all very curious.

Slade must be dead. For some reason, the news had not reached these parts. Maybe he had died further east, in a hospital, where nobody had heard of Captain Slade, the notorious gunman. He was just another hundred dollar funeral and nobody cared.

Ben retired to the bunkhouse. He had nothing else to do so he might as well get some rest. Hardly had he stretched out on his bunk when the door opened and Amos entered. He looked ill-at-ease, his face shiny with sweat.

"Mister Ben." Amos scratched his thigh the way he always did when he was nervous. "There's a fellah askin' to see yuh. He just come in on the coach, gone straight to Cap'n Slade's office. Seems like some sort of a boss. Anyhow, he sure gives the orders and you jumps to obey 'em."

"He wants to see *me!*" Ben was amazed. "Why me?"

"I guess there ain't nobody else much around now that the cap'n's gone. Bosses, they don't talk to stablemen or storemen, 'cept to give 'em orders, an' you're the only one whose reg'lar round here. I said to this fellah, it's Mister Ben you wants to see."

"I'd better see what he wants." Ben ruffled his hair into place and checked that he was presentable. Back in St. Joseph, they insisted that all Pony Express riders wore the designated flowery leggings and jangling spurs. West of Fort Laramie nobody checked. This guy might be looking to enforce company regulations.

"So you're Hollister." The dapper man was seated at Slade's desk going through the pile of paperwork that had accumulated since the road boss's departure. "My name's Ficklin. Major Benjamin F. Ficklin, late United States army. I work for Russell, Majors and Waddell. My office is in St.

Louis." It was a statement of fact, not a boast. No hand of greeting was extended. Ficklin was precise in everything he did or said. He clearly gave orders and expected them to be obeyed.

"I'm pleased to meet you, sir," Ben was nervous, he had never been able to relax in the company of fancy-dressed officials.

"I understand that you are the longest-serving rider on the Rocky Ridge division during the short history of the Pony Express." Ficklin leaned back in the rickety chair, stroked his drooping moustache. "Consequently, I shall be relying upon you for local information. The Indian problem is escalating—that much has been evident to me during my journey here."

"Yes, sir. The Paiutes are on the warpath. There's rumors that Blood Arrow is trying to persuade the Shoshones and the Bannocks to join forces with him for an all-out war on the whites."

"Rumors?"

"Smoke talk. Some of the half-breed stablemen at the stations have read the signals."

"The army will put the Indians down, make no mistake about that." Ficklin was arrogantly confident. "I've come straight from Fort Laramie, where they are waiting for reinforcements. As soon as more soldiers arrive, detachments will be sent out here to take the Indians on. Right now, though, the army has got its own problems with the Cheyenne and doesn't have enough men to spare to mount an all-out assault on the Paiutes. But within a year, take it from me, the Indian tribes will be only too pleased to surrender unconditionally. The army won't stand for any nonsense. If the Indians choose to fight, then they'll be wiped out to the last man. The best way is to deprive them of their food supplies, kill all the game, fell the timber. Starving warriors won't put up much of a fight."

Ben was reminded of Sam Booker's words. It wouldn't be

wise to put that side of the argument to Major Benjamin F. Ficklin.

"I'm taking over here temporarily as Division Superintendent." Ficklin leaned forward, "And I shall need your help, Hollister. I've heard that you've accounted for a few Indians yourself, and that they've named you Slayer Who Rides With the Wind." He winked. "I've also heard that your family was wiped out by redskins, so you don't exactly love Indians, eh?"

Ben grunted in a non-committal manner. He wasn't prepared to put his cards on the table. Anyway, he wasn't exactly sure where his own sympathies lay—at least not until he discovered Sarah's fate.

"I can use you, Hollister, until such time as the army arrives in numbers," Ficklin continued. "We have to do everything we can to protect the stations on the Rocky Ridge division as well as the telegraph construction camps. The way things are at the moment, as soon as a line of wire goes up, the Paiutes chop down the poles and steal the wire. Progress has ground to a halt."

"We don't have the men to give that protection, sir."

"But we have *guns,* Hollister. Arrows are no match for guns. They reduce the odds when you're outnumbered."

Ben didn't argue, he wouldn't have gotten anywhere if he had. Ficklin had been well indoctrinated by his eastern superiors and by the army.

"I understand that the horse stealing problem has been sorted out." Ficklin permitted himself a faint smile. "Jules Reni has been hanged. However, I find it rather insulting that a ramshackle settlement still carries the name Julesburg after a horse thief. Rest assured that it will be changed before long. Doubtless many names will be changed once the Indians have been defeated. However, our priority is to see that communications between east and west are not broken. There is a strong possibility that this country may be divided by a civil war. The Pony Express will serve a vital role in carrying important dispatches. I want you to continue with your job as a despatch rider. I have heard that you are one of the best in the company's employ."

Ben showed no reaction. The other was not showering him with praise for nothing. Ficklin had an ulterior motive.

"With Slade no longer around, both Paiutes and outlaws will think that they have a clear field. Your job, Hollister, in between riding with the mails, will be to carry on where Captain Slade left off. Harass the Indians, play them at their own game. Get out into the hills, kill em whenever the opportunity presents itself. Have 'em looking over their shoulders, not knowing when a bullet will strike 'em down. Make 'em so goddamned scared that they'll leave the settlements and stations alone." He thumped the table with his fist, avalanching a heap of papers. Then he added, almost as an afterthought. "And make life difficult for the outlaws, too."

"What's the news on Slade?" Ben's mouth had gone dry, he had not expected to be given a free-ranging killing role by the company.

"Very little." Ficklin waved a deprecating hand. "I hear they transported him by stage as far as St. Joseph. Miraculously, he survived the journey, but he was more dead than alive by the time he arrived. He was taken from there to a hospital in St. Louis. I haven't heard since then. He may well be dead, it wouldn't surprise me. Certainly, he will not be coming back here." He began shuffling the spilled paperwork back into some semblance of order, "But he did an excellent job during his short time here. The Overland Trail through the Rocky Ridge division was kept open. In that respect, he served his purpose. You have a hard act to follow, Hollister."

Ben stalked angrily back across the compound. Right now he hated the company and the army and everything that they stood for. Still, he would stay until the telegraph lines were joined up and the Pony Express was disbanded—because he needed a job. And if the job demanded that he kill Indians

then he would do just that. And when it was over he would
go looking for Sarah.

Only then would he know his feelings toward the people
who had inhabited this continent since time immemorial.

Ben's relays were to take him westward as far as the home
station at Platte Bridge. After a night's rest he would then
bring the eastbound mail back to Horseshoe.

It was a relief to be away from Ficklin, if only for a couple
of days. Ben could live with Slade, in spite of the ex-road
boss's unpredictable raging furies, but Ficklin was objection-
able in a different way. He never raised his voice, he did not
need to do so. It wasn't what he said but how he said it. It
also seemed that the official had singled out Amos for most
of those jibes and insults. He seemed to bear a grudge against
the negro who always tried to please him, anyway. Ben
thought that possibly Ficklin came from a family of slavers,
and in his own way, he was punishing Amos for running
away. Clearly Major Benjamin F. Ficklin hated all non-
whites, and Ben despised him for that most of all.

Ben was anticipating Indian trouble as he rode out through
the gates of his home station. Against company regulations,
he carried two revolvers, the .45 holstered and the .36 stuck
behind his belt. He had contemplated booting a carbine but
decided it was too unwieldy for a fast rider who would have
need to shoot from the saddle. The Adams would fulfill all
his needs.

The summer heat was fast building up to its peak. Ben
maintained a fast but steady pace. He would only push his
mount to its limits if the need arose.

He changed mounts at La Bronte and again at Box Elder.
He had noticed plenty of Paiute smoke talk in the hills but
had not yet glimpsed any Indians. Maybe Blood Arrow was
keeping a low profile. Isolated attacks on Pony Express riders served little purpose apart from the theft of a thorough-

bred horse. When the time came, the Paiutes would take all the horses they needed.

Ben was conscious of an added tension on his relay rides now that Slade was gone. The road boss's reputation had been enough to make outlaws and Indians think twice before attacking a Pony Express rider or a stage on the Rocky Ridge division. It had been much safer to make raids elsewhere along the trail. In a strange sort of way, J.A. Slade had been like a guardian angel. Or devil.

Without warning, Ben's horse lurched and stumbled. He heard the heavy report from the nearby bushes even as he was kicking himself free. His mount was dead—an ambusher's bullet had penetrated a vital organ.

Ben reacted as fast as ever Slade would have done. A lightning draw had his .45 out of the holster even as he was throwing himself clear of the saddle. Maybe whoever had shot at him was no marksman, had aimed for the rider and killed the horse instead. Whatever the target, the mails were the reason for the ambush. Ben had to save them at all costs.

Ben's survival instincts had him rolling, making as difficult a target of himself as possible. But there was no way he could avoid a lump of jagged rock on the road as his head made contact with it. He experienced a second of pain, exploding bright lights, and then everything went black.

He could not have been unconscious for more than a few seconds. He stirred, everything starting to come back, filtered through a throbbing headache. His gun was lying several yards away where it had been thrown from his grasp when he hit the rock. He grabbed for the .36 behind his belt.

"Leave it or I'll blow yer brains out!"

Ben turned his head with great difficulty. His vision was blurred and streaked with crimson. For one moment he thought he was about to black out again. He squinted and tried to focus. He could just make out a silhouette—a squat, powerful man, a ragbag desperado wearing a close-fitting cap, shoulders hunched as though he had a deformity. There was no mistaking the heavy Hawken .54 rifle trained on Ben.

"Jest lay there'n count yerself lucky that I shot the hoss instead o' you."

That didn't make sense, Ben thought. The outlaws who worked the Overland Trail were not particular about killing folks. They were hanged for robbery as well as murder—they had nothing to lose by shooting their victims. This one wasn't wearing a mask and made no attempt to hide his face. His features were vaguely familiar, and Ben thought he had seen him around somewhere, but he could not be sure until his vision steadied. He had heard that voice, too—the thick nasal growl and the rasping of nicotine-soaked lungs.

"Yuh know who I am?" It was a boast as much as a question.

Ben shook his head. His vision steadied and he was unable to disguise his shock, his disbelief. There had to be some mistake. An identical twin or a double, a lookalike. Or somebody deliberately dressed up to look like . . .

"*Jules Reni!*" Ben Hollister whispered. The very name conjured up an image of a corpse come to life again in a resurrection that defied the laws of Man and God. "No, I don't believe it. It's impossible!"

"Look fer yerself. Look closer." The misshapen figure shambled nearer, but the rifle barrel never wavered for an instant. "But don't try nothin'. Jest look at *this* if yer still don't believe what yer see."

The stubby, grimed fingers of the gunman loosened the collar of his filthy hide shirt, exposing the fleshy neck ingrained with dirt. There was a blue-black weal encircling the neck where the skin had been chafed by a hempen rope.

Ben recoiled from the spectre of the horsethief that he had helped J.A. Slade hang.

"It's . . . impossible!" Ben denied what he saw. It had to be an hallucination caused by hitting his head. "I don't believe it."

"Didn't reckon yuh would." The thick lips parted in an obscene grin. "Mebbe others won't. At first. But you've gotta tell 'em. That's why I shot your hoss instead o' you. You're the luckiest fellah alive, mister. Luckier than the great Cap'n J.A. Slade."

"So *you* shot Slade!"

"Yep. Sure did!" Even more blackened and broken teeth came into view. "I stepped right out in front o' him, challenged him to draw. And beat 'im! With a shotgun. Killed 'im stone dead afore he hit the ground."

That part of the story did not ring true with Ben. Nobody had ever matched J.A. Slade when it came to gunplay. Reni had shot Slade from cover. The outlaw was convinced he had killed the road boss outright. There were no witnesses and Slade had not regained consciousness to Ben's knowledge, so who was to dispute Jules Reni's claim? Only Slade himself and from what Ficklin had said the ex-boss of the Rocky Ridge division had died in a St. Louis hospital. Slade would not be contesting Reni's boast.

"He tried to hang me." Reni kept the rifle pointed at Ben as he retrieved the fallen Adams revolver. "He couldn't even manage that!" He laughed coarsely again. "So he tried to gun me down, but it was him that ended up full o' shot."

Ben licked his dry lips. His head was still pounding but he knew now that Reni was no figment of delirium. Somehow the horsethief had escaped alive from the noose.

"Easy now." Reni's grin had faded. "Take that gun outta your belt'n toss it over here. No tricks. You helped Slade to hang me, Hollister, so I ain't gonna be too fussed 'bout blowin' yore head off, perticularly as you'n Slade kilt both my sons. But there's jest one reason why you're gonna live, so don't blow it. And don't fergit, even Slade couldn't beat me to the draw."

Ben considered a rapid draw, changed his mind. The Hawken was held too steady to argue with. Reni might not be renowned for his gunfighting skills, but he soon would

be. Ben drew the .36 out of his belt very slowly, held it by
the barrel and tossed it towards the other.

Reni stuck both revolvers in the belt around his bulging
waistline. With surprising deftness, he lifted the mochila off
the dead horse.

"Next time I see you, Hollister, yore dead. There's only
one reason you're alive, fellah. Go and tell the Pony Express
that you wuz robbed by the guy even J.A. Slade couldn't kill
no ways. Let the word get around so's everybody who rides
the Overland will be tremblin' case they might meet up with
Jules Reni. Get it?"

Ben got it. Reni saw a means whereby he could become
the most feared outlaw from St. Joseph to Sacramento. Stagecoach crews wouldn't chance their luck when he held them
up. Maybe even the Paiutes would revere him for slaying
their most hated foe. Killing Slade was something to be capitalized upon.

"You gotta long walk back to Box Elder," Reni sneered.
"Jest hope the injuns don't get yuh on the way, else I might
as well've had the pleasure o' killin' yuh myself. Mebbe one
day I will. An' when yuh git back, Hollister, remind 'em that
Jules Reni didn't just kill Slade, he held up the one they call
Slayer Who Rides With the Wind. Coulda kilt him, too, 'cept
this time he had a reason not to."

Then Jules Reni vanished into a clump of cottonwoods.
Ben shook his head in disbelief and then started out on the
long trek to Box Elder.

Ten

J.A. Slade would have raged and shouted at the news Ben Hollister brought in with the westbound mail. Benjamin F. Ficklin's anger was cold and calculated. He seethed, his tongue a whiplash that cut deep into anybody within earshot.

"Somebody must always shoulder the blame" was one of his favourite sayings, a leftover from his army days. Another was "There is no such thing as luck; you make your own luck, good or bad."

"You have lost the mails, Hollister." Ficklin stood with his back towards Ben, hands clasped behind him. It was a posture that both demoralized and humiliated. He had learned that from a colonel in a Chicago regiment of dragoons. "Furthermore, you have invented an unbelievable and outrageous lie in an attempt to detract from your stupidity. This man Reni cannot possibly be alive. If he was, and he held you up, he would have killed you. I have my own views on the matter."

"Might I ask what they are, sir?"

"It seems to me that the mails are stolen, supposedly by a man hanged for horse stealing, and yet *you* are spared when most outlaws would kill to avoid being identified later. *You* are unharmed. The company has lost a valuable consignment of mail and one of their mounts. The fact that you walk back in here with a preposterous story can only raise suspicions in my mind. Of course, there is no proof. I cannot, at this stage, make any accusations."

"It's plain enough why Reni didn't kill me." Ben was breathing fast, the implication was not lost on him. "Reni wants fame as the man who shot J.A. Slade."

"I see." Ficklin whirled to face Ben, using another ploy he had learned during his military service. Alternation of moods unnerved a suspect—sometimes.

"I think we shall all be aware of Reni's return to the living before long, sir."

"I await further developments with interest, Hollister," Ficklin snapped. "You are on the early eastbound ride tomorrow, Hollister. Beware of Indians. And outlaws."

Ben took a .44 and a carbine from the armory. Only now did he mourn the loss of his own weapons. At the first opportunity he would go after Reni. The outlaw had to be holed up in a new hideout. It would not be located easily.

Ben wished more than ever that J.A. Slade was around. That was another reason for killing Jules Reni.

Ben was fully alert as he rode with the mails between Scott's Bluff and Mud Springs, despite having slept little the previous night. He tossed and turned in his bunk as he tried to work out how Jules Reni was still alive. There was only one possible explanation.

Ben and Slade had driven the survivors of Reni's gang into the woods behind Julesburg. Perhaps the outlaws had not gone far, remaining hidden until the two Pony Expressmen had left. Then they had crept back and cut down Reni. If Reni's neck had not snapped, he would have died slowly from strangulation. If the French-Canadian was still alive, the gang would have attempted to resuscitate him. Reni recovered and went looking for revenge.

Having killed Slade, it occurred to him how his ambush could turn him into one of the most feared gunmen in the west. Robbing express riders and stagecoaches was much more lucrative than selling horses to the Pony Express and stealing them back again. His new reputation would make highway robbery much easier. Everybody would be afraid of him.

Ben rode fast and low in the saddle. The French-Canadian would have no further use for him now, and Reni was still looking for revenge for the deaths of his sons. He would not aim for the horse next time.

Ben's horse suddenly snickered and shied. He crouched even lower in the saddle and kicked its flanks. Ben braced himself for a bullet or a hail of arrows from a clump of cottonwoods to his left, but none came.

The horse had almost certainly heard or smelled something to alarm it. As he raced at full speed alongside the trees, Ben saw a horseman in their midst. It was just a momentary glimpse of an outline of a man sitting astride a big roan. It could have been Reni but Ben was convinced that it was not. The stranger sat his mount with a straight back and did not seem obese or misshapen.

Another road agent, perhaps, one who sought a bigger prize than he might find in the mochila of a Pony Express rider. The westbound coach was due in a couple of hours. Ben would leave a warning for the driver at Mud Springs.

All the same, an icy shiver prickled its way up Ben Hollister's spine. He had an uneasy feeling about unknown horsemen these days. Returning from the dead was an unhealthy occupation for all concerned.

Amos sat by the palisade gate and watched the trail that went down to the river below the wood where the evening shadows were already lengthening. The last rider of the day was due in within the hour. A fresh mount stood in the stable, fed and watered in readiness. The incoming eastbound rider would probably be Jay Kelly, and after he was on his way again, Amos would close and bar the heavy gate. There were reports of a large Paiute war party in the vicinity, and the telegraph construction gang had already arrived at Horseshoe station to spend the night in the comparative safety of the stockade. Their own small cabin was too vulnerable in the event of an Indian attack.

The rider was indeed Kelly and he was on time. He was a wiry youth who wore a permanent expression of determination and only spoke when it was absolutely necessary. Within a couple of minutes, he was back in the saddle and on his way again. Amos led Kelly's tired horse across the compound towards the stable. After he had tended to it, he would close the gate for the night. He glanced apprehensively in the direction of the office building. A lamp was already burning, and he could just make out the silhouette of a man seated at the desk.

Amos hurried on by, praying that the door did not suddenly open. Ficklin had given him a hard time these past few days. The stable's cleanliness, apparently, was not up to the standard demanded by one who had once supervised U.S. Cavalry horses. It must be mucked out daily, regardless of whether or not it needed it. Horses must be groomed as well as fed and watered. Ficklin inspected both stable and horses every morning, and he always found something that Amos had neglected. And even if the negro had completed his designated chores to the other's satisfaction, there were other jobs around the station that must be done. The office needed cleaning—that was one aspect in which Ficklin's predecessor had been neglectful. Now, after the temporary Division Superintendent had retired for the night, it was Amos's duty to sweep the office floor and dust the sparse furniture.

Benjamin F. Ficklin made it clear that, by escaping from his master, a slave did not enjoy the freedom he craved. The boundaries of captivity were not simply the perimeter of a plantation. A negro's role in life was to serve, and he would never achieve any other status.

Amos ventured back outside. The deep dusk was blending into darkness. Maybe Ficklin planned to work right through to the early hours like he had done one night last week. Amos would have to wait up to finish his chores. His sleeping hours had become shorter and shorter. A stableman was expected to be at work at first light.

Amos stood by the gate and stared out to where the landscape sloped gently down to the river. Beyond the opposite bank, there was a dark fir wood that was even darker with the coming of night, the kind of place where a Paiute war party might gather in preparation for an attack on the station at dawn.

Amos thought he detected a movement on the edge of the pines but could not be sure, the shadows across the river were too dense. He heard a splashing of water, there was no doubt about that. It might just have been the current swirling on the rocky watercourse—at this time of year the river was very shallow. No, something was splashing its way across, iron clinking on stone Amos tensed. He knew it was a shod horse picking its way carefully across the uneven riverbed in the fast failing light. Then it was scrambling up the near-side bank.

Horse and rider were silhouetted against the dusk sky. Amos strained his eyes. The last Pony Express rider of the day was gone on his way, no incoming riders were scheduled before morning.

The mysterious horseman was coming this way, not hurrying as though he had ridden far and the end of his journey was in sight at last. It was definitely no Indian. Amos experienced a surge of relief. Some lone traveller in Indian-infested country seeking sanctuary for the night, then? He would have to request Major Ficklin's permission, in that case, for there were outlaws along the trail and strangers were not welcome unless they were able to identify themselves.

Amos contemplated closing and barring the gate. He would be able to speak with the newcomer from the safety of the stockade. Then, if he was not satisfied with the other's explanation, he could go fetch Major Ficklin.

But it was too late now to do that. The rider was not slowing his pace as he approached the gateway, as if he was already familiar with his surroundings.

"Who comes?" Amos voiced the customary challenge in shaky tones, hardly recognizing his own voice.

The rider never slowed, he might not even have heard. He passed through the open gate at a fast canter, drawing level with the stableman.

A shaft of light from the office window fell full on the horseman. Amos stared, fear rooting him to the spot. He would have screamed his terror had not his vocal chords refused to function.

Then the mysterious horse rider was past him. Amos watched him dismount stiffly in front of the saloon and hitch his horse to the rail.

The stranger adjusted his hat, brushed invisible flecks of dust from his clothing with his hands and then strode purposefully in the direction of the lighted office. The stride, the posture, were only too familiar. There could be no possible doubt concerning the other's identity and that was the most frightening thing of all for Amos. Now his trembling limbs were capable of movement and he fled for the stable doorway.

"Lord, please don' let him come a-lookin' fer me," he prayed as he hid in a corner. His papa had once told him a story about a distant land called Haiti, where men died and were buried, and then rose up from their graves and went back to work in the fields.

Jules Reni, the horse thief, had been hanged and he had returned from the dead. And now it had happened again . . .

Benjamin F. Ficklin glanced up from his desk as he heard the door click open. He was annoyed at the disturbance. He was also angry because an employee of Russell, Majors and Waddell had dared to enter without knocking. It was probably that negro looking to clean the office so that he could get to bed, Ficklin thought. The fellow was lazy and now that he had fled his overseer, he was becoming cheeky, too. Well, he was about to be taught a short, sharp lesson—army style.

The oil lamp on the desk shone in Ficklin's eyes as he looked up, dazzled him so that all he saw was an outline framed in the open doorway. It certainly did not look like the negro but, whoever it was, they had no business just walking in here at this time of night. Or any other time.

"Get out!" Ficklin snarled, shading his eyes against the glare. There was something disconcerting about the figure behind the lamplight. It was also familiar. And arrogant.

"D'you hear me? *Get out!*" Ficklin's tone lacked its usual ring of authority.

The newcomer stepped forward into the lamplight and Benjamin F. Ficklin recoiled in shocked surprise.

"*Slade!*" It was almost a gasp of fear.

"*Captain* Slade, to you." J.A. Slade stood there, he might never have been away, maybe just popped across to the saloon for a couple of whiskies. There was the beginning of a pink flush on either cheek. His hand rested on his high-belted 44. "*You* can get outta *my* office, Ficklin." He spoke softly but menacingly. "You've no business in here."

"I . . . I . . ." Ficklin stammered and then, with a supreme effort, he regained his composure. "I came out here to take over in your absence, Captain Slade. I wasn't expecting you back."

"No?" J.A. Slade sneered. "You *hoped* I wasn't coming back. You *hoped* I was dead."

"The news was that you were very badly shot up . . ."

"I was." Slade cut a grim figure in the light from the flickering, smoking oil lamp.

He didn't look any different from the last time he'd seen

him, Ficklin thought. Maybe that frock coat was a mite dustier.

"But it takes more'n a charge o' buckshot to put me under."

"So I see."

"Then move off that desk, I got work to catch up on."

Ficklin had stood up and moved back before he realized it, and he hated himself for it. He was not used to obeying orders, particularly from one who had occupied a lower rank in the army. "All right. But you didn't exactly make a good job of hanging Jules Reni, did you? He's back on the Rocky Ridge division operating as a road agent."

"I know." Slade's eyes mocked the official from back east as he fumbled in the pocket of his frock coat and tossed something on to the desk. "See that?"

Ficklin's mouth went dry, bile burning his throat. He almost retched. The object was a mass of bloodied dark hair—a freshly lifted scalp.

"Reni?" Ficklin tempered his revulsion with hope. Reni's scalp would solve a lot of problems for the pony riders.

"No." Slade's lips were a stretched bloodless slit, his killing look was not pleasant to behold. "Not yet, anyway. But I'll bring it to you before very long, you can count on that. This one comes from a half-breed, one o' Reni's old gang I happened to meet up with along the trail. He told me all I wanted to know before I shot him. And scalped him."

"Then you know where Reni's hiding out?"

"Uh-huh."

"I'll organize a posse. They might even be able to spare some soldiers from Fort Laramie. This time we'll hang him *properly!*"

"No!" Slade's short neck was thrust forward, the blotches on his cheeks had spread. "This has become kinda personal between me'n Jules Reni now, an' I never start anythin' I can't finish. I'll see to Reni, and this time there'll be no mistake. Now, seein' as you're here, you might as well make yourself useful. Go tell Hollister I want him ready to ride with me at daybreak. If he's scheduled for a run, organize a replacement. Got it?"

Ficklin nodded, hoping that Slade did not notice how he swallowed. "All right."

"Now, get the hell outta my office, I got work to do."

Ficklin obeyed without question. It was a relief to step outside. He knew that for a few seconds he had stared death in the face. Slade was in a killing mood and thank God that Jules Reni had not hanged or else somebody else might have ended up dead. The road boss would kill someone before the sunset tomorrow, for sure, even if it was only a hunting Indian. And Indians didn't count.

Tomorrow morning, Ficklin made his decision before he even reached the saloon, he would take the stage back east and inform his superiors that everything was back to normal on the Rocky Ridge division. Slade would take care of Reni, Ficklin had no doubt about that. And maybe the warring Paiutes, too.

Eleven

"What the hell are yuh doin', Hollister?"

Ben looked up in surprise as the bunkroom door was kicked open and J.A. Slade stalked in. Amos had conveyed the news of the road boss's return in faltering tones to Ben late the previous night. Ben had retired to his bunk, his confused brain reeling from the shock. Then Ficklin had walked in and conveyed Slade's orders that Ben must be saddled and ready to ride at daybreak.

Ben had slept fitfully, and it was still dark when he awoke. There was at least half an hour before dawn broke and Amos would have a horse ready. In the meantime, Ben busied himself. He had plenty of time.

Ben pored over his task. The candle which he held at an angle over the table gave him enough light to see. As it burned steadily, tallow dripped into an open paper cylinder.

"You're early, Slade." Ben moved on to another cylinder. "You'll have to hang on for a few minutes until I'm finished. I'm all ready, apart from this, and a horse will be waiting for me in the stable."

"What tomfoolery is this?" Slade moved across to the table, the flickering candlelight gave his features a cadaverous look. "Those are them new-fangled shotgun cartridges . . ."

"You've got it." Ben moved the candle so that it dripped into the next cartridge. "I'll doctor half-a-dozen, that should be enough. I take it we're going after Reni and his gang?"

"This is no time for scatterguns." The road boss's tone was harsh. "What're yuh playin' at? You brought a shotgun along the last time an' never had no cause to use it."

"Because I didn't have any shells like these." Ben began closing the cartridge ends, pressing them down and sealing them with hot grease. "A little trick o' the trade—it can be dangerous, but I've checked the gun and it's open bored so there won't be any choke to cause a barrel burst. The tallow holds the shot together. It won't begin to separate until it's reached thirty yards, maybe even forty. Up until then, it's like a rifle ball. After the shot spreads, anybody at fifty or sixty yards gets blown apart like they'd been standing at only ten or fifteen. A guy trying to gun you down with a handgun doesn't stand much chance. He'll underestimate you, think you've only got a scattergun, and at worse, all he'll get is splattered. Too late by the time he finds out—if he ever does! These shells are loaded with number five shot. Birdshot. They'll make a tidy mess of anybody who gets in the way."

"Huh!" Slade was impressed but he wasn't going to show it. "I got on the wrong end of a charge o' buckshot. It didn't do me no permanent harm, as yuh can see."

"This lot would've done." Ben finished closing the cases, set the candle upright on the table. "Right, I'm ready. Reni stole my guns—I want 'em back."

"More important, you lost the mails." Slade's eyes were like chips of ice in the wan light. "You let Reni rob you."

"Nothin' much I could do about it at the time." Ben turned and met the other's angry stare and held it. "Hit my head on a rock as I rolled. When I came to I was looking down the wrong end of a fifty-four. Come to think of it, you didn't make much of a job of Reni, either, Slade. First you botched the hangin', then you let him shoot you outta the saddle."

"Get your hoss." Slade turned on his heel. "We're leavin' in five minutes."

* * *

The eastern sky was streaked with grey as the two horse-men forded the shallow river below Horseshoe station, with J.A. Slade in the lead and Ben following a little way behind. The former was clearly in a killing mood. Ben had smelled whiskey on his breath. Conversation would be limited to stac-cato whispers and then only when absolutely necessary.

The smoke signals up in the hills had already begun. When it was full daylight, Slade reined his horse into a clump of cottonwoods and studied the signals with a grim expression.

"See what those red bastards are saying, Hollister?" Ben guessed, but he waited for his companion to translate. "They're saying 'Man Who Likes Killing is dead, drive the whites from our land'. I reckon they're in for a goddamned shock before long, but for now, we gotta keep outta their way. Once Reni's dead we can teach them Paiutes a lesson, but it'll have to wait until then."

"You know where Reni's hidin' out then?"

"I wouldn't be takin' you along if I didn't," the Division Superintendent retorted. "A half-breed told me. He mighta died a lot sooner an' a lot less painfully if he'd told me what I wanted to know at the start!" He laughed. "Came to the same thing, though. After I'm through with Reni, I reckon they won't call that cluster o' shacks Julesburg no more. We'll take our time. There ain't no hurry—Reni won't be goin' nowhere, 'specially as he still thinks I'm dead. But we don't want a run-in with any injuns an' any shootin' that might warn him. We'll take to the hills north o' Julesburg, approach that way. They won't be expectin' nobody to come in that way."

It was clear to Ben that Slade knew this country like it was just back of Horseshoe, following game tracks and In-dian trails and making numerous detours. Once a war party passed within a hundred yards of the two riders. Slade and Ben waited until the braves were gone before continuing on their way.

"Bannocks," the road boss muttered when they were out

of earshot. "They're mebbe on their way to council with Blood Arrow."

The evening shadows were lengthening by the time Slade and Ben sat their horses in a clump of trees on the edge of a bluff. Beneath them was a small valley screened on all sides by wooded mountains, the kind of place a traveller would only come upon by chance unless he knew it. It was the perfect hideaway for a gang of outlaws. Jules Reni had chosen it well. Wisps of sweet-smelling woodsmoke hung in the still atmosphere. There were a couple of unroofed timber shacks in the early stages of construction and a fenced off area where some horses grazed.

"Probably no white's ever set foot in the valley, jest Reni and his gang," Slade whispered. "You cain't call Reni a white, nor his half-red gang. Guess the injuns know where they are but they leave 'em alone. Reni used to trade with the injuns, probably still does. Renegades can be useful when a tribe's on the warpath. Now, we gotta get down there without bein' seen. At least that 'breed told me the truth and we've found the place."

They came upon a steep narrow track that wound its way down to the valley below. There was no sign of either footprints or hoofprints, it was only used by wild animals. Doubtless the outlaws used a much easier way in and out. And that was fine by Ben and Slade.

"Which means that they won't be expectin' company." In the darkness, Ben almost imagined that Slade grinned.

There were a couple of campfires burning, the outlaws were confident that their hideout was well hidden and there was no need for caution. All the same, a sentry was posted. It was habitual of all who camped out in the wilderness, the only way in which they slept easily in their blankets.

"We'll have to take that sentry out if we're goin' to get in close," Slade whispered. "You reckon' you can do 'im, boy?"

Ben nodded. Clearly Slade was putting him to yet another test.

"Make sure there's not a squeak outta him. Cut the squeak afore it starts."

Ben moved along the narrow track with all the stealth of a stalking cougar, tested every bit of ground in front of him with an outstretched foot before putting his full weight upon it. The crack of the smallest dead twig would sound like a pistol shot in the stillness of a warm night.

The sentry was leaning up against a tree. The flare of a match as he lit a cigarette illuminated a hint of Shawnee features, then the darkness swallowed them up again. A rifle was propped up against the tree trunk. There had never been any problems here, the army was too busy chasing and losing Cheyenne war parties around Fort Kearney, and the Paiutes wouldn't trouble those who supplied them with guns and liquor. There was no real need for a guard . . .

Ben reached round the tree and slit the half-breed's throat wide and deep with his skinning knife; in almost the same movement the Pony Express rider caught him as he fell, helped him quietly down to the ground.

Slade materialized out of the darkness, nodding his approval of a job well done by his protégé. The road boss was a harsh critic—in his book praise was a signal for complacency. However well one had done, it was always possible to do better.

They crept nearer to the camp. The fire had burned down to a dull glow. There was just enough light to make out the shapes of bedrolled outlaws, although others might lay beyond the radius of the firelight.

J.A. Slade squatted with his back against a tree. Ben joined him, it was going to be a long night. They dared not risk opening fire on the sleeping bandits until they knew just how many of them there were.

At long last, the stars began to fade, the sky gradually turned grey, and the cold light of early morning revealed nine sleeping forms. Slade tried to determine which rumpled dirty blanket hid Jules Reni. It was impossible to be absolutely sure. The road boss's greatest fear was that Reni might die without knowing whose bullet had slain him. Or, worse, the French-Canadian might fall to Ben Hollister's gun. That was all that prevented Slade from opening fire on the gang as they slept.

A blanket stirred, a face showed. The features were half-Indian and that was good enough for Slade. A .44 ball entered his forehead and threw the man back on to his bedroll.

Men came awake instantly, rolling for cover. Outlaws jumped up and ran, weaved and ducked. Slade's barking revolver clicked on a spent cylinder; he had counted three down, the one had died in his bedroll and he was certain he had hit a fifth who had made it to the surrounding bushes. The latter would not have limped into cover if the road boss hadn't run out of powder and shot.

Ben dropped one. He knew that with the Adams he would have gotten two or even three, but cocking between each shot was unfamiliar to him and slowed him down. He emptied the Colt into the bushes and grabbed up the shotgun.

"Leave Reni to me!" Slade yelled. A hail of bullets answered his command, but he was already behind a tall cottonwood.

Ben had not yet determined which of the outlaws was Reni, or even if the French-Canadian was among the gang, so fast and furious had been the exchange of gunfire. If Reni was shot, then that was tough. On both the outlaw and the man who sought a terrible revenge.

Ben watched and thought that a bush about sixty yards away quivered—there was no breeze to rustle its leaves. He cocked the 10-gauge, lining the front sight centrally on the moving foliage.

The report was deafening compared with that of rifle or revolver, the powdersmoke thick and villainous. A scream answered Ben's shot and a blood-splattered figure lurched into view, the face now unrecognizable. The upper half of the bandit's clothing was torn and ribboned. He pitched forward, then lay motionless.

Ben smiled to himself as he reloaded. The tallowed shot charge had not failed him. It had held together for much of the distance, then spread and inflicted sheer carnage. He crawled to another vantage point. Beyond the bushes opposite was a stretch of open ground and then a steep cliff face; there was nowhere else for the gang to flee. They were trapped in a patch of scrub. Slade and Ben might have been faced with a lengthy stake-out—except that Ben had the shotgun and a supply of "doctored" shells.

Ben watched carefully for the slightest movement, the rustle of a branch in the windless atmosphere. Before long the stillness of the small valley was shattered by a second thunderous roar. Another body thrashed and groaned behind the bush which Ben had blasted, then died.

Crack-crack. Slade fanned the hammer of his army revolver. Ben's shotblast had prompted one of the outlaws to crawl for a safer refuge. Slade spotted him and the ruffian stretched full length and did not move again.

There could not be many more of the gang left. Ben began a mental count of the slain, but it was too risky to make a move until the last one was accounted for.

A shout came from the thicket. Jules Reni was attempting to bargain with them.

"No deal," Slade answered. "Come out with your hands where we can see 'em. Else Hollister starts blasting away with his scattergun—you've seen what that can do!"

There was silence. Probably the French-Canadian was weighing up the lesser of the two evils. Which was worse, shooting or hanging? But while there was life, there was hope. Maybe a chance to escape would present itself.

Ben fired another blast into the scrub, making sure it was well wide of where Reni's voice had come from. To have killed the gang leader would have incurred the wrath of the Division Superintendent and even Ben wasn't risking that.

Reni shambled into view, a humped and bedraggled figure with his hands held high. There was blood on his face, but it was only from a thorn scratch. His cap was gone and his matted hair straggled around his neck.

"I kin do a deal," he grunted and then stared in disbelief at the dark clad figure which confronted him. *"No! You are dead!"* He backed away in terror. He had strong beliefs concerning the undead. His foot caught in a trailing briar and he sprawled to the ground.

Ben started forward with an exclamation of delight. He recognized the revolvers stuck behind the bandit's belt. There was no mistaking the heavy Adams and the lighter Naval .36. Ben grabbed them. Whatever else happened today, he had been suitably rewarded.

"Tie him to that tree over there," Slade barked. He had waited a long time for this, it was the one thought that had kept him going during those weeks when he had lain in a hospital bed in St. Louis.

Jules Reni protested but did not resist. He had expected to be hanged again, but being roped to a tree signified that he was being taken prisoner.

Ben did not understand Slade's order, either, but he obeyed. The outlaw was roped to Slade's directions, his wrists tied separately to an overhead bough.

J.A. Slade was clearly in no hurry for whatever he had in mind. He reloaded his .44 meticulously, handling it almost lovingly. He was savoring these few moments. He had waited a long time for them.

Reni watched, the color draining from those parts of his features which were visible through the mass of hair. His thick lips quivered.

"Take a better man than you to kill J.A. Slade." The road boss seemed relaxed now, stood directly in front of his prisoner. "Even from ambush yuh couldn't manage it.

"I . . . uh . . . look, we kin do a deal," Reni stammered. "I got some gold . . ."

"We'll find it." Slade's eyes were like those of a bird of prey that had just swooped on a cottontail. The thrill of the hunt was over, now it was time to kill. His eyes never moved from Reni as he spoke. "Hollister, go look around. Find those mail pouches, mebbe the loot from a stage hold-up. An' when you've found em, start scalpin' those 'breeds. Ficklin will surely want proof of what we've been doin'."

Ben stiffened. As fast as he came through one test, Slade put him to another.

Crack.

Ben whirled around at Reni's scream, saw the outlaw had slumped in his bonds. A second scream came from the very depths of the French-Canadian's evil soul. A leg was twisted at an unnatural angle, a sliver of bloody bone protruding through the ragged trousers.

Slade's second shot shattered Reni's other knee. The bandit writhed, shrieked for mercy, straining at the ropes which secured his wrists to the overhead branch. But even if he had snapped them and somehow managed to free his ankles, his legs would not have supported his bulky body. The outlaw's full weight was suspended by his bound wrists. His legs dangled uselessly.

"What're yuh gawpin' at, Hollister? Go find those mails," Slade said, just like he was issuing routine orders from his office. The .44 bucked and spat again, smashing Reni's right foot; the left one splintered a few seconds later.

"Any sign of them mails, Hollister?"

The pouches were strapped to one of the tethered horses. A studded box lying close by had clearly come from an Overland stagecoach.

"Reckon these are them, Slade."

"Make sure, then start scalpin'."

Reni had run out of screams—he was barely conscious. Another shot and a shoulder shattered, then the other. J.A. Slade paused to change the cylinder.

"The mail's all here. There's gold dust in the box."

"Get scalpin', then."

Ben's guts churned as he grabbed a handful of wiry half-breed hair. He tasted bile. He would have closed his eyes except that he might have cut himself. The blade was sharp. He made an incision in the loose skin and was surprised how quickly and easily his knife completed the circuit. He pulled, almost toppled backwards as the bleeding scalp just lifted clear. It was as easy as that.

His revulsion subsided as he moved on to the next renegade. This one was even quicker than the last. What bothered him most was the calculated way in which he carried out the grisly task assigned to him. It was far easier than skinning a shot rabbit—like it was something he'd done ever since he was a kid. All the same, he despised himself, not just for doing it, but because by the time he had finished scalping, he did not really mind it much. If there had been another dozen corpses, he would have carried on scalping. He knew he could do it again and probably would. That was the most frightening part of all.

"You done yet, Hollister?"

"All done." A pile of scalps thudded at Slade's feet. The road boss did not even look, he was staring at Jules Reni.

Ben was sure that the outlaw was dead by the way he hung limply from the branch above, every bone in the pathetic, bedraggled body smashed.

Then an eyelid lifted and a bloodshot eye squinted from beneath a bushy brow. There was no mistaking the fear and the helplessness, the pleading to be put out of his misery. Ben stood watching and thought he understood. Maybe the scalping had helped. This was how it was west of Fort Laramie. He had had to wait until now for his own initiation.

J.A. Slade stepped back a pace. This time he took careful, deliberate aim. He did not need to, he could have fired from the hip. This was the final moment to savor. The single eye closed and the entire broken body shook.

Click!

That eye flickered back open as if to scream mutely, 'You bastard, you knew the gun was spent!'

Slade did not hurry as he changed cylinders. Reni's eyes were closed again, and he sagged in his bonds. He might already have died. But, for his tormentor, he was still alive.

The final shot was an anti-climax, there was nothing left in that body to jerk or twitch. Ben Hollister tasted blood on his lip.

Slade thrust his gun back into its holster. Skinning knife in hand, he stepped close to his victim. Twice he slashed, cutting off an ear with each stroke. Then, in almost the same movement, he scalped that mat of greasy hair.

He walked across to where the horses were tethered and stuffed the pile of scalps under a saddle. Something on the ground caught his eye and, almost as an afterthought, he stooped down and picked it up. It was a nail cast by a horse's shoe.

Slade might have been posting a notice to riders or stablemen on the board outside his office at Horseshoe station, so matter-of-factly did he tap the nail into the tree trunk above Reni's remains, driving it through a fleshy severed ear. He stood back, admired his handiwork, and nodded his satisfaction, not just to himself and Ben Hollister, but to the whole of this big country.

"Just in case anybody says I didn't kill Jules Reni this time," he laughed in his own peculiar flat manner. "A scalp and an ear." He tucked the second ear into the pocket of his frock coat. "And anybody who happens along this way will know for sure who did it. Right now, the Paiutes are saying 'Man Who Likes Killing is dead'. Tomorrow they will say 'Man Who Likes Killing' lives. Slade is back."

His mood changed—killer became Division Superintendent. There was a narrow borderline dividing the two on the Rocky Ridge division. "Hollister, them mails are way overdue. Saddle up the best o' them hosses, that one over there looks like it once belonged to the Pony. Get that mochila to

Box Elder by sundown. An' tell Wheeler that J.A. Slade sends his compliments and that he hasn't lost any mails on his division yet. I'll take the gold dust back to Horseshoe with these horses. Next stage through can take it on east."

Ben hastened to obey. His mind was in a turmoil still because of what he had done and how easily he had done it. The Indians had named Slade, Man Who Likes Killing. They called Ben, Slayer Who Rides With the Wind. Both meant much the same, there was very little difference.

Certainly not anymore.

Twelve

It seemed that for the moment there was not going to be an alliance between the Paiutes, the Shoshones and the Bannocks. The smoke signals had threatened, there had been councils, but no mass uprising against the whites had resulted. Some said that J.A. Slade's return to the Rocky Ridge division had a bearing upon this. More likely, Blood Arrow had not yet succeeded in obtaining the full backing of all the tribes.

Ben was on the westbound run from Cottonwood, working his way back to Horseshoe. He was barely a mile out of the station at Lodge Pole Creek when a war party of a dozen or so Indians pursued him. He was not unduly concerned. The Pony Express mount rapidly pulled away from the mustangs and over the next two miles he left them behind. Badeau's was his last change before an overnight stop at Ward's.

Sam Booker had a fresh mount ready, but the old stableman's attitude towards Ben was openly hostile even before the latter had dismounted.

"Heered you'n Slade've bin on the rampage." Booker lifted the mochila off the sweating horse and on to the fresh one. "They say *you've* taken to skelpin' now."

"Who says?" Ben was shocked that the news had travelled. The renegade scalps had been displayed at Horseshoe, and the road boss had boasted of his protégé's prowess, taking the credit for it. Ben should have felt guilty, a few weeks ago he would have. He didn't now.

"They says." Booker jerked a thumb westwards, he did not elaborate. "Injuns skelp their victims, allus have done 'cause it lets the spirits of the dead go to the happy huntin' grounds. It's a way o' life to them, allus will be. Not to us, though. We're supposed to be *civilized*. If'n we take to skelpin' then we're wuss than them 'cause we know better. We're savages when we don't hev to be."

"We're fightin' a war." Ben felt a need to justify what he had done. For Booker's sake, mostly.

"We're stealin'!" Booker spat in the dust. "Stealin' their land and now their customs. And killin' 'em, too. We're murderers and the army and the government are tryin' to make it seem right, brainwashin' us. In the end, the whites'll wipe out the injuns, them as are left will be given the sourest, driest stretch o' land to live on. They'll be so crammed in that they'll die o' starvation an' disease. The white's win, all right, no doubt 'bout that, and a lot o' them will get kilt in the winnin' an' I cain't say I'm sorry 'bout that. I'm jest glad I'm old and nearly ready to go. Damn whites even took the mountains. Kilt all the beaver so's an honest trapper didn't have no livin' left. Go on, carry on killin' and scalpin' if it pleases yuh, and see what's left fer yuh at the finish!"

Ben swung up into the saddle and kicked his horse's flanks. He hadn't time to stand around arguing the rights and wrongs of the Indian war with Sam Booker. He knew, also, that Sam Booker spoke the truth, but it wouldn't make any difference. When Ben found out what had happened to Sarah, it might just change his way of thinking. But not right now.

Horseshoe station was becoming just too damned overpopulated for Ben's liking. Some of the wagon trains were making their night halts in close proximity to the Pony Express stations; it offered added defensive strength in the event of an Indian attack. It also gave the movers an opportunity to stock up on their supplies. The storekeepers were doing a roaring trade and welcomed the additional custom. There were saloons to oblige the menfolk with liquor, and also the other kinds of entertainment that went with these places.

Relay stations would one day become towns, and pioneers were already staking claims to land along the Overland Trail. Not everybody wanted to go all the way to California.

One day the saloon at Horseshoe would be given a name. Right now it was just called "The Saloon." Sep Dwyer ran it and had helped to build it out of pine trunks dragged across the river from the forest. He was already contemplating extending his establishment. The lean-to shack, which he had erected temporarily at the rear, was handy for the women who travelled the Overland working the saloons. Sep took a commission, naturally. It boosted his trade.

Only last week a battered old piano had come on one of the wagons from St. Louis. The new girl, Mollie, could play it tolerably well. Sep had an awful lot of plans, but they would take time.

Ben sometimes ate in the saloon. Old Sep put on a varied menu that was a welcome relief from the standard fare of pemmican stew and beans and bacon that was always on the stove in the bunkhouse. Rarely, though, did he frequent the saloon at nights. He was mostly too exhausted after a day's hard riding.

Slade had put up the weekly schedule on the board and Ben was surprised to note that he had a couple of "free" days. Depending, of course, on other riders successfully dodging Indians and outlaws and not falling sick. Ben's luck held and, for once, he found himself with time on his hands. Boredom was a new experience for him so, on the first night, already having caught up on his quota of sleep, he went across to the saloon.

Slade was seated at a table in the far corner. He looked

like he had been there for some time, Ben decided, judging by the way the level in the whiskey bottle had dropped.

The room was crowded and the only space on the sawdust strewn floor was around the Division Superintendent. Most folks had learned to keep clear of J.A. Slade at all times, but especially when he was drinking.

Ben pushed his way to the bar and bought a beer. The liquid in the glass was cloudy, flat and warm. Sep brought in hops and yeast and brewed his own. Over the months his customers had gotten used to it, forgetting what beer tasted like in the bars back east.

Ben thought about joining Slade, then changed his mind almost as soon as the thought crossed it. Slade was a good man to have with you on the trail, fighting Indians and outlaws, but socializing with him could be a dangerous occupation. Ben had heard how Andrew Farrar had gotten himself shot in a bar in St. Joseph. Every man was an enemy to a drunken J.A. Slade.

An overpowering sickly sweet, unfamiliar smell assailed Ben's nostrils, wafted by the voluminous skirts of a large woman. Her huge bosom threatened to overflow her low-cut neckline; scarlet lipstick plastered her lips and several layers of powder hid her wrinkles. It didn't stop the drunken settlers from groping her, and she laughed and squealed in a high-pitched voice.

"Hi, there, rider!" She had spotted Ben and pushed away a man who was in the process of trying to lift up her skirt. "They tell me you can ride *anything!*" She laughed loudly and her whiskey-fumed breath was hotter than the wind that blew off the Great Salt Lake. Her fleshy fingers found Ben's thigh and remained there.

"My rest day," Ben said expressionlessly. "Right now, I'm not riding anything."

Somebody nearby overheard and laughed coarsely. The woman snatched her hand away, her smile becoming an instant scowl. She muttered "bastard!" and moved across to a table where some movers were playing blackjack. Often the winner took all, everything she had to give him—and that was plenty.

The honky tonk was silent. Ben wondered idly where the player piano was. Music of any kind was an unaccustomed treat to a Pony Express rider.

A tall rawboned man wearing a fringed hide shirt and matching leggings came in through the door. Shoulder length black hair spilled from beneath a wide brimmed hat. His features were lean and cleanshaven. He stood there eyeing the whole room like he was looking for somebody or maybe just somewhere to sit and enjoy a quiet drink away from the crowd. Ben noted the two belted revolvers were both Walker Colt .44s, like the U.S. Army were issued with. It could be that the stranger was a scout from Fort Laramie, just passing through.

"Hey, that's *Pinner!*" A small man with a squeaky voice spoke in awe. 'Takin' that big wagon train through, prob'ly, the one that's circled up between here'n Ward's."

Ben recalled talk of Pinner when the Hollister family had been looking to join a wagon train going west. If they had gone with Pinner, then his parents might still be alive. And Sarah might . . .

It was a train of thought that brought with it a morose mood. Ben looked at the wagon master across the room with a sense of regret. Pinner had probably been to California and back three or four times since that fateful year. And he still lived and walked.

Pinner spied the vacant seat he was looking for—at Slade's table. He moved across to it with the ease and arrogance of a mountain lion. Slade looked up, the flush on his cheeks was a deeper red, and that boded ill for somebody by the time the road boss had drained the last dregs out of his whiskey bottle.

Ben's attention was diverted as an attractive young woman came in through the door, straightening her jet black hair.

She paused to fasten a button on her corn yellow dress and smoothed some crumples out of it. Her pretty features were flushed and when she looked up again, Ben read guilt in her expression.

Men laughed and spoke coarsely to her as she threaded her way through the throng. Hands pawed her, and she pushed them away. A drunken settler tried to kiss her. She evaded him, laughing in case she caused offence.

Then she was seated at the piano, hammering out a catchy tune as best the untuned instrument would permit. A sing-song started up:

She ain't got a ring on her finger,
Her rings are all under her eyes.

Ben pushed his way through the crowd until he found himself leaning up against one end of the piano. The girl did not look up, over-acting her playing to prevent being interrupted.

Ben guessed that she was a few years older than himself, perhaps twenty-four or five. She wasn't as young as she had looked at first glance, like she had had a hard time working the saloons just to survive. But there was something about her that held his interest, set her trails apart from the big red-headed whore and the other girls who had drifted in here.

Ben had never dated a girl. He had been too young when his family lived in England and after they emigrated, all his time was spent in his father's workshop. He hadn't minded, as he hadn't really thought about it. Sure, he had those feelings that every boy gets when he reaches puberty, done things to himself that afterward made him feel guilty. He had often wondered what it was like to lie naked with a woman. He couldn't imagine his parents ever doing anything like that, but they must have done because they'd had two children. It was something that embarrassed him just thinking about it.

Ben began to get those feelings right now but in a different kind of way. He didn't see the honky-tonk woman in the same way that those guys who had pawed her did. He wanted to touch her. Hold her. Kiss her. But at the same time to show her tenderness and respect. He probably would never do any of those. He would not know how to, anyway. It was Sep's tepid beer making him feel this way, that was all.

She glanced up, noticed him looking at her and smiled at him in the quaintest way he had ever seen a girl smile. In the same sort of way that Sarah used to smile at him when she had been rowing with their parents and she needed somebody to turn to.

Ben was aware that he was blushing. His cheeks felt as if they were on fire. The girl changed the tempo but her eyes never shifted from his own.

"What's your name?" He lip-read her because it was impossible to hear above the din in the saloon.

"Ben."

"Mollie." The smile came with it, warmer and wider than before.

She was looking back down at the keyboard, their brief exchange had embarrassed her, and she was blushing a deeper hue. He tried not to look down her cleavage but it was impossible.

Now they were both blushing.

She changed to a medley, glancing at him several times then looking away like she ought not to. The leering audience had drifted away as some more whores had come into the saloon.

"Maybe we could go outside." The guilt flooded back into her expression. "I mean . . . maybe we could talk some."

He nodded. His pulses were racing and he was trembling a little.

She finished the number she was playing, slid off the stool and headed straight for the door. Heads turned. Ben's legs felt weak as he followed her. He thought they might buckle beneath him and throw him to the floor. All eyes were on him, a ripple of laughter ran round the room.

The night air hit him, cooled him somewhat. He stood outside the door, waited for his eyesight to adjust to the darkness. He could not see her anywhere. Somewhere, not too far away, a man was grunting and a girl was giggling.

Ben almost ran for the bunkhouse. It was safe in there.

"Over here." Mollie's voice came to him on the night breeze, soft and almost musical like her playing. Then he made out her silhouette in the corner of the palisade.

Her breath smelled sweet—no waft of alcohol or tobacco. There was a cleanliness about her that was a rarity out here. Ben was glad that he had washed and shaved earlier.

"You're kinda different from the others," she whispered as if she was afraid that somebody might hear and see them standing together. "I guess you think I'm cheap. I am. I don't have any choice, playing the piano doesn't clothe and feed you. Men don't pay just to listen to your music. D'you understand?" There was a pleading in the way she asked the question as if the answer was all-important to her.

"I understand." He did but he did not know how to convey his own feelings. He would never have the courage to put them into words. "Really, I do. I wasn't lookin' for . . ."

"I know you weren't." Her hand touched his, stayed there. "That's why I . . ."

"You stayin' around?"

"I . . . don't know. Depends. I'm travelling on the wagon train that's camped between here and the next station. When they move on . . . you see, I don't have anywhere to live except in my wagon."

"I . . . you on . . . on your own?"

"Yes." He imagined that her eyes had filled with tears because her voice had gone husky. "I wasn't to begin with . . . when we set out from Fort Kearney. My husband . . . we'd only been married a few months. We married in St. Louis . . . he wanted a new life, a farm in California." Her voice broke off, and then Ben was holding her to him just like it was something that was natural to him. "Indians attacked the wagon train. It was only a small war party. A skirmish. The men fought them off easily enough. An arrow, just one. It got Sam."

Ben held her tightly, felt how she shook. He let her cry without saying anything because there was nothing more he could say. He had no idea how long they clung to each other, it seemed that they had always been that way.

Whores and drunks were coming and going, the shack on the end of the saloon was a busy place tonight.

"I'm sorry." It was all he could think of saying when she was done with crying.

"I guess it happens to a lot of folks who decide to go west." She dabbed at her eyes with a handkerchief. "You don't understand until it happens to you."

He almost said "it happened to me" but it would have been too painful and spoiled everything. Instead, he said, "I want you to stay, Mollie. Please don't leave."

"I'd like to but . . . I don't have any place except the wagon and the only way I can earn money is by . . ."

"We'll find a way."

Her lips went in search of his and found them, and for Ben Hollister it was the most heady experience of his life. They might just have stayed that way for the rest of the night.

Except that a shot split the night like a clap of thunder. Silence followed—it lasted perhaps half a minute, then folks were stampeding out of the saloon, clustering in the open compound. Men shouted and women screamed. Everybody was panicking.

"Stay right here till I get back." Ben pushed Mollie into the safety offered by the corner of the stockade and ran towards the saloon. A man bumped against him, cursed. Ben ignored him. He guessed what he might find in there, prayed that he was wrong. Men were drunk, and quarrels were plenty. It could have been any one of them.

Ben stood just inside the doorway. The saloon was empty except for J.A. Slade standing over by the table which he had occupied all evening. The whiskey bottle stood in the center—it was empty. Sep Dwyer might have been crouched down behind the bar. If he was, then he stayed out of sight.

Slade's cheeks were flushed, his gun was in its holster but a faint spiral of black powdersmoke trickled up from it, its acrid stench drifting across the room. He did not look round, he might not even have been aware of Ben's presence.

Slade's expression was just how Ben dreaded seeing it—the twin red cheekspots, the tight slitted mouth, the fixed stare. The look of a predator who has just killed.

A man lay face downwards on the floor. Ben could not see his face but he recognized the hide clothing, the fallen wide-brimmed hat, the long flowing dark hair. Blood was seeping from beneath the inert body, forming a pool on the rough floorboards. A Walker .44 was clutched in his outstretched hand.

Ben did not move. He did not speak. There was nothing to be said. Slowly, he backed out through the door and when he looked in the direction of the corner of the palisade, there was no sign of Mollie.

J.A. Slade had gunned down Pinner, the wagon master who had become a legend from Fort Kearney to Sacramento.

Now there was big trouble brewing.

Thirteen

"The cap'n's bin and gone and done it now." Amos was skulking in a corner of the stable, shivering like he was cold and wet. "They won't let him get away with killin' the wagon master. The law'll come for him now, fer sure." His eyes rolled. "Boss Slade is likely to shoot any one of us, Mister Ben, when he gets the whiskey inside o' him. And maybe Boss Ficklin will come back here after they've hanged the cap'n."

Amos's greatest fear was the return of Benjamin Ficklin. Ficklin might hand him over to the bounty hunters who roamed the land looking for escaped slaves.

"I don't think so, Amos." Ben became thoughtful. "Nobody will try to hang old J.A. and he won't stand for Ficklin interferin' on the Rocky Ridge division. Slade is boss here, everybody is scared of him the length of the Overland, not just on the Rocky Ridge. The company won't sack Slade. He's doin' too good a job here on the Indians and outlaws. They can't do without him. And outside of this division, everybody'll be more than happy for Slade to stay here. They don't want him on their stretch. Myself, I don't think there will be any changes until the telegraph is working from coast to coast. Once the Pony is disbanded, it's anybody's guess what'll happen to him. Or the rest of us. Take a tip from me, live each day as it comes and forget tomorrow."

"I guess you're right, Mister Ben." Amos began forking

hay for the horses. "You wuz in the saloon last night. What happened?"

"Don't rightly know." Ben averted his eyes, "I wasn't facin' the right way at the time. Slade and Pinner were sharing a table, and Slade had drunk a whole bottle of whiskey. You know what he's like when he's drunk, the slightest disagreement and he's grabbin' for his gun." He sighed. "Guess that's what happened."

"S'pose so." Amos was still agitated. "If it'd bin anybody else the cap'n'd shot, some troublemaker, nobody've hardly noticed. But that feller, Pinner, they say he's the best wagon master in the business."

Ben turned towards the doorway. His keen ears had picked up the sound of horses' hooves coming up from the river. They were shod so it definitely wasn't Indians.

Ben watched about a dozen horsemen approaching the palisade gates, a motley assortment of buckskin-clad figures, some wearing clothes that they had bought back east, sitting their mounts with the postures of novice riders.

"Trouble," Ben muttered. "Seems to me this is a posse from the wagon train. They've either come to collect Pinner's body . . . or else they've come for Slade!" His practiced eye noted the assortment of weaponry carried by the newcomers, booted Hawkens and carbines and a variety of handguns.

The riders reined in the center of the compound. A heavily-built bearded man, who was clearly their leader, looked around with an expression of anger and arrogance on his swarthy features. "Hey, you!" His gaze rested on Ben in the stable doorway. "Where's this bum who shot Pinner? Bring 'im out!"

Ben straightened up, stood with legs slightly apart, thumbs hooked in his belt, hands close enough to his guns if he should need them. He was in no way cowed by this deputation of movers and scouts and he wanted them to see that. "I haven't seen Captain Slade this morning. I don't wetnurse him."

"Fetch the bastard out!" The rider's hand dropped threateningly to the butt of his holstered gun. "We ain't got all day. If he's hidin', we'll pull this place apart till we find 'im."

The horsemen bunched threateningly. There was safety in numbers.

"Somebody lookin' for me?" Slade appeared on the verandah outside his office door. He looked the same as he always did, his frock coat flapped in a gust of wind and the watchers saw that his hand rested on his Army .44. They were not close enough to see those menacing grey eyes and the twin red spots on his cheeks meant nothing to them. Most of them had never even heard of J.A. Slade.

"You murdered Pinner," the bearded man growled, "an' now we ain't got no wagon master. We gotta rope, though!"

"Turn around and ride back to your wagons." Slade spoke softly but everybody heard him. "Pinner's body is back o' the saloon. Take it with you. Any trouble and you'll be burying a few more alongside him."

There was a moment of tense silence. One of the dudes at the rear pulled on his reins as if to obey. Whoever this man dressed in black was, you got the feeling that he was not one to be tangled with.

The big man gave a sudden roar of rage and grabbed for his gun.

Crack.

Nobody saw Slade move. One second his hand was resting on his .44, the next the old revolver belched powdersmoke. The wagon train scout never even cleared his holster. He jerked upright, his expression one of total disbelief and sudden pain. Then, with a glazed look in his eyes, he slid sideways from the saddle, thumped on the ground, rolled once and slay still.

The trouble was over before it had begun.

"Anybody else got anythin' to say?" The road boss's gun

moved in an arc across the stunned posse. Riders were backing off, some having difficulty in controlling their horses.

Nobody protested. Nobody spoke.

"No?" Slade smiled in that rictus manner of his and only then did he raise his voice. "Then get the hell outta here, and take Pinner an' this bum with yuh!"

Amos was peering from the safety of the stable doorpost. Boss Slade had stopped a whole posse with just one shot. The others were frantically loading both corpses onto the riderless horse, feverish in their haste to be gone from here.

Amos saw that Ben's hand still rested on his gun. If there had been a shoot-out, the Pony Express rider would have defended his Division Superintendent. It was worrying for Amos how these two men were becoming so alike, almost as if Slade was grooming his successor in readiness for the day when he might have to take over. When another Jules Reni had better luck. For the only way anybody would ever gun down Slade would be in a cowardly ambush.

The men rode out through the gates. They would not be returning.

Ben approached the circled wagons cautiously. Away to his left, he saw two fresh mounds of earth. The burials were less than a day old. Memories would be recent and bitter and anybody remotely connected with the Pony Express might receive a hostile reception. This was hardly the best time to come paying his respects. It would have been better to have left his visit for a few days, but by then the train might have moved on, and he would have been too late. It was now or never—it was a chance he had to take.

There were between sixty and seventy wagons camped, and there was no way of knowing which one was Mollie's. He would have to ride alongside, maybe inquire. As he rode closer, heads peered out from beneath canvas awnings, watched him. He pretended not to notice.

"Lookin' fer somebody, stranger?" A tall man repairing a wagon wheel looked up. His expression was deadpan but his hand rested on a rifle propped up beside him.

"A lady called Mollie." Ben reined in.

"Mollie?" The other's lips pursed. "Now, as fur as I knows, there's three Mollies on this train an' I don't know half these movers yet. Could be six Mollies, fer all I knows."

"She plays the piano," Ben said.

At his words a canvas flap pushed outwards and a woman's bonnetted head was thrust through the gap. Her eyes blazed, her lips curled scornfully, and she snarled angrily. "He means the whore, an' you know it, Jed Matthews. You're as bad as the rest o' the men on this train, sneakin' off to bed her an' thinkin' that us wives don't know what's goin' on!"

"It's a lie!" The man called Jed Matthews protested unconvincingly, his features reddening.

"You're the liar, Jed. An' a whorer! I guess this young feller's lookin' to do just the same 'cept he's brazen about it, don't care who knows or sees. Well, stranger," her gaze centered on Ben, "you'll be doin' every woman aboard this train a service while you're keepin' our menfolk from the likes o' *her.* So go to her, take your time, stop as long as yer like. 'Bout six wagons up, the one with the blue canvas. Yuh can't miss it." The head was withdrawn and the flap closed. A muffled shriek followed Ben as he moved on. "One o' these days us God-fearin' women'll tie her to a wagon wheel, flog her with our menfolk's bullwhips. Mebbe stone her, too, like they did in the Bible days. You enjoy her, stranger, while she's still able!"

The wagon was a large one, the blue canvas torn in places. A broken arrow shaft protruded from the tailboard. This had to be the one, Ben decided. His guts balled, that raucous woman's words still echoed in his ears. He hoped that he had not made a mistake. He could have turned and ridden away and nobody would be any the wiser. He didn't. Instead, he called softly, "Mollie?"

The flaps were pulled open and then Mollie was squeezing her way past a pile of baggage, clambering over on to the front seat.

"Ben!" Her surprise was not altogether convincing. Her delight was.

He sat his horse, aware that all eyes were on him from the adjacent wagons. They hated him for what J.A. Slade had done as well as what he, himself, was about to do. The hatred and contempt of those unseen eyes burned him like branding irons.

"It's risky here for you, Ben," she whispered, anxiety coloring her pleasure at seeing him again. "They haven't forgotten what happened last night. They've only just buried Pinner and Schaffer. There's angry talk amongst the menfolk. They want to form a big posse to go get Slade."

"Nothin' to do with me," he smiled. "That's Slade's problem."

"But you . . . you can't stay here, Ben."

"Wasn't figurin' on stayin' long, Mollie. If we get this wagon hitched up, we can roll right out of here and never come back. If you want to, that is," he added nervously.

"Where'll we go, Ben?" Her smile came back, her lower lip quivered. She was suddenly close to tears.

"Horseshoe station for a start. There's room for a wagon inside the stockade. Damn it, movers are stopping over all the time. I'll have to ask Slade, of course." That might be the hardest part. "Back o' the station there's a shack that was used by trappers years ago. Needs some restoring but there's plenty o' timber at hand. It'd make a real cozy little place once it was finished. Close to the station but not too close. There's some open land that would plough up, maybe keep a cow or two, grow a few crops. Mind you, I'm going to be busy with the mails for a while, but once the telegraph's finished I'll have time on my hands. I can hunt, too. We won't go short o' meat."

Ben had not intended to pour out all the plans that he had

made on the ride out here, but if Mollie was going to ride out with him it was best she knew what he had in mind. There, he'd said it all, the rest was up to her. He didn't give a cuss about the watching, listening movers.

Mollie was smiling and blushing, and Ben knew then and there that his instincts had not let him down. She gave him a hand to hitch the team and soon they were rumbling away from the encampment.

"An' good riddance!" The wife of the man called Jed Matthews screeched after them as they pulled away. "But don't you bring her back here, mister, when yuh get tired o' her!"

Ben drove, his horse hitched behind the wagon. Mollie was seated beside him, her arm slipped through his as if it was something they had always done. Soon they were out of sight of the wagon train, and they would both try to forget that they had ever been there.

Ben's only cloud was up on the far horizon, a puff of woodsmoke that slowly dispersed in the mountain breeze. Without the threat of Indians, his life would have been as idyllic as it was possible to get.

Surprisingly, J.A. Slade raised no objection to Mollie's wagon being parked in the compound.

"I've got a wife." That was the nearest he had ever come to talking about his private life, but he did not elaborate any further. Perhaps his wife was living somewhere on her own, or staying with relatives, waiting until the Pony Express was disbanded and her husband would join her. Or else she had left him because of his drinking bouts, and he still hoped for a reconciliation. It was hard for Ben to imagine Slade having a woman.

"Preachers pass through from time to time on the coaches," Slade continued. "I guess we could hold the stage up for a few minutes while one of 'em married you."

"Thanks, Slade." Ben was taken aback by the other's generosity. It was totally out of character.

"*Captain* Slade." That rare spark of humanity died as quickly as it had come. "Just because you've gone and got yourself a woman don't mean there's goin' to be any special treatment for you. Schedules have to be kept. If a rider gets killed yuh have to take over like before. You can fix that old cabin in your spare time—if you get any."

"Well, we've got ourselves a home." Ben returned to the wagon and gave Mollie the good news. "I'll start knockin' that cabin back together tomorrow. I gotta rest day—unless something crops up. Meantime, you're best living in the wagon here, at least until this Indian trouble's over and I guess that won't be until army reinforcements arrive at Fort Kearney."

"And you, Ben?"

He avoided her gaze, tried to hide his embarrassment. "Slade says that next time a preacher passes through, he'll get him to marry us. It's best that way."

"As you wish." Mollie failed to hide her disappointment. She wondered if it had something to do with her having worked the saloons along the trail.

"My folks were religious. I guess I owe it to 'em." It did not sound convincing. Sooner or later, he would have to tell her that he had never slept with a woman. It might make her feel guilty about her own past and that was what worried him most.

Ben worked on the restoration of the old cabin whenever he had a spare moment. Most of the original timbers were still stout, those that were not he replaced. He put in a wooden floor with some surplus planks he bought from Sep Dwyer, who still talked about extending the saloon.

Mollie helped Ben, filling buckets of soil for him to carry up on to the roof. "Just in case the Paiutes get any ideas about firin' it," he explained. "They might burn it to spite us even though we're not living in it yet." Because they knew it was to be the home of Slayer Who Rides With the Wind and his woman.

Ben did not plan to start ploughing the land until after he and Mollie had moved in. He would not have any time to devote to farming while the Pony Express was still running, and it would only grow over with weeds again in the meantime. He wanted to have their home ready before the winter snows came.

One morning, Ben and Mollie were working on the inside of the shack when Slade appeared in the doorway. Ben figured one of the riders had either fallen sick or been injured and an urgent replacement was needed.

"Westbound stage has just come in." The road boss was not one for small talk. "There's a preacher travellin' on it. Says he'll marry you. Stage's due back out in half an hour."

"Oh!" Molly looked down at her soiled working clothes, her face and hands were streaked with dirt. "I'll have to wash and change, and . . ."

"No time." Slade turned abruptly on his heel. "Not if yuh want to get married today. Could be weeks before another preacher passes through. Can't hold up the stage."

Ben and Mollie followed Slade across to the station. He walked fast. They almost had to run to keep up with him. His priority was that the stagecoach should leave on time. A wedding was of secondary importance.

The preacher—they never found out his name and nobody seemed to know it, was ready and waiting in the Division Superintendent's office. A small, balding man, he gave them a cursory nod and began the ceremony straight away. He, too, did not wish to be delayed on his journey.

Slade witnessed the marriage and the ceremony was completed within a few minutes. Then the stage was rumbling on its way westwards, and Ben and Mollie watched its departure as man and wife. The office door slammed shut behind them and the road boss returned to his work.

"You'd better start moving your things out of the bunkhouse and across to the wagon." Mollie kissed her husband.

"Guess so." He shuffled his feet awkwardly, looked down at them. His stomach knotted. He was more scared than the time he had looked down the barrel of Jules Reni's .54. The moment of truth he had been dreading for weeks had arrived.

"Scared, huh?" There was a half smile on her full lips.

"Yeah, scared to hell."

"I thought you were," she laughed. "I guess I'll have to teach you, and we'll start right at the very beginning."

At which they both laughed.

Mollie taught Ben that night in the cramped bunk of the wagon. She taught him real good.

Fourteen

Williams's station was situated fifty miles east of Lake Tahoe, on Bolivar Roberts's section, one stop from Virginia City. It might have vanished in the mists of history, except for the events of those few fateful days in May, 1860.

A full-scale Paiute uprising was inevitable. After weeks of talks between the Paiutes, the Shoshones and the Bannocks, which had come to nothing, Blood Arrow was prepared to wait no longer. It was just a question of when. Indians were unpredictable—it might be today or tomorrow, next week or next month, but it was likely to be sooner rather than later. The hills were full of smoke signals, but they gave nothing away to the white invaders.

Little did Ben guess when he left Mollie in their bunk in the wagon to ride west on that bright morning, that it would be weeks before he saw her again.

Ben rode far beyond his scheduled relays. Sporadic Indian attacks had caused seven injuries and two deaths among the dispatch riders, and there was nobody to take over from him at Millersville. So he carried on to Sutler's Store, which was situated within Fort Halleck. Here, fortunately, another rider waited to take the mochila so Ben rested up, otherwise he would have had to carry on as far as Diamond Springs.

Had Fate dealt him a cruel blow and compelled him to ride on still further to Williams's station, he might not have returned.

* * *

That day Paiute smoke signals were conspicuous by their absence. The previous day they were to be seen all around, today there were none—which meant that the talking was done, everything the Indians had to say had been said. All that was left was the waiting.

Jack Williams was Division Superintendent at Williams's station. Small and lean, had he been born ten years sooner he would have ridden the mails himself. He limped when he walked; an Indian arrow had severed a tendon which had forced him to quit the army. He had few distinguishing features and average talents. He could ride and shoot as well as most, but no better. He qualified as a road boss because he could read and write reasonably well and the job entailed routine paperwork.

The company had named the station after him because they could not be bothered to think up another name. In hindsight, it was an epitaph. Jack Williams's name would be etched indelibly in the annals of the Pony Express and his own insignificance would be overlooked.

There were four other men within the palisade at Williams's that morning, a stableman and three riders whose relays had not arrived. Until they did, nobody was going anywhere—there were no despatches to carry.

The gate was kept shut at all times these days, only opened to let riders in and out. After dark, a sentry took his post. The station was under-manned, and even though the Sacramento office had promised increased manpower a week earlier, reinforcements had not been forthcoming.

"Where's them goddamned riders got to?" Williams had spent the night dozing fitfully in his office chair and his limp was more pronounced because of his cramped posture. Nobody slept a full night. They dared not try.

"Injuns got 'em, I s'pect." Lander, one of the riders, was becoming edgy with his forced stay here. If he could only make it as far as Virginia City, he could relax. But not here—those woods out there were probably full of the devils.

"Huh!" Williams grunted, "then there ain't no point in sendin' out any more riders until these damned redskins've bin taught a lesson. Can't understand what's takin' the army so long."

"Still busy chasin' Cheyennes and losin' 'em back east." Lander squinted through a spy-hole in the stockade.

Dick Egan and John Burnett walked across the sun-baked compound. They carried a brace of Walkers and a carbine each. The armory was the only place that was fully stocked because—so far—there hadn't been any Indians to shoot at. The supply wagon from Carson was two days overdue and food was running low.

"If Russell Majors got any sense," Williams began as he lit a stubby pipe and puffed on it, "they'd suspend the Pony until the injuns are sorted out, but they won't 'cause it might cost 'em their contract. It's all about money, not lives. Same goes fer the telegraph—as fast as the poles go up, the Paiutes chop 'em down. Costin' a fortune and achievin' nothin', but the company don't see it that way. Doesn't alter the fact, though, that we're stuck here. Nowhere to go, an' even if we had, we couldn't get there. They've just abandoned us. If we get attacked then there won't be no help comin' our way."

Bilton, the stableman, was an optimist. If he had not been, he wouldn't have had two mounts saddled and waiting. The incoming riders, both eastbound and westbound, would show up before long, he was certain. Then, all he had to do was to help them swap the pouches from the tired horses to the fresh ones. The Indians were all smoke talk, he insisted. It was just a bluff. He had succeeded in convincing himself, but he had not convinced the others.

"Wonder what them redskins are up to?" Williams asked the unanswerable question because nobody had spoken for over an hour and the silence was making him edgy.

He got his answer. A shower of arrows arced into the compound.

No specific plans had been made in the event of an attack, other than to shoot and keep shooting. Even had Williams outlined any tactics, it is doubtful the outcome would have been any different, for the station was undermanned and the defenders heavily outnumbered. Many miles away at Horseshoe, every man knew what was expected of him, the position he had to take up on the palisade and his area of fire. At Williams's station the occupants simply returned the fire, and if the palisade was stormed then they would retreat to the bunkhouse and its adjoining living quarters. It was the only place that would give them any kind of protection if they had to make a last stand.

Miraculously, that first hail of arrows did not hit any of the men caught out in the open. Instead, the feather-tipped missiles embedded themselves in the ground all around. It was worth a try as far as the Indians were concerned. Just one lucky strike would have reduced the defenders by a fifth.

Lander took up a position by the gate. If the Paiutes tried to storm it, he could either shoot through the hinged flap or take them as they clambered over.

Bilton's responsibility was the horses. They must not fall into Indian hands. At worst, with the gate broken down, he would stampede them into the open.

Williams, Egan and Burnett sought safety in the bunkhouse. The defense was flawed from the outset, there was no retaliatory fire from the stockade. Lander would not be able to hold off the attackers single-handed.

The Paiutes had spent the night hours crawling from the woods to within easy arrow range of the station. They had lain undetected in the surrounding scrubland until they were ready. By not attacking at first light, the attackers had lulled the whites into a false sense of security. Even now the defenders thought there were only fifty warriors out there. Instead, two hundred had come to fight, and Blood Arrow himself led them. They did not holler and try to rush the small force. They did not need to—time was on their side. They could afford to wait. It was a victory to be savored.

Towards evening, Williams smelled smoke on the warm breeze that blew off the desert, and he knew only too well what the Paiutes were going to do next.

Fire arrows smoked and burned themselves out on the stable and bunkhouse roofs where the soil was at least a foot deep. The acrid stench hung heavy in the air, but no harm was done.

"Smells almost as bad as that pipe o' yours, Jack!" Egan joshed. The others forced themselves to laugh.

Lander thought that the fire arrows were all part of a demoralizing process by the Paiutes, to convince the defenders that they were in for a long siege. He was partly right, that was the message the chief intended to convey. But Blood Arrow was more cunning than that; his braves were massed and ready for an all-out attack, which the whites should not be expecting. He was prepared to sacrifice a few braves. After all, it was an honor to die in battle.

The chief, heavily daubed with war paint, retreated to the safety of some thorn bushes on a small hillock. It was an excellent vantage point from which to survey the fall of Williams's station. He was not risking an unlucky bullet from one of the guns, for this was a mere skirmish. It was only the beginning of the war which would sweep the whites from the Paiutes's land. Blood Arrow had no wish to die before it had begun, for one day he would be honored by all the tribes for leading them to victory.

He gave the signal and a horde of bronzed figures rose up out of the scrub.

Lander used his revolvers with devastating effect as the Paiutes swarmed over the gate. Two fell back, a third hung over the top, blood pouring from a gaping wound. Standing directly beneath the gate, the Pony Express rider was an almost impossible target for the bowmen.

Two braves jumped down. Lander shot them as they landed. He swivelled downed another one who was climbing over the stockade to his left. A snap shot accounted for one to his right. He loaded fresh cylinders, and had he had a ready supply of these he could probably have kept the Indians off the gate and along the stretch of palisade on either side of it. Corpses were strewn around him but his problems began after those cylinders were spent.

The carbine missed, it was no close range weapon. He would almost certainly have killed the brave who hurtled down upon him had his .44 been loaded. Lander reversed his grip on the carbine, swung it by the barrel like a club but the Paiute grabbed it. As they wrestled, more Indians spilled over the gate and Lander went down beneath them. Knives glinted in the late afternoon sunlight as they hacked and stabbed.

Bilton fired from the stable doorway, emptying his second Colt at some braves who were astride the palisade on the other side. Two dropped, a third clung on precariously, one arm shattered. The stableman's revolver clicked—he had used up his reserve cylinder. Three braves jumped down inside the compound, ran for Bilton, screaming and brandishing knives and tomahawks. He tried to bar the door but sheer weight of numbers pushed it inwards.

Those defending the bunkhouse heard Bilton's screams. They swung their carbines to cover the smashed door, a hail of lead cut a swathe through the blood-splashed bodies that spilled out of it. Indians sprawled in a writhing heap. Something fell from among them, rolled and came to a halt in the dusty compound.

It was Bilton's severed head, his staring eyes pleading with his companions to come to his rescue.

"Jesus!" Egan unknowingly had just witnessed his own fate.

Williams and the other two had so far managed to hold back the oncoming horde at the rear. The air was thick with powdersmoke but the men needed time to recharge their weapons. The Paiutes did not give them time, they were now coming over the top so fast that they might have queued on the other side.

The hollering was at full pitch. Beyond the station, up on that hillock, Blood Arrow followed the course of the battle by the sounds and smiled in satisfaction. Even so, he waited until the gate was thrown open, and his warriors revealed the extent of their triumph, before he emerged from his place of safety.

Five scalps—it was a good start. There would be many more. This was only the beginning of a tidal wave of bloodshed which would destroy the whites.

Blood Arrow gave the order for the station to be torched.

During the week following the attack on Williams's station, isolated settlements in the region of Honey Lake and the Truckee River were wiped out by the Paiutes. Five more Pony Express stations were attacked and razed: Cold Spring, Smith's Creek, Reese River, Simpson's Park and Dry Creek. Fifteen pioneers who had survived the dangers of the Overland Trail died in their Promised Land. In all, the Pony Express lost seventeen employees and over a hundred horses.

The Paiute War had broken out much further west than anybody had anticipated. Blood Arrow's cunning was not to be underestimated. He was totally unpredictable and had fooled both the army and the Pony Express.

Soon the war would gather momentum and spread east. The Bannocks and the Shoshones would undoubtedly join forces with the Paiutes and, possibly, the Arapahoes and the Cheyennes.

Blood Arrow's vow of vengeance spread before him. He would drive the whites from this land, and the scalps of men like Man Who Likes Killing and Slayer Who Rides With the Wind would hang in his lodge.

After a week of killing and looting, the Paiutes headed toward the Great Salt Lake to hold council and plan their next wave of attacks. Their early success was due entirely to their locating weak points to attack. They had hit the whites where they were least populated and in areas which the soldiers had not yet established their forts and military strategy. The Indians knew that they must do the same again to outwit the army.

Blood Arrow permitted himself a short time to savor his victories—and to go to the squaw who prepared his food and shared his blanket. His pleasures here were such as he had enjoyed with no other woman. His emotions were a mixture of carnal delight and of inflicting pain upon his woman. He worked himself up into a frenzy, grunting his delight in time with her cries. He had ridden and broken many a wild desert mustang but never had he straddled one with such ferocity as he did this squaw who had once been white. She was now as Paiute as she would ever be, the Cheyenne had broken her before Blood Arrow had traded some Pony Express horses for her. But he had made her what she was today. That was perhaps his sweetest victory of all over the hated whites.

She was neither Indian nor white now, instead only a mixture that was hated by both races. Her sobs were a compliment to Blood Arrow's massacres of the settlers, her screams an echo of his victims's pleas for mercy at the torture stake. She made his blood course fiercely and brought out the very depths of savagery within him.

He degraded her in every way he knew and then he drifted into a satisfied sleep, her sobs a sweet lullaby. She was an integral part of the revenge which he was exacting on those who had stolen his people's land and destroyed their food. She would pay for the white race's crimes for many a year to come and long after their bones whitened in the sun.

She did not have a name—that was the greatest insult of all, both to her and her kind. She was just a squaw. One day, long after the whites had been vanquished and his vengeance was complete, and he had no further need of her, he would probably kill her.

Slowly.

Book Two

When guns speak, death settles dispute.

Charles Russell

"Not snow, nor rain, nor heat, nor night keeps them from accomplishing their appointed courses with all speed."

Histories, book VIII, 98
Herodotus
c. 500 B.C.

Book Two

One

News of the Paiute uprising reached Ben while he was holed up at Sutler's Store. The relays had been seriously disrupted, and it was three days before an eastbound rider clattered in through the gates of Fort Halleck.

Ben watched as the rider dismounted, and even at a distance there was something vaguely familiar about the other. His figure was slight, almost boyish, and even after a ride of over a hundred miles, during which he had had to make several lengthy detours in order to avoid war parties, he still walked with a suppleness which belied those long hours in the saddle.

Ben followed him into the bunkhouse where recognition was mutual.

"Will Cody!" Ben extended a hand.

"Ben Hollister!" The other's grip was firm. "Where you bin hidin' since we both showed 'em how to ride in Sacramento?"

"Mostly around Rocky Ridge." Ben poured coffee for both of them. "I wouldn't be this far west if there were enough riders. I hear a dozen or more have been killed and others have refused to ride until the army does something about keeping the Paiutes in check. You're the first rider in here for three days, Will."

"Don't reckon any mails will be goin' further'n Fort Bridger from now on." Cody sipped his coffee. "In which case, there ain't no point in sendin' 'em out of St. Joseph.

The company don't have no choice but to suspend the Pony until things are back to normal, but Majors will only do that as a last resort. The Utes are sure to join up with the Paiutes, which'll mean the Shoshones and Bannocks will go on the warpath, too. None of this would've happened if Numaga had still been chief of the Paiutes. He would've settled for some sort of treaty, which wouldn't've done the injuns much good, but at least we wouldn't have had a full scale war on our hands. Blood Arrow's been after war for a long time an' now that he's got his way, there won't be peace until the injuns've been whupped. But that won't happen fer a while yet. There ain't enough soldiers west o' Fort Laramie. Just look around yuh. Here we are in Fort Halleck and it ain't got no more than a handful o' soldiers here to defend it if it was attacked. But the injuns won't win, take it from me, but a lot o' folks will be killed on both sides. You can almost git to feelin' sorry for the injuns, if you think about it long enough. Best not to. We're fightin' a war an' you just hev to remember which side you're on."

Ben nodded. Cody had weighed it all up and made his choice, just as Sam Booker had made his. Still, you had to push injustices to one side when you found yourself caught up in a war.

"I can hear a rider comin'." Cody was on his feet in an instant, moved across to the doorway. Even now there was no trace of weariness in his body; it was almost as though he had rested up and was ready to ride again. "Westbound rider." He shaded his eyes. "Looks to me like it's Pony Bob Haslam. He's one of the best riders in the Pony. If anybody's gonna get through, Bob will."

The stableman appeared leading a fresh mount. No orders had yet been issued that relays were to be suspended and, until they were, it was the duty of every employee of the Pony Express to maintain the service which he had pledged.

"There's somethin' wrong with Bob!" Cody pushed past Ben and broke into a run.

The incoming rider was slumped low in the saddle, the reins were trailing loose, and he hung on to the mane. As the horse came to a standstill, he slid sideways, hit the ground and sprawled. He tried to rise and fell back again.

As Cody and Ben rushed toward him, they saw an arrow shaft protruding from his shoulder. His shirt was saturated with blood.

In spite of his tiredness, Cody beat Ben to the injured man and knelt down. Pony Bob Haslam moved, but he did not have the strength to sit up.

"Easy, Bob," Cody spoke reassuringly, "you'll be okay. Just a flesh wound."

"I made it." Haslam's face contorted with pain but he still managed a weak smile. Delivering the mails safely was his priority. His wound came a poor second. There was no mistaking his determination even with an arrow sticking in him. "Damned red bastards've learned a new trick . . . stretched a rope across the trail . . . just saw it in time, hoss jumped it. But they got an arrer in me, all the same. Got . . . got two stages to go yet."

"Which you ain't gonna ride." Out of the corner of his eye Cody saw men spilling out of the bunkhouse. They were stablemen and settlers who had moved in to Fort Halleck for safety. None of them were riders. "Hey, you fellahs," he shouted across to them, "give Pony Bob a lift into the bunkhouse an' find out how deep this arrow's gone. With a bit o' luck it ain't too deep. All the same, he won't be ridin' no mails for a week of two."

Willing hands lifted the wounded rider and began to carry him across the compound. A couple of soldiers watched from a distance, shaking their heads. There was nothing they could do about the Indians, at least not until reinforcements got this far.

The stableman lifted the mochila on to the fresh horse and looked from Cody to Ben questioningly. There were Indians all along the trail, but nobody had given orders that the mails were to be suspended. One of these two would have to ride on with them, and Cody had already done three times his quota.

"I'll go." Cody snatched the reins. "I'll git as far west as I can, can't do no more."

"No!" Ben grabbed Cody's arm. "You've just ridden a hundred miles, Will."

"An' I'll ride another hundred if'n I hev to!"

Ben's grip tightened, he swung the other round to face him. *"I'll* go, Will."

The stableman backed away. These two were crazy hotheads. He'd heard all about both of them. Any moment they were going to start throwing punches over which one of them was going to ride out there to get himself killed.

Will Cody had never backed down to another man before in his young life. For a moment, his eyes blazed into Ben's, then slowly his fingers relaxed their hold on the reins. It wasn't backing down—it was just letting a friend do you a favor. He would have done exactly the some if Ben Hollister had ridden in here after a hundred mile stretch. The Pony Express was all about comradeship; you learned to give and take. This time it was Cody's turn to take.

"All right, if you're damn fool enough, Ben. You'll have to ride off the trail in places, mebbe for miles, follow animal tracks and jest hope that mebbe they'll bring yuh out in the right place. Yuh could get lost, that's the best that can happen to yuh. Worse is yuh'll probably get kilt."

"Which I probably will, anyhow." Ben released the other's arm, checked that he had both revolvers and a spare cylinder for each. The stableman had already booted a carbine. "I'll just keep ridin' as far as I can until there's somebody to take over at one of the stations. Or until I run out of fresh mounts."

Cody turned away without another word and walked across towards the bunkhouse. The weariness that he had fought against for so long now began to show. He had no reason to fight it any longer. His feet dragged and his shoulders stooped. There was nothing more to be said. He would have done exactly the same in Ben's situation. Nobody gave or expected thanks for it—it was all part of the job.

Ben kept the horse at a steady canter. He had to conserve its strength and stamina, as he had no idea where or when he would find a change. Schedules had gone to the wind. Riders were expected only when they showed up, and west of here probably nobody was expecting to see one at all. If the Paiutes had taken to stretching ropes across the trail, it would be foolhardy to ride at full speed. He would only push his horse to its limits if he was pursued.

He made it as far as Needle Rocks by nightfall. There was no rider waiting to take over, just a stableman and a fresh mount still in the stable. The mount could enjoy an extended rest, Ben told the other, he would not be setting out again until daylight.

"Makes sense," the man grunted, "but it don't make sense to go on west. Yuh'll hev to sleep in the stable, there's no accommodation here. This is just a swing station. I'm closin' it down tomorrow. You're the first rider I've seen for four days. Reckon the best thing I can do is to take the hosses on to Muddy Creek. What chance does a man stand on his own if the injuns come? Don't even know if Muddy Creek is still standin' or any stations west o' there. No word's got through. Don't expect it will."

"You do as you please." The station was just an adobe building that served as both stable and cramped living quarters for the man in charge. "I'll take my chance ridin' the mails. It's no more risky than holin' up somewhere."

Ben cursed himself for being a fool, as he stretched out on a blanket on the stable floor. Twelve hours ago, he was all set to ride back east to Horseshoe and Mollie. Even Horseshoe, with its fortifications and J.A. Slade, would not be able to stand the might of the Paiutes and any other tribes who had joined them, but at least that way he could have died with Mollie. He could have ensured that she did not fall into

Indian hands. He had let her down. He had done it for the Pony Express and the men who rode the mails. For Cody. This time Ben had gotten his priorities wrong.

"Don't let them redskins take yuh alive," the stableman's voice came out of the darkness, as if he had read Ben's thoughts. "Save a bullet fer yourself. If yuh get time, that is. Heard stories 'bout what they do to whites afore they kill 'em. Men are luckier than wimmen, at least they'll be kilt eventually. Wimmen ain't so lucky—they git tortured but kept alive. Their minds go, they think they've bin born and raised injun but they don't get treated like injun squaws. The injuns treat 'em far worse. Whores' n slaves, that's what becomes o' white women. Mostly the chiefs keep white women fer themselves."

It was all that Ben could do to stop himself from yelling at the other to shut up. But the stableman was only speaking the truth.

The next day, Ben had his first look at the Great Salt Lake. If ever there was a hell on earth, he decided, this was it, a shimmering wasteland for as far as the eye could see. It was inhabited mostly by the Gosiute Indians and somehow they survived—or some of them did. They lived on nuts and berries, and they were as peaceable as any tribe was ever likely to be. Because the whites did not want their land, there was nothing worth stealing. Nobody, would kill for a tract of arid, burning land.

Ben rested up in a patch of shade among some straggling thorny undergrowth, drank the last of the water from his canteen and ate a handful of biscuits. This was the hottest time of the day, he dared not risk his horse for another two or three hours. Then, with luck, he might make it as far as Roberts's station by nightfall. If there was no rider there to take over, he would continue on to Carson City in the morning. So far he had not caught sight of an eastbound rider, but that was not surprising because he had made several detours. All the same, he got the feeling that nobody was riding east any more. And he was the only one fool enough to ride west.

There was no rider waiting at Roberts's but at least there were a couple of fresh horses in the stable. There was no sign of Bolivar Roberts, just a young negro stablehand who shrugged his shoulders. "Help yourself. Nobody else'll want a hoss. 'Cept me, 'cause I'm ridin' out tomorrow. Goin' east. Only a fool would go west, that was what Boss Roberts said, and he's ridden west. Told me to wait till tomorrow, jest in case anybody got through, then to lit out'n look for myself. The boss, he reckons the injuns are scared o' black people. Mebbe, then, I'll be okay."

When Ben awoke next morning, the stablehand was gone, along with one of the spare horses. Ben wondered whether the other had struck out across the desert, or if he had followed the trail back east. Either way, the negro was likely to find out if Indians were scared of black folk or not.

Ben put the mochila on the spare mount, left the one which he had ridden in on free to wander. It would find enough grazing. Sooner or later, the Paiutes would find it. He had contemplated shooting it, decided against it. It had brought him a long way. One thoroughbred mount would make little difference in an army of mounted warriors.

That afternoon, he came upon the first of the razed stations. Cold Springs was a gutted, burned out shell. Two scalped and charred bodies lay in the compound, and everything else was either burned or stolen. Only the well remained intact, and he drank gratefully and refilled his canteen.

Ben tethered his horse and rested up in the brush that night. From now on the going would be very slow. Caution was his priority. He might have turned back, except that he knew what lay behind him. His only hope was to make it as far as Carson City.

Smith's Creek was razed, too. So was Reese River and Simpson's Park. And Dry Creek.

Ben walked his horse, rested up frequently. His only thought was to make it alive to Carson and it did not matter when he arrived. Nobody would be looking out for him.

He spied a party of Gosiutes in the distance. They were on foot, gathering wild scrub fruit. They looked anything but warlike but he was taking no chances.

He wondered where the Paiutes were. They had left plenty of evidence of their presence along the Overland, from Wyoming into Utah. They had destroyed every Pony Express station from Cold Springs westward, but not once did Ben so much as glimpse one of their warriors. They had either pushed on east or right now they were massing in the Great Salt Lake, preparing for a mighty onslaught against the white invaders.

Ben prayed that Slade had already evacuated Horseshoe and taken Mollie further east. Just how far east did one have to travel in order to be safe from the Indian uprising? Ben wished that he knew the answer to that question.

It was on the fourth day that Ben sighted Carson City. In some ways, he thought, it resembled Julesburg, except that it was much larger and the conglomeration of shacks were in a better state of repair. There was an orderliness about the place, and his relief at arriving safely was overwhelming. And yet, at the same time, he experienced a slight sense of unease which he was unable to account for.

There was *something* wrong, he could not decide what it was. Something . . . abnormal.

There were people around, a group had clustered to watch his approach. They were chattering to one another. It wasn't excitement, their gesticulations told him that even when he was several hundred yards away. They were agitated. Distressed. *Frightened.* He noticed how they huddled, cowered. Pointed at his approach.

Obviously it was because the Paiutes were attacking every

white settlement in the region. Even Carson City would not be able to withstand a concerted Indian attack.

The watchers began to walk towards Ben. Some of them broke into a run. Whatever tidings they had were obviously of great importance.

It was then that Ben realized that those figures scurrying towards him were all *female*. Bonnets were clutched, skirts lifted so that the wearers did not trip over them. Young women with children, older women who couldn't keep up. Still more were crowding the gate to watch the arrival of a stranger.

Ben's unease became concern. Where had all the men of Carson City gone?

TWO

Ben sat his horse and waited as the female deputation approached. At a distance, the woman in the lead might have been mistaken for a man. She wore baggy homespuns, her hair was cut short in a ragged trim like she had done it herself and had not used a mirror. Her upper lip grew hair that on a younger face might have been unshaven puberty. A single black hair sprouted from a wart on her fleshy cheek. She breathed hard from her exertions and a dribble of saliva swung from a thick lower lip. Even her voice was deep and masculine.

"Wal, I'll be . . . If it ain't the Pony Express!"

The others gathered around her. She was clearly the spokeswoman of the group, and young and old, they stared in disbelief at Ben, as though the opposite sex was an extinct species in this part of Utah. Ben sensed a moment of embarrassment. He might even have raised his hat if he had not been wearing the riders's skull cap.

"I'd appreciate a change of hoss, if you ladies could arrange it." He spoke politely, looking beyond them. There was not a man in sight. More women had emerged from the cluster of buildings and were staring in his direction.

"Ain't a goddamned hoss left in Carson City, mister," the hairy woman answered gruffly.

"But . . . but there's a Pony Express depot here, ma'am." Ben knew now that his hunch had not been wrong, there was something very strange here. "This is the prime station in Nevada. Take me to Washoe, he's Division Superintendent here."

"Was." She stood there, hands on hips, legs apart. "Washoe's ridden out, along with Major Ormsby and all the other menfolk. There's not a man left in Carson, 'cept the old-timers, and the city's all the better fer that. Men!" She spat and the dribble swung like a pendulum. A blob of tobacco juice hit the dusty ground. "There's only one thing they want, an' they ain't never gotten it from me in fifty-four years!"

Ben believed her.

"Wasn't expectin' no more Pony Express riders." Her eyes narrowed and her lips pouted as she masticated. "Most o' the stations east o' here have been burned by those murderin' savages." She spat again. "Except mebbe Roberts'."

"Bolivar Roberts has gone, abandoned his station." Ben wiped his mouth with the back of his hand. Salt stung his lips. "I was hopin' to find a relief rider here. Or, at least, a fresh horse so that I could carry on to Fort Churchill."

"Ain't neither riders nor hosses left here, mister. The men needed every hoss they could lay hands to. Major Ormsby said his need was greatest an', in any case, the mails wouldn't be able to get through until the Paiutes'd either been kilt or driven out o' Nevada. He took all our menfolk with him, 'bout fifty. Guess the Paiutes are high-tailin' it right now. Them as haven't bin shot, that is."

"Looks like I'll have to ride on to Fort Churchill on the hoss I got, then." Ben wheeled his mount. Whoever this Major Ormsby was, he was downright arrogant thinking he could quell a full-scale Indian uprising with fifty men. Or stupid. He was probably fresh from the east and had learned his soldiering from some academy where they taught military tactics from books and maps. These women had been left to fend for themselves in the meantime, and somebody as cunning as Blood Arrow might just realize this and double back and storm Carson. Or kill the posse first and take the women and kids afterward.

"Yuh kin either come in and rest or ride on. You please yerself, mister."

The other women huddled, spoke in whispers. Doubtless, they had thought that Ben was one of their menfolk returning with news of Ormsby's posse. Their disappointment and concern was only too apparent.

"You ride on, mister, if you've a mind to. It's all the same to us, whatever you choose to do."

Ben decided this was as good a time as any to continue on his way. The Paiutes were occupied right now and his horse would make it as far as Fort Churchill.

The women stood and watched him go. He felt as if he was running out on them, leaving them to their fate, but his staying would not have made any difference. If the Paiutes attacked, Carson would be left a smoking ruin and there was nothing Ben could have done about it. He would have been just one more scalped corpse in the funeral pyre.

Fort Churchill had, until recently, been a few scattered adobe buildings that was known as Buckland's station. Captain Stewart and a small detachment of cavalry were in the early stages of establishing it as a fort. A stockade had been completed, encompassing the array of shacks and, in due course, military buildings would be erected. During the time when Numaga had been chief of the Paiutes, some of his braves had assisted the army in their efforts to establish an outpost here. But, with Numaga's fall from power, the braves had left to answer Blood Arrow's call for war. Now those peaceable Indians might well help to destroy that which they had built. Certainly, the skeleton force of soldiers would in no way be able to defend it against the Paiute warriors.

The soldiers had ridden out in search of Indians, leaving the fort in charge of Frederic Dodge, the Indian Agent for the region. A small, lithe man, he might have made a despatch rider had he been ten years younger.

"Wasn't expectin' you." He emerged from the building he used as an office and looked like he might have been snatching some sleep. "Soldiers are away lookin' for Paiutes and probably won't find any. Injuns are headin' east by all accounts. All the stations east of here have been razed, I'm told."

"Some of 'em." Ben dismounted, looked over towards the stables. A man in the doorway was clad in Pony Express attire but he was making no attempt to lead out a fresh horse. "I managed to get through, all the same."

"There'll be nobody takin' the mails on from here," Dodge snapped.

"The Pony ain't been suspended. Yet."

"Not officially. I make the decisions here. It's too risky to ride. Anyway, the men are refusin', an' I can't say I blame 'em."

"We're paid to take risks."

"Not the way things are now. Put the mails in the office. When the trail's open again, they'll go. Not until."

"Bring me a fresh horse," Ben called across to the rider in the stable doorway.

"You're crazy!"

"Cold Springs and Smith's Creek are burned down, so I'll ride on to Reese River."

"The sun's got to yore brain."

"Maybe, but I signed the pledge and I'm stickin' to it until I get official orders not to. Now, are you goin' to bring out a horse or do I have to go fetch one myself?"

The rider who had refused to continue brought a fresh horse out of the stables. If this guy wanted to go get himself killed, that was fine by him. That way they wouldn't be sending anybody else.

The horse had been confined for the best part of a week,

and was raring to go. The others stood back, watching as Ben transferred the pouches.

He was riding out in under the two minutes allotted for a change-over.

Sand Springs and Cold Springs were still smoking when Ben passed them. He didn't bother to make a detour; there was nothing left for the Paiutes to come back for. On this stretch he made better than average time.

The final run from the ruins of Smith's Creek was the most tiring. He fought against falling asleep in the saddle. If there had been a rope stretched across the trail he wouldn't have seen it in time. The only Indian signs were the devastation they had left in their wake. Maybe Major Ormsby and his ragtag vigilantes really had got the Paiutes on the run.

Ben cantered into Reese River in the late afternoon and almost fell from his horse. Apart from swift changes of mounts, he had been in the saddle for 18 hours without a break. He had covered 190 miles.

Ben slept for six hours. The eastbound rider was due at eight the following morning. He probably would not show up, but Ben made sure that a fresh mount was ready.

A few minutes after eight there was a drumming of hooves along the trail.

It was a rider whom Ben had not seen before, a youth with a hairlip and pale blue eyes. The expression of determination on the other's lean features designated him as one of the few who were prepared to carry on at all costs.

"Injuns?" Ben grunted as he transferred the mochila.

"Not a sign," the weary rider said as he shook his head. "Leastways, not a fresh one. But they're up to somethin' somewhere, you can bet on that. Quietest I've known it for weeks. Reckon the outlaws have run fer cover, too, in case they lose their scalps."

Ben swung away and picked up speed. The two torched stations he passed were no longer smoking. They were as dead as the men who had tried to defend them. There was a fresh mount awaiting him at Carson Sink, and he was on his way again within a couple of minutes. Everything had gone well, but he wasn't going to relax his vigilance.

On impulse, Ben decided to make a detour through a tract of desert. Just a hunch, he did not argue with it. It was simply that from hereon there were no signs of Paiute raids. Had the Indians decided that this was as far as they were going or were they lurking in the hills and forests in readiness for their next surge eastward? He didn't know, but they would hardly have given up. The wooded hills might have concealed a thousand warriors, the desert offered less chance of an ambush. He turned off the trail. He had played hunches before, and they had proved to be right, which was one of the reasons he was still riding the mails.

He slowed his horse to a walk. He had made good time so far and it was foolhardy to tax a mount in the desert heat. Carson City was his last stop. He wondered how the posse had fared. The menfolk had probably returned by now after a fruitless chase. It would not matter if Ben was late because the mails would not be going anywhere for a while after Carson. He had done everything that could be expected of him.

Ben's horse snickered, and his gun was instantly in his hand. The only cover was a clump of thorn bushes some thirty yards to his left that he had scarcely given a second glance. An Indian was sitting in the scant shade, just watching. He had probably watched Ben's approach for the last mile.

It was an old Gosiute, sitting cross-legged with his back against a gnarled trunk. A hide blanket was draped around his wasted body, blending him perfectly with his surround-

ings. Ben might have ridden on by without even noticing
him if the horse had not warned him. The old man's expression was stoic, but his keen eyes missed nothing.

Ben rode slowly over to where the Gosiute sat. The severest winter for many years had taken its toll, and the old man
was scratching an existence until it was time for him to go.
He had no reason to fear anybody.

Ben lifted his hand, forefinger upraised to signify that he
was alone. The other nodded very slightly to show that he
understood. Only then did his lips move.

"Big battle." The Indian pointed out across the desert with
a hand that was near skeletal. "Much shooting. Many killed."

"The white men shot the Paiutes?" Perhaps this Major
Ormsby wasn't such a fool as Ben had thought. The Paiutes
only had a few guns, traded from renegades. If there was
shooting, then it had to come from the vigilantes.

"No." The Gosiute's tone was a kind of recitation almost
as though he wasn't taking sides in the war. "Whites all
killed. Ambushed at Pyramid Lake. Paiutes have plenty guns
now. Bad shots, but bad white men ride with them so shooting is good sometimes."

Ben dismounted. This latest piece of news was decidedly
worrying.

"Tell me." He reached a biscuit out of his pocket, handed
it to the other. The Indian snatched it with surprising speed
and chewed on it voraciously with toothless gums.

"Gosiutes like peace." Crumbs sprayed with the words
and the hand stretched out for another biscuit. "No war for
Gosiutes, we live in desert, trouble nobody. Blood Arrow
loves killing. His buffalo robe carry many scalps. More now.
All white. But if Gosiutes anger him, Gosiute scalps will
hang from his robe. Or bad white men will shoot us. Young
Gosiute braves will follow Blood Arrow now. I have come
to die in peace in desert. Always has been my home."

"Tell me about these bad white men." Ben found another

biscuit and held it just beyond the other's taloned outstretched fingers.

"Man called Brent. More whites and bad halfbreeds ride with him. About . . ." the Indian became thoughtful then held up both hands, fingers and thumbs splayed.

"Ten of 'em, uh? Can't say I've heard of this guy Brent, but a war will produce the worst on both sides."

"Mogoannoga and some bad Bannocks ride with them, too."

"Have the Bannocks joined the Paiutes against the whites?"

"Not yet. Soon, perhaps. Mogoannoga try to persuade his chief to go to war. Roaring Water say 'no'. So Mogoannoga take those with him who want war. Maybe the rest will follow. That is how it is."

"And they killed the whites who were hunting the Paiutes?"

"I watch battle. I see dust, many horses, whites riding after Paiutes. But more Paiutes, Bannocks and bad whites are hidden in arroyo." The emaciated hand pointed again out into the desert. "Whites caught on both sides. Guns. Arrows. Then knives and tomahawks. No chance. Soon all over. Many scalps taken. You go look and you will see that I speak the truth."

"I believe you." Ben had no wish to go and look for himself. He thought about the women occupants of Carson. It did not look good for them now. "Which way did the Paiutes go after the ambush?"

"Back into the desert. Camp somewhere, not sure where, desert big place. Perhaps they stay there for some time. Perhaps they ride out at next sunrise to kill more whites." The Gosiute shrugged his scrawny shoulders. "No can tell with Blood Arrow."

"The whites who were killed," Ben spoke softly, "all their women stayed behind in Carson. Just children and old men with them."

"Bad." The previously stoic expression became grim. "Very bad. Tribe on warpath like to take white women captives. Big prizes." He made some explicit hand signs which churned Ben's guts. "Plenty that. Some die, others live. Even worse for them. Much work. Much pain. Then they are killed, too. Slowly. Scalped. Then Indians go look for more white women. Mogoannoga, he have white woman."

Ben tensed, his pulses began to race. "What is she like?"

"Very young still, captured as a child. She die soon."

Ben was trembling, a mixture of relief and disappointment. Mogoannoga's woman clearly was not the one Ben sought. He prayed that Sarah was already dead, but he had to know for sure.

"Blood Arrow have white squaw, too."

"Young?"

The Gosiute was uncertain. He had not seen her himself, but he had spoken with an old Paiute who had. "White women become Indian squaws very quickly." He tapped his head, "Often go crazy. They think they have always been Indian, forget whites. They have papooses, half-breeds. Indians do not like half-white papooses. Often kill them, cut throats or smash heads with rocks."

"What about Blood Arrow's woman?" Ben demanded. It was all he could do to stop himself from shaking the old Indian.

"Indians always kill half-breed papooses if white man has been in squaw's blanket." The Gosiute was unmoved, he would say all he wanted to say unhurried. "Not always if Indian has lain with white woman." The bony shoulders shrugged. "Sometimes. Depends."

"Tell me about Blood Arrow's woman." Ben knelt down, thrusting his face close to the other. "How long has he had her?"

"Not long. A few moons."

"Where did he find her?" It could not be Sarah, Ben thought, but he had to eliminate every possibility. This was how it would be for many years to come, maybe for the rest of his life.

"I do not know. Perhaps in raid on white settlement, men killed and women taken prisoner." He regarded Ben with curiosity for the first time. "Why do you want to know about Blood Arrow's woman?"

"My sister was taken by the Cheyenne a long time ago."

"Then she is dead by now. Cheyenne very cruel. She maybe have papoose and Cheyenne kill them both. Most likely. Not likely she now with Paiutes."

"No, probably not. But I have to know for sure."

"Best not to know. Once white woman becomes Indian squaw, always Indian. Many Indians have white squaws. Too many. Bad for Indians and white women."

"Thanks." Ben gave him the last biscuit and a strip of dried salted meat which he carried for emergencies. "May your tribe not join up with the Paiutes."

It was growing dusk when Ben rode slowly down the dusty slope towards Carson City. He had completed a round trip of 380 miles in 36 hours.

The gates were dragged open as he approached. The whiskered woman stood there watching him, but there was no trace of her former arrogance. Her gaze averted his own as he rode on past her. Further down the street a group of women were huddled on the saloon steps. They did not even look up.

The warm breeze wafted their weeping towards Ben. One of them was hysterical, and they were all grieving.

The news from Pyramid Lake had travelled on ahead of him.

Three

The Paiutes had left their desert stronghold and were swarming east. This time nothing could stay the tide of bloodshed, Blood Arrow swore.

Ben first heard the news from an eastbound rider. Millersville had been sacked. Holmes, the station boss, and his men had fled just in time to avert a massacre. Jack Robinson's trading post had been looted and burned and that wasn't far off South Pass, which was too close to Slade's section for Ben's liking. He was desperately afraid for Mollie's safety. He would not rest until he was back at Horseshoe.

An eastbound relay took Ben as far as La Bronte, a swing station that comprised a single log building. Prior to being taken over by the Pony Express it had been a trading post for mules and horses.

Ben was not prepared to linger there. Horseshoe was little more than a four hour ride away, and there was a spare horse in the La Bronte corral. Nobody would be needing it. He took it and was back on the trail within minutes.

He pushed that horse almost to breaking point. He thought only about Mollie. He wanted to hold her. This time he rode with greater urgency than he had ever done when carrying the mails, but the journey seemed to be taking an eternity. Familiar landmarks were tantalizingly distant, and he convinced himself at one point that he would never reach his destination. His tight-fitting clothes clung damply to him, his face was streaked with dirt and sweat, and his mouth was as dry as the desert he had left a few days ago. Would Horseshoe station still be standing, or had the Paiutes somehow cut across the mountains and beaten him to it? Was Mollie still alive? He would rather she was dead than taken as a white squaw.

His horse stumbled in a rut, went lame, and he was forced to slow to a walk. He trembled with sheer frustration. Beyond the next wooded rise, about another mile, he would look down upon the river below Horseshoe. He almost believed that the river would have gone, too, that he would gaze upon an unfamiliar landscape, like this was all a fevered nightmare.

Telegraph poles were down. Those that still stood looked stark and dead. Some had cut wires trailing from them. The Paiutes had left a trail of destruction in their wake.

There was no sign of the telegraph construction gangs. They had probably fled to Fort Laramie or Fort Kearney. Work would not begin again until there was peace with the Paiutes, if ever. It would be a long time before the Pony Express was no longer needed.

Ben topped the last rise and looked down upon the river. It was little more than a muddy trickle. The entire landscape was parched, brown and dried up in the grip of the longest and fiercest drought for many years.

Ben sighed with sheer relief and almost whooped his joy aloud. Horseshoe station still stood beyond the river—it looked just the same as when he had last seen it. The gates were closed, preventing him from seeing inside the compound, where the wagon with the patched and torn blue canvas would be standing in the corner. It *had* to be there. He knew it was.

His horse limped behind him as he embarked on the final downhill stage. The animal sensed that food and water and rest were waiting for it.

Amos dragged the heavy gate open, flashed a set of pearl white teeth and whooped *"Mister Ben!"* for all to hear.

Ben barely nodded to the negro, as he had eyes only for . . . thank God, the wagon still stood in the corner of the palisade. It had a fresh rip in its side and some clothing was strung out to dry on a line at the rear. He saw all the signs he looked for. All he needed now was . . .

"Mollie!"

Ben ran to her clumsily, tripped and almost fell. It didn't matter. Nothing else mattered.

"Ben!"

They held each other close, their bodies trembled together. They wanted to cry their relief, but they would save it for later.

"I knew you'd come back, Ben." She didn't. She had almost given up hope of ever setting eyes on him again. Those weeks had seemed like years.

"I got delayed down in Nevada. Injun war held me up." He tried to make light of it.

"I know, that's what worried me."

They climbed up on to the box, just sat there, their relief at being reunited overriding everything else.

"The Paiutes are close, and the Cheyenne and the Arapaho are giving the army a hard time around Fort Laramie. The wagon train's gone there for safety. We'll maybe have to evacuate this place. Slade's holdin' on, says he ain't runnin' from no goddamned injuns!" She laughed, but it sounded forced. "But you're back safe, Ben, and that's all that matters."

"Where's Slade?" Ben looked towards the office. The door was closed.

"Rode out early this morning. Like he does most mornings. Comes back at nightfall, usually with a scalp or two danglin' from his saddle. It's small war parties which are the trouble around here right now. At the moment, Slade's givin' them a hard time. But even he won't be able to stop the main lot when they get here. But try tellin' him that."

"Somebody's comin'!" Ben heard the approaching hooves before he saw Amos opening the gates again.

J.A. Slade rode in. His dark clothes looked grey in the failing daylight, horse and rider were filmed with trail dust. Something bumped and swayed from the saddle. Ben knew only too well what it was. The section boss hadn't drawn a blank today.

Slade dismounted and tossed the reins to Amos. The road boss looked around, then started to walk towards the wagon.

"So you're back. At last." He stood there eyeing Ben, but there was no hint of a greeting, no stretching of those thin lips. Ben had been gone weeks—he might just as well have been an hour overdue on a run from Ward's or La Bonte.

"I've been carryin' the mails. Like I'm paid to." Ben met the other's stare. "You go where you have to when there's no other riders available. I ended up in Nevada."

"Nobody'll be ridin' any mails for a while." Slade might not even have heard, he spoke flatly, expressionlessly, like he was just repeating a despatch which had come in. He probably was. "The Pony is suspended until further notice. Mails, riders an' hosses've bin lost. Not on the Rocky Ridge division, though. No bandits or injuns've stolen anythin' on my stretch an' got away with it."

"So, I'm out of a job," Ben said.

"You're still on full pay, and you'll earn every damned cent of it!" Slade's head was thrust forward, his grey eyes blazed. "Just because there ain't no mails to carry don't mean there's no work to do. My job is to keep this division clear o' injuns and outlaws, and you won't be sittin' around on your ass like everybody else while I'm out there!" His arm made a sweep of the land beyond the stockade. "I give the orders around here, you obey 'em."

Ben was aware of how Mollie tensed.

"What about the army, then?" Ben asked.

"The *army!*" In the deepening dusk Slade's mouth became an invisible slit. Had he not been in the company of a woman, or had he been drinking, Slade might have spat. Sober, though, he was courteous where the opposite sex was concerned. "The army! All they're doin' is chasin' after small war parties, losin' 'em in the hills, and afore they know it, the injuns've doubled back and attacked a settlement. They're chasin' shadows and it's all part of Blood Arrow's game, only they can't see it. Until the government gets enough troops out here, that's how it'll be. In the meantime, we gotta make life difficult for the Paiutes. I got three more today. It keeps 'em nervy, every one o' them blasted injuns out there don't know whether it'll be his turn next, whether he'll see tomorrow. A few months ago, they were celebratin' the death of Man Who Likes Killing. Now they're scared to hell of him, and you'n me are gonna keep it that way, Hollister."

Slade took a deep breath, let it out slowly, like he had been saving all this up for Ben and now he had got it out of his system.

"You reckon we can hold out here against Blood Arrow's main war party, Slade?"

"We ain't runnin' from no damned redskins!" Slade's thin lips curled in contempt. "Every man on this division is stayin' right here in Horseshoe. The rest can stay or leave, as they please. We're stocked up on supplies. We got enough powder'n shot to kill every last one o' them Paiutes if they were lined up in front of us. An' all the time every savage'll be lookin' over his shoulder, in case I suddenly appear behind him. Or in case he doesn't even hear the shot that gets him."

Any other man would have been boasting. Ben knew that J.A. Slade wasn't. Every Indian out there was terrified of the black clad figure. Slade was their nemesis. Around Slade, they only found their courage in numbers. But nobody knew what those numbers were. And numbers might be the deciding factor in the ultimate confrontation between red and white men.

"We'll ride out tomorrow, just you'n me." Slade turned to go. "Split up or stick together, whichever suits. We'll do some scoutin'. There's a bunch o' renegades tacked on to the Paiutes now."

"Brent and Mogoannoga," Ben said.

"You heard, huh?"

"Talked with an old Gosiute in the desert. They wiped out a fifty-strong vigilante posse from Carson. Not a single survivor."

"If we can kill the pair of 'em," Slade began, his voice was loaded with menace and hatred, "and mebbe Blood Arrow, too, then the rest'll have no stomach for a fight. Blood Arrow's roused the rabble—he's like a war god to 'em. With him dead, there's a good chance they'll turn back to Numaga. And he's yeller, don't like fightin'. Doesn't mean, though that we'll let up on 'em even if that happens." He laughed in that strange flat way of his.

"He just likes killing for the sake of it," Mollie said after Slade was out of earshot. "And sometimes, I get the feeling that you're the same, Ben. It's revenge for what the Cheyenne did to your folks that you want, isn't it?"

Ben fell silent. He wished that he hadn't told her what had happened to his parents. Or to Sarah. She had lost her husband in the same way, but she didn't hate the Indians for it. It made him feel guilty.

"Well?"

"No." He squeezed her hand, "I don't hate them for what they did to Mom and Dad, but I might for what they might've done to Sarah. Maybe I won't know how I feel until I find that out."

"Which you most likely never will."

"Mebbe. Mebbe not. It might be better not to know, but I'll never rest till I do. There's a lot o' white women livin' with the Indians, I've heard the kind o' things the savages do to 'em. I need to know Sarah's fate, however terrible."

"Just don't get like Slade." Mollie stared straight ahead of her. "I couldn't live with that, Ben, no matter what."

"I want us to build a new life for ourselves." He pulled her to him, sensed that suddenly she might have resisted him. "Maybe we'll grow crops, raise animals and I'll hunt for meat. I can fix guns, too, and there'll be plenty of that out here."

"That's how I'd like it to be, too, Ben."

He could not see her eyes in the darkness, but he sensed that she was close to crying. "Mend guns, maybe use 'em for hunting. But not for killing people."

There were things that maybe she should have told Ben soon after they first met. Mollie had anguished over them during the weeks that Ben had been away. She consoled herself that she hadn't lied, hadn't deliberately kept them from him. It was just that he hadn't asked. If he had, then she would have told him. At times, she thought, it was better for him not to know, he wasn't ever likely to find out, and that way it might be better for him. But it would eat into her like a cancer for the rest of her life.

"There's things I got to tell you, Ben." Her voice quavered as he climbed into the bunk alongside her and turned down the lamp.

"Sure. Go ahead." He felt his stomach knot. It sounded like a confession, something that had gotten too much for her to bear alone any longer. Something she had done in his absence. She had worked the saloons before and, since almost every settler within a hundred mile radius had moved into Horseshoe for safety, there were clients aplenty.

"I've got a son, Ben. I should've told you before."

"Tell me if you want to." The wagon seemed to gyrate in the darkness. Mollie was holding on, too, but not to him. He knew her face was turned the other way.

She told him how she had been born and raised in New

York. Her father had been a drunkard. He had died when she was too young to remember him. Her mother had taken a job cleaning and cooking for the Tripps who lived in a big house down by the harbor. Walter Tripp moved in high society, ran a music academy and was part owner of a theater. His wife, Thelma, spent most of her time socializing with the other socialite women in the fast growing city.

When Mollie was home from school, her mother used to take her with her when she went to work at the Tripps's. Much to her mother's embarrassment, Mollie used to sing out loud and, on one occasion, Walter emerged from the class he was teaching. He stood and gazed at the child, but instead of admonishing her, he said, "That child has a marvelous voice. She's talented, too. With training, she could become a professional singer. Let me train her, I promise you it won't cost you a dime."

Mollie joined the children of the privileged at Walter Tripp's academy. As she grew from childhood into adolescence, not only did her voice enthrall but so did her looks. Young men turned their heads when she passed by, but she was too wrapped up in her ambitions to notice. Even when Walter suggested that she go for private tuition at his home in the evenings, she was too innocent to be suspicious.

She fell in love with a man thirty years older than herself. Or perhaps she fell in love with the prospect of a glittering career that her lover's influence would make possible. She was seventeen when she became pregnant, and even then, she was foolish enough to believe that her mentor would marry her. Fame and fortune beckoned.

But it did not work out that way. Walter Tripp did not divorce his wife. Instead, he arranged an adoption for the baby. Perhaps he thought that everything would carry on as before, and that he could continue to enjoy the best of both worlds. Thelma was adamant that he could not.

She told Mollie never again to enter their house and Mollie's mother was fired from her job to ensure that Walter had no further contact with his young mistress through her mother.

Soon afterward Mollie's mother took ill with consumption and died the following year. Mollie's world collapsed, but she was still determined to capitalize upon the training which her baby's father had given her. Nobody could take that away from her.

She attended audition after audition, but always she was turned down. In the end, she accepted that she was not good enough, and maybe Walter Tripp had extolled her talents for his own ends.

Eventually, Mollie found happiness with Sam, a store clerk, and they married. Sam had ambitions, too, but he would never realize them in New York. The newspapers were full of the Big Trek westward, agencies advertised deals for prospective movers. The Promised Land beckoned and Sam and Mollie answered the call.

Like the Hollisters, though, Sam and Mollie's dream died west of Fort Kearney.

Perhaps, by telling Ben, she could finally bury the past and pick up the dream where she had left off. She prayed that her husband might be persuaded to do likewise.

"Before I married Sam, I tried to look for my baby." Her voice broke at last, "But I never found him. If my mother knew where the Tripps had fostered him, she didn't tell me before she died. I called him Tom. Maybe the folks who took him called him something different. I thought I'd like to see him just once. I wrote to Walter, but he never replied. I guess it's . . . it's best that way, Ben. Some things you have to leave behind when you start a new life."

Ben pulled her to him and kissed her long and hard. He didn't know how to put it into words, but he thought that was the best way of letting her know that it didn't make any difference between them. He let her cry until she was done.

"Thank you, Ben." Her voice was steadier now. "There's something else I have to tell you."

He tensed and his heart started to pound again.

"Ben, I think I'm going to have a baby. I'm not absolutely sure. Near enough, though."

Ben trembled in the sultry darkness of the Wyoming night. Elation flooded over him, but it was tinged with guilt. Mollie had finally buried her past but he knew that he could not bury his. Not yet, anyway.

And her worst fears might be fulfilled. Ben might become like Slade. If he was honest with himself, he was part of the way there already.

Four

Ben rode out with Slade most days now. He didn't have any choice, at least, that was what he told Mollie. He told himself, too, but he gave up trying to convince himself in the end.

They slipped out through the gates before daylight, wraiths in the darkness, just in case the Paiutes were watching from the woods beyond the river. The signs so far were that the Indians were still some distance north and west. Ham's Fork, a vacated swing station, had been looted and burned to the ground and some cattle bones were whitening in the scorching sun. Lewis, the station boss, Slade informed Ben with undisguised contempt, had fled to Ward's Central. From there he had probably gone on to skulk in Fort Laramie.

"Where'd you learn to ride?" Slade asked Ben once and maybe there was Just a hint of admiration for his companion's horsemanship in the road boss's tone. Slade did not make small talk.

"Back in England when I was about twelve," Ben answered. "My father's gun business brought him into contact with other sporting activities. One of his customers was a Master of Foxhounds. Dad had done a job on Mister Houghton's gun, and he was very pleased with it. He asked if Dad would like to ride to hounds one day. Dad didn't ride, but I'd already had some riding lessons, so he said I could go."

"Shootin' from the saddle, huh?" Slade was curious.

"No guns," Ben explained. "The hounds get on the scent of a fox, chase it for miles. Most times they lose it, but occasionally they catch up with it. Kill it. You have to be able to ride, jump fences and ditches. I came off a time or two, but eventually, I learned to stay in the saddle. I rode with the hounds regularly for one season. There's no better training."

"Sounds crazy to me," Slade grunted. "Easier to shoot the foxes, I'd say."

He lapsed into silence, his curiosity satisfied. Ben had learned to ride and shoot in a strange way. But he had made the grade, as far as Slade was concerned, and that was all that mattered.

Slade and Ben took to going further afield. They packed supplies in their saddlebags. They would camp out for two or three nights. West of South Pass was where the Indians were likely to be and there was no way of knowing how far the section boss might decide to travel. Ben groaned inwardly, knowing that meant he would be parted from Mollie again, just when she needed him most.

They saw roaming bands of Indians from time to time. It was on their third scouting trip together that Slade and Ben came upon a band of five Paiutes. The Indians were clearly hunting. They wore no war paint. The two men took cover in a patch of scrub and waited for the band to approach.

The Paiutes were oblivious of the danger and every one of them fell in the hail of bullets. Slade claimed four to his own gun, scalped the dead and handed the fifth tuft of bloody hair to his companion.

"I'd have had all five if I'd bin alone," he remarked as he climbed back in the saddle.

Ben was sure that he had dropped two—he and the road boss had fired simultaneously. Only by digging the bullets out of the corpses would it be possible to prove which calibers had killed them. Ben let Slade's claim go unchallenged.

There were enough Indians in these hills to satisfy both of them.

"Shod hosses!" Slade's keen eye had spotted some faint hoofmarks on the dusty track ahead of them. He dismounted, knelt to examine them more closely.

The hoofprints headed out of a narrow gulch towards the wooded hills.

"Brent an' his gang o' breeds." The killing look appeared on Slade's pallid features. "They must be hidin' out somewhere in these hills. It's impossible to track 'em from hereon 'cause the ground's all rock and shale. Blood Arrow's mebbe somewhere on the edge of the desert and his tracks'll be covered, too." He looked thoughtful. "Reckon' the time has come fer us to split up. If we're close to either the renegades or the injuns, we don't want to give our presence away by shootin'. Don't shoot unless yuh run into trouble. Find the outlaws' hideout and mebbe where the main lot o' injuns are, that's what we have to do. Once we know where they are, we can make plans."

"Smoke!" Out of the corner of his eye Ben glimpsed smoke on the far northern mountain ridge.

Slade shaded his eyes, studied the signals, his expression grim. "Bannocks," he muttered, "an' they're askin' to meet up with Blood Arrow. The main Paiute force is movin' in to South Pass an' they'll be comin' this way, mebbe this time plannin' on sweepin' right down to Fort Laramie."

"And Horseshoe's right in their path!" Ben's guts knotted. "Maybe we should evacuate to Fort Kearney."

"Like I said," Slade grunted, "kill Blood Arrow an' they'll stop. Numaga would never make full-scale war. Let's ride. You take the desert area, I'll take to the mountains. Make cold camps, no fires. See yuh back at Horseshoe in a few days."

Ben stood and watched Slade ride away. It sounded like an impossible mission. But he had already learned that nothing was impossible where J.A. Slade was concerned.

* * *

On the first night, Ben camped in some scrub on the edge of the desert. The night was cold, and he was grateful for his blanket. He thought about Mollie. She would be frantic with worry again and she did not like him riding with Slade. But he had signed the pledge and he was still on full pay and the Division Superintendent allocated the duties.

Somewhere, Mollie had a son. He might be alive or dead. She had succeeded in putting her past behind her. Ben only wished that he could do the same.

He slept uneasily and was fully awake before the stars had paled. He ate some biscuits and dried meat, took only a sip from his canteen because he would need all his water later. He set off, walking his horse, taking note of his bearings for it was easy to become lost in the desert. To the south were hills and canyons and pine forests; to the north the scrubland stretched away until it blended into the Great Salt Lake. Within an hour or two it would become unbearably hot.

The atmosphere became stifling and windless. In places scrub grew thickly and offered ample cover for tracker or those he tracked. Ben stopped frequently to listen. There was no sound, no sign of life of any kind except . . .

A movement, a tiny speck so high in the sky that it was only just visible, attracted his attention. A bird—it floated on moth-like ragged wings. Ben shuddered in spite of the heat. A buzzard was watching him. Waiting. It was hungry for carrion. As if it had a premonition of death.

His death.

In one place Ben found some unshod hoofmarks, but they soon petered out. Just a breath of night wind in the desert was sufficient to blow sand and cover the prints. From now on it was all a question of luck. Just as the Paiutes might spot him first.

The buzzard was still up there.

The sky was turning saffron, and Ben decided to make

camp in a clump of thorn trees, it was as good a place as any he was likely to find out here. Hidden among some bushes was a tepid water hole, no more than three feet across. He filled his canteen and drank thirstily. Any place else it might have tasted sour, here it was real good.

A watering hole in an arid land is a communal meeting place for all forms of life: animals, large and small, birds. And humans. He would need to be wary but to have travelled on might have found him stranded without cover.

Ben slept more deeply than he had intended, the desert heat had taken its toll on him. Somewhere, deep in his slumber, a horse snickered. Just once. He stirred restlessly but did not awaken.

Until strong hands seized him and a weight of bodies, pinioned him to the ground.

"What . . ." He was unable to grab for his guns. They had been snatched from him, anyway. In the half light of a desert dawn he stared up into the cruel, gloating face of a Paiute warrior in full war paint. Two other braves were sitting astride Ben, rendering him powerless even to struggle.

"Slayer Who Rides With the Wind is careless." One of the Paiutes was examining Ben's guns with undisguised curiosity. "Likewise, without his guns he is as a mountain lion without fangs and claws. He is small," he sneered, "and sleeps heavily. He does not even awake when his horse warns of danger. He pretends to be brave, but he will not be when he begins to die slowly. Even now I can hear his screams for mercy!"

Ben somehow kept every nerve under control. The Indians were gloating, trying to search out a weakness in this much-feared white. The slightest sign of fear was regarded as cowardice. Ben had been told that in his Butterfield days. His heart was pounding and his mouth was as dry as the desert all around. He took a deep breath, let it out slowly, and when he spoke there was not a tremor in his voice. He did not even swallow in his nervousness.

"You crept up on me in the darkness because you were afraid to face me by daylight." He might even have spat his contempt had he had any saliva. "You are afraid of Slayer Who Rides With the Wind except when there are several of you and he is helpless."

The Paiutes stiffened, their painted faces becoming grotesque masks of anger. For one awful moment, Ben thought that they might plunge their knives into him or mutilate him with their tomahawks. They might just have done that except that each one of them earned the wrath of Blood Arrow if they did not bring this sworn foe alive to him.

"We shall soon see how brave Slayer Who Rides With the Wind is," a warrior grunted. "His screams will echo across the stillness of the desert. First, though, we shall take you to face Blood Arrow." He turned and spoke in the Paiute tongue to his companions. "Bind him and put him across his horse. We have a long journey ahead of us."

They travelled slowly for most of that blistering hot day. Ben was slumped over his horse, head downward, his hands and feet bound tightly with hide thongs. He could scarcely breathe in the mid-day heat. Several times he passed out and came to again.

One of the Paiutes led the horse, the other two walked behind. They seemed impervious to the heat. They had lived most of their lives in and around the Great Salt Lake and it was no hardship for them.

The tall Indian in the rear was still examining Ben's revolvers as he walked; fascinated by them. So *these* were the sticks that banged and killed! The white renegade and his halfbreed gang carried guns like these. They had traded some to the Paiutes already, but the Indians were wary of them. Fear did not make for good marksmanship. Arrows were swifter and more accurate. And quieter.

It was full dark by the time the party reached a scrub oasis deep in the desert. Possibly no white man had ever set foot here. The Paiutes had discovered it generations ago, Blood Arrow's father had told his son about it. It was an excellent place to hide or to prepare for battle with the whites.

Ben's captors tipped him from the horse. He fell heavily. His hands and feet were numb where his bonds had restricted his circulation.

He lay there sizing up his surroundings. The Indian encampment was a sizeable one. Small fires burned but not enough to show up across the huge expanse of desert. Silhouettes passed to and fro. Beyond the fires Ben made out some shelters erected from poles with animal hides stretched over them. He was aware of an aroma of cooking but all he wanted right now was water. Clearly, the Indians were not going to allow him to drink.

Blood Arrow was tall. Very tall. At least 6 feet, 4 or 5 inches, Ben estimated as the Paiute chief arrived to inspect his prisoner. The Indian was strong and muscular, not an ounce of surplus flesh on his body. His feathered head-dress, hooked nose and capacious buffalo robe gave him the appearance of a giant bird of prey. A kind of half-Indian, half-eagle look. His expression was merciless.

Ben remembered the buzzard that had followed him into the desert. It had surely been an omen.

"So at last we have Slayer Who Rides With the Wind," Blood Arrow sneered. "Pah! I expected a tall, strong warrior. It makes no difference, he will scream long and loud before long!" He leaned over Ben and his eyes narrowed. "Where is Man Who Likes Killing?"

Ben would have shrugged his shoulders, except he was trussed too tightly. He moved his head from side to side. "Who knows? Does anybody know where Man Who Likes Killing is? One moment he is here, another there. One moment you are alive, the next you are dead. Perhaps right now he is watching from the shadows beyond your fires."

Blood Arrow turned his head and looked across in the

direction of the shadows beyond the camp fires. Ben's suggestion had clearly disturbed the chief.

"Even Man Who Likes Killing would not dare to venture into the Paiute war camp alone." Blood Arrow's tone lacked conviction. His eyes moved from side to side. He did not trust the darkness of the desert night and what it might conceal.

"He'll come." Ben played on the other's lurking fear. "Maybe not tonight. Nor tomorrow. But sooner or later, he will come after you."

A thoughtful look crossed the Indian's cruel face, a narrowing of his dark eyes, a pouting of his lips that merged into a kind of smile. It was disconcerting to look upon if you happened to be tied up and at his mercy.

"Perhaps you are right," Blood Arrow muttered. "Yes, perhaps you are right, Slayer Who Rides With the Wind. Man Who Likes Killing may come to the Paiute camp sooner than even you hope."

Blood Arrow leaned forward and extended a bronzed hand. Ben flinched at its touch, the way it grasped a finger of his left hand. A tug: Ben's tight-fitting gold wedding ring yielded under protest, scraping the flesh of his finger as it was torn free.

The Paiute held the ring aloft. It glinted in the soft light. He looked closely at it, intrigued by the scroll engraving.

"So the Paiute chief is a thief as well as a butcher of women and children!" Ben snarled. "Give it back to me!"

"I shall need it." Blood Arrow passed the ring to one of the watching braves. "You may never see it again. That will depend upon Man Who Likes Killing."

Ben shuddered involuntarily. The chief's expression sent a chill through his body, the hairs on the back of his neck prickled. What cunning plan was the other hatching now?

One of the fires crackled, some dry brushwood sent up a tongue of flame. The eerie orange glow had the shadows retreating and a circle of bright light briefly illuminated the scene.

Ben had a clear view of Blood Arrow now. The half-light had not played tricks, the other was everything that Ben had thought he was. And worse.

Ben had thought at first that the chief's robe was fringed, some fancy finishing by a woman who saw her man as not like other men—regalia fit for a chief, cut and sewn, the craft of their people. So it had looked in the half light and the shadows. Now he saw that the fringes were not fashioned from the original garment but had been crudely attached to the edges. They hung down, straggled and matted where a brownish substance had congealed and dried.

Blood Arrow's robe was adorned with human scalps.

Ben tasted bile at the back of his throat. He retched. Had his stomach been full he might have spewed and drowned in his own vomit. Even though he, himself, had taken scalps, the wearing of them was an obscenity to a civilized race.

"You choke, Slayer Who Rides With the Wind?" The Paiute mocked his prisoner.

"I'm fine." Ben overcame his revulsion. "Just the heat, I guess." Doubtless many of the trophies worn by Blood Arrow came from the slain at Pyramid Lake as well as from raids on settlements and Pony Express stations. Maybe even his own parents' scalps hung there.

No! He reassured himself quickly. That was not possible— his folks had been massacred by the Cheyenne. Braves did not trade scalps. They were personal trophies, proof of a warrior's bravery and fighting prowess.

"I think that Man Who Likes Killing will come here." Blood Arrow was obviously pleased with the germ of an idea. "I know that he will. Perhaps two or three days from now—it is a long ride from his camp. I will send a messenger to summon him."

Ben was following the other's train of thought. Blood Arrow had a hostage. It gave him bargaining power. Whites were considered crazy by the savage tribes of the west. Chivalry, where a comrade or relative was concerned, was considered a weakness. An Indian warrior died bravely. He did not rely upon help from his own kind, as it would neither be asked for nor given. But whites had been known to sacrifice their lives for others . . .

Ben smiled at the irony of Blood Arrow's thinking. J.A. Slade was not like others—the road boss didn't give a heap of hoss shit for the lives of his men, stagecoach passengers or anybody else. All that mattered to him was his reputation. He was obsessed with his brief record in the Pony Express. Possibly, he cherished his renown as a gunfighter most of all. Whatever his values, they were selfish ones. There was no way he would lay down his life in order to save a fellow human being, most certainly not to a hated foe. He might have risked it to recover stolen mails, but Ben had not been riding with the mails. There was no reason to expect the section boss even to attempt Ben's rescue. Slade had his own code. Only he understood it and he would live by it.

Even if Slade *did* come to the Paiute camp, there was no way Blood Arrow would set Ben free in return. The Paiute chief traded in treachery. He would delight in slaying both of his hated foes. Slowly.

"Well, you'd better try asking Slade," Ben managed a grin. He knew what the reply would be. In all probability, the messenger would not return alive. All the same, it would give Ben time. There was always the slim chance that an opportunity to escape might present itself.

"In the meantime you will remain here." Blood Arrow was definitely pleased with himself. "Do you have a woman, Slayer Who Rides With the Wind?"

"I have a wife."

"Then I shall see that you do not spend the night alone." Blood Arrow turned and signalled to two braves who stepped forward and lifted the trussed man off the ground. "No-Name is," Blood Arrow said, pondering over a means of communication, then tapped his head, "crazy. She hates whites. As you will find out. I shall send her to your tepee later."

Blood Arrow's scalp-adorned robe swirled as he strode haughtily away amid an array of cooking pots and tepees.

Ben was borne towards a tepee which stood apart from the rest. He had misgivings over what the night ahead held for him.

Five

The stifling darkness of the small tepee was heavy with the mingled stench of cured animal hides and stale cooking. Ben's captors had not untied him. His arms and legs were numb and he longed to stretch them. His head still throbbed from the heat and the long journey, and his mouth was dry and his tongue felt swollen. He had not been given even a sip of water, and he knew it would have been futile to request a drink. It would have been considered a weakness. Ben knew only too well the dangers of dehydration.

He did not hear any approaching footfalls. His first realization that somebody had entered was a rustling as the hide flap was pulled open. He had a momentary glimpse of a silhouette against the glow from the dying fires outside. It could have been either a brave or a squaw—there was no way of telling. The hair was cut short and the body was clothed in a baggy hide jacket and leggings, so that the wearer could have been fat or thin. Bare feet enabled the newcomer to move silently.

He decided that it must be a female—Blood Arrow had spoken of a squaw. Stale body odors and sweat wafted over him. He heard quick breathing as though the stranger was anticipating this meeting with relish. Ben's fears mounted.

A laugh, a throaty chuckle. It was definitely female. It was also far more terrifying than if she had snarled or cursed. Anger was not long in following, expletives muttered in the

Paiute tongue. Ben did not need an interpreter—they were explicit enough in themselves.

Now she was behind him, bending over him. Her breath was fetid, and he felt the warm wetness of spittle on his face. He closed his eyes even though he was unable to see much in the gloom. Far rather would he have been left alone with Blood Arrow than . . . *this.*

"White trash!" Her calloused hands with their ragged fingernails raked through his hair, bunched and pulled it until he was sure that she was trying to rip it out by the roots. Not a single gasp of pain passed his lips because he knew that was what she was seeking.

Something sharp nicked his scalp. *Oh, God, she was about to scalp him while he was still alive!*

He felt a warm trickle of blood on his forehead. He had scalped men himself and knew just how easy it was. He also knew what his victims had looked like afterward. Ultimately, it would make no difference because the Paiutes would kill him when they had finished torturing him. Right now, though, the prospect of death was inviting.

She did not scalp him. Another nasal laugh came out of the darkness and the blade was withdrawn. She had merely taunted him.

But this was only the beginning.

"Paiutes scalp. So do whites. Blood Arrow has vowed that your scalp shall hang in his lodge."

Her words were basic, staccato. As if she had been taught only the rudiments of the white man's language. Or else she was attempting to remember a tongue which had once been her own, but she had not spoken it for many years.

"Whites torture Paiute women . . . rape them."

Which was certainly true, Ben thought. There were many stories of captured Indian women being subjected to the ultimate humiliation after they were taken prisoner. Women were the victims of war on both sides. Ben did not try to deny it. It would not have made any difference, anyway.

He was amazed at her strength. She gripped his clothing and pulled. There was a ripping sound and he felt a coolness on his sweating loins.

"You not rape again!"

Her fingers gouged down into his torn pants. Had her weight not been pinning him down, he would have rolled over onto his stomach. Her laughter was maniacal, the blade of her knife was like a sliver of ice on his heated flesh. He almost screamed in anticipation of what she was about to do.

She didn't do it.

She knelt back then rose to her feet. Her laughter was shrill, hysterical. It stopped as suddenly as it had begun. He sensed her walking around him—clockwise, then counter-clockwise, like a trapper who had discovered a catch in one of his traps, a wounded beast that had to be despatched and wondering how best to kill.

Ben grunted and he almost cried out as a bare foot drove into his side. Again. And again. The strength and force of those kicks were unbelievable. Then she stepped upon him, stood there, slowly forced out any breath that still remained in his lungs.

Ben fought for breath, wheezed and rasped. Streaks of red arrowed before his eyes like lightning in a stormy sky.

He fainted briefly. When he regained consciousness he saw that she was standing over him, watching him in the sliver of outside firelight flickering through a gap in the flap opening. He saw how she breathed fast and shook with rage and hatred for the white man who lay before her.

One of the fires outside blazed up suddenly, fully illumi-nating the interior of the tepee. Ben saw her face clearly for the first time. His agonized gasp had nothing whatever to do with the pain that racked his bruised body.

Her features were horrifically scarred—a jagged wound that had long healed ran the length of one cheek, disfiguring her lips into a perpetual snarl. Her nose had been broken at some stage and was pushed to one side so that her nostrils flared cavernously. Her eyes burned insanely with hate, glowing red in the reflection of the flames like some ancient goddess of evil.

Ben almost shrieked her name aloud. There was no doubt in his mind, even those disfigurations could not completely change the face he had known, grown up with, watched mature from childhood into adolescence.

God above, no! Not this!

He tried to tell himself that it was a nightmare brought about by his ordeal. His exposure to the desert sun had snapped his reasoning and had created this monstrosity which he somehow likened to . . .

"Sarah!" He croaked.

It couldn't be. It wasn't.

It was.

"White trash!" She screamed at him, delivered another barefooted kick to his side. "Slayer Who Rides With the Wind."

His brain spun. The unthinkable, the unbelievable, had become stark, awful reality. The physical resemblance between this crazed Paiute woman and his own sister was barely recognizable. But it was enough. Sarah stood before him, the shadows raced back as if to spare him the terrible sight. Physically, she was here. Mentally, she was gone. Only a demented savage stood as a reminder to him of what once had been.

"Sarah? It's me. Ben. Your brother." He had to try to get through to her. He knew he would not.

She did not appear to understand. Those lips were bared in an animal snarl. Instead of sparkling white, even teeth, there were broken, blackened stumps. That slim figure which had once graced the floors of dancing schools had filled out with muscles hardened by menial labor. The shoulders were hunched from years of stooping over cooking pots or tilling barren ground. Slender hands had calloused into virtual claws.

Sarah existed no more. There was no way back for her. These savages had destroyed all that Ben remembered so tenderly, had turned his sister into *this*.

"Don't you remember, Sarah? Our parents? Me?" He knew it was futile but he had to try. He would not abandon years of searching lightly.

"You will die!" Her spittle sprayed over him, she slobbered like a wild animal. "I would kill you, but my husband, Blood Arrow, would be angry with me. Tomorrow you die. Or after the next sun sets and rises. Blood Arrow will decide."

She was crazed, frenzied. He opened his mouth to plead again with her but a kick drove into his ribs and only a gasp of pain escaped his bleeding lips.

Then she was gone, as silently as she had come. Outside the fires died down, the glow of their ashes dulled. Ben was left alone in the blackness of a tortured night. Perhaps he had imagined it all, he clung to a vain hope.

He knew he had not.

Ben's captors came for him at first light, two warriors with stoic expressions who did not speak as they dragged him outside. A knife was produced, he thought for one moment that it was going to be plunged into his exposed loins where the woman called No-Name had ripped his clothes. Instead, he experienced the agony of returning circulation after his bonds were cut.

He was handed a bowl of food, a mixture of wild berries, persimmons and choke cherries and freshly peeled wild thistle stalks. Ben ate, then drank from a hide gourd filled with brackish water, but it tasted cool and refreshed him somewhat. Now that the agony of his blood flowing again was over, he began to ache in every limb. Especially where the woman who had once been his sister had kicked him.

All around Paiute women were busy cooking, using vessels fashioned from hide and stretched between upright poles. To make the water boil, they dropped heated stones from the fires into it, lifting them from the ashes with shovels pillaged from wagon trains or white settlements. Scalps hung from every lodge.

As he ate, Ben scrutinized the encampment. There were no more than thirty warriors and as many squaws. Nowhere could he see Blood Arrow's woman, No-Name. Neither was there any sign of the Paiute chief.

After he had finished his meal, Ben was left sitting there. A guard wearing a hide shirt and leggings stood watching him from some distance away. Ben saw that the brave had Ben's own two revolvers attached to a thong around his waist. All that the Paiute probably understood about the guns was that if he pulled the triggers, they made a bang and killed. He would have no knowledge of marksmanship. Ben hoped that the other would not idly play with his newly acquired guns, for there would be greater danger from an accidentally fired bullet than an intentional one.

Clearly, the Indians were not in any hurry to do anything to him. Their messenger was already on his way to deliver an ultimatum to Slade at Horseshoe station. Ben reflected that the chances of that brave returning were slim. By sunset, his scalp would probably be amongst the grisly collection in the Division Superintendent's office. All the same, it gave Ben a 24-hour respite. The Paiutes would not do anything to him until their courier failed to return.

Ben stared longingly at his guns on the sentry's waist. The other was watching him, too. He would not relax his vigilance no matter how long he stayed there. There was no question of him dozing in the desert heat. A sudden rush by Ben would have been both foolish and futile.

Ben saw that his horse was tethered in the shade of some

thorn trees on the edge of the village. It might as well have been back in the stable at Horseshoe for all the good it was to him.

Still, an opportunity to escape might present itself later. Right now there was none and all he could do was bide his time.

He stretched himself out in a patch of shade afforded by a tepee and slept. Whatever lay ahead of him, he would need all his strength.

The Paiutes came for Ben at sunset. Two braves hauled him to his feet and, as if he had been watching from somewhere close by, Blood Arrow strode haughtily into view. None of the Indians spoke as Ben was pushed along in front of them and made to walk the length of the village and out as far as the edge of the scrub oasis. Beyond, the desert shimmered after the heat of the day.

Four wooden stakes had been hammered into the parched ground. A sudden push from behind sent Ben sprawling. His arms and legs were seized, each limb was tied to a stake, spread-eagling him at full stretch.

The braves stepped back and Blood Arrow strode forward, standing over Ben like a bronzed and angry colossus.

"Your life depends on Man Who Likes Killing," the chief grunted. "He has until sun-up to come. See." He pointed behind him. "That is where your death will come from if he does not answer my summons."

Ben lifted his aching head as best he could. Beyond Blood Arrow, outlined against the deep red of a desert sunset, he could just make out a mound some four or five feet high.

"Ants!" Blood Arrow smiled cruelly. "Creatures that have the intelligence of redmen and who also build and fight with their armies. And they eat any living thing in their path!"

Ben understood only too well. He did not answer—there was nothing to be said.

A fourth Paiute approached. It was the guard from the camp, still with the guns hanging from his waist thong. He was carrying something which he set down on the ground. Ben saw that it was a gourd like the one from which he had drunk earlier.

"Ants hunt the scrublands for nectar." Blood Arrow gestured around him. "They search for the hives of wild bees. When they find a hive, messengers are despatched to bring the entire population to feed. I have witnessed them on the move, a trail longer and wider than our village and moving with the speed of a horse. I have also seen them strip a horse down to its bones, such is their greed. They can smell honey from a great distance."

"I get it." Somehow Ben forced a grin, the last thing he must do was to reveal his terror to these Indians, "I'm to be the honeypot."

"When the sun rises above the mountains in the east, if Man Who Likes Killing has not come, then the honey will be poured over you. All that remains then is for the ants to scent it and find you. That will not be long. Pray to the white man's God this night, Slayer Who Rides With the Wind, that our most hated enemy will come unarmed to our camp. One of you will be dead before the desert heat rises tomorrow, that I swear."

Blood Arrow turned abruptly, stalked away in the direction of the camp. Two of his braves followed at his heels. The third one, the sentry, seated himself cross-legged under a nearby bush. He fixed the prisoner with an unwavering stare and remained motionless. He would stay like that throughout the coming night hours.

Ben closed his eyes. He knew that there was no way that J.A. Slade would surrender himself to the Paiutes. He would not falsely raise his hopes by even thinking that the road boss might come. By now the Indian messenger had an Army .44 ball in his head and his scalp was hung up to dry.

Ben resigned himself to his fate. He would be dead by the time the sun reached its zenith.

Six

Mollie watched Slade ride back alone into Horseshoe station in the gathering dusk. She had been sitting on the wagon seat, watching and waiting, since late afternoon. Amos opened the gate, the road boss dismounted, handed the reins to the negro and marched straight over to his office.

Where had Ben got to? She stood up, looked down the trail as far as the river. There was no sign of anybody else. Why hadn't Ben ridden in with Slade like he always did? She consoled herself with the thought that, if any mishap had befallen her husband, Slade would have informed her right away, which meant that Ben had remained out there for some reason, alone in a land that crawled with hostile Indians.

All the same, the road boss should have let her know why Ben hadn't come back with him. She slid down off the seat. Everybody else around here was scared of J.A. Slade, but she wasn't. Goddamn him, she would go right across to his office and demand to know where Ben was, and she wasn't leaving until he told her!

Slade was sitting at his desk poring over a pile of papers when Mollie pushed open the door. His hand was on his gun even as he looked up. That was the way he lived, otherwise he would have been dead long ago. The expression of irritation on his sallow features softened a little when he recognized Mollie. He was a gentleman because he was sober and she was a woman. Without alcohol in his blood, he respected the opposite sex.

"Where's Ben?" The question came out in a rush, her eyes blazed. Like Slade, she had no time for small talk. "You came back alone . . ."

"We split up." There was a hint of a smile. "He's scoutin' the desert area, could be gone two, three days. That boy can look after himself, you mark my words. He'll be back afore long. If he finds the Paiute camp, he'll keep clear, ride back to warn us. Then we'll teach 'em a lesson they won't forget."

Mollie nodded, her relief that nothing awful had happened to Ben brought a smile to her lips. She stepped back outside, pulled the door shut. There was nothing else she had to say to J. A. Slade.

All she could do now was to wait and she knew all about that. Waiting was the worst part of all.

"Injuns!" The lookout shouted from the gate early the next morning.

There was a scramble from the bunkhouse. Partly dressed men appeared, guns in hand. It was the warning they had been dreading for days.

"Jest one. On his own, cain't see no others."

Sam Booker was among the crowd. Only yesterday he had ridden back in from Ward's Central. If the Indians were going to kill the whites as far as St. Joseph, then there wasn't much point in trekking all the way to Fort Kearney. At least there was still work at Horseshoe, as most of the horses had been brought in here. Amos couldn't manage them on his own, and Sam had to live somehow. He didn't have a gun in his hand. There were more than enough men around to do the killing. He didn't want blood on his hands. If the Paiutes were going to kill you, then there wasn't any point in taking a few of them with you, it wouldn't make any difference in the long run.

Booker chewed on a plug of tobacco. An Indian on his own was real interesting. Maybe this was the start of the peace talks.

The watchers heard the office door scrape open and J.A. Slade emerged. He looked as though he might have worked all through the night and just got up from his desk—or he had dozed in his chair. However he had passed the nocturnal hours, he looked no different now than he did at any other time, with his frock coat held back so that his hand rested comfortably on his gun. A puzzled look appeared on his grim features. He had eyes only for the gates. Paiutes usually kept well clear of the home of Man Who Likes Killing. This one had to be plumb crazy.

"Open the gates." The section boss spoke softly but his voice carried to all corners of the palisade. A deathly hush had descended upon the gathering of riders and settlers.

The bar was lifted, the heavy wooden gate creaked open. Somewhere a gun was cocked with a menacing click. This might be a trick of some kind.

The Paiute rode slowly into the compound. He sat a blanket on the back of a mustang that was streaked with sweat and dust. He had ridden hard through the night. He was dressed in plain hides; no trappings of war were visible. He carried neither bow, lance nor knife. His features were not daubed with paint. An upraised finger signified that he was alone.

"He's come to talk peace," Booker spoke his thoughts aloud. "It's us who oughta be makin' peace with the injuns after all we done to 'em."

Nobody answered him. This was no time to enter into an argument over the rights and wrongs of the Paiute War.

The brave halted about ten yards from Slade. An upraised hand signed that he came in peace. He waited. Everybody watched and waited.

"I come from Blood Arrow," he said slowly. "I bring a message from the Paiute camp."

Slade drew himself up to his full height. His lips were a bloodless slit and a flush was beginning to appear on either cheek. His eyes never left the other. "Spit it out, then. It'll be lies, but let's hear 'em."

"I speak the truth." The Paiute's eyes flashed angrily. "Slayer Who Rides With the Wind is a prisoner of Blood Arrow."

"That's a damn lie fer a start." Slade's legs were apart, his fingers had curled around the butt of his .44.

"It is the truth!" The brave snapped. "Look!" He tossed something on to the verandah. It bounced, rolled and stopped at Slade's feet.

Mollie had been watching from the wagon seat. Even at that distance she guessed what the Indian had thrown in front of Slade. The way it glinted and clinked and rolled, it looked like a ring.

She could restrain herself no longer. She leaped down, ran across the compound and retrieved the ring even while Slade was standing staring at it. He had guessed, too, but he wasn't going to grovel and pick up some trinket thrown by a damned Paiute.

Mollie examined it. She didn't want to find the scroll engravings. She clung to a forlorn hope that it was just a plain ordinary gold ring. Then it wouldn't be Ben's.

The engravings were there as she feared they would be. She almost fainted as she turned to Slade, clutching at any reason why Ben might not be a captive of Blood Arrow. In the end, she had to accept the truth.

"Slade," she was almost hysterical. "It's . . . it's Ben's wedding ring. *The Paiutes have got him!*"

J.A. Slade was staring fixedly at the mounted warrior. The road boss's eyes were chips of ice, his cheeks had blotched red. "Where'd you get that ring, scum?"

"It was taken from the hand of Slayer Who Rides With the Wind. He is our prisoner. He is alive and unharmed—for now."

"Slade," Mollie screamed. "They've got Ben!"

"Be quiet!" It was the nearest Slade had ever gotten to being rude to a woman. His expression was terrible to behold as the killing look grew. He met the brave's gaze and held it. "Why do you come to tell me, red bastard?"

"I come with a message from Blood Arrow."

"I'm listenin'."

"Slayer Who Rides With the Wind is a captive of the Paiutes at a camp which no white man has ever found."

"Except Brent."

"Slayer Who Rides With the Wind will die at sunrise tomorrow, the flesh eaten from his bones by soldier ants, unless . . ."

Mollie screamed and nearly fainted again.

"Unless what?" Slade stepped a pace closer to the Paiute, dropped into a half crouch, his grip tightened on the butt of his gun.

"Unless Man Who Likes Killing rides unarmed with me to Blood Arrow. If he does that then Slayer Who Rides With the Wind will be set free. Blood Arrow gives his word."

"And nobody would take Blood Arrow's word, red or white," J.A. Slade sneered. "All injuns are liars, 'specially Paiutes. And Blood Arrow's the biggest goddamned liar o' the lot."

The Paiute stiffened. "I speak the truth. So does Blood Arrow. Ride with me, Man Who Likes Killing and . . ."

Slade seethed with rage. The watchers noted how the veins on his forehead stood out, he might draw his gun at any second. The Paiute messenger stared death in the face.

Maybe Slade was within a second of drawing, pumping a cylinder of .44 balls into the Indian's defenseless body. Had that happened, the road boss would almost certainly have scalped him as he twitched his death throes. But it did not happen because a distraught Mollie flung herself between the two men.

"Slade!" Her scream rose and hung in the still atmosphere

of early morning. "Slade, they'll torture Ben. Kill him. Please go with this Indian, at least try to bargain. Anything. *Please!*"

"Shut up, woman!" Slade spoke without taking his eyes off the Paiute. "Blood Arrow has no intention of letting Ben go, whether or not I surrender to the red scum. He jest wants to trick me into goin' along so's he can kill us both. It ain't no 'either or'."

Mollie wrung her hands together in frustration and helplessness. She turned to the Paiute and spoke in a trembling voice, "Take me instead."

"You damn stupid fool!" the Division Superintendent sneered. "They'd like you, me'n Ben to make a real party of it, no doubt 'bout that."

"You *have* to save Ben."

The Indian wheeled his horse. He realized only too well that he had stared death in the face. The white woman had saved him from the man who was the nemesis of all the tribes. It would be foolish to linger here. Man Who Likes Killing would not ride out with him to the Paiute camp. He had never believed that he would.

The Paiute kicked his pony's flanks, lay low across its back and streaked out through the open gate. He fully expected a bullet and he did not feel safe until he was splashing his mount back across the river.

Slade pushed Mollie from him, it was all he could do to stop himself from hitting her. "Now look what you've gone and done. That injun's got away."

"You'd let Ben die just because you're afraid to risk your own skin!" She covered her face with her hands and sobbed. "You could've tried to rescue him, but now we'll never know where they're holding him."

She turned and stared out through the gates. The galloping Indian was a mere speck in the distance across the other side of the river. Soon he was lost in the woods beyond.

Heads turned but there was no sign of J.A. Slade. The

door of his office was closed again. He had been interrupted and now he had returned to his unfinished work.

It was about an hour before Slade showed himself. He came out of his office, closed the door behind him and walked unhurriedly across towards the stable—just as though he had caught up on his routine paperwork and now he was going for a ride.

"Saddle me a hoss," he ordered Amos. "An' if anybody asks after me, I've gone out on business. An injun jest got away, thanks to a damnfool woman, but mebbe I'll find me one or two more out there jest to set the record straight."

Then he was gone out through the gate, riding easily.

Mollie watched him from the wagon, her eyes red from crying. "And I hope they get you, Slade!" She shook a fist after him. "I hope they do to you what they'll do to my Ben, you bastard!"

Seven

Ben lay and watched the sun go down beyond the desert. He had always had a fascination for sunsets, but this one was fast losing its appeal. This was stage one of his torture and slow death. Stage two would begin when it rose again behind him. Slade would not come, but the ants sure would.

He closed his eyes. The cool of the night was a welcome relief after the heat of the day—his only consolation. Exhausted as he was, sleep eluded him. The night hours would be slow and agonizing.

Through half-closed eyes, Ben could just make out the Paiute guard watching him, a motionless figure seated in the shadows of the thorn bush. The other might have been asleep, but Ben knew that he wasn't. The Indian had not moved a limb since he had taken up his post, sitting there cross-legged just staring at his prisoner. Ben marvelled at the warrior's self-discipline—he neither shifted a leg to ease its cramped position nor fidgeted. He must have been tempted to examine his recently acquired revolvers again, just to hold them in his hands. They were a worthy prize for any Indian. But they remained at his waist. He had been entrusted with a duty by his chief, and he would carry it out in the only way he knew how. He would watch the white prisoner throughout every second of this night.

Ben needed to stretch, to change his position, but it was impossible even to flex a muscle. He was staked out as taut as a Paiute bowstring. He would remain that way until daylight.

As his body cooled, his mental torture began. His first emotion was grief because he would never see Mollie again, nor their baby when it arrived. That was harder to accept even than the prospect of torture and death. He only wished that he had not seen Sarah, that she had remained hidden from him. The old Gosiute had been right, so had Sam Booker. Their warnings of what he might find if his search proved successful had proved chillingly true. Reality was a thousand times worse than any of those awful nightmares which he had suffered since the day when the Cheyenne had snatched her from the wagon train out of Fort Laramie.

The horror of it all had Ben's features contorting in the desert darkness. He tried not to think about what she had suffered but his thoughts plagued him unmercifully.

Doubtless Sarah had been beaten and raped by that Cheyenne brave. Perhaps his chief had demanded the beautiful white girl, even murdered for her. That was when Sarah's "conditioning" would have begun; menial tasks, beatings, humiliation and degradation. Decivilized. Ben prayed that her mind had snapped in the early stages, it would have been easier for her that way.

Why had the Cheyenne rejected her? It could have been because of some inter-tribal treaty with the Paiutes, something to do with a unification of all redmen against the white invader. Sarah might even have been kidnapped by Blood Arrow. More likely she had been traded as had already been rumored, barter was a way of life for the savage tribes—captives or horses.

It was really of no consequence how Sarah came to be with the Paiutes. One tribe was as bad as another in its treatment of white prisoners, they despised them even after they had become as near to one of themselves as they were ever likely to get. They called her No-Name, the ultimate in degradation for a squaw. Possibly she was barren and would have been put to death except that Blood Arrow saw her as a symbol in his attempts to unite the tribes against the whites. Both sides would witness the Indians's ultimate in humiliation of their hated foe, to see how the redmen were superior to the whites. It would strike terror into white women. They would plead with their menfolk to flee before Sarah's fate became their own.

Consequently, Sarah had become what she was, a whore to taunt the white males. And when she was of no further use to the Paiutes, her reward would be death in some way which Ben tried to shut out of his mind.

Slade would not be coming. Ben had already resigned himself to the fact. Would Ben himself have walked unarmed into a Paiute camp if the roles had been reversed? If he was honest with himself, then he knew he would not. He didn't blame Slade. But, by God, Slade would make 'em pay for this, there was no doubt about that. He had struck terror into the hearts of roving bands of Indians, his tally of scalps was already formidable. It would be nothing, however, compared with the revenge that J.A. Slade would take after this.

Ben smiled to himself in the darkness just thinking about it. Once he had almost seen Sam Booker's point of view. Not any more. Not here. You couldn't bargain with Indians because you couldn't trust them. Treachery was bred in them, it would never change. Slade was right in his thinking, the way he fought them. Even if he had been foolish enough to keep his side of the bargain, and surrender himself to Blood Arrow, then both white men would have ended up as honey-pots for the ants.

Ben tried not to think about the ants. He had always disliked the little bastards. Once a few had found their way into his bunk soon after he had joined the Pony Express. They had stung him. He had gotten up in the middle of the night, boiled some water on the stove and scalded them. He'd sworn that they had screamed as they sizzled. Now the ants were going to take their revenge on *him*. He shuddered at the prospect.

It wasn't their fault; he blamed the Paiutes. No, not just the Paiutes—all the Indian tribes. There wasn't much to choose between any of 'em, Slade had once told him that. They just had different customs, killed in a variety of ways and tried to devise even slower and more painful methods than their rivals.

"The only good injun is a dead 'un with his scalp hanging up to dry," Slade had said. At that time Ben had thought that was going too far. He didn't now. He understood what motivated the road boss, what had made him what he was. Do-gooders like Booker preached from a safe distance. A lot of them might change their views if they got caught in the middle of a full-scale Indian war.

Ben found himself watching the stars. He had even begun to count them, and that was damned silly. Right now they were bright and sparkling. It was when they began to pale that he had cause to worry.

He heard a movement close by, a faint scuffling that stopped, started. Stopped again. His flesh crawled. Maybe the ants were hungry for human flesh already, a kind of night starvation and to hell with the honey. Or they had scented it in the vessel over by the Indian guard. Go eat *him*, then.

No, whatever it was, it was far too big for ants. It might be a snake. Ben went cold at the thought. He listened, held his breath until he heard the sound again. It wasn't a snake, it didn't slither, it moved in quick darts. It was right behind him now.

Whatever species it might have been, it remained motionless for some time beyond his range of vision. Then it scurried away. It did not sound heavy enough for a gopher—maybe it was just a lizard that had satisfied its curiosity.

His thoughts turned to that buzzard which had followed him into the desert. Damn right, that bird had sensed all along what was going to happen to him, but it looked like being out of luck on this occasion. By the time the ants had finished with Ben there wasn't going to be much left in the way of carrion.

The stars had become fainter. Ben had dozed from exhaustion because when he looked for them they weren't sparkling like they had been. He had lost all track of time, he had prepared himself for a long wait, but it had to end sometime. He stared at the stars, thought maybe he was imagining that they had paled. They definitely were not as bright and the dark void beyond them was lighter, too.

Ben strained his eyes to look sideways without moving his head. The Paiute's silhouette was plainer now, but his face was still in deep shadow. He might have been a wooden totem carving, not so much as a muscle moved.

Ben shuddered. He knew the brave was still watching him with those unseen eyes, just like he had been doing all night. It was creepy, the worst part of all. If the Indian had gotten up and walked around his prisoner, taunting and goading him, Ben could have mustered up a personal hatred that might have overridden his mounting fear. The guy wasn't human—he was a zombie.

Ben's terror was beginning for real now. He knew that he might start screaming for mercy when the torture began. Most certainly he would go crazy before he died.

The ants would be waking up soon, scurrying to and fro in frenzied activity. Ben shifted his eyes in the opposite direction. He could just make out the big mound in the early dawn light. It looked to be moving.

Then the Paiute moved. It made Ben start, he might have jumped in alarm if he had not been staked out so tightly. His eyes flicked back to where the Indian sat.

The Indian had fallen forward. Just pitched and slumped, sprawled face downward as if he had dozed and toppled over in his sleep. Except that he did not wake, continuing to lie there motionless.

The other must've suffered heart failure, Ben decided. Just

died. But it would not make any difference, there was no way Ben could escape and there were plenty more Paiutes to carry out the slow torture.

Ben heard another sound, one that he could not identify. It came from beyond where the Indian lay, a rustling of foliage as if somebody or something moved amidst the foliage. A figure materialized out of the bush, moved with the stealth of a wraith and was barely visible against the dark background.

Whoever it was blended with their surroundings and the shadows perfectly. Only the faint pale blur of indiscernible features told Ben that it was no Indian.

The figure moved swiftly and silently, passed beyond Ben's restricted arc of vision. The silence surged softly back. He listened, and after a time he thought he detected faint movements but he could not be certain. Now he sensed rather than heard barely audible footfalls which told him that the other had circled round and was now somewhere behind him.

Ben felt the sweat on his body, smelled his own odors. This was another Paiute trick. They were trying to drive him mad before they left him screaming as the ants poured over him. Any second he was going to crack.

A sudden slackening of tension on a thong that held an outstretched wrist was Ben's first realization that one of his bonds had been cut. He heard a faint *twang* as his other arm came free. He lay there, stared up in shocked amazement at the crouched figure slicing through the hide shackles on his ankles.

There was something tantalizingly familiar about the shape, the movements, its calculated decisiveness.

Ben lay there in his slack bonds, closed his eyes. The Paiutes had driven him crazy, after all. So subtlely. You're free to run, Slayer Who Rides With the Wind. Go now. Then they would seize him, drag him back down, stake him out again. The ants were merely the finale in this game of life and death. Ben closed his eyes, did not move. He wasn't going to join in this cruel game, he'd spoil it all for them.

"Yuh cain't jest lay there, Hollister. Git up!" Those gruff, commanding tones left nothing else to speculation. Ben opened his eyes, forced himself up on an elbow that was devoid of feeling and trembled violently.

"Slade!"

It was J.A. Slade, all right. Even in the deep gloom of a pre-dawn desert there was no mistaking the Division Superintendent of the Rocky Ridge division.

"My hoss is back there," the other said in a hoarse whisper. "We'll have to ride double. Not much time, it's gettin' light and the camp'll be stirrin' any minute."

"My horse isn't far away. I know where it's tethered." Ben made to get up but his legs buckled beneath him, threw him back down to the ground. It was all he could do to stop himself from crying out aloud as his circulation began to flow again.

"Take these, they're yours." The road boss handed Ben his guns. "I ain't got no spare cylinders, though. Jest forty-fours. How cussed can yuh git, usin' a forty-five an' a thirty-six. Knew the time'd come when it'd cause a problem."

Ben massaged his ankles furiously. The feeling started to come back into them. It was getting light fast now and he looked across to where the Indian sentry lay motionless. A pool of thick dark fluid was seeping out from beneath the body.

"Cut his goddamned throat." Slade wheezed a laugh as he wiped the blade of his heavy skinning knife on the ground. "Long and deep, almost cut his head off. He never guessed till it was too late and by then he hadn't got nothin' left to scream with." It was a statement of fact, not a boast. Slade had no need to boast. "Now, hurry, get up on the hoss behind me an' we'll git as far as we can afore they realize you're gone."

"We'd never make it, even a Pony horse can't outrun Indian mustangs with a double load. I tell you, my hoss is less than a couple o' hundred yards from here."

Slade hesitated. He knew only too well that Ben spoke the truth, but he was reluctant to venture back towards the Paiute camp while they still had the chance to skirt it and get a head start on their pursuers. But his own mount had ridden all the way from Horseshoe station to here. The animal was far from fresh and two burdens would have slowed it considerably.

Ben did not wait for him to agree. He turned, began walking unsteadily in the opposite direction. With every step his legs became stronger. They mighty just make it in time.

Overhead the sky was streaked with grey. Voices came from the direction of the camp as the Paiutes awoke and stirred. Every brave was eagerly anticipating the white man's torture. If Man Who Likes Killing did not arrive before the rays of the sun bathed the distant mountains to the east, then the torture would begin. It would begin, anyway, the only question was whether one or two victims would be screaming in agony as the ants stripped flesh from bone.

"There it is!" There was no mistaking the relief in Ben's voice when he spied his horse grazing the sparse tufts of coarse grass on the edge of the oasis. He stumbled forward, fumbled with the tether. Even now, they might still escape unseen.

Until J.A. Slade's .44 shattered the dawn stillness, its vivid flash momentarily illuminating their surroundings. Ben had a glimpse of an Indian with a strung bow crumpling to the ground. They heard the body crash down into the dry undergrowth.

"Must've posted a guard," Slade cursed beneath his breath. "Get up on that hoss, Hollister, an' ride like you've never ridden them mails in your life."

The Paiutes had left the horse still saddled and bridled. Unbelievably, the carbine was still in its boot. Indians had little faith in guns. The Paiutes had not been impressed by their own marksmanship with the rifles they had used at the battle of Pyramid Lake. Ben swung up, grabbed the reins.

All hell broke loose in the Paiute war camp.

Indians were almost never taken by surprise and, on those rare occasions when they were, they reacted quickly. Warriors leaped from their tepees, stringing their bows as they ran, zig-zagging in the direction of the shot.

Crack-crack-crack.

Slade fanned the hammer of his Army Colt, two darting shapes fell, the others scattered. Arrows hummed hopefully in the direction of the two mounted men. Ben and Slade had the advantage of being hidden by the still dark background of trees. For a few seconds, the Paiutes were caught out in the open.

Ben's .45 bucked and boomed. A warrior was thrown back against a tepee. The expressman fired at another, missed as the Indian dived full length. Slade's hammer was clicking—he calmly changed the cylinder. He was out of the fight for perhaps ten seconds.

Even so, Slade was the first to spot the tall Paiute wearing a feathered head-dress, his hide robe adorned with the scalps of his own victims, as he stepped from a tepee.

"Blood Arrow!" Slade yelled, still in the act of reloading. "Shoot the bastard, Hollister. Kill him!"

Recognition brought a numbness to Ben's reflexes. He froze for a few seconds as his fury boiled. He recalled what this savage had done to Sarah. Hatred dominated over cold reasoning as the long dreamed of opportunity to avenge his sister presented itself.

Even so, he still had time to put a ball into Blood Arrow's crazed brain. Until a second figure emerged behind the chief, one which instantly distracted Ben, brought back all the pain and sadness, those emotions which had shocked him only a short time ago. In those few brief seconds the desire for revenge was secondary.

For it was Sarah who moved to one side of Blood Arrow.

Or rather, it was the human shell that had once been Ben's sister.

Ben saw his own sister clearly in the dawn light, more grotesque and pitiful than ever she had been in the glow from the camp fires. He called out to her, but if she heard him, then she gave no sign. If she had answered, stumbled towards him, then he would have gone to her for one last time. He knew in that instant that there was no way back. Whatever Blood Arrow and the Cheyenne had done to her was irrevocable.

Ben's reaction equalled the speed of mountain lightning, all he saw now was a demented squaw who had inflicted upon him pain and humiliation. A cur that it was kindest to put down.

The Adams revolver crashed. Twice. The first ball took her in the bosom and spun her round. The second shattered her skull as she teetered.

Sarah was at peace. No-Name did not exist anymore.

Even then Ben might still have had time to shoot Blood Arrow. Slade's revolver snapped shut. A wave of grief and remorse engulfed Ben even as he watched that monstrosity sprawl prone. Only then did he swing his gun on to the Paiute chief.

Ben and Slade fired simultaneously but it was too late. Ben's distraction had cost them dearly. Blood Arrow dived with the alertness and agility of a buck at bay, flung himself back into the tepee entrance, rolled as he hit the ground. Balls ripped through the hide shelter but the white men's intended prey was lost from view. A lucky ball might have struck him—both men knew with that instinct peculiar to marksmen that it had not.

"Fool!" Slade was beside himself with fury. "You had him for the taking. Instead, you shot the squaw and let him escape!"

There was no time for explanations. Even had there been, Ben could not have put it into words. Paiutes were running from all directions. Some came on foot, others ran to where the mustangs were tethered.

For one moment Ben almost did not flee. He had an impulse to turn his mount, gallop back towards that tepee, try to get a shot into Blood Arrow before they cut him down and then die alongside his sister's corpse.

But it would have solved nothing. Reasoning infiltrated his emotions and then he was riding alongside Slade and out into the desert. They had only a short lead and they needed to increase it.

They did not look behind them. They heard the Indians coming, that hollering that had often made the blood of movers and settlers run cold. Arrows were fired wildly after the fugitives. Some fell short, while others overshot their intended mark, but there was always the possibility of an unlucky hit.

Slade and Ben drove their mounts to their very limits and beyond. Yard by yard, they forged ahead until they were beyond the range of those arrows. Likewise, the Paiutes were out of revolver shot. The two fugitives left their carbines booted, for to have felled a couple of braves would have made little difference. Worse, they would have lost ground while they wheeled to shoot. Powder and shot were saved for a close encounter.

Much later, they saw the woods where the desert ended and the mountains began. Ben thought they could make it now. Slade's horse was tiring but they had still put maybe a quarter of a mile between themselves and their pursuers. He glanced at his companion. The road boss's expression was inscrutable. If those cheeks were flushed, then a layer of desert dust hid the tell-tale signs of his killing lust. The section boss had savored every moment of his mission. It had been successful, not in rescuing a Pony Express employee from torture and death, but in keeping his own self-imposed record intact. There had been an element of failure, too. Blood Arrow still lived in spite of the chance that had arisen to kill him.

As far as Ben could tell, none of the pursuing Paiutes had been wearing an imposing feathered headdress. Blood Arrow had not joined the chase after the two hated whites, much as he coveted their scalps. Maybe the shots that had ripped through the tepee had killed or wounded the chief? Ben doubted it. More likely, Blood Arrow was right now urging the main Paiute war party to sweep east, killing, plundering and burning. Perhaps he realized the futility of chasing after riders mounted on thoroughbred horses. Personal vengeance was secondary to the mighty war he planned. His sworn enemies would be accounted for then, anyway.

There were many reasons why the chief might have decided not to ride after Slayer Who Rides With the Wind and Man Who Likes Killing. None of them mattered right now.

The Paiutes turned back where the desert met the greenery of fertile land. Only then did Slade and Ben slow their pace and, eventually, rein in their mounts. There was still a long way to go, steep winding tracks which would bring them to the Overland Trail.

"Thanks, Slade." It had to be said, even though Ben knew that it would not be appreciated.

"You could've got Blood Arrow." It was something that would fester with Slade for a long time. Perhaps forever. "Instead, you shot a *squaw!* You don't miss like that, Hollister!" Slade's grey eyes were accusing.

"I had my reasons." Ben was tight-lipped. He felt like he had aged ten years during these last few hours. He owed nobody explanations. Only he had to live with what he had done this day.

Surprisingly, Slade did not press the issue. Blood Arrow would keep. Perhaps he was glad that Ben had not killed the chief. That was one killing that would be very special to J.A. Slade. He did not count Indians in his lifelong tally of those who had fallen to his gun.

Thoughts of revenge smoldered inside Ben on that long slow ride back to Horseshoe. Deep inside him, he cried five years of grief that finally had culminated. Sarah was dead. She had died on the day of the wagon train massacre beyond Fort Kearney. Someone else had lived on. Now she, too, was at peace.

But it did not end there. Ben was glad that they had missed Blood Arrow today, for when the time of reckoning came he wanted the Paiute to know who had killed him. And why. In the meantime, Ben did not want Slade to kill the chief, and that was another good reason for sticking close to the Division Superintendent from now on. Where Slade went, Ben would go, too. The Paiutes had a lot to answer for to the Pony Express, but Blood Arrow's debt could only be paid to Ben.

"Tell me," Ben said as they were fording the shallow river and Horseshoe was in sight, "how did you find me, Slade?"

"The Paiutes sent a messenger." Slade did not turn his head. "I sent him packin'. Guess it never occurred to him that I might be tailin' him. Which was why I let him get a good start on me. I picked up his trail, got to the camp when they were least expectin' me. You, too, I guess."

"It was damn close."

"An' don't ever feel grateful 'cause I didn't do it for you. Not personally, anyhow. Right now, the Pony can't afford to lose men who can ride an' shoot, even if you've still got a lot to learn. One lesson you've learned today, Hollister, you don't shoot squaws until all the braves've stopped writhin' and kickin'. Don't ever forget that."

As they rode in through the gates Ben saw that a detachment of U.S. Cavalry were camped in the compound. The long-promised reinforcements had finally arrived.

Eight

Mollie's relief at Ben's safe return was tempered by his moroseness and his long periods of silence. Previously, they had talked in their bunk long into the night, but now it was as though Ben didn't want to talk any more. He had been back three whole days and he had not even asked how she was faring with their unborn child. He must have heard her throwing up in the back of the wagon this morning.

She told herself that this was the result of his ordeal at the hands of the Paiutes. They had done something to him which he hadn't told her about. Physically, he seemed fine. Mentally, he was deeply affected.

On the fourth night, she was awoken by his crying, his body shaking with uncontrollable sobs. She slipped an arm around him. He tensed, for one awful moment she thought that he was going to push her away.

"Ben, what is it? What's wrong?" The time had come for talking.

"Nothin's wrong," he made an effort to control his sobbing, turning his head away from her.

"There is and it's no good keeping it from me. Whatever it is, we're going to share it. Is it something the Indians did to you while you were a prisoner? Is it something I've done? Or haven't done? We've had three whole nights together since you got back and you haven't even touched me. You've hardly spoken. Something's happened, and I want to know what it is. We can't go on like this."

"It's not what's happened now, it's what happened five years ago." He stared into the darkness. He had hoped to keep it all from her. He realized now that that was impossible. There was no way a man could conceal a tortured mind from his wife. "Nothing can ever put it right. I did the only thing I could, I didn't have time to think about it. I'll always wonder if I did the right thing, there's no way I'll ever know. I won't ever get over it, I just hope to God that in time I'll be able to live with it."

Slowly, falteringly, he told her about the grotesque creature that had once been his own sister. It took a long time, and he let her hold him every time he broke down. In the end, it was a relief to get it out of his system. At least Mollie knew— that might make it easier in years to come. He hoped she understood.

"Oh, Ben." She pulled him close and held him tightly when he had finished. Crying inside wouldn't get the grief out of him, it had to be shared. She cried with him, not just for the awful fate of a woman she had never even seen, but for Ben who had to bear the burden of it all. Even then Mollie knew it was not all over. It was something she would have to learn to live with, too.

Maybe the baby would help Ben, she thought. The three of them had to make a new life for themselves, leave the past behind. But nobody was going anywhere until the Paiute War was over.

The next morning, Ben and Mollie sat drinking coffee on the step of the wagon. She glanced sideways at him. It was hard to tell whether or not their long talk into the night had helped. He seemed to have aged, but maybe that was her imagination. At least they were talking now. It might be a

slow process, helping him back to normal life, but she would
see it through.

The compound was a busy place, army wagons drawn up,
soldiers standing around talking. In this small area, there
looked to be more than there were, she had already counted
them—twenty-four, including the two officers. It gave an
added feeling of security, if you didn't stop to think how
many Indians there were out there. Everybody hoped that
this was just the first of many detachments of troops. At
least the government was beginning to take the Paiute War
seriously.

Mollie looked nervously in the direction of the Division
Superintendent's office. The door was shut. There was no
way of knowing whether Slade was inside or not. Perhaps
he had ridden out at first light, as he often did. Mollie hoped
he had. Her greatest worry of all was what Slade was doing
to Ben.

"The cavalry rode in yesterday afternoon." It was important to keep up a conversation, however trivial. Ben had
talked, he must be kept talking. Silence was like a cancer
eating him away. "I overheard the soldiers talking. There's
two more detachments following. They're headed for Fort
Bridger. They're trying to establish fully manned military
outposts as far as Carson. That way, with plenty of troops
already west of here and more at Fort Laramie and Fort
Kearney, they hope to get the Indians between them. They
reckon they can defeat the Paiutes by the end of the summer."

"I got some Indians to kill, too." It was as if Ben spoke
to himself rather than to Mollie. He was staring fixedly ahead
of him. He might not even have been aware of the military
presence in the station.

His words hit Mollie with the force of a physical blow,
like he had slapped her. It wasn't just what he said, it was
how he said it. It was not anger spoken in the heat of his
recent ordeal—it was cold and calculated. She knew that he
meant what he said and it was no idle threat.

"Ben, that's the army's job, killing Indians." She almost added "and Slade's" but she checked herself just in time. Where the section boss went, Ben would go, too. Their last expedition had made her husband the way he was now. She cast another apprehensive glance in the direction of the office. The door was still closed, thank God!

"I get my orders from Slade. I have to carry 'em out, he's the boss."

"Because you *want* to carry them out." She avoided his gaze. Her stomach muscles had contracted and she felt sick. This time it was nothing to do with the baby.

He did not reply.

"You can't blame a whole nation for what happened to Sarah, Ben." She meant it to come out kindly, instead it sounded like an admonishment.

"Can't I?" His tone was terse. "You didn't see her, Mollie, and I wouldn't wish that on you. If you had, you'd understand what I have to do. Blood Arrow degraded my sister. It could have been any Indian, any tribe. There's no difference."

The pain was getting worse. She knew she would have to go inside the wagon and lie down, but not until she had said what she had to say. Ben had to hear it now, rather than later. "The whites are just as bad, Ben."

"You been talkin' to Sam Booker?" His lips curled in a sneer.

"No, but I lost my husband to Indians, don't forget. And I'm not burning with hatred towards the whole Indian nation. And I don't want to lose another husband that way, Ben."

"They killed your man, Mollie. That's bad enough, but it's nothin' to what they did to my sister."

"It's *war,* Ben. Both sides are slaughtering. And worse. I overheard one of those soldiers yesterday boasting about how they'd tracked a Cheyenne war party to a village north of Fort Kearney. The soldiers attacked the village, massacred men, women and children. Some of the women they took alive and . . . well, you know what they did to them before they shot them."

"But they *killed* them, Mollie. Within a few hours. Those women didn't suffer for years. That's the difference. And when it happens to somebody close to you. . . ." He left the sentence unfinished.

Mollie leaned back in the seat, closed her eyes.

"You understand what I'm gettin' at, Mollie?"

"I see what you mean, Ben, but that doesn't make it right. It won't wipe everything clean for you. It'll fester on and on inside of you. Come next spring we're going to have a baby. Hopefully, this war will be over and the Pony Express disbanded. We'll have a home and a family. Isn't that more important to you than killing Indians and maybe getting killed yourself, so's the baby won't have a father? Oh, Ben, where will it all end?"

"I'll still be around." Ben spoke without looking at her. "By then, it'll all be over and I'll settle down for good."

Mollie got up and went inside. His promise had a hollow ring to it. As Ben had said, one day it would all be over—one way or another.

The following morning, the soldiers saddled up and rode out. The occupants of Horseshoe station crowded the gate and watched them go.

Ben sensed a different atmosphere within the station. It was almost euphoric. The soldiers would deal with the Paiutes, and soon everybody would be safe. Somebody threw a cap up into the air and a cheer went up from those around him.

Ben had his reservations. He had seen for himself the vastness of the country from here to the Great Salt Lake. There was plenty of wilderness to hide the Indians. They had lived and hunted these mountains and deserts for centuries. They knew every arroyo and canyon, every mountain and forest. Every ambush place.

He was glad he wasn't wearing a blue uniform and riding out with that detachment.

"That's right, kill the injuns and steal their land!" Sam Booker, leaning on the rail outside the stables, shouted across at the gathering by the gates. "They're only pertectin' what's rightfully theirs, an' has bin since God fust put 'em on this land."

"Go kick yer own ass, Sam!" one of the men called out.

The jeering died away as suddenly as it had begun. All eyes were on the office. The door swung open and Slade stood there on the step. "You fellers got nothin' better to do than to stand gawpin' after a bunch o' soldiers?" There was silence, except for the shuffling of feet in the dust.

"I got some news fer you." Slade did not have to raise his voice to make himself heard. Everybody was listening intently, apprehensively. "As from tomorrow, the Pony runs again. East an' west. First rider's due in 'bout mid-day. There's a schedule goin' up." He held up a sheet of paper. "An' you better check it out, see when you're ridin'."

Sam Booker stayed as quiet as the rest of them, he had a job to look after. Or maybe, he was scared of Slade, too.

Slade's eyes roved the group, came to rest on Ben. "Hollister, I want a word with yuh. In private."

Mollie had been watching and listening from the wagon seat. Her mouth went dry at Slade's words, she almost yelled for her husband to come back as he started to walk over to the office. Ben was becoming more like J.A. Slade with every passing day.

The Pony Express was back to normal. It almost seemed like it had never been disrupted. Ben stood waiting and ready to ride as the westbound rider splashed across the shallow river below Horseshoe station. It would not be shallow for very much longer, Ben reflected, for already the leaves were taking on a golden tint and the nights were cooler. Last night there had been a hint of the first frost. Late summer had eased gradually into fall, almost unnoticeably. In another few weeks the rains would come, a forerunner of gales and blizzards, creating yet another hazard for the Pony Express riders.

The army was still fighting the Indians. Reports were unreliable. Some said that the Paiutes had been driven north beyond Fort Kearney. There were stories of raiding bands of Indians around South Pass and, on occasions, the dispatch riders had been forced to outrun them.

Another company of cavalry had passed through Horseshoe only a week ago. Whatever effect the soldiers were having on the Paiute War in real terms, at least they gave the settlers and movers a feeling of safety.

Ben suggested to Mollie that they move into the cabin before winter set in. It was now habitable and cozy. Ben had put in a lot of work on it while the mails were suspended. It would be a good idea, he had told her, to set up a permanent home there before the baby arrived in the spring. They were close enough to the station for safety and the Indians in the region were mostly small parties who wouldn't venture close to a large station. The mighty uprising which Blood Arrow had planned seemed to have been thwarted by the army reinforcements moving westward—for the time being, anyway.

"It's Cody." Amos stood alongside Ben, holding the fresh mount.

Will Cody slid from his lathered mare. He had ridden it hard, Ben noticed. Maybe too hard by the way it was blowing.

"Injuns," Cody grunted, " 'bout a dozen, between Badeau's and Ward's. I left 'em standin'." He patted his horse affectionately.

Ben was not unduly concerned. The war party Cody spoke of would not catch up with him. There might be others up ahead, though.

Amos lifted the mochila on to the fresh horse and Ben climbed up into the saddle. "I'm only scheduled as far as La

Bronte," he said, "provided there's somebody waiting to take over, that is. I'll be back tomorrow on the eastbound run."

"Slade around?" Cody looked toward the saloon. That was the last place you hoped to find the road boss.

"He rode out early this morning." Ben touched the horse's flanks with his heels and it needed no second bidding. "Huntin' injuns and outlaws, or maybe just checkin' on riders—who knows?" Only Slade knew where he went during the daylight hours.

Then he was away, thrilling to the feel of the strength and speed of the animal beneath him. He was looking forward to this ride. He had spent his rest day working on the cabin.

The air was heavy with the scent of pines and dying vegetation, a sour-sweet smell that brought with it distant memories for Ben. Back in England, autumn had always been his favorite time of year. That was when he rode with the hounds, hunted foxes and thrilled to the chase. Sometimes, he went with his father to shoot woodpigeons as they flew in to feed on the carpet of acorns in the big wood beyond the city, or went at dusk to wait for wild ducks that flighted in to a secluded reed-fringed pond. Days that had been carefree and happy. Until . . . he managed to push the more recent years out of his thoughts.

The coming winter would be the hardest he had ever experienced. When he had been riding stages for Butterfield, if the snows were bad, then the coaches didn't run. It wouldn't be like that with the Pony Express. The mails had to get through against all odds. He relished the challenge. He would meet it when it came.

By next fall, there probably would not be a Pony Express. There was talk that with the Paiutes on the run, the telegraph crews were making good progress, sometimes as much as twenty-five miles in a single day. The westbound construction gangs had already progressed beyond Fort Kearney and the eastbound lines were well out of Carson City. Wrecked lines had been repaired, and new ones were being strung as fast as the poles went up. The winter would delay the work, but Slade was optimistic that the telegraph would be operating from coast to coast by the end of the next summer.

Ben had considered going back to gunsmithing. There would be plenty of work out here now that the army had arrived. He relished the prospect and thought again about brass cartridges for rifles and revolvers. Maybe he would work on the idea and patent it before somebody else did.

His thoughts, the tranquility all around him, had relaxed his customary vigilance. Today was perhaps the first time that he hadn't brooded.

Even so, it was doubtful whether he would have been able to dodge the volley of gunfire that rang out from a clump of cottonwoods on his right. He felt the horse slump beneath him but he threw himself from the saddle before it collapsed.

Ben experienced a sense of *deja vu* as he lay stretched out behind his dead mount. But it wouldn't be Jules Reni this time, because the French-Canadian's ear was as stiff as a piece of cured hide on J.A. Slade's desk.

The shot horse provided scant cover. Ben lay perfectly still. In all probability, the road agents thought that they had got him as well as his mount. Ben should have been lying there riddled with bullets but Fate had spared him—temporarily, at least. He lay perfectly still, watching and waiting, his .45 in his hand. He did not intend to toss his good fortune to the autumnal winds.

Three men emerged from the trees on foot.

Ben watched through half-closed eyes. His body was shielded by the shot horse, and the bandits would have to circle round if they wanted to make sure of him.

They were halfbreeds. They wore hide clothing that was filthy and torn as well as wide-brimmed hats. Each carried a handgun, probably .44s. Doubtless these men belonged to Brent's gang.

Ben weighed up the odds. It was 3-1 against in a shoot-out. He had surprise on his side because they probably thought that he was already dead. They would pump his body full of lead just to make sure. Consequently, he had no option but to open fire on them.

Ben took the nearest outlaw. If the man knew what hit him then he had only a split second to bemoan his fate.

Even as the first man fell, the second was swinging his gun. Had Ben been using the standard manually cocking Colt, he might have been dead before he could thumb the hammer back. As it was, he fired a split second before the other. His ball took the bandit in the chest, knocked him off target even as he squeezed the trigger. The halfbreed's ball shredded some leaves on an overhead branch as it whined skywards.

The second halfbreed crumpled to the ground.

Slade might have downed the third man with his Army .44 by fanning the hammer. Ben was fast but not quite fast enough. The squat man fired a split second before Ben swung to him. Ben knew that he had been hit even before he heard the crashing report of the other's gun. The force of the ball threw Ben back and there was a blinding pain in his shoulder.

Ben switched gun hands, the instinct to survive transcending his pain. He fired left-handed and saw his snapshot spin the gunman round. Ben's second shot took the other in the back.

The road agents sprawled on the trail. Ben struggled to prop himself up against the dead horse, watching for the slightest movement but there was none. They were dead, all right, all three of them. If there had been a fourth, Ben knew that he, himself, would be lying there stretched out by now.

He felt sick and dizzy, and he became aware of a warm stickiness inside his shirt. The ball had smashed into his right shoulder. He had no idea how badly he was hurt. His vision fogged, and he thought that he might faint. He must not, there might be other bandits riding the trail or a party of marauding Paiutes might find him.

Ben's horse was dead, and there was no way he was capable of making it on foot to La Bronte—or even back to Horseshoe.

A movement attracted his attention and, even as his gun swung round, he spied the outlaws's horses tethered amongst the cottonwoods. Somehow he made it up on to his feet. With even greater difficulty, he got the mochila off the dead horse and dragged it with him as he staggered across to the trees. The horses watched him. They were not in the least concerned. Gunfire was an everyday noise to them.

Ben stared. Again Fate was offering him a helping hand. Two of the animals were mustangs but the third was a Pony Express horse the gang had probably stolen.

"Hey, fellah." Ben stroked it as he slipped the mail pouches on to its back. "Reckon you're back workin' again."

He surveyed the slain outlaws. If he had had the strength he would have scalped them. They were half-Indian and every scalp went a little way towards paying the savages back for what they had done to Sarah. He seethed with hate. This time he would leave the bastards for the buzzards and any other scavengers that happened along. He hoped they would make a good job of tearing the flesh from the bones.

Ben rode at a walking pace, slumped on his mount, clinging to its mane. Somehow, he made it as far as La Bronte. The waiting rider and stableman spied him from a distance and rode out to help him. They were just in time to catch him as he passed out and began to slide from the saddle.

"Road agents!" The stableman tore open Ben's shirt while the relay rider transferred the mails. "Jest a shoulder wound by the looks of it. Nothin' too serious, seems to've caught the fleshy part an' missed the bone. I'll get 'im patched up. Knowin' Hollister, there's some corpses lyin' out there somewhere between here'n Horseshoe. They say he's as fast as Slade, mebbe even faster. An' gettin' as mean, too, by all accounts."

Nine

The Paiute smoke signals could be seen in the hills once more. Ben watched them from the window of the bunkhouse at Red Butte where he was temporarily forced to rest up.

His gunshot wound was worse than either he or the stableman at La Bronte had guessed. The ball had gone deep, ploughing through the fleshy part of his shoulder and chipping the bone on the way out. It was an ugly injury. Ben had been transferred by stage to Badeau's station, where Badeau himself had cleaned and stitched the wound. It was a crude job but adequate enough. Had Ben been fully conscious when they loaded him onto the coach, he would have insisted on being taken back to Horsehoe and to Mollie.

A few days later, Ben had taken on the mails when the westbound rider came in with an arrow sticking out of his thigh. It was Nick Wilson, and he was in a much worse way than Ben had ever been.

"I'll take the mails," Ben said lifting the mochila off the one horse on to the other with his uninjured arm. "There's nobody else here to ride." He felt he would manage once he got in the saddle.

"You ain't oughta be ridin' for another week, at least." The station master's protest wasn't as strong as it might have been. His duty was to see that the mails weren't held up at his depot. He bit on his pipe. Ben was right—there wasn't anybody else. "That wound o' yours might open up again."

"I'll take it steady."

Pony Express riders never took it steady. All the same, Ben was unable to ride at his usual speed and he was behind schedule by the time he made it to Ward's Central.

There was no relay rider waiting there, either.

Weary as he was, Ben was glad to be continuing because the next stop was Horseshoe: home and Mollie.

"You're not fit to be in the saddle." Mollie was waiting by the gate with Amos. She reached out to help Ben from the saddle. Had it been anybody else he might have pushed them away.

"I'm fine now. I've just ridden two stops, I'd've gone on to Red Butte if there'd been nobody to take over."

She didn't argue. She knew only too well that not even she could stop him doing anything he had a mind to do. She admired him for that. It also frightened her.

Ben was in no way fit to resume duty but he did. The wound was looking fine, even Mollie thought so—until the stitches burst open two days later, five stops from Horseshoe, at Red Butte. It looked uglier now than when the .44 ball had first ploughed through it.

There was no question of Ben returning to his base station. The fever was the worst part—for several days he tossed and turned and soaked the blankets on his bed with sweat. But again fate was on his side, just as it had been in that shoot-out.

The first snowfall of autumn lay upon the land and the westbound stage from Platte Bridge got through with difficulty. The driver stated in no uncertain terms that he was not prepared to risk going on as far as Three Crossings. They had seen Indians, too, and he had passengers to consider. One of them was a doctor travelling as far as Sacramento.

"Damn fool, ridin' with a wound that's scarcely had a chance to heal!" Doc Velantry was a taciturn grey-haired man from New York who had recently lost his wife and had decided to make a fresh start in new surroundings. "Way I'm going right now, I'll get to Sacramento when it's time to retire!" He had already been delayed in Fort Laramie helping the army doc to treat some soldiers who had run into a skirmish with Paiutes.

Ben groaned. In his fevered state he imagined that the dark clad figure bending over him was J.A. Slade. The last thing he wanted was the road boss cutting him up with a knife. Knowing Slade, he might lift his scalp, too.

"You fellers will have to come and hold this man down for me." Velantry gave up struggling with his patient and called over to a couple of resting riders by the stove. "Either that or you'll be using picks to dig a grave in the frozen ground out there! And who the hell is this Slade this man thinks is me? The guy who shot him?"

"If Slade had shot Hollister," one of the men grunted as he struggled to hold Ben down, "then it wouldn't be a stitchin' job. We'd be diggin' out there, an' no mistake!"

The doctor treated and re-stitched the wound. Afterward, Ben slid into a deep sleep. He slept for two days.

More snow came with the bitter eastern wind, small flakes that drove horizontally, the kind that would drift and pile up in sheltered places and make the trail impassable. It looked like the stagecoach would not be continuing on its way for some days. Early snowfalls were treacherous. They came unexpectedly and viciously, thawed just as quickly and left swollen rivers in their wake. In the dead of winter the snow was deep and unrelenting, but at least everybody knew what to expect.

It was impossible to predict what the weather would do in the next few days. Or the Paiutes.

Blood Arrow had re-grouped his warriors and re-thought his strategy, assisted by Brent and Mogoannoga. The Gosiutes also had reluctantly joined them. Their only defense against the soldiers was a union of the tribes.

The army pressed westward. The Indians split up, filtered

back behind them. This much was evident to the Pony Express riders as they fought against snowdrifts and flooded rivers. Slade was spending most of his days along the Overland Trail on the Rocky Ridge division. There were few nights when he did not return to his headquarters with an Indian scalp swinging from his saddle. Paiute or Gosiute, they were all the same to him. These days, he was in a perpetual killing mood.

The trails were blocked by snowdrifts, the coaches were temporarily suspended. The weather would change again before the onset of winter. This was just a taste of things to come.

Meanwhile, Ben made a rapid recovery under the watchful eye of the marooned Doc Velantry. The wound had completely healed. All he was left with was a soreness and stiffness. His thoughts turned to Mollie. He was well enough to ride all the way back to Horseshoe and convalesce there, surely.

"You ain't gettin' on no hoss for at least another week!" The doctor shook a stern finger. "And neither am I goin' anywhere, judgin' by the way this weather's behavin'. So I'll be around for a while yet an' I'll see to it that you are, too!"

Ben reluctantly agreed. The days were long and boring, and with all the unaccustomed inactivity, he found it difficult to sleep at nights. He spent some time dissecting a shotgun cartridge and trying to envisage similar ammunition manufactured out of brass cases which would fire in a rifle or revolver. The Adams .45 seemed to him to be the most adaptable. Once the cartridge problem had been overcome, the weapon itself would require modification to fire it. Combined with its self-cocking mechanism, the Adams would be capable of very rapid fire. And if Ben's invention incorporated rifles then that would surely herald the end of the Indian wars for good.

When not working on his idea, Ben sat by the bunkhouse window and watched the expressmen come and go. The powdery snow had drifted up against the gate and a liveryman had to shovel it away every couple of hours in order to be able to admit incoming despatch riders.

Sometimes the relays were several hours late. Only the leaden skies with their persistent snow prevented Ben from seeing the smoke signals in the wooded hills all around the station.

Two nights later, Will Cody arrived. He seemed to have matured even more, Ben decided, as Cody entered the bunkhouse, brushing snow from his fringed buckskins. It seemed like he had aged five years these last few weeks.

"It's bad out there an' I don't just mean the weather." Cody helped himself to a plate of venison and beans off the stove, talking as he ate. He was starving, swallowing the hot food with relish. "Hills are full of injuns. Paiutes, mostly, an' a few Gosiutes hangin' on. I ran into a sizeable party, but managed to dodge 'em and outrun 'em. My guess is they could've caught me if they'd really wanted. They mebbe hoped my hoss'd go lame, or they'd get me with a stray arrow, but they weren't goin' to bust their guts runnin' me down'. Some of 'em had Pony hosses, too. No doubt they got 'em from Brent and his gang. Like I said, if they'd wanted me real bad, they'd've got me."

"Why didn't they, then?" Ben was curious.

"You don't shoot a duck swimmin' close to the bank when there's a raft of 'em downstream that you can stalk, do you? No point in catchin' me when they can have me an' a few more whites besides, if they jest bide their time."

"You think they're goin' to attack Horseshoe, then, Will?"

"No. My feelin' is that they'll start on the swing stations, knock 'em off one at a time like they did in Nevada and Utah. Williams's first, followed by half-a-dozen others. That brings the army hell-fer-leather, and then what's Blood Arrow do? He takes off into the desert where the army won't find him, splits his braves into small groups so they can travel unnoticed, and turns up in Wyoming, all ready for war agin. That way he'll strike devastating blows at the whites by just chipping away at 'em until he's finally ready for the big sortie."

"You reckon he might make a start with Red Butte, then, Will?"

"Could be. There's enough Paiutes hereabouts to raze a station the size o' Red Butte. Or p'raps Willow Springs or Sweetwater, just to light the torch. One of them three, I'd say. Then all of 'em. Horseshoe afterward. This weather favors the injuns. They mostly fight on foot so the snow won't worry 'em like it would the cavalry. But the cavalry won't be arrivin' till after a thaw, and by that time, the Paiutes'll be hell-raisin' elsewhere. Me, I'd be a mite uneasy if I was stoppin' in Red Butte more'n a day or two . . ."

"I'm plannin' on joinin' Mollie back at Horseshoe soon as the snow and the doc let me ride. Doc says I'm not to get in the saddle for at least a week."

"If'n I were you," Cody said, with a grave expression, "I'd get up on the back o' one o' them hosses out there in the stable and hightail it fer Horseshoe, no matter what the doc says. This place has good fortifications, but it lacks manpower. Countin' stablemen and coach travellers, you can't muster more'n fifteen men to defend it. There could be two, three hundred injuns hollerin' fer your scalps on the other side o' the stockade."

"I guess you're right, Will. I'll talk to Doc Velantry about it tomorrow."

"If'n I was you, I wouldn't wait fer tomorrow. Me, I got to, 'cause I'm on the first relay in the mornin'. Westbound as far as Three Crossings. I'll be comin' back with the eastbound the next day. I jest hope that you're either still safe here or else gone by the time I git back, Ben. I'll mebbe see yuh at Horseshoe in three to four days."

Cody stretched out on his bunk and pulled a blanket over himself. He was asleep within minutes. It was a knack he'd learned. You made the most of rest periods. You didn't waste good sleeping time.

The snow had eased up by dawn. There was six inches lying on the flat, but drifts up to six feet deep had piled up in sheltered places. Will Cody knew that the trail would be blocked in parts and that he would have to make numerous detours. He would travel as fast as conditions would allow, but safety, both for himself and the mails, was paramount. For once, the schedule came second.

During the earlier months, he had frequently followed wild animal tracks in order to avoid bands of Indians. Somehow, he managed to locate these same trails even though they were buried beneath a layer of soft powdery snow. Overhead, weighed down branches brushed his head and saturated him with countless miniature avalanches as he passed beneath. The discomfort went unheeded. He had eyes and ears only for his surroundings. He was a born scout as well as a magnificent rider.

When he came upon snow flattened by hoofmarks, he stopped to listen. But there was only the silence of a dead, white land. The prints told him that several horses had passed this way only a short time ago, the disturbed snow had not yet had time to freeze solid. The prints were those of shod mounts, so they could only belong to the renegade Brent and his gang. Had Cody followed the tracks they might have led him to a remote hideout somewhere in this white wilderness. He resisted the temptation—his duty was to the mails. By the time an opportunity arose to return here, the snow would probably have thawed.

He proceeded with extra caution, and once he was away from the tracks, he thought about them no more. Otherwise, they would have distracted him from other perils.

Will would change mounts at Willow Springs and again at Sweetwater. The stablemen at both stations were surprised to see him. They were not expecting any riders until the thaw started. There were reports of small roaming Paiute war parties but, so far, there had been no raids.

Cody spent the night at Sweetwater and set out for Split Rock some time after daylight the next morning. Travelling by night in these conditions would have been impossible. As it was, the journey took him most of the day. Several times he had to dismount and walk his horse through drifts that reached up to his waist. It was too dangerous, also, to ride down steep slopes. All of this took up valuable time. All the Indian signs had petered out, and that could only mean that the war parties were heading east, which bode ill for those at Red Butte and beyond.

In the late afternoon, Will Cody came within sight of Three Crossings on the Sweetwater River. Originally, it had been built as a Mormon settlement but was now used as a home station. It was considerably smaller than Horseshoe but its comforts were far superior, mainly because the station was run by a woman. Mrs. Moore had cooked and cared for the relay riders during the period when her husband was station boss there. After his death, she continued to live there and, although the company had not given her the status which her late husband had held, they continued to pay her for her services. The liverymen carried out all the heavy chores and the station continued to run efficiently. Her cooking was famed throughout the Rocky Ridge division and Three Crossings was a favorite stopping place for most of the expressmen. Cody decided to stay overnight. He might even rest up for a couple of days, as this was his last stop. Will Cody had completed his scheduled relays and had covered 116 miles since leaving Red Butte.

Once there had been a swing station at Sweetwater River, but it had been abandoned at the beginning of the Paiute War and had not been used again since the Pony Express had resumed service. Possibly, Russell, Majors and Waddell had considered it was unnecessary, as it lay between two stations that were already within relay distance of each other.

A stablehand transferred the pouches on to the next rider's mount and Cody headed for the eating house. Ma Moore insisted that the riders ate in a shack away from everybody else, so she could tend to their needs personally. They were the sons she had yearned for but had been denied.

She was strict, though. No alcohol was allowed on the station. It went against her Mormon upbringing and that counted for a lot more with her than did the Alexander Majors Pledge. And those who smoked did so out of her sight and also ensured that she did not smell their tobacco smoke.

"Wal, if it ain't young Will!" Ma Moore always claimed to show no favoritism toward the riders, but she made an exception in Cody's case. "The trail's fit for neither man nor beast. Get seated, and yuh don't move from here until yore belly's so full that yuh kin hardly make it across to the bunkhouse."

"That's fine, Ma." Cody sat down at the table. "I don't have to ride for a coupla days so I'll be samplin' a fair bit o' your cookin'!"

"An' welcome to it, yuh are." She served him a heaping bowl of venison stew. "An' there's apple pie to follow. All us did think that yuh don't carry enough weight fer yore age. I got ma doubts 'bout yore years, though!" She laughed deeply.

"Never mind my years," Cody answered, "a hundred an' thirty-five pounds is the only limit they're strict on fer riders an' I'm some way off'n that."

"An' I'm thinkin' yuh haven't stopped growin' yet, Will."

Ma Moore went out back and Cody ate in silence. The room was deserted, and he was glad of that because he wanted to be alone with his thoughts. He got to thinking about Red Butte. Worrying. He was sure that the Paiutes would take that station first, raze it, and then mass for an all-out attack on Horseshoe. He was worried about Ben Hollister, and Cody had never worried about any man in his life, not after his father had been killed. You had to admire Hollister. He'd come out here from England, a greenhorn, and made his mark. But Ben had been learning too much from J.A. Slade, and that was a matter for concern. There was no doubt that Slade enjoyed killing for the sake of it, redmen or whites. Hollister had fast picked up from the road boss and there were stories along the Overland that something was driving him on to kill Indians. Something a lot more sinister than war or survival. Once a man began taking scalps, there was no way back.

Will turned in. He slept late simply because he had no need to rise early. Ma Moore's breakfast would be there for him whatever time he strolled into the eating house.

The new day had dawned with clear skies, and the snow on the ground crunched beneath Will's hide boots as he walked across the compound. He took his time over breakfast because rest days could be long days and you had to fill the time in.

He sat there long after his second plate was finished wondering how to fill his day in. He'd probably read and see if there were any chores that needed doing. Already boredom was hovering on his horizon. Then Ackerman, the stableman, came looking for him. Nobody disturbed anybody in Ma Moore's eating house unless it was something urgent.

"Ron Rivers has been kilt, Will." Ackerman spoke in a low voice in case Ma Moore should hear him out back. "Injuns, I guess. Hoss came in with the mails, but no rider."

Cody knew what he was being asked to do and in a strange way, it came as a relief, even though he mourned the loss of a rider. Death was all part of life in the Pony Express. Will's only regret was missing the next grubstake but, in truth, he would sooner be out there riding than sitting around here killing time.

"Put the pouches on a fresh horse," Will ordered.

"They're already on."

Rock Creek was the next westbound stop, a distance of 75 miles. In between stood two swing stations where fresh mounts would be available. It was probably the toughest run on the Rocky Ridge division in normal conditions. In snow, it was near impassable, except for the most experienced riders. Will Cody was mounted and on his way out within three minutes.

Within fifty miles of the westbound ride, it was clear that weather conditions were much less severe. The blizzards had been mainly confined to the east. Snow lay on the ground, but the drifts were small. Detours were not necessary; he was able to keep on the trail.

All the same, even Cody was saddle sore by the time he reached Rock Creek. He was relieved to find the relay rider ready and waiting to take over. Cody's feet dragged a little as he made his way over to the bunkhouse. Already he was wishing that he was back at Three Crossings, as he helped himself to a bowl of pemmican stew.

Rock Creek was one of the most desolate stations on the entire run. It consisted of a single large structure built from timber hauled from the nearby forest. The building had been divided in the center. One half was the living quarters, comprising pole bunks and a table which Stiler, the station boss, used as his office. The other half was stabling. An aroma of horse dung permeated the accommodation section.

Stiler was drunk most of the time, and his drinking had gotten worse during the months he had been at Rock Creek. Will noticed him lying on one of the bunks, snoring loudly. Mostly these days, the running of the station was left to Palker, the stableman.

"Glad it's you, Will." Palker came through the adjoining door from the stable, bringing a fresh waft of dung with him. "Jest afraid it might be one o' the others."

Will raised his eyebrows.

"We ain't got no eastbound rider." Palker shifted uneasily and glanced towards the sleeping station boss. "Thomson rode back to Dry Sandy after he'd completed his run this mornin'. Says he ain't goin' no further east, not with the weather and how the injuns are thataways. Mebbe we won't see him agin."

Will scraped out his bowl and licked the spoon. "So?" He was determined to have the satisfaction of making the other put his request into words.

"Mails've gotta go through to Red Butte, Will."

"Guess so."

"I was wonderin' . . ."

"If I'd get right back in the saddle an' ride?"

"That's about the size of it. Ain't nobody else. I'd do it myself . . ." He inclined his head towards the still snoring Stiler. " 'Cept I cain't leave the station unmanned."

Will poured himself some more coffee. He would take the mails east when the rider from the west arrived. "Tell me," he said regarding Palker thoughtfully, "Hollister's run, the one that's rumored might be a record, how far was it?"

"Some say three hundred and eighty miles. Don't know fer sure. Doubt anybody really does, 'ceptin' Hollister himself."

"When's the eastbound rider due?"

"Half an hour, thereabouts. It's Causler from Dry Sandy. No way he'll go on further."

"Get a hoss ready. An' make a note in Stiler's book. Jest in case anybody wants to argue about it afterward."

Will was already making mental calculations as to how far he had already ridden.

The snow held an advantage on the eastbound run. Without it, Will Cody might have waited for morning. The reflection from the carpet of white gave him adequate light to see by. He rode at a steady canter—the snow was frozen and he dared not risk his horse slipping.

He was motivated by Ben Hollister's reputed record ride.

The time and distance would be disputed, argued in bunk-houses and saloons the length of the Overland Trail. Hollister had completed his run in a shorter time because conditions had been good. Cody's conditions were atrocious. They might, or might not, be taken into account in years to come. But the Pony Express kept few records. The mammoth feats would be passed on by word of mouth, embellished. Stories would grow into legends. Years hence, they would just be whispers of legends because there would be nobody left to tell them firsthand.

The further east he rode, the deeper the snow became. A few miles beyond Sweetwater the trail was blocked by 6-foot-high drifts. Will dismounted, somehow pulling and coaxing his horse through. From now on, the going would be much slower.

If there were any Indian tracks, then they would be buried beneath the snow. The Paiutes were probably camped up somewhere in the hills, but there was no way of telling. Cody was vigilant at all times but not unduly concerned. The Indians had more important things on their war-frenzied minds on a snowbound night than waiting in ambush in the forlorn hope that a lone rider might show up.

Daylight came with a greyish reluctance. There was no roseate sky to greet the morning. Will knew that he was less than two miles from his destination. So near, yet so far. The last stretch would be the hardest of all. Every bone and muscle in his body ached and he had to fight to stop his eyelids from closing.

Then the stillness of that grey morning was broken by the sound of gunfire. A distant volley—its echoes were still rolling across the hills and canyons when the second salvo came. From then on, the shooting was spasmodic.

Will shrugged off his weariness like he might have cast off a surplus garment and kicked his horse's flanks.

A mile further on he heard the hollering of Indians intermingled with the gunfire and he knew that his worst fears had been confirmed.

Red Butte station was under siege.

Ten

Ben knew that, without a shadow of doubt, the Paiutes would come. If not today, then tomorrow. Or the day after. Soon. The occupants of Red Butte were trapped; there was no chance of going anywhere. The trails and mountain tracks were blocked by snowdrifts. There was even less chance of the army arriving. Whatever had to be done, the defenders had to do it alone.

He wished that Slade was here. Logically, another gun would make very little difference, however fast and accurate, but somehow it was difficult to envisage the road boss ever being on the losing side. But Slade would have his own problems before long. As Will Cody had pointed out, the Paiutes would test Red Butte and other small stations before massing for an all-out attack on the larger ones. Horseshoe would eventually experience the might of the Paiute nation and any others who joined them.

Ben was restless. He had to busy himself in some way, and he was determined to utilize his enforced stay here to its best advantage. He checked the armory on the rear wall of the bunkhouse. There were five Pony Express standard issue Walker .44s and some spare cylinders. He counted five carbines and four Hawken .54s. Rifles were not widely used by the dispatch riders because they were weighty and cumbersome. In the far corner were a couple of ten-gauge shotguns, the ends of the barrels cobwebbed. Every station carried a scattergun, primarily for shooting small game for food. Nobody ever seemed to get around to hunting, though, at least not here. They relied on the supply wagons. But no supplies would be arriving, either.

The shotguns were breechloaders. Ben also found a small unopened crate of paper-cased rimfire cartridges, an assortment of shot sizes ranging from buckshot down to fives for jackrabbits. He then went in search of candles.

"What in tarnation are yuh doin'?" Doc Velantry came into the bunkhouse and stared in amazement. Ben was seated at the table, shotgun shells lined up in front of him like toy soldiers on parade, the ends pried open. He was holding a lighted candle over them, melted wax dripping steadily from it into the open cylinders. "Yuh better go an' lie down, Hollister, that infection's got to your brain, seems to me."

"Don't worry." Ben smiled. "It's just a little trick I learned in England."

"Never did get to understanding the English." The doctor drew up a chair and sat down opposite Ben. "Snow's eased up some. Yuh reckon the Paiutes'll come? Mebbe they'll hold off until the thaw."

"They'll come." Ben used his knife to close a cartridge, pressed the end in firmly. "I did a count up. We got forty men, all kinds, some of 'em won't be a lot of use—they've probably never fired a gun in their lives. Coach passengers from back east and stable hands don't usually make good marksmen. So, we'll have to make the most of what we've got. Women and kids will stay indoors, and you'll be kept busy tending the wounded. Myers, the station boss, is organizing the defenses. He's posted lookouts and men are detailed in twos to man the four sides of the palisade. Reloading is going to be the problem when the fightin' heats up." He refrained from expounding his cartridge theory—the doc wouldn't understand.

"You got some trick up yore sleeve?" The doctor watched Ben wax another line of shells and close them up.

"Yeah, but it's limited against the odds we're likely to face. We could use a dozen shotguns. We only got two, so we'll have to make the most of what we've got. All depends how many braves attack. Could be Blood Arrow reckons a small station is a push-over and only sends a war party of twenty or thirty. Maybe he's split his forces, goin' to attack other stations at the same time. We won't know until the time comes. He might not play his full hand until he's taken Horseshoe and moved on east. He's dodged the army so far, but he won't want to take them head-on until he's got a sizeable force willing to fight and die for him. My guess is he's bankin' on the Cheyenne and the Arapaho joinin' up with him, but they won't do that until he's got a few of the stations under his belt and he's proved himself to them. Once he's seen to be winning, other tribes will follow him."

"Yuh got it well figured out, fer somebody from England, Hollister." There was admiration in Velantry's tone.

"Learning as I go." Ben reached for the candle again. "I've had some good tutors."

"Yuh better git some o' Ma Moore's grub down yuh. An' some rest." The doctor turned towards the door. "A man can't fight till he's got some food in his belly and he's rested up."

The day dawned grey and damp, and with it came the Paiutes. About fifteen had crawled in close under cover of darkness. The first warning the sentry on the gate had was when they began swarming over. His first shot alerted the rest of the station to the attack.

More braves were scaling the palisade at the rear. Fortunately, the sentries there were off-duty riders who were wise to the ways of Indians. They were also fair marksmen. Revolvers barked and spat fire in the half light. Three Indians on the gate fell back, a fourth slumped and hung there. Dead.

A hail of .44 fire ripped into those braves scaling the stockade at the rear. A couple dropped back; three jumped down into the compound, arrows already notched. Hurried gunfire left them unscathed.

Ben came out of the bunkhouse low and fast just as Rykard, the storeman, went down with an arrow in his chest. Ben's .45 ball took the Paiute in the throat. An arrow thudded into the side of the building where Ben had been standing a second earlier. He fired again and the other Indian fell kicking.

The attempt to take the defenders of Red Butte by surprise had failed. The Paiutes drew back and lay unseen in the scrub beyond the palisade.

Doc Velantry was kneeling over Rykard, shaking his head. "Got him straight through the heart," he muttered as Ben approached.

"Don't waste your time on the dead, Doc," Ben grunted. "There'll be plenty o' patchin' up for you to do before this day's done."

"You reckon we can hold 'em off?"

"Who knows? Judgin' by the first attack, there ain't too many of 'em out there. At least, not as many as I was expectin'. Probably the rest of 'em are attacking other stations west of here, and when they're done with that, they'll join up with those that haven't managed to over-run the depots under siege. And that's when the trouble really begins."

Doc Velantry and Ben dragged Rykard's body under cover and draped a blanket over it. The first casualty count could have been a lot worse. They were lucky—so far.

Ben fetched the shotguns, filled his pockets with as many doctored shells as they would hold. He made his way across to the gate and mounted the rickety ladder up to the raised platform. From here he had an unrestricted view of the surrounding landscape. Keeping his head low, he scanned the scrubland.

There was not an Indian to be seen, but he knew they were out there, lying low amid the snow-laden bushes. He watched and waited. They would come again soon, so far they had only been testing the fire power of the defenders. They might or might not change their tactics; it depended upon their numbers. Every warrior was prepared to sacrifice his life to take the station, and by this time, they were fully aware that only a handful of whites were defending Red Butte.

The sun rose above the hills to the east, its rays were hazy through the clouds. A low-lying mist screened the river from Ben's view. If the mist thickened, the Indians would use it to their advantage. They would sneak close, like wraiths, risking everything in one concerted rush.

The mist was certainly thickening. Ben continued to watch, never relaxing his vigilance for a single second.

A single rifle shot rang out from the rear of the stockade. One of the defenders thought that he had detected a movement amid the snowy foliage. If an Indian had been lying beneath that weighed down bush, then the ball might just have struck lucky. Maybe the sentry had been mistaken and there was nobody there. Nothing moved, so there was no way of telling.

"Save your shots," Ben called out. "You'll need 'em before long."

The mist began to disperse, wafted by a light westerly breeze. The Paiutes began storming the station before the grey vapor cleared altogether, while they still had cover.

Warriors rose up from every place Ben would have bet his wages an Indian was skulking. Wet snow clung to their hide clothing; some had dug in the open ground, leaving the bushes to draw any impatient white fire during the long wait.

They rose and rushed in one movement, letting a hail of arrows fly at the defenders on the ramparts. One quivered in a post within a foot of where Ben crouched. He felt a rush of air as two more passed above his head.

Then he cocked the 10-gauge.

Fifty braves streamed towards the gate, ignoring the other three sides of the stockade. Their attack was concentrated—

sheer weight of numbers designed to breach the defenses in one place only. Some would die, but many more would make it over the top.

Shotguns were a favorite with stagecoach guards. The weapons allowed for any error of marksmanship when Indians were closing in on a swaying coach. They were close range guns—except when the shot charges had been congealed with a blob of melted candle wax.

Ben resisted the temptation to pull both triggers simultaneously. One of the charges would have been wasted. He looked for the greatest concentration of oncoming hide-clad, snow-daubed bodies. The Paiutes were about seventy yards away, closing the gap as they leaped and ran.

Ben picked a brave at the head of a bunch of half-a-dozen. The shotgun boomed and the villainous smoke cloud momentarily obscured Ben's vision. But he heard them screaming as they fell forward into the snow.

He swung on to another group. They were closer now. Bunched. One barrel was all he needed.

It was as if a leaden hailstorm had struck the onrushing Paiutes. The shot charge held well, parting just a few yards before it smashed into flesh and bone. It cut a bloody swath right through the attackers.

Three warriors fell, kicking and writhing. Another staggered, shrieking from a ruined face. The far spread peppered those following behind. Their charge was checked, thrown into a wild disarray as bodies clutched at a multitude of wounds.

Ben grabbed up the second shotgun and swung the barrels through the meleé. The double report echoed across the snowbound scrubland. More braves staggered and fell, then crawled. One lay motionless on his back, arms outstretched. He had a gaping abdominal wound.

Ben reloaded and fired. Reloaded and fired again.

"Boy, whaddyer hit 'em with?" A grizzled stablehand clambered up alongside him, a smoking Colt in his hand.

"Forget that." Ben pointed to the handgun, scooped a handful of shells out of his pocket. "Load 'n fire this spare scattergun. As fast as you can."

Now two of them were loosing charge after charge of tallowed shot at the Paiutes. The powdersmoke thickened, drifting in the breeze. Ben and his companion were shooting at silhouettes, shambling, confused shadowy forms. Indians were yelling and more were going down.

A tall brave emerged from the smoke, staggered towards the station. His eyes were gone and his lips were stretched wide in a screech of pain and defiance.

"Aiyee!"

He came on blindly. Ben waited, let him get to within ten yards of the gate. It was like shooting a sitting jackrabbit. But in war there were no scruples. The Paiute's scream was cut off as surely as he was decapitated, and the waxed shot had not yet begun to part.

"Don't waste a shot!" Ben checked his companion just in time. The Paiute pitched forward and lay motionless.

"Hold your fire!" Ben shouted to the others who lined the stockade.

The defenders waited for the pall of gunsmoke to clear. The snow covered ground in front of Red Butte station was spattered crimson. Some bodies still crawled. Maybe a dozen or more lay still.

The surviving Paiutes were retreating, and some were already swimming the swollen river, clambering up the far bank to seek the safety of the nearby woods.

A volley of gunfire raked them.

Ben stared, straining his eyes. He recognized the crack of a .44, but the shots were too fast to count. Paiutes scattered, leaving their slain where they had fallen. The current caught the corpses, sweeping them downriver.

There was a brief respite in the shooting. Whoever was hidden on the fringe of the tall pines was changing the cylinder in his revolver.

Crack-crack-crack.

"Only two men kin shoot that fast," somebody along the line muttered. "Slade an' Hollister. An' Hollister's right here . . ."

A figure emerged from the trees, partially obscured by the dispersing mist. But even at that distance Ben knew that he was not J.A. Slade. He was too slight, his step too light. He ignored the fallen Indians as he turned and led a horse out of the wood, mounted it and coaxed it into the water. Slade, however, would have stopped to scalp every brave who had fallen to his gun.

Will Cody's saturated clothing clung to his slim frame. His features were muddied and, as he approached the gate, it was the only time Ben had ever seen the man's shoulders stooped in weariness.

"Seems you managed okay without my help." Cody slid from the saddle, leaned up against his horse. "I was goin' to ride on to Platte Bridge, to see if I could muster up a posse. No need. That some new-fangled gun yore usin', Ben?"

"Just a shotgun." Ben smiled. "Pony Express issue, cheapest on the market. But I can make you up a few special shells, if you're interested."

Cody headed for the bunkhouse, shaking his head as he went. He would leave it until later to tell Ben Hollister that he had broken the other's record by just four miles.

Eleven

The snow thawed rapidly in the damp, mild air that came with the prevailing winds. The ice melted and the Overland Trail became thick with slush—but it was passable.

Will Cody and Ben rode out to check on the conditions. "It'll do." Cody nodded. "The mails have to go on as far as Horseshoe, but I doubt I could've made it until today. Much as I'd've liked to extend my record over yourn by more'n four miles, Ben."

They both laughed. Right now records didn't count for much. Staying alive was their priority.

"We'll get everythin' we can loaded up into two wagons and the stagecoach." There was an urgency about Will now that he had established that the trail was passable. "Smoke signals I passed just west of Red Butte spoke of a mighty injun gatherin'. Doubtless Brent and his renegades are with 'em. I guess they counted on that war party razin' Red Butte to pave the way for 'em. Didn't anticipate no problems. Wal, they gotta shock and now Blood Arrow'll be madder than a grizzly with a swarm o' bees stingin' its ass. We ain't got much time, we gotta get away from here. Let's start loadin' up."

The river crossing brought back memories for Ben of that fateful Cheyenne ambush. However, the river here was not so deep and the wagons and the coach were floated across safely and finished up a hundred yards downstream on the opposite bank. Every available horse had a rider, and a couple were ridden double. The mist had cleared and the mountain skyline was clearly visible. It was dotted with smoke signals.

"They're still callin' the war parties in." Cody shaded his eyes, easily reading the signals. "I reckon' we gotta coupla days afore they hit the warpath proper. We'll make it to Horseshoe."

"The Lord has preserved us," Ma Moore said piously from the seat of one of the wagons. She had not forgotten her Mormon upbringing. Nor the Mormon War and J.A. Slade. "I'm not stoppin' a moment longer'n I have to at Horseshoe," she called after Ben. "And I'll not cook a single meal for Captain Slade. He's a murderer. Justice is mine, saith the Lord. He hasn't forgotten, neither."

Horseshoe station was crowded. It seemed that every mover and every settler within a fifty mile radius had moved in there for protection.

"Oh, Ben!" Mollie ran to greet her husband, embraced him and didn't give a damn who might be watching. "I feared the worst. Especially after Ed Kine's horse came in riderless. All that Slade was worried about was the mails, not you."

"That's Slade's way." Ben kissed her. "Times like these, though, we need him around."

"So's you two can go killin' injuns together?"

"There's a lot of Indians going to get killed soon." Ben's expression hardened. "Leastways, I hope so, 'cause if there ain't our scalps are goin' to be dryin' in their camp."

"I wish we could move down to Fort Laramie." She pressed herself tightly against him. "Or further, to Fort Kearney. But the mountain passes are still blocked with snowdrifts. That's why no soldiers have reached here yet."

"We'll be okay." Ben hoped that he sounded more reassuring than he felt as they went inside the wagon. It was good to be home. He would have preferred to have been back in the cabin, but anywhere outside the palisade was at risk. He only hoped that the Paiutes didn't burn it. They knew it was the home of Slayer Who Rides With the Wind.

"Hey, Ben!" Will Cody's voice came from outside.

Ben extricated himself from Mollie's arms and pushed his way out through the flap.

"Slade wants to see yuh, Ben," Cody said. "Asked me to tell yuh."

Mollie's misgivings flooded back.

"Yuh healed and rested and able to ride now?" J.A. Slade looked up as Ben entered the office. The section boss's complexion looked deathly white in the light from the oil lamp. Apart from a hint of twin red spots on his broad cheeks.

"You'd better ask Doc Velantry." Ben closed the door.

"I'm the boss here." Slade was clearly angry. "Well?"

"I can ride."

"And shoot, I hope." Slade's lips were compressed. "Go get a good night's sleep and be ready to ride outta here before daylight."

"I take it I'm riding the mails?"

"The mails can wait. They'll have to. Unless we sort out Blood Arrow and these renegades, the Pony is likely to be suspended again. This time, it won't run again, they'll go bankrupt."

"You mean . . ."

"There ain't no more soldiers gonna reach here. Not in time, anyhow. So we're gonna have to give these red bastards a nasty surprise." Slade's eyes narrowed. "Somethin' they won't be expectin'. Accordin' to Cody, and he'd make one of the best scouts around, the Paiutes are gatherin'. There's goin' to be a big parley at Green River. They might already've started to move this way. They know that most of the soldiers are cut off by the snowdrifts between here an' Carson, so Blood Arrow'll be a mite arrogant. He'll be over-confident. He'll think Horseshoe is here for the takin'."

"But . . . you can't leave Horseshoe defenseless!" Ben's only thoughts were for Mollie's safety.

"There'll be plenty o' men left here. Ridin' with me will be you, Cody, George Chrisman, Don Rising and Bill Reid. The rest'll stop here to defend Horseshoe. *If* it comes to that!"

"That's . . . that's just *six* men!" Ben stared, thinking he'd heard wrong.

"At least yuh can count, Hollister."

"But there'll be *hundreds* of Indians!"

"Maybe three, four hundred. Even five."

"It's crazy."

"That's why they won't be expectin' it, an' we'll hit 'em harder'n a detachment of cavalry. Now, go get some sleep, don't want anybody fallin' asleep in the saddle. Be saddled and ready half an hour before daylight."

Ben turned to go. His pulse was racing.

"Hollister?"

"Yeah?" Ben turned back in the doorway. J.A. Slade was a sinister silhouette beyond the lamplight.

"Bring that shotgun o' yours along. Everybody'll be bootin' shotguns rather than rifles. Cody tells me yuh got some o' those doctored cartridges o' yours. Share 'em out. They might be useful. I heard what they did to the injuns at Red Butte."

The posse slipped quietly through the gates before the dawn was even a hint of grey in the eastern sky. There was still some patches of snow, and it gave the riders just enough light to see their way. J.A. Slade rode at the head of the column, a squat silhouette that was terrible to behold if you stopped to think about everything he had done and what he planned to do now.

Ben had told Mollie that he was going on a scouting mission with the others. She had not taken it quite so badly that way. In a way he had told her the truth. The posse would take a looksee, ride back to Horseshoe and report. In between there would be shooting and killing.

Ben knew in his heart that he could not have stayed behind. Blood Arrow was somewhere out there. The Paiute chief had a lot to answer for, his blood would stain the melting snow crimson. This time Ben would call the shots. Not Slade. Not Cody. Nor any of the others.

Ben's hand strayed to his holstered Adams .45. He fingered it almost lovingly. This mission, for him, had become personal.

They were arguably the six best horsemen in the employ of the Pony Express, and probably the best marksmen as well. They made it as far as Little Muddy by nightfall on the first day and struck a cold camp. They were back in the saddle again before daylight. There were very few smoke signals to be seen, but they told the riders all they needed to know.

"Paiutes've broken camp." Slade reined in to brief his followers. "Looks like they've burned Platte Bridge an' are headed this way. There's a narrow canyon 'bout five miles west o' here. They'll have to use it or else take the long way round through the mountains. My guess is they won't do that, they don't have no need for detours. That suits us fine, provided we get there first."

The canyon was between a mile and two miles long, its sides and floor deep with unmelted snow, as it was shaded from the sun. The snow would still be lying there when the plains and hills were brown and green again.

The riders paused at the mouth of the canyon to listen. Ben could hear nothing, but Slade's eyes met Cody's and the two men nodded.

"The injuns are headed this way, jest like I thought they would." The road boss sat erect in the saddle, his expression was only too familiar to those around him. "They couldn't come no other way and we've beaten 'em to it."

"What's the plan?" Bill Reid was clearly nervous. Six against several hundred was sheer madness. At least, back at Horseshoe, you'd get killed in plenty of company.

"My plan." Slade was haughtily arrogant. "We sit our hosses out o' sight among them trees over there. And wait. From then on, yuh follow me, and don't nobody get any crazy notions of his own." His eyes flicked over Ben and Cody.

It was a long wait. Several times Ben thought that perhaps the Indians had turned back or had decided to take the mountain route, after all. The stillness was broken by the distant sound of voices, then silence again as hollows and bends muffled all noises within the canyon.

A jay screeched and flew out of a snow laden bush. It had delivered its warning and fled. Man was coming. Slade sat his horse, not a muscle in his broad features so much as twitched. He was the grim reaper waiting to beckon the doomed.

At last, the watchers spied the column struggling through the deep wet snow. The Indians were two or three abreast, floundering. Those with horses led their mounts. The line wound on back round twists and turns. On they came, there seemed to be no end to them. Ben gave up trying to count.

Everybody was watching Slade. They would follow whatever he did. They had no choice now, anyway.

The Paiutes were almost at the mouth of the canyon. They were jostling, four or five abreast now. Soon they would be out on the open flat land where only patches of snow remained and the footing was firm.

Ben looked for Blood Arrow, but there was no sign of the chief nor Brent. Some halfbreeds mingled with the braves, distinguishable by their fur caps and long barrelled rifles slung across their shoulders.

J.A. Slade waited until the head of the massive war party was almost clear of the canyon, spilling into the widening exit. That was when he sent his horse plunging forward, holding the reins with one hand, his .44 in the other.

Crack-crack-crack.

His three shots sounded as one and two of the halfbreeds pitched forward into a snowdrift. He had singled them out because they carried rifles and could probably use them moderately well. Five horsemen followed in his wake, galloping in a line across the head of the advancing Indians. Ben was close behind the road boss, followed by Cody, Chrisman and Rising. Ben Reid brought up the rear.

Revolvers barked and the echoes rolled on into the canyon and magnified, rumbling to a crescendo like a charge of detonated explosives. Guns were emptied, thrust back into holsters, and spare revolvers tugged from belts. The gunfire was continuous.

Mustangs reared and plunged. Some fell, kicking, rolling on Indians around them. Braves staggered and dropped. There was no hiding place from the deadly hail of lead.

"Aiiyee! Man Who Likes Killing!"

"Slayer Who Rides With the Wind!"

The Paiutes panicked. They turned to flee, floundered in the snow, trampling those directly behind them. Chaos reigned, the air was filled with the screams of wounded horses and Indians. The snow all around was splattered and streaked with blood, bodies lay on top of one another.

Some arrows were notched and fired by the Indians at the rear but the posse was in little danger. The range and panic did not aid their marksmanship.

Worse was to follow for the Paiutes. J. A. Slade's 10-gauge boomed as he pulled both triggers together. A bloody swath of death and disfigurement cut through those still standing. Only those behind the first bend were safe. Then he wheeled his mount and galloped away.

It was akin to a sideshow shooting gallery at a rodeo. Customers queued to fire, moved on to make way for those behind when they had emptied their weapons. Ben fired his shotgun, one barrel to the right, the other to the left, decimating the fringe of the melee. Then Cody, Chrisman, and Rising. Reid was last, a freak arrow missed him by a foot but he got his shots off and streaked after his companions.

Behind the riders, a milling horde of shocked and wounded Indians staggered among the slain. The panic stretched deep into the long narrow canyon. The air was filled with the screams of the wounded and cries of rage from those who had been unable to vent their hatred upon their deadliest foes. Man Who Likes Killing and Slayer Who Rides With the Wind had struck with terrible devastation.

At the rear of the column Blood Arrow and Brent cursed helplessly. They swore that every white habitation would be burned to the ground and scalps would hang drying in the wind and the sun. None would be spared. Even the distant ocean would turn red with the blood of the slain.

Blood Arrow set about restoring calm and order. Humiliation had been inflicted upon his leadership, and it could not go unavenged. He had lost at least forty warriors and he left them where they lay. The wounded could tend to the wounded. They would be but an encumbrance on the big push east.

What was this terrible weapon which the whites used, that caused injury and death, and inflicted a multitude of wounds from a distance? Rifles he understood. He had fired one himself with no success. A ball either hit or missed, it slew with a single wound. But *these* . . .

"Shotguns." Brent was stocky of build, his filthy hide clothing like an additional layer of skin; it was a long time since he had last undressed. The garments smelled sour and sweaty and his unkempt beard and hair were infested with lice. "Leastways, they sounded like shotguns and them wounds are buckshot. Some of 'em are birdshot. Don't understand it. At eighty yards yuh jest git peppered with a scattergun. Them as they were usin' blow great holes in yuh. Must be some new-fangled shotgun from back east."

"Get some for the Paiutes," Blood Arrow snarled, "and we will do to these whites what they have done to our warriors."

"We'll take 'em." Brent's mouth was dry. He knew only too well that once he ceased to be of use to the Paiute chief, he would share the same fate as the settlers they had already slain. The memory of what had happened to that homesteader, who some braves had surprised, and brought in alive, made even Brent's blood run cold. Brent had done some terrible things to his fellow men in his time, but nothing like *that*. "When we take Horseshoe station there's bound to be some o' them guns there."

"And many braves will die before we get the guns. They will cut us down three or four at a blast."

"Use fire arrers. Burn 'em out."

"Their dwellings are protected by earth."

"Not if the arrers hit the sides an' there's enough fires so's they can't be put out fast enough."

Blood Arrow's eyes narrowed. This treacherous white man spoke the truth, but he was not to be trusted. Brent failed to notice the contempt in the Paiute's expression, or else he might have interpreted it as scorn for the white invaders. Nobody respected a traitor, whatever their race or color. Blood Arrow was fiercely loyal to his own kind, in spite of his lust for power. Every white man was a hated enemy, including Brent. But, for the time being, the renegade was useful.

"Firewater!" Blood Arrow grunted. It was a demand, not a request.

"I've got a small cache hidden 'bout two miles from here." Brent surveyed the surrounding land in order to get his bearings.

"Fetch it!"

"Okay, okay." Brent's swarthy features suffused with

blood—he was not in the habit of taking orders from red scum, even if this one happened to be a chief. But Brent needed Blood Arrow just as the chief needed him, if this vast territory was to be over-run by the Indians. That way there would be much to plunder and, afterwards, California was a big new world where nobody would have heard of Brent. "I'll need hosses. My boys will help me. It'll take mebbe a coupla hours."

"Hurry." Blood Arrow turned away impatiently. "My warriors fight better, braver, with firewater in their bellies. That way they will not fear the guns that slay many with each shot. Before the sun sets twice, the scalps of Man Who Likes Killing and Slayer Who Rides With the Wind will hang in my lodge. I have spoken."

He strode away to address his warriors. War talk was very necessary at this moment to boost their flagging morale.

Ben had presumed, as they sped away from the canyon, that Slade was leading them back to Horseshoe station. When the road boss turned off the Overland Trail a mile or so beyond the gutted remains of La Bronte, Ben began to get an uneasy feeling. It was pointless to ask Slade where they were headed. He only told you when it suited him.

The five men rode in single file along narrow wooded tracks until, after several hours, they emerged on to a steep hill overlooking that same fast-flowing river that passed close to their home station. Ben reckoned that they were about ten miles west of Horseshoe.

The shadows were beginning to lengthen and there was a touch of frost in the air. It would be dark in about an hour.

"We'll strike a cold camp here." Slade dismounted without a trace of weariness in his body. "We need to move out before it gets light. Just in case the injuns are watchin'. But my guess is that after the pastin' we gave Blood Arrow, we shan't see 'em much before noon."

"You reckon they'll keep comin'?" Ben had been clinging

to the hope that the war party might decide to return to the desert to lick their wounds.

"They'll be comin'." Slade laughed, a chilling sound in the gathering dusk. "As sure as the sun will rise tomorrow, Blood Arrow will come. He ain't goin' to forgive us fer what we've done to him." He laughed again. "But next time even he might have second thoughts. Providin' we hit him hard enough this time. Kill Blood Arrow an' the rest'll have no stomach for a fight."

Ben tensed, muttering to himself, "Blood Arrow's my meat. His scalp on my belt an' the buzzards are welcome to what's left."

They made camp in silence, and for the second day in succession ate biscuits and dried meat from their saddle pouches. Most of all, Ben wanted Blood Arrow dead and this war finished. Then, with the telegraph completed and the Pony Express disbanded, he could he start a new life. All this, he promised himself, would just be a bad memory that he would try to forget. But none of it would happen while Blood Arrow lived.

The Pony Express men positioned themselves before dawn. The snow was virtually all gone; there was no reflection to see by, just faint starlight. Slade clearly knew this place well and Ben wondered if the other had been here and planned what he might do one day. There was no figuring J.A. Slade.

The river was about twenty-five yards wide. During the summer, it was easily fordable, but now it was a rushing, swirling torrent. A good swimmer would make it if he went with the current, guiding himself across diagonally so that he finished up on the opposite bank about a couple of hundred yards downstream. The others followed Slade, leading their horses along the nearside bank until they reached a small wood. It offered both concealment and an unrestricted view of the river. Ben was beginning to guess Slade's plan.

"We keep outta sight." Slade tethered his horse to a tree and slipped the shotgun out of the boot. "Don't nobody make a move until I do."

"Surely the Paiutes will use the Horseshoe crossing?" Ben whispered to Will Cody.

"No." The other shook his head. "Yuh hev to learn to think like an injun. They've jest had a whuppin' an' they're figurin' thet we'll be lying in ambush at Horsehoe ford for 'em. By white man's thinkin', thet makes sense. We might jest paste 'em there an' then hightail it back inside the stockade to defend the station. So they'll opt to surprise us by crossin' here and then attackin' Horseshoe from the north. Slade's got it right, unless Blood Arrow out-guesses him and goes fer the obvious. Never can tell with injuns. If he does . . ." He left the sentence unfinished.

They lapsed into silence. The dawn came slowly; daylight took its time. The day was mild and cloudy and there was a hint of drizzle in the air. Towards the middle of the day the drizzle turned to fast rain. The branches dripped steadily as the men huddled beneath them. Ben was certain in his own mind that the Indians would not come. They had either opted for the Horseshoe crossing or had headed back towards the desert.

The Paiutes came in the early afternoon, a long line of them, on foot and leading their horses as they approached the river. There were two or three hundred. Ben looked for Blood Arrow, but the distance was too great to be able to recognize individuals.

The Indians gathered on the opposite bank. Ben's pulses raced and his temples pounded as he finally saw Blood Arrow. The chief was wearing a feathered head-dress that made him seem a foot taller than the others. He was talking, pointing and giving orders.

Ben wished that he had a .54 rifle. At that range, he could

have dropped the chief with a Hawken. It would have ruined Slade's strategy, but Ben knew he would have shot the chief just the same. Maybe a chance to kill Blood Arrow would present itself shortly. Ben's real worry was that Slade might beat him to it. That ragbag standing alongside the chief was surely Brent, Ben decided. Slade could have him.

The Indians were acting strangely, Ben could not figure out what they were doing. There was a confidence about them that wasn't just their customary arrogance. Several were beating their fists on their chests. They were whooping when silence would have been wiser. One fell over and had difficulty getting back on his feet.

"Whiskey!" Cody muttered. "They're as drunk as skunks. Guess Brent's supplied the firewater 'cause they need it to boost their morale after that hammerin' we gave 'em. They've lost their wariness, but they'll fight like demons. Works both ways."

The parley was over, and Blood Arrow was shouting. As one, they rushed down the bank and plunged into the icy, raging water. The current caught braves and mustangs alike, sweeping them downstream.

Slade waited until the Indians were almost level with the hidden watchers, then he opened up with his .44.

Every man was firing, emptying his first gun then snatching out his second. Too late the Indians realized that they had fallen into a deadly ambush. Corpses floated, gathering speed as the current sped them away to make room for more. Braves dived below the surface in an attempt to escape the gunfire. In less tumultuous waters, they were capable of staying submerged for several minutes, but not in this raging torrent. Heads bobbed back up only to be picked off by the guns like swimming ducks. To add to the turmoil, there was debris, trees and broken branches sweeping down river and smashing anything in their way with the force of battering rams.

Driftwood and dead bodies tangled. One warrior grabbed

a passing tree trunk and hauled himself up on to it. Somehow he kept his balance, riding it like a canoe. Ben knocked him off with the last shot remaining in his .36.

Indians were clinging to one another in a kind of human raft. Slade fired both barrels of his 10-gauge; it was loaded with birdshot, number fives. The doctored shot charges parted at just the right moment, decimating the leading swimmers.

The Paiutes were fighting the current with drunken futility. A hurtling log cracked open a skull and took its victim with it. Braves were attempting to swim to the opposite bank but the current pulled them back, offering them as easy targets for the Pony Express men.

Ben searched for Blood Arrow and found him. The Paiute chief was raging beyond the far bank where only a .54 ball might have dropped him. The white renegade by his side watched in dismay. A carefully organized plan of war had been overturned. The attackers had never even attacked. Instead, they were the victims of a grim slaughter.

A large party of warriors had shied away from the water's edge. Their greatest fear was that their chief might order them into the river to face certain death. As honorable as it was to die in battle, this was a massacre.

But even their crazed and drunken chief recognized the futility of sending more warriors to their deaths. He could not afford to lose any more.

There was a lull in the shooting. For once, time was on the side of the Express men. They reloaded revolvers and spare cylinders, slipping fresh deadly shells into their shotguns and booting them. They picked off surviving braves at leisure, riding parallel to the flotsam of hurtling corpses and those fighting for survival in the water. It was good target practice. Very few of the Indians in the water would live. They would either drown or be shot. They were powerless to choose.

The posse rode slowly, shooting discriminately. A few Indians had somehow made it back to the near bank and were trying to claw their way out of the swollen river. They were shot at point blank range. There was no further need for the shotguns, the riders were vying for individual targets now.

Finally, Slade yelled an order. Nobody heard it, but they saw him wave an arm and wheel his horse away. It was time to leave.

Ben paused to look back. There was not a single Indian still alive in the river, the last of the corpses were on their way downstream—human debris on their way to a watery grave. Blood Arrow and Brent were no longer visible. They were somewhere among the retreating Indians that were now no more than distant specks. They had witnessed a rout beyond belief and they had no wish to be humiliated further.

Ben wondered if Slade might have a third ambush planned—it was not beyond possibility. Much to his relief, Ben realized that this time they were heading back to Horseshoe station. Powder and shot were running low after two assaults and that was probably the only reason why the Division Superintendent was calling it a day.

Only then did the sheer magnitude of their success become apparent to Ben. Six men had defeated a mighty Indian war party of several hundred braves. Cunning had outweighed the disadvantage of numbers. Only those who had seen it with their own eyes could truly believe it. It was the stuff that legends were made of.

Horseshoe and the other stations further east would not be attacked in the near future. J.A. Slade and his band of men had achieved that which the army had failed to accomplish for months. The Indians had not been entirely defeated, but they would be licking their wounds for some weeks to come. The Express men had bought valuable time for the whites.

Ben's sense of triumph was only soured by the knowledge that Blood Arrow still lived. The Paiute chief had sent his warriors to their deaths while remaining in safety.

One day Ben would catch up with him. He would never rest until Blood Arrow had paid in full for his barbaric crime. The Indian must suffer as Sarah had suffered. And worse.

Only then could Ben begin to live again.

Twelve

Winter brought its hardships for the men of the Pony Express. Many of the stations burned down during the Paiute uprising could not be rebuilt until after the snow thawed. Temporary shelters were erected amid the gutted ruins, just sufficient enough to house a stableman and a change of horses. As a result, many of the runs were extended to accommodate home stations where a rider could finish his run and rest overnight. This often meant that they had to ride further and in poor conditions.

During this time, a meeting took place in the New York office of the Pony Express. There was an atmosphere of tension in the small room.

Alexander Majors, John W. Russell and William Waddell were uneasy in the presence of Major Benjamin F. Ficklin. They ought not to have been, as he was merely an employee of their company, albeit a senior one. Yet they had relied extensively upon him in the formation of the Pony Express, and they valued his experience and advice. The three men glanced at one another, then back at Ficklin.

"I tell you, you've got to get rid of J.A. Slade before it's too late." Ficklin spoke quietly yet his words seemed to crackle in the tension.

"He's done . . . doing a magnificent job." Majors made a deliberate effort to speak forcefully. Strength of personality counted for a lot in gatherings such as this. "With a small posse he virtually put down an Indian uprising—something which the army has been trying to do, unsuccessfully, for months."

"Slade was instrumental in starting the uprising." Ficklin's stoic expression did not alter. He was here at the request of senior company employees. He was their spokesman, and he would not falter in his task.

"That's nonsense," Waddell said puffing out his cheeks. "Slade's been doing what we hired him to do—to clear the Rocky Ridge division of outlaws and Indians and to ensure that the mails and coaches got through safely. No mails have been lost on Slade's division, which is more than you can say for some of the others."

"Very few mails have been lost overall," Ficklin snapped, "but Slade is big trouble for the company. And it looks like Hollister is fast following him. Their names are synonymous the length of the Overland, killing and scalping Indians when we're looking to make peace. My advice to you, gentlemen, is to fire both of them."

"I knew Slade's record when I took him on." Majors' laugh sounded forced. "And, it seems, this fellow, Hollister, is learning fast from him. We need them both until the telegraph is in full operation."

"Slade's murdered one of the best wagon train guides in the business," Ficklin's said, his expression becoming grave. "There's an outcry over it. Some of the movers have signed a petition and sent it to St Louis. They want Slade arrested and tried for murder. I hear also that there's warrants out for him in Illinois and a price on his head. *Twenty-six* killings he's suspected of in that state. Gentlemen, this time J.A. Slade has gone too far. Before long, there'll be a sheriff on his way to Horseshoe station to arrest him. An organization such as ours cannot continue to employ such a man. Our reputation is at stake. We cannot condone what he has done. We risk public outrage."

"Thank you for your concern, Major." Majors crossed and

uncrossed his legs. "Please keep me informed of events. We shall certainly keep a close eye on Captain Slade. In the meantime, he is still Division Superintendent of the Rocky Ridge division. Once spring arrives, and the telegraph work can proceed again, it may not be long before we are disbanded. Until then, I, we do not intend to make any changes."

Ficklin strode haughtily from the room. He had expected J.A. Slade to be fired immediately. He would add his own name to that petition, not as a representative of the Pony Express but as Benjamin F. Ficklin, Major-retired, U.S. Army. It would carry more weight that way.

"Now, gentlemen." Majors waited until the door had closed behind Ficklin before he spoke. "We must get down to more urgent matters." He cleared his throat. "The Pony Express is losing money!"

The others started. This was much more serious than Slade's alleged crimes conveyed second hand.

"The Paiute War has cost us about seventy-five thousand dollars in lost revenue and damage to property," Majors said softly. He never panicked, neither did he duck issues. "We should have been due a sizeable allowance from the Post Office Department for making regular mail deliveries. The suspension of the Pony Express has meant that our deliveries have not been regular. Consequently, the Post Office has refused to pay us."

Waddell sighed and Russell sucked his lips. This was, indeed, bad news.

"Washington is complaining," Majors added.

"If Washington had sent enough soldiers in the beginning, the Paiutes would've been licked. As it is, there still aren't sufficient soldiers and the Paiutes are boiling up for another war. It's the government's fault!" Russell thumped the table.

"Precisely, but Washington will withdraw our six hundred thousand dollar subsidy if there is another suspension. The Post Office is claiming that our suspension has broken our contract with them. It appears, gentlemen, that we can't win either way—and *that* is a recipe for bankruptcy."

"Then we have to maintain the service at all costs," Waddell summarized. "The mails must go through, irrespective of snow, flooding, Indians, and outlaws."

"Precisely." Majors put the tips of his fingers together. "Which is why we need Slade and Hollister to keep the Rocky Ridge division open at all times. It is the toughest stretch of all. If Ficklin makes trouble, I'll fire him. But we have to do even more than just keep the trails open."

Eyebrows were raised. Russell and Waddell waited expectantly, nervously.

"Not only are we losing money, gentlemen," Majors continued, "we are also losing riders. Several have been killed by Indians, many more have left the service because of the danger. We have to enlist many more riders. We must have enough on every division so that there is always somebody available to take over a run, if necessary, and that means raising pay."

"But we're losing money!" Russell puffed out his cheeks.

"Exactly, and the only way to rectify the shortfall is to increase the mail deliveries from one a week to two. If we have enough riders, we can do it. But we also need to keep the trails clear of Indians and outlaws. Slade is our trump card, but even he cannot manage the entire two thousand mile stretch of the Overland Trail. We have other Division Superintendents of a similar caliber, if not so infamous. Bolivar Roberts, Doc Faust, Howard Egan, A.E. Lewis, to name but a few. But I think we can use this Hollister more effectively. He's wasted as just a dispatch rider."

"And he's fast making a name for himself," Russell agreed. "Big names, infamous characters, add to the company's reputation, no matter what the likes of Ficklin say. I think Ficklin's got a grudge against Slade. There was a story about how Slade had 'come back from the dead', ridden all the way from a hospital in St. Louis, full o' buckshot that the doctors daren't risk digging out, back to Horseshoe to resume his job. When he got there he found that Ficklin was in charge. Slade ran Ficklin off the Rocky Ridge, so the story goes. They're probably exaggerated, but Ficklin won't ever forgive him, he's that kind o' man."

"Hollister also has a reputation as something of a gunsmith," Majors interrupted. "I have been making enquiries about him. He rides and shoots as good as most and better than some. He's wasted as a courier."

"Meaning?" Waddell leaned forward.

"I'm going to appoint him officially as deputy to Slade. We've far from heard the last from the Paiutes. The trail has to be kept open and Hollister's the man to help Slade do that. And if," Alexander Majors began, pausing thoughtfully, "the worst does come to worst, and the law goes looking for Slade, at least there'll be somebody to take over."

"Hear, hear," Russell and Majors agreed in unison. The Rocky Ridge division was a long way away, and whatever Slade and Hollister did was no concern of theirs, pledge or no pledge.

The meeting broke up. Alexander Majors believed in the old axiom that confidence bred success. Outwardly, he had to remain confident at all times. Secretly, he had his misgivings about the future of the Pony Express.

"Oh, I see," Mollie said from the bunk where she had been lying down for most of the afternoon. Lately, she had taken to resting in the daytime. She was big and heavy with her child, even though there was still two months until her time. She was very tired.

Ben experienced a disillusionment. He had thought that Mollie would be delighted with the news that he had been made Deputy Division Superintendent of the Rocky Ridge division. As far as he knew, there wasn't another official deputy at any of the section headquarters along the entire length of the Overland. There were bonuses—he would not be riding any more relays, except in a dire emergency, and he would be able to spend more time with Mollie, and his pay had been increased by ten dollars a month.

"Don't get too excited about it, Mollie." He was hurt and angry. "I'll be home more and . . ."

"Less, probably." Her voice was subdued as she turned over to face the wall. "Slade's out ridin' every day, sometimes nights as well. The Paiute uprisin' isn't finished yet. He doesn't want it to be, and my guess is that neither do you, Ben. Yesterday Slade came back with scalps dangling from his saddle. Can't you see it?" She gave way to sobs. "It's a *killing* job they've given you, Ben. Worse'n ever it was before. That's what they're paying you to do. *To kill!*"

He had tried not to see it that way. Mollie had made sure he did. He had carved out his own reputation and now he had to live by it.

Slayer Who Rides With the Wind.

Book Three

Cursed be my tribe,
If I forgive him!

William Shakespeare
The Merchant of Venice
Act I, Scene 3

One

Mollie gave birth on March 11. Ma Moore saw to the delivery. She knew what to do because she had been through it six times herself. On two occasions, she had delivered her own baby because there had not been any other women around to help, and she wasn't goin' to have no man gawpin' where only her late husband had ever seen. It wasn't decent.

"You get back across to the station, Ben," she said, pushing him toward the cabin door when Mollie went into her final labor. "I'll send across for yuh when it's all over. We shan't be needin' yuh meantime, yuh'll only get in the way."

Ben did as he was told. You didn't argue with Ma Moore, if you had any sense.

Mollie's labor was long and difficult. She kept them waiting another six hours. Meanwhile, Ben paced to and fro in the stable, barely hearing Amos's attempts to reassure him. He meant well, but there was nothing anybody could say that would truly help. When word arrived, Ben ran for the cabin.

"It's a boy." Ma was cleaning the baby off. He certainly had healthy lungs. "Mollie's had a hard time, but she'll be all right. Don't tire her out. She needs to sleep now. An' I haven't bin informed yet what Hollister junior's name is."

"Joseph." Mollie's eyes opened and she smiled.

"Joseph Benjamin. I guess folks'll call him 'JB'."

This greatly pleased Ma Moore. Joseph Smith had led the Mormons out here. It pleased Ben, too, for a lot of reasons, but he had one he didn't let on to Mollie. He perhaps never would—because Slade was a Joseph, too. Mollie might have changed the baby's name if she had known that.

The snow had melted, and the trails were clear again. The flooding came after the thaw, but as spring advanced, the river levels dropped. Wagons and stagecoaches splashed their way across to Horseshoe station.

The rebuilding of the razed stations began in earnest. Bolivar Roberts had been appointed Division Superintendent in charge of all the stations east of Carson City. Williams's station rose from its ashes like a phoenix, but it would always be remembered as the place where the Paiute War started.

Sand Springs was rebuilt under the supervision of James McNaughton, and Reynal took over Spring Valley. There was an urgency about the work that ignored the future comforts of those who would live in and use the log buildings. They had just dirt floors and most of the furniture was wooden boxes. There was no glass in the windows, just crude shutters to fasten at night or in bad weather. There were pole bunks and benches for the occupants to sleep on.

Food supplies came by wagon from the east—cured bacon, beans, flour for baking bread, molasses, pickles, coffee beans, corn meal and dried fruit. The armories were re-stocked with the standard issue Walker Colt .44s for the riders to carry, and carbines in case the stations needed to be defended.

The Indian troubles smoldered; they had not been extinguished. Blood Arrow had taken his warriors back into the desert, and no one knew their whereabouts. It was unlikely to be the oasis encampment where Ben had been held prisoner. The Paiute chief was too cunning to risk that again. He would plan a fresh onslaught against the whites.

Detachments of cavalry came westward at frequent intervals. It seemed that Washington had finally gotten the message.

Ben was aware of an atmosphere of haste all around as

the mail deliveries were stepped up to twice a week. The initial contingent of eighty riders had been doubled, and the telegraph construction gangs were working at full speed. At Kennekuk, log chain gangs were felling and transporting elm, hickory and walnut for poles. Rolls of wire arrived by the wagonload almost daily.

There also seemed to be more stagecoaches travelling the Overland than previously. The opening up of the frontier meant that more people were trekking west. Ben wondered how the Butterfield line was faring. The Pony Express had taken the delivery of mail from them, but it now looked as though the stages preferred this route, too.

It was none of his business, though. Another few months and he would be a free man. He had made up his mind to return to gunsmithing. He already had carried out some repairs in the armories at Horseshoe and Red Butte. The carbines were ex-army, and many of them had seen considerable service and were urgently in need of maintenance. He had used the forge in the smithy at Ward's Central. It was primitive but effective.

"Look at this." Ben showed a lock spring to Draper, the blacksmith. "Metal fatigue. There's probably many more on the verge of snapping. If that happens when you're fighting for your life. It doesn't matter how much powder and shot you've got, you're unarmed. Some of the sights are bent, too, and that can put a ball a foot wide of your target, no matter how good your aim. Guns aren't getting checked over because there's nobody around who knows to carry out the work. Faulty weapons cost lives."

Draper nodded, turned back to his forge and tapped on a horseshoe.

"You need proper tools to repair guns." With some difficulty Ben straightened a sight with a hammer and checked its alignment, "Like you've got for shoein' horses. The company sees horses as their priority. Horses throw shoes, wagon and stage wheels come off, so they provide a blacksmith with the necessary tools. But they seem to think that guns just go on for ever. A lot of guns are more dangerous to the users than to their targets by what I've seen so far."

"Mebbe you should set up an' do the job for 'em." Draper withdrew a glowing wheel hub from the furnace, hammered it how he wanted it before it cooled. "Mebbe a wagon all kitted out as a workshop, travellin' the Overland."

"It's an idea," Ben mused. One day he would talk to Mollie about it. After the Pony Express was disbanded.

After Blood Arrow was dead.

Amos was clearly disturbed. When Ben rode back into Horseshoe late in the afternoon, there was no sign of the escaped slave. Ben went to stable his horse and saw the negro sitting in a dark corner beyond the hayrack.

"Mister Ben," he said, "did ya see them three guys on the trail? They wuz ridin' two blacks an' a roan."

"Yeah, I passed 'em heading for Ward's. Why?"

"They's a-lookin' fer slaves, that's what they's a-doin'."

"How do you know that?"

"I could tell. They rode in here for supplies. One o' them spotted me, said somethin' to the other two an' they all turned an' looked real hard at me. They talked. I couldn't hear what they wuz sayin', but I know it wuz about me."

"You're imaginin' things, Amos."

"No, Mister Ben, I ain't imaginin' it. Nick Wilson told me he'd seen bounty hunters at Three Crossings lookin' for runaway slaves. Nick says there wuz a young feller used to help out at Rock Creek an' he jest disappeared. Nobody knows where he's gone. One day he was there helpin' with the hosses, next mornin' he's not there. Them bounty hunters jest came an' took 'im."

Ben stiffened. It seemed that the lad he'd met had run the gauntlet of Paiutes against all the odds, after all. Maybe his question had been answered—the Indians didn't harm blacks. They might even be scared of them. It was rotten luck on the youngster, if he'd escaped the Indians only to be seized by bounty hunters.

"Well, nobody's coming to take you away, Amos," Ben promised. "Me'n Slade'll make sure of that. You work for the Pony, and it's our job to protect you. I heard talk that a lot of things are going to change."

"Like what?"

"California has opted out of the Union. It has banned slavery. A lot of folks want to declare it an independent state, but there's also a good many want to keep it as it always was. Now that Abraham Lincoln's been elected president, there could be a lot of changes. The north and south are divided. Some say it could lead to a war."

The Pony Express had delivered the news bulletin. The Union in California had received an unexpected setback. An organization known as the Knights of the Golden Circle had planned to invade Mexico to take the province of Sonora. They had banked on a north-south split and the new state joining the confederacy.

The secret had leaked. Fifty thousand guns had already been smuggled into Massachusetts for the invasion. Washington had reacted by issuing orders for the defense of the state.

The Pony Express in carrying all the top secret bulletins, had become an integral part of a threatened civil war. No longer was the government using Butterfield's Central Overland route for conveying messages. It took longer and the route was controlled by southerners who were confederate sympathizers. The risk of confidential documents falling into the wrong hands was very great.

The central route had to be the main transportation line because soon the railway would follow. A bill had been submitted to Congress to make the Overland the only official route. The Post Office had agreed to contribute $900,000.

But the bill was destined not to go through. Lincoln, although elected president, would not take office until the late spring. At the moment, James Buchanan was still president, and he was clinging to his own sympathies until the bitter end.

War clouds were gathering.

"There could be a war," Ben told Mollie that night. "Maybe sooner rather than later. It's been boiling up for some time."

Mollie was worried because she knew that if a civil war erupted, Ben would go to fight. She would not try to stop him. It was his duty. Mostly, though, she was worried about little JB. His future would depend upon the outcome of the war.

"Maybe Mr. Lincoln will be able to settle things when he becomes president," Mollie said without conviction.

"He'll settle things, all right," Ben replied. "But there's as many who won't like it as those that will. That's the trouble. We'll have a divided country whichever way things turn out. That's why a war looks likely. In the meantime, we just have to carry on with our lives and see what happens."

Ben saddled up and rode out before daybreak the next morning. These days he had a free ranging role, and seldom did he and Slade ride together. So long as Ben was out somewhere, the section boss was satisfied. Sometimes the two men did not meet up for a week or more. There were few Indians in the area, and even Slade had not brought in any scalps lately.

Ben took the eastbound trail towards Ward's Central. He rode slowly, stopping to listen frequently. There were no Indian signs. He had not expected any. Today he was after a different kind of prey.

The westbound rider thundered past him and raised a hand to acknowledge him. Later on Ben saw a stagecoach. Everything was peaceful; it was that kind of day when you didn't meet with any problems—unless you went looking for them.

The men whom Ben was hunting would not be interested

in Express men or stages. They weren't the ordinary kind of outlaws. They had a much more sinister motive. Ben guessed that they would not have ridden too far from Horseshoe, for they had no need to move with the secrecy of road agents. Nobody had any reason to be looking for them—except Ben Hollister.

A little further on, Ben turned off the trail and followed a narrow track into the woods. His nose warned him of a human presence before his eyes or ears did. He smelled woodsmoke, just a faint whiff in the gentle breeze. His thought was confirmed—these men had no reason to strike a cold camp. They would probably pass themselves off as hunters in search of game. They were hunters, all right, but their intended prey was not deer.

The smell of smoke was stronger now. Ben dismounted, tethered his horse to a tree, and crept forward. He loosened the Adams in its holster.

It wasn't long before his ears picked up the sound of voices. He moved with even greater caution, flitting from tree to tree. The voices grew louder, and he knew that his quarry was not far away. Those whom he sought had not been hard to find.

They had not posted a sentry; they saw no need to. There were three of them in the small clearing, the same men whom Ben had passed on the trail the day before: a huge redbearded man in hide clothing, a brace of revolvers stuck through a belt below the overhang of his belly; a slim, swarthy fellow whom Ben thought might have had Indian blood in his parentage; the third one was young, fresh faced, with a hairlip that gave him a sinister appearance. They were a trio of disreputables at best, criminals at worst.

Their horses were tethered close by. Two blacks and a roan. There was no doubt in Ben's mind that these were the men who had ridden in to Horseshoe station to stock up on supplies.

All the same, he could not go on Amos's suspicions and fears alone. Ben edged closer and hoped that their horses did not give him away. He held his breath when the black's head came up, but it lowered it again and continued pulling at the grass beneath the trees. It wasn't interested in strangers.

The young one reached a coffee pot off the fire and poured three mugs.

"When we movin', Red?" He asked, took a sip.

"We'll hev to wait fer dark." Red slurped his coffee noisily and he belched. "No way are we gonna get that nigga outta there in the daylight. Not with the likes o' Slade around. An' there's that other guy, too, Hollister. He looks like a runt, but I've heered what he kin do with a gun."

Ben smiled to himself. That made him feel good, coming from the likes of these ruffians. Mollie wouldn't have agreed, but she wasn't here to disagree.

"This 'un better be worth our trouble," the dark-skinned one's deep-sunken eyes flashed angrily. "Thet other . . . hundred and twenty dollars, split three ways." He spat into the fire and it sizzled. "Dollar a pound ain't hardly worth it."

"Thet's the goin' rate," Red growled. "Yuh gotta take the good with the bad in this game, an' hope the next'll be big and fat. Thet one at Horseshoe'll be worth it. Trouble, mostly, with escaped slaves is that most of 'em live rough an' keep on runnin' so's they lose weight."

"Like that young 'un." The other's hairlip curled in a sadistic grin. "Yuh heard how he squealed when I larruped 'im. Screamed an' begged for mercy. So I gave 'im another dozen lashes jest for disturbin' the peace'n quiet."

"Which mebbe lost him another pound in weight," Red snarled. "Yuh got no brains, Clip, that's yer trouble. What we need is somewhere to keep 'em and fatten 'em up afore handin' 'em over. Time ain't on our side, though. There's talk o' slavery bein' abolished and all the niggas bein' set free. But, accordin' to what they're sayin', there'll be a war over it fust. So, we jest gotta ketch as many as we kin, meantime."

Ben seethed with anger at their talk. That was when he

stepped into the clearing, the barrel of his .45 moving on to each of the three in turn.

"So you're bounty hunters!" He was aware how his voice shook as his fury seethed up out of his throat. "Scum of the worst kind. I heard you'd been looking Horseshoe over so I thought I'd take a ride out, see what it was all about."

"Yuh ain't got nothin' on us, runt," Red sneered. "Go check around fer yourself. We ain't robbed no coaches. We ain't got no niggas tied up in the bushes."

"No, because you've sold the last one you caught." Ben's hatred for these men and what they stood for was coming to the boil fast. The lad they'd sold was something special to him right now even though he had only met him once. "And the other you're after, you ain't caught yet. And you aren't going to, either."

"You're askin' fer trouble," Red's hand edged a couple of inches nearer to his belted guns. "Jest back off an' hightail it outta here while yuh still can."

The youngest of the trio panicked, grabbing for a carbine that lay on the ground close to where he was squatting. It was the move Ben was looking for. Even at the height of his fury and contempt for them, he could not have gunned them down in cold blood. That was the only difference between him and J.A. Slade.

A .45 ball disintegrated the young bounty hunter's eye, leaving a jagged bloody hole. He did not even cry out. He was dead before he hit the ground alongside the fire. His long greasy hair began to singe.

The breed was a knife man, only using a gun when absolutely necessary. He paid in full for his preference of weapons. Ben fired before the first man was even full length. The swarthy ruffian let out just one scream as his chest was smashed.

The big fellow almost made it. His gun cleared his belt, then Ben's third shot smashed his shoulder, which spun him round. His gun clattered on the ground.

Three down, but Red was still alive. He lay there, his florrid features twisted with pain. If his belly had not been in the way he might have chanced grabbing for his second revolver. No way would he have been quick enough.

"Murderer!" he hissed. "They'll hang yuh fer this, runt."

"Unlikely." Ben's final anger erupted in a mirthless laugh. "There's a good many would hang you vermin. I just got to you first. From what I overheard, if I'd lain up in wait back at the station tonight, you'd've come to me, saved me the ride. Still, it was worth it. You scum are makin' money outta poor folks who've never known anythin 'cept slavery in their lives. And I don't hold with slavery."

"They're jest niggas," Red's eyes narrowed. "Look, fellah, you must be Hollister. I heard o' you. Mebbe we kin make a deal."

"The likes o' you have tried to make deals with me before and wasted their last breath." Ben blasted the remaining bounty hunter's forehead at point blank range.

As Ben stepped back he experienced a sense of satisfaction such as he had never known before after a killing. A job well done. No remorse. No guilt. With road agents, you maybe felt a tiny grain of pity for—they might have some redeeming feature that you didn't know about . . . even Indians—except Blood Arrow—but these kind were better off dead for everybody's good.

The war against slavery had begun. Ben Hollister had fired the first shots. In the ensuing years, there would be much suffering and death before slavery was finally abolished. But, for the moment, Ben had made a good start and he was well pleased.

He knew that he would not hold back when the time came.

TWO

Seven states had seceded from the Union by the end of March, 1861. The war clouds had thickened and darkened. Civil war was only a cannon shot away.

In the New York office of the Pony Express another meeting was taking place. On the last occasion, Alexander Majors had been confident. His confidence had bred success. But it had been only temporary.

Factors beyond his control now influenced the fate of his organization. Their main rival, the Butterfield stagecoach line, was losing money faster even than the Pony Express. On the longer route, the cost of a single letter was sixty dollars. The government was subsidizing it, but they could not afford to pay Russell, Majors and Waddell's company as well. One of them would have to cease operating before very long.

War was expected to break out any day and, as the Butterfield coaches travelled through territory that had southern sympathies, it might well be captured. Washington had poured too much money into Butterfield to close it down, so they ordered that the coaches from now on must travel the Overland Trail.

"Gentlemen," Alexander Majors began, for the first time ever, averting his gaze from his two companions. The note of confidence in his voice, to which they had long become accustomed, was non-existent. "I have to inform you that we are, in effect, bankrupt."

Waddell and Russell stared in shocked disbelief. There must be some mistake.

"However," Majors began, making a supreme effort to overcome his subdued tone, "we have been offered a lifeline. We have no choice. Washington has not kept its promises. We have not been paid in full for our services, simply because they have been heavily subsidizing Butterfield's stage-coaches. That, too, is in dire straits. The only safe transportation route that remains is the Overland Trail, the shortest and fastest transcontinental route for the delivery of mail. We cannot afford to continue alone, but this country cannot afford to be without the Pony Express." His voice quavered momentarily, "Thus Butterfield is to become part of the Wells Fargo Express Company and the Pony Express is to be amalgamated with it. We shall be reimbursed in full. None of us will lose a cent, but we shall lose the Pony Express. It is some consolation that this country is not to be deprived of the fastest and finest method of carrying mail."

Russell and Waddell nodded. They said nothing because there was nothing left to say. Even under the ownership of Wells Fargo, the writing was on the wall for the Pony Express. It would only survive for as long as it took the construction gangs to complete the telegraph.

Alexander Majors hoped that his short-lived organization would be terminated with dignity, and that the telegraph would be finished before war broke out.

On April 12, 1861, Fort Sumter, once the home of Daniel Boone, was attacked by Confederate troops. Fort Sumter, named after General Thomas Sumter, a Revolutionary War hero, stood on an island in the Kanawha River. After South Carolina seceded from the Union, the southerners felt that the fort should be theirs. Their attempts to persuade Washington to hand it over to them failed.

Fort Sumter was under-manned. Major Anderson had less than a hundred troops and a paltry sixty cannons with which to defend it. Supplies were running low, but a ship carrying provisions was expected.

Without warning, a Confederate cannon signalled the siege of the fort. An incessant bombardment had followed, and the approaching supply ship was driven back. The defenders of Fort Sumter were left desperately short of men, weapons and food.

At the end of the second day's bombardment, Major Anderson surrendered Fort Sumter to the Confederates. General Beauregard, who commanded the siege, allowed a steamer to take the U.S. troops off the island. On April 15, President Lincoln issued a proclamation calling for 75,000 troops to fight the Confederacy. War had been threatening for a long time.

Now it had begun.

J.A. Slade took the news of the amalgamation of the Pony Express with Wells Fargo badly. The job of Division Superintendent of the Rocky Ridge division was the best he had ever had. He had been left to his own devices and given a free rein to kill Indians and outlaws. Wells Fargo was unlikely to allow him to continue. They had their own agents, and every one of them was accountable to the company.

The notice came via a dispatch rider, and it was terse and to the point. Wells Fargo would be the new owner of the Pony Express effective from the end of the month. Employees were invited to re-apply for their existing posts.

Slade tacked the notice up outside his office. Riders and liverymen could read it or not, as they chose. He had carried out his duty in displaying it. He would do no more.

Then he called for a saddled horse. Amos had one ready

inside of two minutes, and the road boss rode out through the gates without speaking to anybody. It was only as he crossed the river that Slade became aware of another rider following him—Ben Hollister.

J.A. Slade slowed without appearing to do so. Never in his life had he waited for any man but, for once, he was uncertain whether or not he wanted company. When he found out, he would act accordingly.

Ben drew alongside him. No greeting was exchanged and for some time they rode in silence, ignoring the other's presence.

"Looks like we won't be waiting for the telegraph now." Ben was the first to speak. "Everybody's fired, according to that notice you put up. Can't say I'm sorry. I read in a newspaper from back east, a few days ago, that Russell, Majors and Waddell looked to be going bankrupt. If you ask me, it's all a fix. Congress sold 'em down the line."

Slade gave no indication that he had heard. He wasn't the kind of man to discuss politics.

"When it costs sixteen dollars to deliver a letter, and you only get paid three dollars for it, you ain't goin' to last long, by my reckoning. Washington was aware of this, but they wouldn't increase the subsidy—like they wanted to kill off the Pony to make way for somebody else. Wells Fargo, I guess. The newspaper said that the Pony was being sued—some firm that supplied equipment hadn't been paid, so the court gave the firm all the Pony's Utah livestock as payment. I read that Russell's in trouble on his own count, too."

Slade turned his head. This time his curiosity was aroused.

"Big piece in the paper about it. Some official in Washington stole several million dollars's worth of bonds that were being held for the Indians, pending a peace treaty. Nearly nine hundred thousand dollars's worth of those bonds was found in Russell's office. He's been arrested, and he can't prove title to the bonds. Majors and Waddell are tryin' to raise bail. Maybe Russell's guilty, maybe he isn't, but when your company's gone bankrupt, things like that look real bad for you. Me, I reckon it's a plant, a frame-up, just to make sure that the Pony doesn't get up off its knees. The government won't give Russell a contract now, for sure. Seems that Senator Gwin was the main supporter of the Pony in Washington. Not any more, says the newspaper, because he was known to be for the south and in favor of slavery. I guess all this makes me not sorry that we're goin' out of business. What're you plannin' on doing, Slade?"

"Don't rightly know." Slade was strangely subdued. "But until the end o' the month I'm still Division Superintendent of the Rocky Ridge division, and nobody had better ferget that!"

Ben rode with Slade for three days. There was no sign of Indians, so the two men just kept on riding. Ben figured that perhaps the road boss was checking on his division right to the extent of his territory, a kind of farewell inspection before his contract was terminated. Slade was that kind of man, his reputation mattered most to him. He would leave word that everything was in order before he departed, just in case his successor tried to make out that it wasn't. After that, it could go to hell.

Ben and Slade made overnight stops at Three Crossings and Green River. On the afternoon of the third day they rode into Fort Halleck and checked in at Sutler's Store, an established Pony Express home station within the confines of the fort. Ben thought that the next day they would probably embark upon the long ride back to Horseshoe. But J.A. Slade was unpredictable. If he thought you were guessing on him, then he did his damnedest to out-guess you. He might decide to continue even further west in the morning, maybe pay a call on Bolivar Roberts.

In which case, Ben would go with him because it was rumored that Blood Arrow was still licking his wounds out in the desert. And Ben wasn't going to let Slade out of his sight because Slade could well have that in mind, too. The killing of Blood Arrow would be a fitting finale for the road boss to relinquish his division. It would become yet another legend.

Sutler's Store was owned by Judge W.A. Carter and leased to the Pony Express. Everybody had heard of Carter. He had been one of the first judges west of South Pass. His reputation made him a feared man among outlaws and road agents. If they were unlucky enough to be brought before him, they usually finished up on the end of a rope. The only problem was that there were too few lawmen to catch them. There was a saying that there was only one law west of Fort Laramie—Judge W.A. Carter.

Mostly, the law was enforced by vigilantes, and they had their own brand of justice, which differed little from Judge Carter's except that all too often an innocent man was hanged. It was like that in Virginia City, so Ben had heard. Henry Plummer had been elected sheriff there, but he was the leader of the worst gang of outlaws west of Salt Lake City. None challenged him. He made his own laws, frequently changing them for his own benefit. Plummer didn't send for Judge Carter when a trial was pending. The sheriff acted as judge and swore in his own jury. Afterward, he supervised the hanging. There was no other law—yet.

Judge Carter wasn't in residence at Sutler's Store when Slade and Ben rode in. Webber, the weasel-like station boss, stared apprehensively at the newcomers as they dismounted and hitched their horses.

"Jest look who's arrived, Wal," he remarked to a Pony Express rider who was making ready to take over from the westbound rider. "Damned if it ain't J.A. Slade and that sidekick o' his!"

"They're mebbe trailin' Blood Arrow," Wal Makker answered. With any luck, he would be on his way out of Sutler's within the hour. Nobody was at ease when Slade was around. You could tell that by just looking at the folks who stared from the saloon verandah. Word had it that Hollister was fast getting that way, too.

"Huh, the soldiers can't ketch up with Blood Arrow so's I don't see them two bein' any more successful," Webber sneered but kept his voice low.

"It was Slade an' a handful o' men who routed the Paiutes an' sent 'em scurryin' back to the desert. Yuh cain't take that away from Slade'n Hollister." There was reluctant admiration in Makker's tone.

"Ambushed 'em!" Webber spat. "I got no time fer injuns, can't wait fer the day when they're all either dead or rottin' on some reservation, but it don't alter the fact that Slade tricked 'em. Anybody else coulda done the same if'n they'd hit 'em at the right time an' in the right place. Any fool kin shoot injuns when they're swimmin' in the river with no-where to go and unable to fire an arrey in defense."

"Mebbe." Makker was squinting down the trail. The sooner the incoming rider arrived, the better. Just having Slade around the place was making him nervous.

Sutler's Store was crowded. It was Saturday and many of the settlers within a fifty mile radius had ridden in. After toiling six days a week, they were entitled to let off steam on one night. On the Sabbath, they either slept in or went to church and asked the Lord to forgive them their indulgence. That made it right, and they could do the same again on the following Saturday night.

Already the strains of a honkytonk piano were coming from the saloon. It was the largest building in this straggling settlement, constructed of adobe brick. The door was open and the place was starting to fill up. It looked like one helluva noisy night, Ben decided.

It was the first saloon that the two men had come upon since leaving Horseshoe. Sutler's Store was famed for its wild drinking and Judge Carter made sure that he was not around on Saturday nights. However law-abiding the region might become eventually, drunkenness would still remain a lawful pursuit. It was the fights and killings that resulted from it that were the problem.

And that, right now, was Ben Hollister's greatest concern.

"Maybe we should push on to Muddy Creek. We could be there before sundown," he suggested to Slade. "I've used it several times on overnight stops, the accommodation is better than Sutler's." That was arguable—it just didn't have a saloon.

"Sutler's is fine." Slade was already pushing his way into the saloon. He stood just inside the doorway looking for a vacant table.

There wasn't one. Until two men rose, the smaller one knocking over his chair in his haste and nervousness. It was as if he had suddenly developed a violent dislike for his drink, abandoning a half-full glass of rye whiskey. His companion paused just long enough to drain his glass before following on the heels of the first man in the direction of the door. Whatever their reason for leaving, it was an urgent one.

Ben knew the reason. Slade's reputation was synonymous with saloon fights—gunfights.

Nolan, the saloon keeper, hurried across to the empty table just as Slade pulled back one of the vacated chairs and lowered his stocky body into it.

"What'll it be, Cap'n Slade?" He was small and balding, rubbing his hands together as though he was washing them. A group of men edged away. There was now an empty space around that table.

Slade looked up, his expression was almost mild-mannered, and when he spoke his voice was cultured. To a stranger he might have been a representative of a banking corporation en route to the far west to establish new business. "Bacon and beans." His thin lips nearly smiled. "And coffee. Black, please."

Ben felt his own sigh of relief. "And I'll have the same." He picked up the fallen chair, sat down opposite Slade. Maybe tonight was going to be an exception.

J.A. Slade was no conversationalist. He ate in a manner

that befitted a gentleman, sipping his coffee in between mouthfuls. He had a lot on his mind. Ben did not attempt to interrupt his companion's thoughts.

Out of the corner of his eye Ben noticed a number of soldiers come in through the door. There was a small company based at Fort Halleck whose job it was to try to locate the whereabouts of the Paiutes in the desert, and then defeat them before they had a chance to re-group. There were whispers that it wasn't the real reason for their presence, that it was all a cover-up. Before long the south would be fighting a bloody war with the north and these troops were the beginning of an infiltration into the southern states.

Ben kept an open mind. He had a job to do, until he was informed otherwise.

Nolan appeared at the table and collected the empty plates. Slade nodded. That was the nearest to an approval anybody ever received from him. The saloon keeper was trembling so much that he almost dropped the plates.

"Whiskey." Slade spoke so low that Ben only just caught the word amid the din of the room.

Ben stiffened. Nolan seemed to recoil, recovered himself. "Yes, sir. Right away, Cap'n Slade."

"A bottle."

"A beer, please." Ben enjoyed an occasional glass. Tonight he was making a point. No way was he going to join his companion in a drunken stupor. Maybe after his beer he would leave the road boss to his whiskey and make some excuse about turning in early. You didn't stay with J.A. Slade once he started to hit the bottle.

"I always drink alone, Hollister."

Slade's words hit Ben like a pail of icy water. His initial feeling was one of relief because he didn't have to stay. The other's tone had lost its former courtesy—it was like he was barking an order to a rider in a bunkhouse. It was humiliating.

"I was going to turn in early, anyway," Ben said. That way he didn't lose face.

"Good."

The empty space around the table had filled up. The soldiers who had just arrived took the place of the settlers who had left. Ben rose from the table, began to push his way through the throng.

"Who's your friend, sodbuster?" A hand gripped Ben's arm, holding him. Somewhere, somebody laughed coarsely. It sounded forced. Trouble often began with a laugh.

"I'm Pony." Ben's face was only inches away from that of a moustached corporal. The Express rider smelled drink on the soldier's breath. "And that gentleman seated at the table happens to be the Division Superintendent of the Rocky Ridge division."

"That's Slade," a man shouted. "J.A. Slade."

"Cap'n." Somebody corrected him.

It brought forth a chorus of drunken laughter.

"You sure?" The corporal looked towards the table. Ben shook his arm free. "You mean the guy who picks off drownin' injuns?"

"S'right," the soldier from the crowd called out. "Also shoots wagon masters."

Ben tensed. Out of the corner of his eye he saw that Slade was drinking from a tumbler, tipping whiskey back as if it was beer or sarsaparilla. The road boss's cheeks had taken on a pinkish tinge. He was staring straight ahead of him as if he had not heard.

"You must be Hollister, then."

"That's right."

"A dude."

It seemed that the entire saloon laughed.

"I ride the mails." Ben fought to keep his rising anger under control. Drunken soldiers were no different from drunken homesteaders. Or drunken anybodys. Only a drunken Slade was worse.

J.A. Slade refilled his glass, drank again. The bottle on the table was a third empty.

Ben's eyes roved the soldiers. They all carried guns. At least, he supposed they did, because their holsters flaps were fastened down, army style. They were not trained to draw fast. The military concentrated on marksmanship skills. Soldiers weren't good saloon fighters.

Ben hesitated. If this had started after he had left, his conscience would have been clear. That way he wouldn't have walked out on Slade.

"A dude on horseback, huh!" The laughter came again, even louder. "Mind you don't get throwed. Or else jest fall off."

"I was on the point of leaving." Ben tried to sound casual. "Captain Slade prefers to drink alone."

"*I'm* gonna drink with him." The corporal pushed past Ben, made his way across the room toward the vacant chair. "It's unsociable to let a man drink alone. Bad manners. Ain't that right . . . *Captain* Slade?" He lowered himself into the chair, pulled the whiskey bottle towards him.

"*Leave it!*" J.A. Slade's words were like crackling lightning, the forerunner of a mighty electrical storm.

Both men gripped the bottle. The soldier took the strain, amber liquid sloshed. They stared at each other. Slade's cheeks had gone from pink to scarlet, his lips were a compressed slit. He held on and did not speak.

"I'm gonna drink with yuh," the corporal's speech was slurred. The soldiers had been drinking in their quarters—the saloon was where they had come looking for trouble. "Only polite. We're fightin' these redskins together, ain't we? Only difference, we shoot 'em in the front, fair'n square. You ketch 'em swimmin' in the river or else shoot 'em in the back!"

Suddenly there was silence in the room, except for the creaking of the swinging door where somebody had just left. A haze of tobacco smoke dimmed the lighting. Nobody moved or spoke. Everybody just watched, including Ben.

The corporal exerted all his strength. His knuckles whitened around the swilling whiskey bottle and the veins in his forehead corded. He was breathing heavily, grunting.

J.A. Slade held his ground. The bottle moved not an inch. His features were impassive, not revealing the strain. He was not even breathing fast.

Everybody in the room was hypnotized by the scene before them. Soldiers and settlers craned their necks to see over and around one another. There had to be an outcome soon. Surely, one of the contestants must tire.

Then, without warning, Slade's fingers opened. The bottle was not wrested from his grasp, he let it go. It shot forward with a fountain of spirit that drenched the corporal as he was flung backward. His chair overbalanced, he went over the back of it and sprawled on the boarded floor. The whiskey bottle rolled, leaving a trail of alcohol in its wake, and bumped against the wall.

The soldier just lay there, bewildered, his expression one of utter disbelief. It took him several seconds to realize what had happened.

Everybody began to laugh. It was the corporal's turn to be humiliated. He had insulted J.A. Slade, but it was he who had been made to look a fool in front of his own men.

"You owe me a fresh bottle," Slade said evenly and quietly, only raising his voice to call "Bartender!"

"Why, you . . ." The corporal staggered to his feet, swayed and almost fell over. His features were livid with fury. "If you think you kin make a fool o' me, Slade, an' . . ."

His fingers flipped the flap on his holster. Ben tensed, his eyes flicking to Slade, anticipating that lightning draw, the Army .44 whipped from its high slung holster and fired with deadly accuracy, all in the same movement, a blur too fast for the eye to follow.

Instead, Slade's arm remained outstretched across the table, exactly how it had been since he released his hold on the bottle. He made no move to go for his gun but, for those who had seen it before, there was no mistaking the "killing look" on his broad features.

Ben might just have drawn in defense of his companion. If any of those who stood watching had made a move to help their fellow soldier, he most certainly would have. But nobody did. Ben watched, transfixed, not understanding.

The raging corporal had his gun clear of his holster before Slade drew and shot him— A sharp crack and a puff of powder-smoke. The soldier jerked upright, his back arched. His unfired weapon fell from his nerveless fingers and clattered to the floor. Then he fell forward on to his face, and lay motionless.

All eyes centered on J.A. Slade. His .44 was still holstered, his arm was still extended across the table. But in the deathly white fingers of that outstretched hand, if you looked closely enough, you just made out the tiniest of pistols, from the stubby barrel of which came a faint trickle of smoke.

"Gawd Almighty!" A homesteader at the back of the crowd put everybody's thoughts into words, and enlightened any who might not have seen through the forest of bodies. "He shot 'im with a sleeve gun!"

It was true enough. Ben saw for himself and understood. Slade returned the small weapon to his sleeve. The pistol was a Derringer .22 Colt No. 4, a model which had been launched a few months prior to the formation of the Pony Express. Ben recognized the all-metal frame which enabled the barrel to pivot open.

Slade had probably carried it all the time, but this was the first occasion he had had to use it in Ben's presence. A sleeve gun, as opposed to one carried in a shoulder holster the way many of the passengers travelling on the stagecoaches habitually concealed a small pistol. Nobody would ever have thought of searching a sleeve when disarming a victim. It was a trick the Chinese used. Ben had read about it once. Maybe Slade had, too.

"Barman." Slade did not need to raise his voice, a whisper

would have been sufficient in that room full of stunned on-
lookers. "A fresh bottle of whiskey. Charge it to the U.S.
Army at Fort Halleck. They can take it out of what they
won't have to pay this bum."

Nolan brought another bottle on the run. He was shaking
uncontrollably, as though he suffered from the ague. Slade
poured himself a shot with steady fingers, gulped it down.
He refilled his glass before he spoke.

"Anybody got anythin' to say?" His grey eyes roved the
entire room, burning into every man looking on.

Nobody had.

"Yuh better take him with yuh." Slade's hand rested on
his .44 as he eyed the group of soldiers. "Yuh all saw him
draw on me, so don't any man get sayin' he didn't. Or
else . . ." He tapped the butt of his gun meaningfully.

Then he went back to his whiskey and drank steadily. He
did not even turn to watch the soldiers carrying the limp body
of the corporal out through the door. Slade's cheeks were
flushed. Anybody who stayed around was likely to get shot,
too.

Ben left with the last of the would-be revellers, and walked
slowly across to the bunkhouse. Sleep was impossible; he
lay tossing and turning, listening to the various comings and
goings outside. Waiting. For what, he dared not even guess.

The door opened and closed many times. The bunks filled
up, but there was no sign of Slade.

Ben was tempted to get up and look outside to see if there
was still a light burning in the saloon. But it would not have
made any difference. Sometime toward dawn, he drifted into
an exhausted, uneasy sleep.

When he awoke it was full daylight. He rose, dressed hur-
riedly, and went across to the stable. His horse munched hay
contentedly, but there was no sign of Slade's mount.

"Musta come'n fetched his hoss sometime durin' the

night," the liveryman said, reading Ben's thoughts as he busied himself filling a water trough. "Anyways, his hoss was gone at daybreak. Mebbe it's jest as well on account o' what he gone an' done last night. The army won't stand fer Slade shootin' their soldiers, not when they need every man they got to fight the injuns. Or the southerners."

Ben turned away. Slade hadn't run. He didn't run from any man, not even the U.S. Army. More likely he'd ridden on to wherever he'd had a mind to go all along. He had let Ben ride with him this far, but from now on, he didn't want anybody stringing along with him. Because wherever Slade was headed, he wanted to be alone.

Ben stood staring out across the flatlands to the north, to where a shimmering haze rose as the day began. That was where the desert started. Where the Paiutes were hiding out.

Where Blood Arrow was.

Slade had ditched his partner when it suited him, and he had ridden on. Another niggling thought furrowed Ben's forehead. Slade's days as Division Superintendent with the Pony Express were numbered. Not just the army, but the law, too, might be hunting him from now on.

J.A. Slade might just have killed once too often. He had shot down a man at Sutler's Store. And Sutler's was owned by Judge W.A. Carter, who was determined that from now on there was going to be law west of Fort Laramie.

As far as the eye could see, this was Judge Carter's land. There would be no hiding place for Slade this time.

Ben walked back towards the stable to fetch his horse. There was nothing to keep him here any longer.

Three

Unbelievably, the Pony Express continued to run without any major changes. Employees had not been paid off. Their money came through regularly, and the relays operated fully. Nobody knew whether they were working for Wells Fargo or Russell, Majors & Waddell. Perhaps changes had not filtered out beyond St. Joseph yet. In the meantime, everybody carried on as before.

J.A. Slade was in charge of the Rocky Ridge division. His headquarters were still at Horseshoe station and neither lawmen nor soldiers had come looking for him.

Ben wondered where the road boss had gone after he had ridden out of Sutler's Store that day. It seemed that he had returned to Horseshoe. Maybe just did not want company on the ride so he had left Ben to follow.

"I was hoping you'd be staying home from now on," Mollie said as she fed young JB at her bosom. "That maybe things would be different with Wells Fargo running the Pony Express."

"Right now nobody knows for sure who their paymaster is," Ben replied, "but it won't be long before I'm kicking my heels around here. They reckon the telegraph will be operating all the way from St. Joseph to Sacramento by the autumn."

"Which is still four months away."

"Well, we're all ready, whenever they decide to disband

the Pony." He stood on the porch looking out across an acre of land which he had tilled with a plough borrowed from Sam Eden, their nearest homesteader. The crops were growing well in the virgin soil, mostly potatoes and sweet corn. Before next spring he would cultivate another acre, leave the rest for grazing. He had already made a start on putting up a post and rail fence. He had ordered a small forge from St. Louis and it might arrive on the next supply wagon. Then he would be ready to start gunsmithing. Between the crops and the guns, they would get by.

But he had not forgotten Blood Arrow. He never would. The hatred, the desire for revenge, still smoldered within him.

"Why are you riding the mails again?" Mollie put JB back in his cradle and fastened her plaid blouse. "I thought you were Slade's deputy?"

"Because they're short on riders. From what I hear, they hired extra men to double the relays, but they sacrificed quality for numbers. A lot of those who signed on couldn't make the grade. So the company has to keep up a twice weekly schedule, from St. Joseph to Sacramento, relying on the best of the riders who stuck with 'em. I gotta do the run to Rock Creek tomorrow. I'll be back the next day."

"Unless a rider falls sick." Her tone was resentful, "Or gets shot by outlaws or injuns."

"Injuns are pretty quiet lately," he said and unfolded a newspaper which had arrived from back east only that morning, a flimsy broadsheet carried by the Pony Express riders. "Hmm!" He became engrossed in his reading.

"Something interesting?" She wasn't really interested. She felt ignored.

"Maybe this is why we haven't been paid off yet and given Wells Fargo briefings. We already know that Russell was jailed after a stack of stolen bonds was discovered in his office," Ben was scanning the columns of tiny print on the front page. "The Pony was losing money fast but, apparently,

Russell managed to get a last minute stay, a part subsidy of a hundred and sixty thousand dollars from Floyd, the Secretary of War. They were buddies, so it looks like Floyd pulled some strings. Russell's now been released and isn't going to stand trial. Now, this is really interestin' . . . Bailey, the guy who stole the bonds, was married to Floyd's second cousin, and Bailey has sworn that Russell only borrowed the bonds. Bailey might go to jail for misappropriation of government funds, but it puts Russell in the clear because he borrowed the bonds in good faith."

"It stinks of corruption," Mollie said.

"Maybe, maybe not. But it seems that at the moment Majors, with a part subsidy in the bank, is holding on to the Pony. The paper reckons that he's got to sell to Wells Fargo because Congress had already ordered it. But Majors is fightin' it. Congress is holding fire. The last thing they want right now is a scandal involving the Secretary of War when there's a war just starting. I'd say Majors will probably manage to hold out for another month or so. We'll see." He refolded the newspaper and tossed it on to the table.

"Roll on the telegraph." Mollie got up and put some potatoes on the stove to boil.

Ben made it to Rock Creek without incident. The station had been rebuilt and was much larger, an untidy conglomeration of log buildings which comprised a saloon, store and separate bunkhouse all inside a palisade. The suppliers recognized its potential. One day it would become a small town on the busy Overland Trail.

Horace Wellman was station boss, a rawboned ex-Butterfield stagecoach guard whom Ben had first met during his own stage driving days.

"Yuh'll hev to ride to Dry Sandy in the mornin'." Wellman greeted him, rubbing his angular chin. "Word's jest come through that Stap Bolman's fell off his hoss and broke a leg."

Ben nodded. That was okay by him. It would only delay his return to Horseshoe by half a day or so.

The station master's expression became one of concern. "An' there's injuns west o' here. Weeks without trouble an' now it looks like it's all startin' up agin. Allus said the Paiutes weren't licked proper. There's some poles bin chopped down and the wire stolen. Tell Slade when yuh get back to Horseshoe."

"I'll maybe take a ride out and see for myself when I've delivered the mails." It was part of his job; he was still Deputy Division Superintendent, and he sure wasn't going to go running to Slade every time there was a problem. "Blood Arrow?" He tensed expectantly.

"Could be, don't know fer sure. Sam Walters was chased by a war party. He said there were breeds with 'em and some of 'em had guns. Wild shootin', didn't hit nothin' they aimed at."

"Sounds like Brent's gang. They've been lying low for some time, probably holed up with the Paiutes, wherever they've been hiding."

"They talk 'bout closin' down the Pony as soon as the telegraph's finished." Wellman chewed, spat a stream of tobacco juice. "If'n you ask me, that telegraph'll never be workin'. There'll allus be some injuns choppin' down the poles an' stealin' the wire. This country can't manage without the Pony. Nobody else'll deliver mail cross country inside ten days. New-fangled contraptions!" He spat again. "They'll never learn!"

Ben rested on his bunk, dozed for a couple of hours. Then he was fully awake and had thoughts only for Blood Arrow. Maybe he wouldn't have to go searching the desert for the Paiute chief. Blood Arrow would come to him.

Ben was restless. Since he had been riding relays again, he had adapted to short sleep periods. There was no way he would sleep the night through until it was time to ride again.

He went outside. It was dark, the only light came from the saloon opposite. Voices were raised. Saloons were always noisy places.

There were half-a-dozen men inside the saloon. Ben stood in the doorway eyeing them. Wellman was at the bar engaging in a heated argument with a tall, swarthy man in worn and greasy buckskins. The station boss was clearly angry, shaking a finger.

Saloon quarrels were none of Ben's business. He wasn't going to get involved. His eyes roved the room. Two liverymen drank beers in a corner, they were listening to the argument with interest.

Ben's gaze settled on a stranger seated by himself in the opposite corner. There was something about the other that set him apart from the average homesteader or Pony Express employee. His clothing, for a start. The hide leggings and fringed jacket were worn and dusty, but they were of a quality that bespoke eastern tailoring, fringed and cut to fit, washed regularly so that they had faded a little.

The wearer was clean, too, like he had washed and groomed his shoulder length hair before coming here to eat. He had the finest head of corn gold hair that Ben had ever set eyes on, and that included women. But this man was no fancy dude. That much was evident by his twin revolvers, holstered with their butts reversed. A cross-draw man. Ben was curious. A gunfighter, possibly, or a bounty hunter. Or maybe one who earned his living at the card tables and made enemies doing it. At a rough estimate the stranger was twenty-four or twenty-five, give a year or two.

The man looked up and his gaze met Ben's, a half smile between the neatly trimmed moustache and the goatee beard. A slight nod, an acknowledgment, and he went back to his food. Like Ben, he was a man who minded his own business, but he noted everything that went on around him. He gave the impression that he wasn't one to tangle with.

Ben moved to the bar and got his beer. Now he was only a couple of yards away from Wellman. The quarrel was heating up.

"You get off my station, McCanles," Wellman began to shout. "Ride on an' don't never show yer face here agin!"

"You pay me fer that load o' hay an' I'll go." McCanles's face was dark with fury. He stepped back from the bar. His legs were slightly apart and he bent forward in a menacing crouch. His hand moved close to the gun that was stuck behind his belt. "I don't go from here till I bin paid."

"Hay!" Wellman laughed. "You got the nerve to call that junk *hay!* Some hay, not a lot, mixed up with brushwood in the hope that we wouldn't notice. The stablemen didn't but the hosses sure did!"

"You callin' me a cheat, Wellman?"

"Sure am." Wellman's hands were still resting on the bartop. "Me, the stablemen, an' the hosses 'cause they're the ones that went hungry."

McCanles tugged for his revolver. He was no gunfighter, just a trail drifter who made a fast dollar any way he saw how. Perhaps the draw was merely intended as a threatening gesture. That was something which the occupants of the Rock Creek saloon that night would never know.

A shot rang out. McCanles jerked upright and his gun fell from his grasp. For a moment he stood there at full stretch, his expression of shocked disbelief becoming one of agony. But his pain was only brief, he was dead before he hit the boards. He fell on his back, arms flung wide, his buckskin shirt beginning to saturate with blood from the wound that went right through to his heart.

Ben froze. For a second or two he thought that it was Horace Wellman who had fired, but the station master's hands were still on the bar. Maybe he carried a sleeve gun like Slade. But there was no sign of a Derringer.

Ben turned slowly, in such situations one never made a sudden movement. It might be misunderstood.

The stranger at the far table had a smoking gun in one hand, a fork with a chunk of meat speared on the prongs in the other.

"He'd've gunned you down for sure," the man said softly, giving the instant impression that he had gone the whole way through schooling. He could probably read and write, too. He could certainly shoot. "Trail trash. Nobody'll miss him, but I'd sure be obliged if somebody would be kind enough to bury him for me. I don't have any working clothes with me."

"We'll see to 'im in the morning." Horace Wellman had paled, the realization of how close he had been to death was just dawning on him. "He might've cost the Pony the price of a wagonload o' hay that was mostly brushwood, if the hosses hadn't been a might smarter'n him. Thanks, mister, I'm much obliged to yuh."

The stranger holstered his gun and returned to his meal. Ben took a long swallow of beer. It tasted sour. He wished that he had stayed in the bunkhouse.

"That's a fine looking gun you're toting, mister." Ben's professional eye had appraised the well-dressed man's weapon even in the midst of violent death. It was undoubtedly a .44 and a brand new one at that. Even at a glance from a distance it looked sleeker and sturdier than the Colts which most folks carried in these parts. The other's second gun was identical, probably purchased as a pair.

"Remingtons," the stranger said through a full mouth, "Forty-fours but lighter to handle, and more accurate than Colts. New model. Army issue. That's where I got 'em. Mebbe they ain't got out this far west yet but they will, I guarantee. Walkers are good but they've had their day, unless Colt can improve on 'em." He made no move to offer his guns for inspection. Out west a man kept them in easy drawing distance at all times.

Ben noticed that the guns were cap and ball percussion models. Even Remington had not beaten him to a cartridge firing gun—yet. It would come, though.

"You're army, then?" Ben made it sound casual. Out here men did not take kindly to being asked their business. It was an unwritten code that you didn't enquire. For all Ben knew, this man might have killed a soldier and stolen those revolvers.

"Uh-huh." Which was almost an admission to being on the U.S. Army payroll.

"Army's done a good job." A white lie would not come amiss, Ben thought. "Paiutes are on the run."

"Scattered, not running. They'll re-group, launch one final onslaught in an attempt to overthrow the whites. Won't do no good, but they'll try. My job is to find out where the Paiutes are holed up, what their strength is, what they're plannin'. If it's ever possible to guess what an injun's plannin'."

"Scoutin', huh?"

"Yep. And I'm also plannin' to keep this." He brushed his long golden hair with his free hand. "Grew my hair like this on purpose. The Cheyenne and the Arapaho want my scalp real bad, but they ain't got it yet. Mebbe the Paiutes'll feel the same way when they see it. It won't do 'em no good, though." He laughed.

There was something that Ben disliked about this stranger, a character trait that marred everything else that was good in him. Conceit and arrogance. The killing had not even interrupted his meal. He had eaten through it, almost nonchalantly. Cold blooded. Only J.A. Slade could have equalled him, both in his indifference to death and his marksmanship. There was very little to choose between the two of them.

Here, truly, was another Man Who Likes Killing.

Ben didn't ask the other's name. Names were personal out here, like guns and horses. A man called himself whatever he liked.

"Good night." Ben turned towards the door, gave one look back.

"Sleep well." The stranger did not look up, he was too busy scraping his plate clean with a hunk of rye bread.

* * *

Ben was up early the following morning. He ate breakfast and made ready for his westbound ride to Dry Sandy. As he watched for the incoming rider, Horace Wellman approached him.

"Keep an eye out for injuns." The station boss looked as though he had not slept much. It was small talk—everybody looked out for Indians. "He left before daylight. Guess he's lookin' out fer injuns, too. He's paid to."

"Army scout, I reckon."

"In between gamblin' an' killin'. An' hell-raisin'. Hey!" Wellman's eyes widened. "You tellin' me, Hollister, you don't know who that guy is?"

"Never set eyes on him before last night. Got a fine pair of guns, though."

"Purty's the word where he's concerned. Everythin' about him's fancy. Hand tailored clothes, silver spurs, even washes twice a day! A real dandy. But nobody's ever outshot him. He boasts about it, but it's gotta be true 'cause he's still walkin'. He shot McCanles last night, but it weren't meant as no favor to me. Jest another tally fer him to brag about."

Ben squinted against the morning sunlight. There was a dust cloud down the trail to the east. It was time to go.

"Yeah, but *who* is he, Horace?"

"Lord, can't get over a fellah like you not knowin'. That guy applied to be a Pony rider once. They turned 'im down. Too heavy. Offered him a stockman's job. That's rich!" He laughed. "He went scoutin' fer the army instead. Boy, that's Hickok. They gotta name fer him that fits everythin' he does, wherever he goes. Folks've named him 'Wild Bill'."

Four

Ben was watchful as he rode, as wary as he had ever been. Everywhere was quiet. Too quiet, that was the trouble. If there had been a smoke signal or two in the hills, then he might just have been that bit extra alert.

Not that it would have made any difference when an ambush had been carefully laid before daylight. A dozen Paiute warriors, led by their scalp-lusting chief and a white renegade, waited at the end of a narrow canyon for the first relay rider through.

There was no sign of either Indian or renegade. No sound to warn an oncoming rider. There were no mustangs tethered nearby to make a snort or a snicker. Nothing at all.

Somehow Ben survived the hail of arrows and bullets. At the last second his horse sensed danger, reared just as the ambushers opened fire, becoming an equine shield for its rider. Ben reacted instantly, diving even as the animal died beneath him and rolling for cover.

At least that gave him a fighting chance.

A bullet glanced off a rock, showered him with splinters. A .54, without a doubt, there was no way he would have crawled away if that ball had found its mark. That was Brent, surely.

Ben had a fleeting glimpse of his attackers amid the scattered rocks. A feathered head-dress ducked from view. He had not seen the face beneath it but did not need to. He knew

Blood Arrow was here, leading a war party out of the desert and their first strike against the hated whites was to be a lone rider. Like the "blooding" at an English fox hunt, one sought an early kill, and the hounds bayed for more blood.

It should have been Stap Bolman, but he had fallen and broken his leg. That had saved his life. Now fate was playing the hand that Ben Hollister had prayed for over these last few months and had thrown him face-to-face with Blood Arrow. This could be the final encounter between the two, the ultimate clash between red and white. Only one of them would leave here alive. And the way the odds were stacked right now, it was unlikely to be Ben.

Some of the halfbreeds were using carbines. Bullets whined, the air was heavy with the acrid stench of powder-smoke, but so long as Ben kept under cover, only an unlucky ricochet was likely to score a hit. Boulders were a far better protection than trees and bushes.

So far he had not fired a shot, but it was a stalemate. He was outnumbered, surrounded on three sides and there was a sheer rock face behind him. He wondered how long it would be before his attackers decided to make a long detour and come upon him from behind and above. It might be a trek of several miles to approach him from the rear. They might try that as a last resort, probably after nightfall.

In the meantime, Ben had nowhere to go. He had a full canteen of water and a pocketful of biscuits. His ambushers had time on their side, especially when his water ran out. His carbine was still booted on the dead horse, it would have meant instant death to try to retrieve it. He didn't need it, though, his handguns were sufficient. Both the .45 and the .36 were fully loaded and he carried a spare cylinder for each. He could not afford to waste shots.

The sun rose higher in the sky and the day became unbearably hot. Fortunately, the cluster of rocks, behind which Ben crouched, were shaded by the cliff behind. All the same, he sweated.

After the first couple of volleys from the Indians and renegades, there was a deathly silence. It stayed unbroken. For all Ben knew the Paiutes and the halfbreeds might have crept away. He knew they had not, though. They were masters of concealment. Blood Arrow was unaware who they had ambushed. A rider unskilled in Indian warfare might have panicked, tried to shoot his way out and ended up resembling a porcupine. Ben knew better. It was a waiting game on both sides, and the one whose patience ran out ended up dead.

Ben recalled the last time when he had found himself in a similar situation. Then he had been aloft in the boughs of a tall tree which had given him an advantage over the Indians. This time there was nothing but rocks all around.

His train of thought lead to J.A. Slade. The chances of the road boss showing up this time were negligible. If Slade wasn't a fugitive himself already, he soon would be. You didn't kill a soldier and get away with it. Judge Carter would see to that, Ben thought. He would issue a warrant for Slade's arrest the moment the news reached his ears. The Division Superintendent had enjoyed a breathing space since leaving Sutler's Store only because warrants took time to serve. But one day the law would come for him.

Ben decided that his only hope was nightfall. That would even things up considerably. The Paiutes would try to sneak up on him and he would attempt to crawl away unseen. But his chances were slim. His horse was dead and, even if he managed to escape from this canyon, he was faced with a twelve-mile walk to Dry Sandy.

The mochila was still on his dead horse. He could not leave without the mails. Probably Blood Arrow and Brent knew that and they would be lying with their weapons trained on the dead animal. Everybody waited for somebody to make the first move.

* * *

It was sometime during the late afternoon when Ben's ears picked up a faint rumble. The atmosphere was humid, and his first thought was that it was distant thunderstorm. But the noise was unbroken, a continual roll that was becoming louder with each passing second.

The sound was tantalizingly familiar. He had heard it often but not under these circumstances. Suddenly, he knew and his body oozed additional sweat at the realization. It was the Overland stage from Carson City. It would run right into the Indian ambush. Even speed would not get the coach through because Ben's dead horse was blocking the trail! The crew would need to move it before they could continue their journey. They wouldn't stand a chance—they would be cut down.

Unless, somehow, Ben could warn them first.

There wasn't much time— He made his decision. The moment he heard the stagecoach approaching the canyon, he would leap to his feet and come out of this rock strewn landslip with guns blazing. He would be mown down by a hail of arrows and bullets, but at least the shots would warn the coach. The driver would swing around, head back for Dry Sandy station. With luck, he would make it. It was Ben's duty, and he would not shirk it. By sacrificing his own life, he would probably save several.

The roll of iron on stone grew louder by the second. Ben had ridden this stretch of the trail many times before, and in his mind he logged the coach's whereabouts. It was maybe still a third of a mile from the canyon entrance. The land was flat and open there, mostly scrubland, bushes and stunted trees. Shortly the trail would narrow, the surface would be solid rock from thereon. He would be able to tell the moment the wheels were on it, a grinding sound rather than a rumbling one. That was when he needed to warn the crew, before they entered the canyon itself where there would be no room to turn.

Ben braced himself. He had only an outside chance of survival. He preferred to think of it like that rather than to accept the sheer impossibility of coming out of this alive. While there was life, there was hope. He must leap the rocks at a run, weave and zig-zag, firing as he went. He had to get as many shots off as possible. If there was no gunfire, and the Paiutes dropped him with arrows, his sacrifice would be in vain.

He listened intently. There were about ten seconds to go. He began a countdown. Blood Arrow was somewhere out there, if Ben could only get him with one of his shots . . . His thoughts ran riot as he counted.

Seven. He would never see Mollie and JB again, that was what hurt most.

Six. "Watch out fer injuns." Horace Wellman had warned him.

Five. Ben hadn't watched good enough.

Four.

That was when the shooting started, when the stagecoach was probably still a hundred yards off the flat rock beyond the canyon entrance.

Ben tensed. He heard the double blast of the guard's shotgun, then a rifle. The driver carried one on the box. A staccato roll of revolver fire.

Then whooping and hollering. A splintering crash told Ben that the coach had overturned. The rest was almost impossible to follow by ear in the ensuing din. In his mind Ben saw the coach on its side, wheels still spinning, the horses dead in their traces, and Paiutes swarming and murdering crew and passengers.

Ben felt physically sick. The Indians had out-thought him. Some of them had slipped away, laid their own ambush in the scrubland beyond the canyon, rather than wait for the stagecoach to get this far where Ben's guns might have given a warning.

Ben had been ready to go, every muscle in his small, wiry body tensed to springboard him on a shoot-and-die run. Now he held back, there was nothing left to die for. He thought

of Mollie and JB again . . . and Blood Arrow who was still
out there somewhere. Staying alive had become Ben's priority once again.

Blood Arrow had squatted impassively alongside Brent
these past few hours, an arrow notched in his bow. For the
Paiute chief had caught a brief glimpse of the rider who had
leaped and rolled when he should have died from a score of
wounds. It was Slayer Who Rides With the Wind, and any
warrior who slew him would face a lingering, agonizing
death. Blood Arrow had warned his braves, they would not
lose a single arrow until after their chief had fired his. Neither would Brent and his renegades let off a rifle shot.

Blood Arrow's hatred for the small white warrior had sim-
mered to a boil. This, truly, was the Day of Reckoning for
which he had waited so long. Soon this most coveted scalp
would adorn his lodge and he would become the mightiest
chieftain of all the tribes. Only then would his warriors sweep
down upon the white invaders. Blood Arrow prayed to the
Great Father that he would be victorious this day. Man Above
would not desert him.

If possible, Blood Arrow decided, he would shoot to
wound, to disarm, so that his most hated enemy could be
taken alive. There were still ants in that mighty mound on
the edge of the oasis in the desert.

Slayer Who Rides With the Wind's living skeleton would
writhe and scream. And die. Eventually.

First, though, he would be scalped for, afterward, there
would be no scalp.

Not a muscle of his face moved with his thoughts. He
remained perfectly motionless, for to show emotion, or to
fidget, was a waste of energy. There was no hurry, he wanted
to savor every second. If need be, he would remain here until
Slayer Who Rides With the Wind was weak from thirst and

starvation. Blood Arrow, himself, would not succumb to such human frailties. He was a warrior of the desert.

His foe had slain the squaw they had denied a name. That, in itself, was no loss, for white women captives were plentiful in this land. You either took one, or traded for one. No-Name's death gave no cause for mourning. It was the humiliation of her death at the hand of Slayer Who Rides With the Wind that had hurt Blood Arrow most.

It would be dark in an hour or so, and Ben knew that he had to make his move then. In all probability, the Indians and renegades would be anticipating it, but he could not remain here until morning. It was preferable to go down fighting than to be slain like a beaver in a hunter's trap. The sun dipped down behind the steep cliffs. The shadows lengthened.

It would soon be time to go.

So quiet. Not so much as a breeze moaned through the twisting canyon. Ben could almost have convinced himself that his ambushers had left, that they were content with the loot and scalps from the stagecoach. But he knew better.

And then the first shot split the sultry silence.

Ben flattened himself against a rock, he knew instinctively that the shot had been fired from up above. So his enemies had made the long detour, after all, in order to get behind him and pick him off. Yet the ball did not splinter rock or ricochet anywhere near him. That was puzzling—even atrocious Paiute shooting would only have been a yard or two wide of the intended mark. Ben hugged the only cover that was available to him. Even so, he presented a sitting target to whoever was up there on the cliff top.

Another shot rang out. Then a couple more in quick succession. Whoever it was, they were using a handgun, probably a .44.

A scream came from not far away. Then cursing. The gunfire was returned by the hidden ambushers, bullets chipped splinters of rock from the high cliff face.

Ben was bewildered. The mysterious sniper could easily have picked him off. But the other had ignored him. *He was shooting at the Paiutes and renegades instead.*

It *had* to be J.A. Slade. It could not be anybody else, Ben decided, as he twisted around and looked up. He glimpsed a silhouette, no more, somebody lying flat on the summit of the canyon side in order to make as small a target of himself as he fired downwards.

Another cry came from amid the boulders opposite Ben. He heard a body fall on the landslip slope, roll and start an avalanche of small stones. It thudded against a rock and did not move again.

Two down. At least.

Ben raised his head slowly and cautiously. He spotted a halfbreed looking up, temporarily distracted by the gunfire from on high.

The Adams barked, the heavy .45 ball found its mark, shattering the forehead just below the greasy headband. The renegade slumped and did not move again. Ben ducked. He was just in time; a carbine ball whined off the rock behind where his head had been only a second earlier.

Suddenly, the ambushers were caught up in their own trap. There was scant protection from this aerial hail of lead. There were neither trees nor bushes that might have offered concealment. They were vulnerable amid the scattered rockfall.

Paiutes jumped up from their hiding places, ran and leaped like deer. Shots whined all around them. And then Ben was kneeling up, taking them from the rear as they fled.

Another brave crumpled and fell, a renegade staggered. Their only hope was to make it out of the canyon, but their retreat exposed them to the gunfire from above and below. Ben estimated that there were about twenty of them, Paiutes and half-a-dozen or so renegades.

The guy had to be Brent—he was cursing his renegades,

calling them "yaller dawgs." Ben swung on to him, lined him up. He had just one shot left in the .45, he could not afford to miss. His deliberation deprived him of his kill. A shot rang out from up behind him, and the renegade leader slumped with a ball in the back of his head.

"Damn you, Slade!" Ben yelled his frustration.

It was Slade up there, wasn't it? It had to be. Nobody else could shoot like that—except maybe Ben Hollister.

Ben dropped another running brave with his last shot, ducked down to change the cylinder. When he looked up he saw an Indian standing atop a boulder, drawing back his bow, contemptuous of the danger that threatened from above.

It was no ordinary Paiute. Everything about the brave was majestic, awe-inspiring to behold. Ben caught his breath, he sensed the evil that transcended tribal chieftainship, that of a primeval predator, features that might have been cut from stone, sculpted in the ultimate malevolence.

Only Blood Arrow's eyes reflected his hatred and bloodlust for the one his people called Slayer Who Rides With the Wind. His stance was that of a statue, not a muscle quivered as he drew his bowstring back to its fullest extent. He savored this moment of vengeance. Even the scalping of his victim would not be carried out in a frenzy.

Ben's gaze met Blood Arrow's and he froze in the act of reloading. The .36 was spent, too. Ben did not have a shot left to fire. The Paiute had stayed while his warriors and the renegades had fled. He had chosen his moment to kill with cunning and precision. He neither gloated nor taunted as he took careful aim. His only thought was to put an arrow in Slayer Who Rides With the Wind. He would pick his mark, disarm the other. Only afterward would he kill. Slowly. Then he would give free rein to his emotions.

In those few seconds that seemed an eternity, Ben resigned himself to death. He prayed that it would be swift. This was the encounter which he had pursued for so long and it would end with his own death. Sarah would go unavenged.

It was the way things had worked out. Fate had decreed that he should die. The Paiutes might have starved him out or over-run him. Or captured him as he tried to escape under cover of darkness. Just when things had seemed hopeless, J.A. Slade had come to his rescue. It would be to no avail. That was the cruellest blow of all.

Ben stared head-on at the tip of the arrow. He drew himself up, at least he would not give Blood Arrow the satisfaction of seeing him cringe and beg for mercy.

The bowstring twanged. Ben saw it go slack. He felt a rush of air past his face. He heard the missile strike the rock face behind him, bounce and clatter on the canyon floor.

It was impossible, unbelievable! An Indian boy under instruction could not have missed at that range. *Yet Blood Arrow had fired his arrow well wide of his target.*

Ben stood there, not understanding, looking for reasons. It was a hallucination brought on by the long hot hours. Or a trick of the shadows. The arrow behind him had been fired as a parting shot by one of the fleeing braves. Blood Arrow's was still to come.

But Blood Arrow would fire no more arrows. His bow fell from his hand. Still he maintained his arrogant, fearless stance. Just. It seemed that he swayed, fighting to keep his balance.

His expression had changed. Where previously it had been stoic, now there was disbelief. Was that a flicker of pain in his dark eyes? It might have been another trick of the fading daylight.

The shooting had stopped. The renegades were either dead or their carbines were empty. The survivors had almost made it to the end of the canyon. The man on the cliff top fired one last shot after them, but it was only a token gesture of victory.

The kind of thing Slade would do.

Ben watched Blood Arrow's final defiant stance crumble. Those eyes still blazed and there was a reluctance about the

way the powerful legs buckled. The Paiute fell to his knees
as if he was paying homage to Wakan Tanka who had summoned his soul. His head bowed. Then he fell forward and
rolled to lay staring sightlessly up at the first stars in the
saffron sky.

Ben walked slowly across, stood looking down at the slain
Paiute chief. At first he was unable to detect any wound, it
was as if the other had been struck down by some invisible
bolt. Perhaps slain by his Man Above as punishment for leading so many of his warriors to a futile death. Blood was
starting to seep from beneath the fallen body, a dark rivulet
oozing across the stony ground, trickling into a slight hollow
and forming a pool.

Damn you, Slade!

It was so unreal after all this time, standing there in the
fading twilight, Blood Arrow's corpse becoming just another
shape amid the fallen rocks. Elation did not come, it was all
an anti-climax. He didn't hate Blood Arrow like he was supposed to. Not now. It was like a hunter skinning out somebody else's kill. Impartial. In the end, it hadn't worked out
the way Ben had planned. It wasn't ever meant to.

Ben's hand dropped to his Bowie knife, then fell away. If
he had killed Blood Arrow, then he would have lifted his
scalp. Now it wasn't his to take—that was the irony of it.
He almost felt relieved and that was very strange, indeed.

Ben could not go anywhere, his horse was dead and his
attackers's mounts were tethered somewhere outside the canyon. Slade would make his way down here, take the long
ride round. It would be several hours before he showed up.
Or he was cussed enough to ride on in the knowledge that
Ben was safe. In which case Ben would wait for daylight
and see if he could find one of the mustangs. Failing that,
he would walk all the way to Dry Sandy with the mails.

He retrieved the mochila, seated himself on a rock and
reloaded both guns with his spare cylinders. He drank the
last of his water. And waited.

It was still dark when at last he picked up the sound of an approaching horse. The rider had dismounted and was leading his mount through the canyon. It was too dark to see and the man was not risking riding across the uneven ground.

Eventually, in the faint starlight, Ben made out a silhouette. It might have been anybody, but it could only be . . .

"Slade?"

The other halted ten yards away. His horse snickered. Somehow, the dark shape was not familiar, at least not how Ben had expected to see it, even in the blackness of a canyon night. It was too tall, not stocky enough. The hat was broad brimmed instead of short, the crown was not high enough. All the same, as Ben strained his eyes, the silhouette was not altogether unfamiliar. He got a feeling of *deja vu*.

"Slade?" He called again and held his .45 ready, just in case.

It certainly was not Slade, but it was all he could think of right now. Who else but Slade could shoot like that?

"You got it wrong, Hollister." The other was soft spoken, too. Ben knew that voice, but he could not quite place it. Almost, though. Recognition eluded him. He had heard it recently and he knew for certain that it did not belong to J.A. Slade.

Who, then? *Who?*

The stranger moved forward a pace, stepped into a shaft of faint starlight. It was enough. Ben saw and understood, and gasped his amazement out loud.

"Hickok!"

"Got you pinned down good'n proper, didn't they?" There was a hint of scorn in Hickok's tone. "You musta rode right into their ambush. They seen you comin', but you didn't even smell 'em till it was too late. Me, I sensed 'em further back down the trail, my hoss became uneasy. So I turned back and took the long way round so's I could get above 'em and take a look-see. Coming from the east, that's a long ride. They got the coach, nothin' much I could do 'bout that.

Mebbe they was plannin' on ambushin' it in the canyon, then you rode along an' Blood Arrow saw a way to have both coach and pony. But they failed to kill yuh, and with you holed up here, he couldn't afford to risk yuh warnin' the stagecoach driver. So he sent back a small party to deal with it. No way I could save 'em, but I reckoned I could get you outta that hole." Hickok laughed. "Nowhere for 'em to go and no chance o' me gettin' hit, 'cept by a fluke shot. It was Blood Arrow I wanted. I bin chasin' him fer weeks an' now I've got him!" He slid a hunting knife out of his belt. "The army's put a price on his head. A thousand dollars for his scalp, five hundred for Brent's. He should be lyin' around somewhere. I saw him go down."

"*I* shot Brent!" Ben snapped.

" 'Scuse me while I attend to one or two urgent matters." Hickok gave no indication that he had heard as he vanished into the darkness.

Ben sat and waited. He wasn't arguing over scalps. He had lost the urge to take them. Not even for dollars.

"I was trackin' them Paiutes." A bundle swung from Hickok's hand as he climbed over the landspill. "They were on their way to join up with the Gosiutes and Shoshones, accordin' to the smoke signals I read. Guess they won't be talkin' to nobody now, and with Blood Arrow out of the way, the Paiutes'll want Numaga back as chief 'cause they're done fightin' a losin' war. That way, there'll be a treaty soon. You see if I'm not right."

Things looked to be working out the way Sam Booker had said they would, Ben thought. The Indians would surrender. They would lose their land and would be given some barren tract in place of it and made to stay on it. It wouldn't grow anything, and they would starve.

You couldn't blame Blood Arrow for fighting for what rightfully belonged to the Paiutes. He had treated Sarah how most white women captives were treated by the Indians.

Often the whites treated Indian women a lot worse. It was just that, for Ben, it had become personal.

Now it was all over. Hickok had killed Blood Arrow. Ben didn't have any further cause to seek vengeance. Looking at it that way, he owed Wild Bill. He was welcome to the bounty. Brent's, too.

They rode double on Hickok's horse all the way to Dry Sandy. Ben crawled into a bunk and slept until mid-day. When he awoke there was no sign of his recent companion.

Wild Bill had ridden on. For him, there was still an Indian war to be fought. There would be until the last bullet and the last arrow had been fired. He would not want it any other way.

Five

On May 16, 1861, a notice was printed in the *Sacramento Union*:

"Orders having been received from W.H. Russell, Pony Express Company, I hereby transfer the office, and everything appertaining thereto, to Messrs Wells Fargo & Co. Also letters to be forwarded by Pony Express must be delivered at their office on Second Street, between J & K, Sacramento."

Signed: J.W. Coleman, Agent,
Pony Express Company

The Pony Express was under new ownership at last.

By August of that year, the telegraph was fully operative from St Louis as far as Fort Kearney. The construction gangs had covered ninety miles in two weeks as there was no longer any disruption by Indians. As a result, the Pony Express was abandoned along this stretch. It had become dispensable.

The eastward progress from Carson City averaged twenty miles a day, and the telegraph company forecast that there would be a full coast-to-coast service by October. Congress had pledged $40,000 a year, for ten years, to the new means of communication, and Edward Creighton's telegraph company was eager to secure the contract as soon as possible.

Messages were telegraphed as far as Fort Kearney. With

the wires reaching Fort Churchill, the Pony Express only
operated between Fort Kearney and Fort Churchill. The end
was in sight. A telegraph office had been installed at Horseshoe station and the relays would be reduced further before
long.

Two Division Superintendents of the telegraph company
arrived at Horseshoe station early in September. Ben stood
in the stable doorway with Amos and watched the newcomers
disembark.

There was not a soldier to be seen in or around the palisade. Not a gun was in sight. A notice on the board outside
the road boss's office ordered that no weaponry was to be
displayed. It bore J.A. Slade's signature and was counter-
signed by Howard Baker and Arthur Templeman, the two
officials from the telegraph company.

"I don't like it one li'l bit, Mister Ben." Amos was edgy
and he refused to go outside the stable.

"It's the only way." Ben felt naked without the comforting
weight of the Adams on his hip. The .45, together with his
.36, were on the top of his bedroll in the bunkhouse. They
were easily accessible if the need arose. He prayed it wouldn't.
The Pony Express and the telegraph were playing their last
card today. It had to be an ace. Win or lose, there could be no
compromises. "Here come the injuns now."

"Lord, save us!" Amos said.

"It'll be all right," Ben assured him and watched through
the open gates as a dozen or so Paiutes rode slowly up the
rise from the river. They were nervous, too—everybody was.
Some just hid it better than others. Like Alexander Majors
frequently said, confidence breeds success. But, in the end,
he had lost the Pony Express.

The braves did not wear war paint. They carried neither
bows, lances, tomahawks nor knives. Theirs was a show of
complete trust in the white invaders. Ben did not doubt that

the distant woods and hills teemed with braves in full war regalia, all heavily armed. One slip up, one hint of betrayal or treachery, and Horseshoe station would be a gutted smoking ruin by nightfall.

"Where's Slade?" Amos put into words the question that everybody within the perimeter of Horseshoe station was asking right now. Would Man Who Likes Killing allow his most hated foes to ride unchallenged into his own stronghold? Would he accept a peace treaty that would change his whole way of life? Or was he out there intent on making this day the bloodiest in the history of the Pony Express?

"He's off somewhere, I guess." Ben watched the Paiutes' approach with narrowed eyes. This was all too good to be true. There had to be a snag somewhere along the line.

"Killin' injuns?"

"No. Not today." Surely even J.A. Slade would honor the truce because the completion of the telegraph depended upon its success. If it failed, poles and lines the length of the Overland Trail would be cut down again. The country would be plunged back into an Indian war in which almost every tribe would rise up and unite. Surely, Slade would not risk the consequences of killing even a single brave. At least, not today.

"How can yuh be sure, Mister Ben?" Amos's voice quavered.

"I can't. I'm just prayin'."

The Paiutes rode in through the gates, at their head Chief Numaga, a small wizened figure almost hidden beneath his head-dress and ceremonial trappings. Upon the death of Blood Arrow, the tribe had welcomed their former chief back from exile in the Great Salt Lake. They realized that peace with the whites was their only hope. They would neither forget nor forgive the theft of their lands, but they would attempt to live alongside their conquerors. But, if there was treachery, they would fight to the last man. Everything depended upon the integrity of the whites.

A deputation was waiting to greet the Paiutes. Ben recognized Baker and Templeman, dressed the way they had left St Louis, frock-coated and bowler-hatted. Pompous. These men did not understand the Indian way of life. All they were interested in was the completion of their telegraph and a fat subsidy check. At any price. Right now, though, a treaty with the Paiutes seemed to be the only way of achieving that ambition.

Bolivar Roberts and Don Rising stood close behind them, heading a group of Pony Express representatives. Alongside them was a gaudily dressed man wearing a tall hat and clothes cut from the finest cloth, with jewelled buttons and tie-pin to match. Ben Halladay had been appointed to oversee the Wells Fargo takeover of the Pony Express. He was a Kentuckian who had worked his way up through the company and his checkered career included stints as a mule-skinner and mine owner. He had invested his savings in a stagecoach enterprise that he had sold out to Wells Fargo before returning to work for them. It was rumored that he had taken over from Alexander Majors. His presence here today seemed to confirm that.

Halladay was nicknamed the Emperor of Transcontinental Traffic, a title which served to massage his huge ego. He was renowned for his rages when anything dissatisfied him. Today his quick temper had to be restrained. The situation was a powder keg. The long smoldering fuse had to be snuffed out if there was ever to be peace on the Overland Trail.

The Indians halted. Numaga gave the sign of peace. Bolivar Roberts responded and the Indians dismounted. In spite of his smallness, the chief was a commanding figure. He stood straight and proud, his expression stoic. He would do what was best for his people. There would be no betrayal.

"We have come in peace." Numaga's eyes flicked from one to the other of the whites. "We shall listen to what you have to say and look at what you show us. Then we shall hold council. Our decision will be either peace or war. We shall speak no lies."

The two telegraph men stared in amazement. Neither of them had ever seen an Indian before, just pictures in magazines and newspapers. Men watched from doorways and windows. Guns were within reach if they were needed. Maybe the whole of the Paiute nation would come hollering across the river any minute—the Arapahoes, Gosiutes, Bannocks and Pawnees, too. Peace was just a dream that would never become a reality. Everybody was tense. That powder keg might go off with one helluva blow at any moment.

The Paiutes watched and waited, too. Mutual trust was still a long way off.

"We're gonna show you somethin' you've never seen before." Halladay stepped forward, becoming the spokesman for the telegraph company as well as the Pony Express. "Somethin' you'll hev to see an' hear before yuh believe it."

"We will watch and listen," Numaga answered.

"We'll hev to go into that building." Halladay pointed across to the new telegraph office. "It's all in there." He turned, led his party across the compound. There was a moment's hesitation and then Numaga followed, leading his braves in single file.

Ben Hollister eased himself off the stable doorpost, and unobtrusively tagged on to the column. The Paiutes glanced nervously at him. Slayer Who Rides With the Wind was only too well known to them. They were wary of him. Their eyes roved the compound, checked every face that stared after them. They could not see the one they called Man Who Likes Killing, and that was a matter for concern.

The telegraph office was crowded. A small table, set up against the far wall, was loaded with instruments that were as much a mystery to the whites as they were to the Indians. Only the engineer understood the process of sending and receiving messages. His shoulders were hunched and an eyeshade gave his complexion a greenish hue. The Paiutes regarded him with awe but he seemed oblivious of his audience as he tapped away on a keyboard. He was muttering beneath his breath, shaking his head.

"Don't tell me it's decided not to work!" Templeman was agitated, his pomposity replaced by frustration. Beads of sweat formed on his broad forehead, trickled down his whiskered face. "Of all the days, today . . ."

Then the galvanometer started to move, clicking its way along.

"Thank God!" Baker breathed, mopped at his brow with a polkadot handkerchief. The galvanometer—he had been told what its function was but not how it worked—had to make a complete circuit before it was possible to send a message.

The operator's finger pressed a key. They all heard his sigh of relief. They were now in direct contact with Cottonwood, the next station east of Horseshoe.

The Paiutes had bunched together. This contraption was frightening; there must surely be a demon inside which made it click and move. Was this all trickery on behalf of the whites?

"Now, please allow me to explain." There was no mistaking Howard Baker's relief as he turned to face his audience. He might have been addressing a class of erring children in school. "You have been chopping down our telegraph poles and stealing our wire."

"Make necklaces and tomahawks." Numaga's expression gave nothing away. "Destroy Wires That Speak. There are demons inside them. We have heard them talking. They are bad medicine."

"Exactly. That is why we have tried to stop you cutting the wires." Templeman glanced sideways at his colleague.

"Evil demons," Numaga added. "Very bad."

"But they cannot escape while they are inside the wires." Baker wagged a finger. "They are prisoners there. Until you cut the wires and let them out. Then they run off to make evil in the hills and forests. Your game has died, so have the plants and trees upon which you depend for food. Because the demons have killed them. If you had not allowed them to escape then this would not have happened."

"White men cut down trees to make poles, shoot our game with guns." Numaga was defiant.

"Some of the time." The telegraph official smiled. "But not enough to deprive you of food. It is the demons who destroy your food. They also spread sickness among the tribes. Have any of your people been ill lately?"

Numaga's expression said that they had. "Many have been ill. Some have died."

"There you are, then!" Templeman's tone was almost ecstatic. "The demons made them sick so they died."

"I do not believe you, white man!" Numaga's eyes clouded with suspicion. It was all a trick, after all.

"All right, then, but do you know *why* there are demons inside the wire?"

The Paiutes did not know.

"Let me explain, then. The wires are used to carry the white man's message over the land, a thousand times faster than a galloping horse. Faster, even, than the forked fire that shoots down from the sky during a storm."

"You lie!" Numaga's lips curled. "That is impossible."

"I am going to show you in a minute that it is not impossible." Templeman was showing signs of impatience. "Many messages are sent, many words are spoken by tapping on that machine."

The galvanometer had completed its circuit. Numaga was staring fixedly at it. There was a hint of fear in his dark eyes. It might just be that this strangely dressed white man was telling the truth.

"For every word that is sent out," Templeman said smiling, "a demon is used to carry each one. So, just imagine how many demons are running inside the wire. There are more demons than there are both red and white people in this whole land. Imagine, then, how many escape when your braves cut the wire. The evil demons all run off into the hills and forests to eat your nuts and berries, and kill your game. As a result, your people will starve next winter."

"Prove it to us!" Numaga suspected a trick, this white man told many lies. But if the Paiutes had been lured into a trap then there were ten times as many braves waiting in the woods to attack this station. The defenders would be over-run, slaughtered and scalped.

But Numaga was a peace-loving man. He would give the whites an opportunity to prove that which they claimed. Bloodshed would be a very last resort.

"Show us!" The Indians huddled together. This was the moment of truth.

"Very well." Templeman turned towards the telegraphic equipment. "As you know, Chief Numaga, your son, Oganna, has ridden into Cottonwood station with more of your warriors. You will be able to speak with him there through this machine. Ask him a question, one of which only you and he know the answer to. Await his reply. Then, if the answer is true, will you accept that as proof that demons carry your words through the wires?"

"Huh!" Numaga stepped forward. His companions held back. Their expressions were contemptuous. Surely, this white man did not think that the redmen were so foolish as to be tricked in this way.

Ben Hollister shifted his position against the doorpost. He was tense. Like everybody else in this office. If the telegraph failed to work then they were all in trouble. Big trouble.

"Ask your son, Oganna, a question, Numaga." Baker's words seemed to crackle in the atmosphere.

"Very well," Numaga's expression was one of cunning. "Ask him . . . what beast he killed in the desert to prove himself a warrior."

The Paiute chief stepped back, folded his arms. His smile was smug. Nobody except himself and his son shared that secret. Even these warriors did not know, for Numaga had gone alone into the desert lands, many moons ago, to look for his son when Oganna had not returned after several days. Numaga had found Oganna, a triumphant but badly mauled victor from his ordeal. He had treated his son's wounds and remained with him while they healed. Oganna had almost died. The answer to the question would prove beyond a doubt whether or not these whites were lying.

The operator tip-tapped away on a key. The galvanometer began to move again. Then the sounder told them that the message had been received at Cottonwood station.

There was silence in the room, except for the nervous breathing of those who waited.

Numaga turned slowly, looked at each of his braves in turn and received answering nods. Only Oganna could answer that question. All were agreed upon that.

The message went through. The wait seemed a long and tense one. Nobody spoke.

Then the machine started to chatter again, a click-clacking of sounds that were transferred into symbols on a piece of paper. Heads were thrust forward, everybody watched as the paper unfurled out of the instrument.

The operator waited until the instrument was still and silent. Only then did he withdraw the message. He studied it thoughtfully, his forehead creased above his eyeshade.

"Well?" Tempsleman could contain his impatience no longer. "What does it say? What are you waiting for, man? Read it out!"

The operator cleared his throat, the fingers that held the slip of paper shook slightly. He realized, only too well, the implications if the answer was not the right one. "It says . . ." He squinted as if he was having difficulty in translating the strange symbols, pushed his eyeshade right up into his thinning hair.

"Come on, man! What's the delay?" Tempsleman barked.

Everybody, including the Paiutes, had crowded closer. Ben

thought about his guns in the bunkhouse and worked out how long it would take him to get to them. He glanced back outside. The gates were still wide open, but there was no sign of any Indians closing in on the station. He wondered where Slade was and what he was doing right now.

"It says," the operator began, his voice high-pitched with nervousness, "that Oganna came upon a wounded buffalo in the desert where it had gone to die from wounds from the guns of the white men. It charged him. He leaped upon it and rode it for some distance, stabbing it with his hunting knife. Eventually, it fell from exhaustion. It gored Oganna, but it died before it could kill him. Numaga found his son trapped by a leg under the dead beast and saved him."

"Aiyee!" Numaga shrieked his surprise, leaped back from the telegraph machine. His braves huddled, staring fearfully at the now silent instruments. *"It is true! Only Oganna and myself know what happened in the desert. The evil demons have truly carried our words in the wires."*

For one moment it seemed that the Paiutes were going to flee the telegraph office in terror, leap on to their mustangs and ride out of Horseshoe.

"Wait!" Halladay barred their way. The experiment had proved successful. They could not afford to lose their advantage over the Indians. "The demons have truly carried your question, and your son's answer, over many miles in a matter of seconds, Numaga. But you are safe from these evil spirits, they are imprisoned inside the wires, they cannot get out to harm you. Unless *you* allow them to escape by cutting the wires!"

The Paiutes recovered from their shock. Truly, the Talking Machine was magic. Numaga had spoken with his son at Cottonwood. There were wooded mountains between Horseshoe and Cottonwood, even smoke signals at one were not visible to the other. The telegraph had overcome these obstacles. The whites had spoken the truth even if there was devilry in their Talking Machine. Undoubtedly, the cutting of the Wires That

Speak allowed the demons inside to escape. Far better that they remain inside and were forced to work, carrying the words of messages from place to place. That way they could not destroy food supplies and spread sickness and death.

"We will not cut the Wires That Speak." Numaga was shaken, but he spoke with all the dignity he could muster. "I give you my word. So long as you will no longer kill our braves. Tell *him!*" He had spotted Ben in the doorway. "Also, tell Man Who Likes Killing."

"Your braves will no longer be killed by men of the Pony Express or the telegraph," Halladay promised. "If you leave the wires and our riders alone, we can live in peace. I urge you, also, to make peace with the soldiers so that there can be peace throughout the land. I cannot make promises on behalf of others, only my own men."

"I will do as you suggest." Numaga turned towards the doorway. "But I warn you, white man, if just one of my warriors is killed by your pony riders, then it will be war throughout all the land. I speak on behalf of the Arapahoes, the Bannocks and the Gosiutes. I will keep my promise if you keep yours."

Ben watched the Paiutes ride away. The telegraph officials and Halladay had gone into Slade's office. The door was closed. Doubtless, they were celebrating a milestone in their history. A telegraph message would already have been sent to Creighton.

Yet, Ben was ill-at-ease. Perhaps the celebrations were a little premature As much as J.A Slade wanted to see the telegraph operating from coast to coast, he was a killer by nature. And his killing license had just been taken away from him.

Right now Slade was somewhere out in those wooded hills that were crawling with Paiutes. Ben would have given anything to know what Slade was doing right now.

Six

J.A. Slade had ridden out of Horseshoe station before daylight. Even Amos had not heard him leave. There was no way that the road boss could have taken part in that contrived means to try to win peace with the Paiutes. It was a trick, a gimmick. He sneered his contempt as he rode through the pre-dawn darkness. The only way you achieved peace with savages was by defeating them in the only way they understood and respected. Dead Indians didn't attack riders or stagecoaches. The rest would surrender when they realized they couldn't win, but by then there would be damned few of 'em left! It was the only way.

Slade had not slept. He had remained at his desk, drinking. He had helped himself to one of the bottles of whiskey which the Wells Fargo and Creighton Telegraph companies had brought along to celebrate their foolish hopes of making peace with the Paiutes. Slade's cheeks took on that all-too-familiar flush. After that, only killing would satisfy him.

He had no time for Halladay. The Wells Fargo boss was an arrogant dude. No man could win respect by swaggering around in eastern tailored finery and talking to his employees like they were slaves on some southern tobacco plantation. Halladay had a reputation for hell-raising and gunfighting. He had probably spun the yarns himself, told them so many times that in the end folks got to believing him. Maybe Halladay even believed them himself by this time. Slade laughed mirthlessly and stroked the butt of his Army .44. One day somebody would put a ball in that loud mouth . . .

Around mid-morning Slade picked up the fresh tracks of an unshod horse on a winding animal track a mile or two off the Overland Trail. His weariness evaporated instantly and he stiffened in the saddle. No dude boss from back east was going to give orders to Captain J.A. Slade. Slade had been hired to protect the mail carriers from outlaws and Indians and he would continue to do just that right up until the day his employment was terminated. And that would not happen until the telegraph was operating all the way from St Louis to Sacramento. After that, it looked like there would be another war raging for him to step right into.

Slade estimated that he was about five miles south of Ward's Central. It was too close to Horseshoe to have injuns sneaking around . . .

It was probably a scout spying out Horseshoe in preparation for an attack This peace talk, inviting the Paiutes into Horseshoe could all be part of a Paiute plan to infiltrate the defenses, distract the whites while the main war party closed in. Only a fool like Halladay would take the word of an injun!

Killing Blood Arrow wasn't the answer to the problem. Slade did not trust Numaga any more than he trusted any Indian. Treachery was bred into every one of them, and they wouldn't give up until they were beaten to their knees.

Damn that Hickok fellow! The road boss seethed. Hickok was just another show-off dude with a big mouth. The Indians on the Rocky Ridge division were Slade's responsibility. He didn't need some jumped-up army scout hornin' in. And if Hollister wanted to ride with Hickok, he could go and do just that. Slade would handle the Paiutes on his own. He didn't need any help.

The Indian was not far ahead of him, the tracks were barely drying out yet in the hot morning sun. Slade rode slowly, warily, his hand never far from his gun. He wasn't risking an ambush. Not now, not after all that he had gone through and survived. The Paiutes might remember Hickok slaying Blood Arrow, but they would never forget how J.A. Slade and a handful of pony riders had massacred them in that canyon—and in the river. Slade would be their nemesis for generations to come. They would whisper his name fearfully around their camp fires, glance into the shadows in case he might be lurking there. That was the stuff legends were made of.

Slade's instincts warned him that he was close to the Indian now. He didn't need signs any longer. He could almost smell the other.

The road boss dismounted and tethered his horse. He slid the .44 out of its holster. It felt good, like it was a part of him. It was.

A snapped twig on an overhanging branch told him that his intended prey was tall, an average sized rider would have passed beneath it. The tracks had disappeared now because the ground was stony from hereon. Slade moved from tree to tree, if he did not catch up with his quarry soon he would have to go back for his mount.

Around the next bend, the woods opened up into a clearing. The Indian had stopped to make camp. He was collecting dead branches to make a fire. He was not expecting to be followed, and in any case, there was a big peace parley taking place today.

A mustang stood close by, grazing on the sparse grass. If it sensed Slade it gave no sign. It looked weary, as though it had been ridden far and could not even be bothered to snort an alarm. There was a carbine roped on to it. The gun was probably stolen from a slain soldier.

Slade's observations were proven correct. The man was tall, wore dirty hide clothing, and his long black hair straggled round his shoulders. His back was towards the hidden watcher, and it was impossible to see his face. Which didn't matter a damn, Slade reflected, because all Paiutes looked alike.

The Indian got his fire going, squatting with his back towards Slade. The Division Superintendent looked for bow and arrows, perhaps a lance. There were none. Just the carbine.

And a revolver. Slade was surprised to see a handgun stuck behind a hide belt around the other's waist. That, too, had probably come from an army victim. Gun-toting Indians were more of a menace to themselves than to their enemies. Slade smiled his killing smile and his thin slips virtually disappeared.

J.A. Slade was in no hurry. It seemed an eternity since he had last killed. His temples pounded, the twin flushes on his cheeks darkened. It had been too long. Far too long.

Had the other been an outlaw, a horse thief or a road agent, Slade might have stepped out into the clearing, letting the man reach for his gun. But, with Indians, it was pointless—you killed 'em where you found 'em. You didn't waste time. It was the tally that counted.

Slade fired. Just once. The sound of the shot was ear-splitting beneath the surrounding, overhanging cottonwoods. The Indian's skull split open with a jagged bone-splintering sound.

The body hunched and fell forward. The bloody head started to sizzle as it lay amidst the crackling flames of the recently lit fire.

Only then did Slade move swiftly. Three strides took him to the dead man. He grabbed a moccasin-clad foot and dragged the corpse well clear of the camp fire.

He holstered his smoking revolver and slid his skinning knife out of its sheath. Whoever, wherever, he killed, he claimed his trophy. It was pointless without it; it was the only way to keep an accurate count.

Slade smiled grimly to himself as he lifted the bundle of bloody, singed hair clear of the head. Right now those fools at Horseshoe would be parleying with the Paiutes. Maybe they were already congratulating themselves on having made some kind of truce.

If they had, then it was already broken. Slade laughed aloud at the thought.

Seven

"You damned fool, Slade!" Ben had stood by the open gates of Horsehoe station and watched the road boss ride up all the way from the river below. Even in the deepening twilight the mass of long bloodied hair swinging from the saddle was unmistakable for what it was. "You've gone and ruined everything now. We've finally got a treaty with the Paiutes. Even if it is only a temporary one, it might've lasted just long enough for the telegraph to get joined up. Now even Numaga won't be able to hold his braves in check. And neither will we. They'll come here lookin' for you and they won't rest until they got you. And me as well!"

Slade was like some squat demon silhouetted against the darkening sky, "Trouble with you, Hollister, you're gettin' to be an injun lover, like the rest of 'em. You think you can talk peace. Yuh can't. There'll only be peace when all the injuns that is left are on a reservation and glad to be there 'cause that's the only place they won't get killed. The dead 'uns are the only real peaceable ones."

Slade nudged his horse forward. Ben stood there, trying to get his anger under control. Amos took the section boss's horse and led it into the stable. Slade walked across to his office, entered, and closed the door behind him. The only thing he understood was killing. And just when everybody was congratulating themselves that the killing was over, it looked like it was about to begin again.

* * *

JB was now taking up much of Mollie's time. He was a big strong baby. He would grow to twice his father's size one day, she jokingly told Ben. If the Pony Express ever started up again in years to come, young JB certainly wouldn't fit the bill on account of his size.

"But I just hope that he doesn't get to liking guns too much," she added, her smile fading.

"He'll be helping me to mend 'em, not fire 'em," Ben reassured her. He had not told Mollie the outcome of Slade's hunting trip in the hills. She was still rejoicing over the prospect of peace. He didn't want to spoil it for her. That would happen soon enough. "Look what I got here."

She squinted in the lamp light of the kitchen, tried to figure out what it was that her husband held up between forefinger and thumb. "Looks like a piece of cut-off pipe to me."

"Which is exactly what it is." He held it horizontally so that the solid end was visible. "It's copper casing, the telegraph wires are joined up with it where one roll of wire finishes and another starts. This is just a cut-off end."

"Whatever d'you want that for?" She was mildly curious. He probably intended to fix something around the place with it.

"I'm goin' to start work on that idea I've had in mind for years." There was a slight tremor of excitement in his voice. "Dad used to talk about it, maybe I can put some of his theories into practice, even improve on 'em. This fits a .45 cylinder just like it'd been made for it. I'm going to try fixin' a percussion cap in the base. Then I'll pack it with powder. I'll have to make a ball in the forge, shape it sort of 'nosed', I reckon. After that I'll have to work on a .45, see if I can get a cartridge to line up right. Make the action revolve on a self-cocking basis so that each shell lines up with the barrel."

"Oh!" She didn't really understand, only that it was an

experiment that might go seriously wrong. "Ben, it might be dangerous."

"Don't worry." He reached up and put the sawn-off cylinder on a shelf where JB could not reach it. "When I test it, it'll be a line pulling the trigger an' I'll be standing well away. Maybe round the corner of the cabin."

Mollie laughed her relief aloud.

"But it'll take time." He slid onto a chair at the table. The plate of venison stew, loaded with vegetables from the plot outside, looked and smelled the most appetizing meal he had ever sat down to. "Once the Pony's disbanded I'll start work on making a metal shell. There ain't too much time to sit around just thinkin' about it. Maybe right now there's somebody, somewhere, thinkin' along the same lines. And the first one to register it won't be growin' crops for a livin', that's for sure."

J.A. Slade's mood had swung like the uncertain pendulum it was. Yesterday, he had been out hunting Indians, today was for reorganizing relay runs now that Horseshoe had become the furthest telegraph station west of St. Louis.

If he left his office door ajar, he could hear the constant clacking of the operating key across the compound. He did not understand how it worked. He was not interested in learning; all he knew was that it received messages from back east.

Mostly these days, the messages concerned the war and how it was escalating. Urgent dispatches arrived and had to be relayed to the next telegraph point by Pony Express riders. The Union was gaining support daily. Never before, in its short history, had the Pony Express played such a vital role. Even so, its future would be short-lived. The telegraph would soon take over. The speed with which bulletins were delivered was the criteria.

The Pony Express was laying off riders almost daily. Only

a few relays remained until the telegraph was joined up. Ben Halladay was not popular with his employees. Benjamin Ficklin resigned after a quarrel with him and many of those riders, whose names were already legendary, walked out. Will Cody left to become an army scout, later to be known as "Buffalo Bill" throughout the west because of his reputation as a buffalo hunter. The army needed meat for the soldiers and Cody spent his time depleting the sizeable buffalo herds to satisfy this demand. Thus food became even more scarce for the Indian tribes.

Bolivar Roberts quit along with Warren Upson and Don Rising. Soon there would be only a handful of riders remaining. The best of them were largely gone.

Ben debated quitting. As soon as the next telegraph station at Deer Creek was operating, Horseshoe would cease to be a Pony Express depot. Then there would only be a few hundred miles of relays left. Unless, of course, the Paiute War flared up again. And that might happen any day after what J.A. Slade had done.

"You'll take the last dispatch out of here tomorrow, Hollister," said Slade looking up from a pile of paperwork as Ben entered the office. "Day after, Horseshoe will be just another telegraph office. Livestock and equipment are being moved up to Rock Creek. That'll be the new division headquarters of Rocky Ridge until the eastbound telegraph arrives from Millersville. That'll happen around early October, if they keep to schedule. After that . . ." He left the sentence unfinished.

"And the Paiutes?" Ben noticed the grisly bundle of bloody hair, which Slade had brought in, suspended from a hook in the far corner of the room. "Maybe it's too late already." He nodded towards the scalp.

"Guess not." Slade smiled in that peculiar way of his, slitted his mouth. "That there," he said, jerking a thumb, "came off Mogoannoga. Renegade Bannock, Brent's sidekick. I reckon the Bannocks won't mind and the Paiutes are already doin' a special dance. I read the smoke signals in the hills this mornin'. Always did wonder what'd happened to Mogoannoga till I picked his trail up and caught him makin' camp. He won't be tradin' any more whiskey and carbines, nor waylayin' coaches an' riders."

Lady Luck had, indeed, smiled upon J.A. Slade that day. But her moods were unpredictable. Already they were beginning to change.

Ben carried the last mochila out of Horseshoe station the following morning. In some ways, he was glad to get away. There was an atmosphere of finality, of sadness, about this place which had been the headquarters of the Rocky Ridge division for the past eighteen months. Wagons were being loaded up with supplies and equipment, and Amos was meticulously grooming the horses in the stable. Tomorrow every animal would be transferred up to Rock Creek. Slade's new office would be a temporary affair there for the final month or so.

Ben reached Rock Creek in the late afternoon of that hazy, late September afternoon. The station buzzed with activity. Two additional cabins were being built, and a number of wagons were camped outside the palisade. He noticed a group of negroes in ragged clothing huddled in a corner of the compound. Ben had seen some others on his ride, both at Platte Bridge and Sweetwater. Escaped slaves on the run, and good luck to 'em. There would be more, many more, before this war was over.

A stagecoach had pulled in and, judging from the sweat-streaked team which the liverymen were unhitching, it had not arrived long ago. Probably, the passengers were stopping overnight because it was too late in the day to continue their journey.

"Gettin' wuss'n St. Louis here," the stableman grunted as he took Ben's horse. "An' I ain't never bin to St. Louis, jest heered tell 'bout It. If'n it's anythin' like as crowded as this, I'll keep away."

Everybody had a mind to head west, Ben reflected. One day perhaps the west would be more densely populated than the east. But that would not happen until the railroad arrived. He had heard that the iron tracks were following hard on the heels of the telegraph. Everything was changing, but the big changes wouldn't happen until this war had been fought and won.

"You goin' on from here tomorrow?" The stableman asked as he began tending to Ben's horse.

"No, I'm headin' back to Horseshoe. Got a wife an' son an' a home back there."

"Settlin' down, huh?"

"Maybe."

Nobody had any real thoughts on settling down until the war was over. Lincoln was calling for still more volunteers. Ben had just brought the telegraph notices with him.

He would have to talk seriously to Mollie about enlisting when he returned to Horseshoe. She would understand—it was his duty. He stood there watching the negroes in the corner of the palisade. Folks were donating food and clothing. Some settlers were talking to the runaways.

Feelings were running high. Lincoln would get his volunteers, all right.

Ben ate in the crowded saloon, beans and bacon washed down with tepid beer. He looked around him. It might have been a Saturday night with all the homesteaders ridden in from afar. There were some soldiers, too, a detachment passing through on their way to Fort Churchill. This time, though, they weren't chasing Indians. The war against the south would be much harder and longer. And bloodier.

Ben pushed his empty plate away, finished his beer, and contemplated another drink. It had been a long and thirsty ride. The bar area was crowded, so he decided to wait a while. He had a long night ahead of him.

Two men eased out of the throng and came towards his table, like they had been awaiting their opportunity to speak to him.

"Mind if we join yuh, stranger?" The taller of the two pulled back a chair, glancing furtively at his companion. There was something about them that was purposeful rather than the chance meeting of casual acquaintances, Ben thought. It made him wary and put him on his guard.

"Pony Express, ain't yuh?" The tall man had an angular face with a neatly trimmed moustache. Ex-army, perhaps, Ben surmised, on his way to Fort Kearney to re-enlist. A brief glimpse of a holstered gun as the other sat down revealed an identical weapon to the one which Hickok had carried, a Remington New Model Army .44.

The stranger's companion, a short thickset man with an unkempt dark beard, packed one, too. Army issue. The army did not issue guns to anyone until they enlisted. Ex-army again, then. Somehow, it did not quite fit.

Ben became even warier.

"Heard Horseshoe station's closed," the tall man said, sipping a whiskey. His keen grey eyes never left Ben. He was sussing him out, all right.

"Today." Ben was curious, he would sit this one out, fetch his drink later. "Everythin's being moved up here."

"You're Hollister, ain't yuh?"

Ben nodded slowly. Somebody had probably pointed him out to these men. "That's me."

"Heard o' yuh." The other's expression was deadpan. Ben could not envisage him ever smiling. "Quite a reputation yuh've done gone and built fer yourself. Slayer Who Rides With the Wind, that's what the injuns call yuh, ain't it? Others, too, by all counts."

"Hopefully, we've done with Indian fightin'. The Pony and the telegraph have made a treaty with the Paiutes."

"And Cap'n Slade?"

Ben tensed, his pulses speeded up a little. A lot of folks asked about Slade. He would probably go down in folklore, his name whispered in awe. All the same, these men weren't the type to interest themselves in anybody without good reason.

"He's still Division Superintendent of the Rocky Ridge division. Will be until the Pony is disbanded."

"Folks say there's nobody faster with a gun. 'Cept mebbe Wild Bill Hickok. And you." Both men's eyes narrowed.

"I've never been put to the test and hope I never will be." Ben felt as if their eyes were boring into him like smoldering branding irons.

"J.A. Slade's killed a lot o' men. Red and white." It was a statement, not a question.

"Stories get exaggerated. That's how legends are made."

" 'Cept in Slade's case it's true. A lot o' folks have seen him shoot and kill. An' I'm not jest talkin' 'bout killin' injuns. You rode with him, you must've seen fer yourself?"

"I've seen him shoot outlaws." Ben's pulses changed up another gear. "That's his job."

"An' soldiers?"

"Never seen him shoot a soldier." A bead of sweat trickled down Ben's forehead and stung his eye.

"They say you wuz at Sutler's Store with him when he gunned down a United States Army corporal."

The sweat on Ben's brow chilled. "Who says I was there?"

"Some folks we spoke to at Fort Halleck."

"It was a fair fight. The corporal taunted him, went for his gun first. Take a tip from me, mister, don't ever goad J.A. Slade."

"Them folks we talked to reckon it weren't no fair fight. The soldier had his holster buttoned. That makes it murder."

"Why're you fellahs askin' me, huh?"

"Jest curious." The tall man stroked his moustache, his eyes gave nothing away.

"Wuz Slade at Horseshoe station when yuh rode out?" This time the question was abrupt, demanding an answer.

"Yeah, but that don't mean he's there now. The Rocky Ridge is a big division. Slade spends most of his time out ridin' the trail, checkin' on the other stations. Most times nobody knows exactly where he is. Till he shows up all of a sudden."

"But he don't have to check no further east now the telegraph's got as far as Horseshoe."

Ben tensed even more These men were trying to establish Slade's whereabouts, there was no doubt about that. Gunfighters looking to make a reputation for themselves? Bounty hunters from Illinois following up warrants issued long ago? Or seeking revenge for some friend or relative who had fallen to Slade's gun? Any might have fitted. Except for the Remingtons—they had an official look about them. If these guys weren't army then they might be . . .

"I take it you're lookin' to meet Slade?" It was Ben's turn to fire a direct question. He hoped maybe to catch them off guard.

The cold eyes blinked but again they gave nothing away. "Guess everybody's lookin' to meet Slade, if only jest to catch a glimpse of him so they'll be able to tell their children, or their grandchildren, one day that they saw J.A. Slade with their own eyes. Like you said, mister, it's how legends are made. Ain't that right?"

It was a lie. These men wouldn't boast about anybody except themselves. "I guess that's so. Now, if you gentlemen will excuse me, I'm goin' to turn in. It's been a long hot day."

They watched Ben until he was out the door. Only then did they turn to each other, give faint nods of satisfaction. The tall one gave the very faintest of smiles, and it had been a very long time since he had done that.

* * *

"The two guys, a tall one and a short one, who are they?"
Ben asked Lowndes, the station boss, who was still sorting
out his quarters in readiness to hand over to Slade.

Lowndes took his time answering, he looked uneasy.
"Why d'you ask, Hollister?"

"Just curious."

"Me, too. I asked one of the passengers on the coach those
two came in on jest the same question. I was curious, too."

"Well?"

"Lawmen."

Ben was not surprised, he had half-guessed. All the same,
the news came as a shock.

"Sheriff and a deputy." Lowndes lowered his voice and
looked to make sure that the door was closed. It was. Even
so, the men of whom he spoke might be crouched down
outside the window, listening. "Sheriff Lawson from Carson
City. Don't know the deputy's name. Doesn't matter, anyhow.
They're lookin' fer Slade. They got a warrant fer his arrest
from Judge Carter. Fer that killin' at Sutler's Store. A corporal. Army's mighty mad 'bout it. Reckon them two'll go
on with the coach in the mornin' as far as Horseshoe."

Ben left the office, forcing himself to walk as casually as
he could across the compound. Just in case Sheriff Lawson
and his deputy were watching from the saloon. Fortunately,
the stable block was situated in a patch of shadow.

Ben knew that if he rode hard through the night he could
make it to Horseshoe soon after daylight. The stagecoach
would not arrive until later in the day. Time was on his side
but he could not afford to waste any.

Slade had saved Ben's life once. The very least he owed
the road boss was a warning that the law was coming for
him.

Ben rode as hard as he dared with only the starlight to
guide him. He knew the trail well enough and he judged that
he was making good time. Night riding was always slower
then travelling by day. He had a schedule to keep that was

suddenly more important than any mail delivery he had ever
undertaken.

A few miles beyond Split Rock his horse stumbled in a
rut and went lame.

Eight

There was no way Ben was going to make it even as far as Split Rock. His horse was so lame that he had to slow his pace as he led it. He considered tethering it, leaving it and going alone on foot to the next station. That would take several hours. Or he could wait for the stagecoach and hitch a lift on it. Then, when he alighted at Split Rock he could borrow a horse, ride at breakneck speed, and still beat the stage to Horseshoe.

But those lawmen would be aboard the stage, and they would guess his intention. It was a chance he would have to take if he was going to warn Slade.

He led his mount off the trail in search of a suitable place to leave it until he could return for it later. The animal hobbled slowly, painfully. Even in his own desperate situation, Ben was determined that he was not going to let it fall into the hands of horse thieves or Indians. He still worked for the Pony Express and he had a duty towards them.

Ben was some fifty yards from the trail when he heard the drumming of hoofbeats. The riders were travelling fast in spite of only having the starlight to see by. They were obviously in a hurry. There was no chance of stopping them, maybe persuading them to let him ride double on one of the horses. The clattering of hooves slowly died away in an east-bound direction.

On reflection, perhaps it was best that he had not managed

to attract the attention of the unknown horsemen, for outlaws and ruffians were abroad in the dead of night. Ben sat down on a tree stump by the side of the trail to wait for daylight.

Time passed agonizingly slowly. He tried to curb his frustration. He consoled himself with the thought that as long as the stagecoach did not pass him, then J.A. Slade was safe.

It was mid-morning before his ears picked up the rumble of approaching wheels. The coach must have been late leaving Split Rock, it should have been here a couple of hours ago. In the long run, though, it wouldn't make any difference. He would still be able to beat Sheriff Lawson and his deputy to Horseshoe station. Ben stood up and made sure that the driver would see him when the coach rounded the bend.

The driver spotted him, the wheels locked and slid in a cloud of dust, and the foam flecked team came to a halt a few yards beyond where Ben stood.

"Wal, if it ain't Ben Hollister!" Sam Brierley had been a Butterfield's driver during Ben's time with that company. "What're yuh doin' hossless out here, boy?"

Ben explained briefly, glanced at the passengers looking out of the windows. There was no sign of Lawson or his deputy.

"Climb up on the box with me'n Sep, boy."

Sam Brierley had the coach rolling again almost before Ben was seated alongside the shotgun guard. It jerked him forward and he had to grab the rail to keep his balance.

"We wuz late leavin'." Sam had to shout to make himself heard. "Two of the goddamned passengers took off in the night, never said nothin' to us that they wouldn't be travellin' with us. We waited fer 'em, went to look fer 'em but there weren't no sign of 'em. Then the stableman found that two of his hosses were missin'. If they'd been jest ordinary hoss thieves I guess there'd've been a posse out huntin' 'em, strung 'em up when they caught 'em. But, seein' as they were lawmen, I guess they musta had a reason to . . ."

"Lawmen!" Ben's stomach churned and not just because

of the way the stage was swaying from side to side. "You
mean . . ."

"Yep, a sheriff an' a deppity. They wuz supposed to be
travellin' with us as far as Horseshoe. Like too many folks
these days, they musta got impatient, couldn't wait, took off
in the middle o' the night. Musta bin in one damn big hurry
to get to Horseshoe. Guess they had a reason."

Ben did not reply. Mentally he was urging the team to go
faster. And faster.

It might already be too late.

Amos was up and about before most people were awake.
The horses had to be fed and watered in readiness for their
move to Rock Creek. It might be the last time he tended to
them. It wasn't just a sad thought, it was a worrying one.
There were already liverymen employed at the new division
headquarters, they maybe would not need any more. He had
no idea where he would go then, the company would not let
him hang around if there was no work for him.

Some negroes had passed through yesterday, a man and
his wife with two children. They looked half-starved. Amos
had given them some cornmeal and water to drink. They
were just running and had no idea where they were going.
All they wanted to do was to put as much distance between
themselves and where they had come from as possible. They
were terrified of bounty hunters on their trail.

Amos was glad to see them go in case they's led the bounty
hunters to him. Without the protection offered by the Pony
Express, he was vulnerable.

He blamed himself for escaping the way he had. It had
been a spur of the moment decision. An opportunity had
presented itself while he was out working in the fields, and
he had taken it. And left his wife, Annabel, behind. That was
downright despicable, and he would have to live with it for
the rest of his life. He had even thought about going back,

begging his new master for forgiveness. But his pleas would have fallen on deaf ears. They would have put him in chains, flogged him—maybe even have shot or hanged him because he was getting too old and fat for work. They preferred the young negroes who had been born and raised on the plantations and had never known anything different. They would certainly have made an example of Amos as a deterrent to other would-be runaways.

It was full light when he heard the sound of horses coming up from the river, iron on stone and men's voices talking in low tones. Amos paused to listen. There were no more dispatch riders due, the new-fangled telegraph had seen to that. Homesteaders didn't come to Horseshoe this early in the day, not unless there was an emergency, and they would have been hollering and banging on the gate.

"Open up!" The voice was commanding.

Amos looked around nervously but there was nobody else up and about in the compound. He was all alone. He thought about going across to the bunkhouse and waking somebody up. It would not have been a popular move.

"Open this gate!"

Amos trembled. The admittance of callers was ultimately his responsibility. If he let anybody in he should not, then the wrath of J.A. Slade would descend upon him. On the other hand, if he refused to admit anybody of importance then he was also in trouble. He couldn't win either way.

He approached the gate and lifted the cover of the spyhole. He saw a tall man and a shorter one mounted on horses which were Pony Express stock. The strangers might be Wells Fargo officials checking on their new company.

Or bounty hunters on the trail of that negro family.

"What're you gawpin' at?" The tall one had seen Amos's face at the lookout. "Get this gate open!"

"Who . . . are . . . you?" Amos's voice came out as a stammer. He slammed the hatch shut because he was frightened of these strangers just looking at him. They were bounty hunters, all right. They were after *him*.

"None o' your damn business. Open this gate or you'll be in big trouble."

They were *definitely* bounty hunters, Amos decided. He was faced with a dilemma. His strict orders were not to open the gates to any unauthorized callers. Oh, Lord, if only Mister Ben had been around, he'd've known what to do, for sure. But Ben was over at Rock Springs, he wasn't due back till later. Maybe Amos should call Cap'n Slade. He quaked at the thought.

Sheriff Lawson and his deputy had banked on gaining easy and inconspicuous entry to Horseshoe station. They did not want to draw attention to themselves until they were ready. They had planned to take J.A. Slade by surprise. With hindsight, it would have been better to have arrived by stagecoach, posing as ordinary passengers. But they had had to change their plans because they knew that Hollister had ridden to warn Slade. They had watched and waited in the compound at Rock Creek and seen him leave. There was only one possible reason why Hollister had ridden out after dark. It was strange that they had not caught up with him along the trail but there was no way he could have gotten here first. Nobody could have ridden as hard and as fast as they had through the night hours.

They did not have time to hang around. Neither did they want this negro announcing their arrival to the entire station.

"Sheriff. Utah County." Lawson spoke in a rasping whisper. "Here are our credentials. Take a peek."

Amos took a peek. Two warrant cards were held up, too far away for his failing eyesight. But there was no mistaking those shiny metal badges that were pinned to the insides of their vests when they turned them back.

"Now, willya let us in without any more fuss?"

Amos deliberated again. The men claimed to be from Utah but this was Wyoming. Did they have any authority to demand entrance here? There was nobody around to ask. But lawmen weren't bounty hunters, and that was one very good reason for lifting the heavy bar and dragging back the gate.

The men pushed their way inside, giving Amos no more than a cursory glance. That, in itself, was a big relief.

They draped their horses' reins over the hitching rail in front of the saloon. They did not secure them, a sure sign that they did not intend to stay long.

They looked the cabins over, their keen eyes missing nothing. Their gaze stopped on the small building with the sign above the doorway that said "Division Superintendent: Pony Express."

The men looked at each other. The taller one nodded and they began to walk towards Slade's office. They had spread out, their postures a half crouch, vests pushed back so that their holstered guns were within easy reach. Every step was slow. Menacing.

Perhaps they intended to sneak up on the cabin, one of them on either side of the door, kick it open and go in shooting. Or wait there for Slade to emerge.

Amos was the only one who saw them, and he knew without any doubt that, at long last, the law had caught up with J.A. Slade. The negro ducked down behind the nearest water trough. Cap'n Slade was in there, all right, and there was going to be trouble. Big trouble.

Whatever the two lawmen had in mind, Slade beat them to it. They were still some ten yards from his office when the door burst open, crashed back on its hinges. One second it was closed, the next it was open, and J.A. Slade stood there framed in the doorway.

He looked just the same as he always did, and that was what Amos found so terrifying. The escaped slave averted his eyes.

The silence was oppressive. Somewhere, across the river and over the woods, a hunting buzzard *mewed* plaintively. It was the only sound. Slade just stood there, watching and waiting. Perhaps he guessed who these men were and why they were here. Maybe he didn't look for reasons. They were stalking his office and that, in itself, was reason enough. Only the beginnings of a flush on his pallid cheeks revealed his innermost thoughts. But he wasn't going to make the first move. He never did.

"You're Slade?" Lawson made it sound like he wasn't sure. It was the wrong thing to say to J.A. Slade.

"*Captain* Slade."

"Yeah, oh, sure," the sheriff said, his voice faltered, then recovered. If it hadn't been for that damnfool negro, they would have caught the road boss asleep on his bunk.

"You want something?"

"Judge Carter sent us."

"Seems to me like the judge ain't too particular 'bout who he gets to run his errands these days." Slade's voice was a whisper, like he was talking to himself, but in the early morning silence of the compound his words carried, hung in the still air as if they were unwilling to disperse until they had been heard and understood.

"We got a warrant. All we're askin' yuh to do, Cap'n Slade, is to come back with us to Carson City. Then yuh'll be able to talk to the judge yourself, state your case'n, mebbe it's all a mistake, after all."

"What's a mistake?" Slade's steely grey eyes never shifted from the two men.

"The . . . uh . . . the shootin' at Sutler's Store. Fort Halleck. A United States Army corporal. Corporal Benbow. Yuh killed him."

"Who says so?"

"Plenty o' folks say so."

"Name 'em."

Lawson slicked his lips "Uh . . . Hollister was there. He told us so."

"He'll tell yuh that soldier went for his gun first. Ask Hollister, get it straight."

"We've asked him."

"And?"

"He said just that."

"So you don't have no case, then." Slade gave the impression that he was about to turn around and walk back indoors.

"Yuh can tell that to Judge Carter. Bring Hollister as a witness. All we're askin' is fer you to come to Carson with us."

"You got it all wrong." J.A. Slade's voice was even softer but they heard him all too clearly. "Judge Carter sits in Carson and Salt Lake City. That soldier got shot across the border in Wyoming. You go back, tell the judge to haul himself up off his ass and ride to Fort Laramie. Mebbe I'll talk to him there. Mebbe."

Slade swung on his heel as if to go back into his quarters. But he continued to swing so that it brought him around in a full circle, facing the two lawmen again.

By which time Sheriff Lawson and his deputy had their guns clear of their holsters.

Nobody saw the shooting that morning. There were no witnesses. Only hearsay and speculation, bare facts embellished with the telling over the years.

Amos had his eyes tightly closed and kept them that way for some time afterward. At least until he had finished praying and thanking the Lord for his salvation. He heard two shots, it might have been three, they were all so close together that it was impossible to count them. Not that counting was one of his strong points, anyway.

His nostrils flared, the air was thick with powdersmoke. Every nerve in his body trembled violently. Without daring to look, he mumbled, "Oh, Lord, they bin and done an' shot Cap'n Slade. Have mercy on his soul, Lord, and forgive him his many sins."

They hadn't shot Slade, as Amos discovered, when he finally plucked up enough courage to peer out through splayed fingers around the water trough. There was no sign of J.A. Slade, whatsoever. The office door was closed again. The road boss had apparently gone back indoors.

Sheriff Lawson and his deputy lay in an untidy heap. Somehow they had fallen against each other when Slade had shot them, almost as if they had tried to cling together for protection. They had died that way. Ugly head wounds seeped blood and their guns lay beyond their outstretched hands—unfired.

Men came out of the bunkhouse and stood looking. But none ventured near the corpses. You didn't interfere with J.A. Slade's victims until he was finished with them. Sheriff Lawson and his deputy still wore their hats.

Some time later, Slade came out of his office and headed for the stable. He didn't shout for Amos to saddle him a horse like he usually did, he took one and saddled it himself.

The road boss did not say where he was going. Nobody asked him. He might have been going hunting outlaws. Or Indians. Or just checking on the few remaining stations that were still under his jurisdiction. It was nobody's business where he was headed.

Nobody found out where he went that day. If he had resigned from the company, then he did not inform them of his decision. Neither did he collect his final pay packet. He did not return to Horseshoe station and was never seen on the Rocky Ridge division again.

Like the buzzard across the river, J.A. Slade was a predator. Indians and outlaws were his prey, and the Pony Express no longer offered him an abundance of killings.

Folks whispered that he had moved on to fresh hunting grounds. It is doubtful whether the arrival of the law, with a warrant for his arrest, influenced his decision. It just happened to coincide with his time of departure.

For J.A. Slade, the time had come to move on.

Nine

October 24, 1861

The last gap in the telegraph wires was finally joined up, and the latest means of communication stretched, unbroken, from east to west. Creighton had achieved his ambition as well as met his deadline.

A handful of riders and horses were retained in case of emergencies, but on November 20, the last rider on the last run handed over the mails in San Francisco.

Then the Pony Express ceased operation.

Horseshoe station was fast growing into a small township. The original palisade had been taken down and log buildings straggled beyond the old perimeter. Another saloon went up, and a hardware store was built next to it. Before long, it was rumored, the railway would reach here. Communication quickly had opened up this vast continent. The telegraph clacked twenty-four hours a day.

But, for the moment, the war between north and south, where brother fought against brother and father fought against son, dominated everybody's lives. There were few young men to be seen around Horseshoe or any of the other towns along the Overland Trail these days. Most of them had answered Lincoln's call. They were in uniform, fighting what was to become a long and bloody war.

Ben Hollister had not enlisted yet. His expertise in gunsmithing had spread as far as Fort Kearney and Fort Laramie, and beyond. Rifles and revolvers were in constant need of repair. Sights became twisted and needed re-aligning, and stocks became broken in hand-to-hand fighting. He cut and fitted new ones and kept a supply of seasoned walnut in readiness. Trigger springs yielded to metal fatigue. New ones had to be forged and fitted. Precision was the difference between killing and being killed.

"You're fighting the war just the same as if you were shootin' Confederates," Mollie told him one day. She had not failed to notice how restless he had become. "Look at it this way, every gun you mend helps the soldier who fires it. He kills an enemy. If it wasn't shootin' right, then he'd miss and probably get shot himself. You've probably accounted for more Confederates lives, and saved more Union lives, than if you'd been out there yourself fightin'."

"I guess so," he sighed. The way Mollie put it, it made it feel almost right for him to be staying back home. "At least it's better'n doin' what Will Cody did after he left the Pony and before he went buffalo huntin' for the army."

Cody had looked for excitement, whether it was fighting Indians, riding the mails or making war on the Confederacy. It was all the same to him. Missouri had been carrying on a long-standing feud with Kansas long before war had broken out. Cody had joined up with the Kansas Red Legs, who were no better than outlaws and carried out raids on Missouri farms and settlements. They rode by night, plundered and burned. They raided under the flag of the Stars and Bars, using the Union cause as an excuse.

Right or wrong, Will Cody had a reason for joining the Red Legs. As a boy, Will had emigrated from Iowa with his parents, and they had settled in Kansas. Soon after their arrival, trouble flared up. Many of the settlers were from Missouri and some had brought their slaves with them. But the Kansas people objected to slavery being brought into their area.

Will's father joined the Free Soil Party and prepared to fight for what they believed in. While speaking out against slavery at a trading post, Will Cody Senior was gunned down.

Just as Ben Hollister had wanted revenge on all Indians for what a few had done to his sister, so young Will Cody sought vengeance against a state where his father had been murdered. He saw the raids on the Missouri settlers as a means of achieving this.

Ben couldn't really blame him. He knew how he, himself, had felt. But it didn't make a wrong right. Maybe Cody, too, had seen the error of his ways and enlisted with a Kansas regiment. At least that made it legitimate, if it didn't alter the reason for killing.

Ben finished fitting a new hammer spring to a Remington .44, cocked it and clicked it on an empty cylinder. One mended a gun but never knew who it was going to kill or for what reason. It was best not to think about it.

Little JB had just taken his first step. Just one. He had tumbled and decided that maybe crawling was safer. It was exciting just waiting for him to try again. It might be a long wait, and that was another good reason for staying in Wyoming repairing the army's guns.

Amos was living in a room that Ben had allowed him to build at the rear of the cabin. In return for food and shelter, he tended the crops and helped Mollie with some of the chores.

The days were shortening; the first snowfall was already late but it would not be long. They had an ample store of root crops, and there were supplies across at the store. Ben knew that he had made the right decision in renovating that old trapper's shack so close to the station.

Amos was used to gunfire and it no longer made him jump, but this was an excessively noisy day. Ben had fired more shots than he'd ever done before, testing the guns he'd mended.

Amos peered out of his room, his curiosity about the shots getting the better of him. Even Mister Ben couldn't repair that many guns in a day. Whatever was Mister Ben up to?

Ben had a revolver tied securely to a fence post some distance from the cabin, the barrel fixed skywards so that the ball would shoot into the air. Amos rubbed his eyes. It was no hallucination—Ben had a length of rope attached to the trigger, unravelling it as he walked backwards. Amos counted the paces as best he could. Eighty, or thereabouts, only then did the rope become taut.

Amos covered his ears with his hands. He had no idea what was going on, but this one sure looked like one helluva bang, otherwise Ben would have fired the gun the same way as he did all the others.

Amos shut his eyes tightly. The report didn't sound any different from any of the others. He opened his eyes and saw that the revolver was still lashed to the post, a trickle of powdersmoke coming from its barrel.

Whatever it was, it had excited Ben like Amos had never seen before. Ben was running forward, feverishly untying the .44. Checking it over, talking excitedly to himself. Lord, he must've taken leave of his senses. Maybe, Amos thought, he should go fetch Mollie right away.

Mollie was standing in the cabin doorway, young JB laughing and gurgling in her arms. He liked bangs. Even at this very early age, he was showing a fascination for guns that she found somewhat disconcerting.

Ben let out a whoop and punched the air with the smoking revolver. "It works! It works! I always knew it would."

Amos kept his distance, embarrassed because Ben and Mollie were embracing. JB was sandwiched between them, his tiny insistent hands trying to get at the .44.

"I'll need to register the patent right away." Ben was breathless like he had just run a mile. "There's no time to lose, there's probably others working on cartridge revolvers and rifles. I have to be the first."

Had Ben remained in his birthplace back in England, and pursued his apprenticeship in gunsmithing, he would have been fully aware of the fervent efforts within the trade to produce a cartridge-firing revolver. He knew that in 1812, Johannes Samuel Pauly, a Swiss gunmaker, had patented a center-fire metal cartridge, and that the original idea was rejected by the gun trade. Other munitions firms had experimented, but all had failed to overcome some flaw or other which prevented their inventions from being manufactured commercially.

The Birmingham gunsmiths realized that cartridge-firing rifles and revolvers would revolutionize future wars. A variety of patents were already registered, but none had proven to be infallible. It was still preferable to have a reliable cap and ball weapon than a new invention which might fail in the heat of battle.

Ben Hollister was close to revolutionizing cartridge-firing weapons. Had he remained in England, he might well have done so. Ben didn't know it would be another five years before Colonel Edward Boxer would produce a coiled brass cartridge, very similar to his own. However, a solid-drawn brass cartridge would finally provide the answer and remain unchanged thereafter.

The winter came and went, and after the thaw, the trees and bushes sprouted new growth. Amos had begun tilling the soil in preparation for sowing seed and JB was finally walking, tottering around the cabin and holding on to items of furniture to support himself.

Another cycle had begun.

Elsewhere, there was bitterness and bloody fighting. Settlers were trying to leave Missouri, taking their slaves with them into Kansas. Many were killed, and their slaves often escaped into a frightening new world.

Mollie remarked to Ben that lately Amos had become morose. Rarely did he chat like he used to while going about his chores. It was a long time since she had heard his deep, rumbling laugh.

"Is anything the matter, Amos?" Ben asked one evening when he looked in on Amos as he always did.

It was some moments before Amos replied, and when he looked up, his eyes were misty. "I ain't oughta gone and done it, Mister Ben." His voice shook. "I should never've run out on Annabel and ma family. If I'da waited a little while longer, mebbe we could all've gone to Kansas like a lot of the other slaves."

"There's bloody fighting there, Amos." Ben shook his head. "And there's no knowin' what might've happened to you. Nobody knows what the future holds for them. Looking back is all too easy. If my family hadn't left England, chances are my ma and pa, and my sister, would still be alive today."

"There's a difference, Mister Ben. You wuz a boy then. You didn't have no say in stayin' or leavin'. I did."

Ben nodded. That was true enough. He had blamed the Cheyenne for his parents's deaths and sought revenge on Blood Arrow for what had happened to Sarah. If he wanted to go back blaming others, then it was his father's fault for bringing his family west. There was no point in blaming anybody. It was too late now.

"Every night I lies awake wonderin' what's happened to ma family. Are they alive or dead? Free or still slaves? I'll never rest till I knows fer sure, Mister Ben."

"You can go and look for them if you want to, Amos." Ben felt a tremor in his own voice. "You're a free man, you've never been a slave here. I won't try to stop you. The choice is yours. Choice is what freedom is all about. I reckon that one day all slaves will be set free."

"I reckon one day all slaves will be set free." Amos stood up, moved to the doorway and stood looking out across the patch of ground he had ploughed up that day. "There's a fellah named John Brown, we heard stories 'bout him on the plantation. He wants all slaves freed and he's fightin' for 'em. Last we heard he'd captured a military arsenal on the Shenandoah. Mebbe he's still holed up there, we never did hear, the master wouldn't tell us nothin', even if he knew. But this John Brown, he'll arm the slaves with the guns he's took, an' there'll be an uprising one o' these days, yuh can take it from me."

"Everybody's taking up guns to free the slaves," Ben said. "Except the Confederates. You go and look for your family, if you've a mind to, Amos."

"I'll think about it." Amos moved back inside. "While I'm a doin' the sowin'. After that I might go. And if I find 'em . . ."

"You're welcome to bring them back here, Amos." Ben's voice was husky now. "This is your home, you can stay as long as you want to."

Sometimes Ben's thoughts turned almost affectionately to Slade. In a strange sort of way, he missed not having him around. He was glad that the law had not gotten the road boss, a rope would have been an ignominious end for one who had survived innumerable gunfights. J.A. Slade had lived by the gun, and at the very least, he deserved to die by it. It was anybody's guess where he was right now. Maybe he, too, had gone to fight for whatever cause he supported. Only one thing was certain: J.A. Slade would not be returning. In all probability, Ben would never see him again. Ben shrugged off a feeling of sentimentality—Slade would not have thanked him for it. Their trails had crossed and parted. It was best that way.

Like Amos, Ben had a decision to make. It was only fair

to Mollie that he made it soon. Whether to go to the war or to stay here repairing guns for the soldiers. It was a simple enough choice and only he could make it.

But, like Amos, he would think on it until the sowing was finished.

"A grateful people acknowledges with pride its debt to the riders of the Pony Express. Their unfailing courage, their matchless stamina knitted together the ragged edges of a rising nation. Their achievement can only be equalled—never excelled."

Abraham Lincoln

WILLIAM W. JOHNSTONE
THE PREACHER SERIES

ABSAROKA AMBUSH   (0-8217-5538-2, $4.99/6.50)

BLACKFOOT MESSIAH (#7)   (0-8217-5232-4, $4.99/$5.99)

THE FIRST MOUNTAIN MAN   (0-8217-5510-2, $4.99/$6.50)

THE FIRST MOUNTAIN MAN: (0-8217-5511-0, $4.99/$6.50)
BLOOD ON THE DIVIDE

*Available wherever paperbacks are sold, or order direct from the
Publisher. Send cover price plus 50¢ per copy for mailing and
handling to Penguin USA, P.O. Box 999, c/o Dept. 17109,
Bergenfield, NJ 07621. Residents of New York and Tennessee
must include sales tax. DO NOT SEND CASH.*